THE CHILDREN
GROW UP

THE CHILDREN
GROW UP

by

BEATRICE KEAN SEYMOUR

THE BOOK CLUB
121 CHARING CROSS ROAD
LONDON W.C.2

This edition, 1950
By special arrangement with
William Heinemann, Ltd.

PRINTED AND BOUND IN GREAT BRITAIN BY WILLIAM CLOWES AND SONS, LIMITED
LONDON AND BECCLES

To
GERTRUDE AND ARTHUR
WITH MY LOVE

CONTENTS

BOOK ONE

April, 1945

Chapter One

ON A fine sunny morning in April, 1945, Lydia Hampton might have
been seen walking with her two young daughters through George
Street, Richmond, in which town lived her aunt, with whom they
were all on their way to lunch.

The elder girl, who wore the uniform of a second officer in the
Wrens, carried a basket containing the usual assortment of edible
odds and ends which, in that year of grace, it was usual to take along
when bound for a meal at someone else's table. Her sister, Fryn,
whose chestnut-brown hair hung in a thick plait down her back, was
clearly not old enough for the Services, and secretly hoped the war
would end before she was. For even in contemplation the communal
life which Meg so much enjoyed considerably dismayed and alarmed
her younger sister.

They were a nice-looking trio and attracted not a few interested or
admiring glances as they moved briskly along—a fact of which Meg
was pleasantly aware. But Fryn looked as if her thoughts were far
away, whilst Lydia's attention was focused upon not missing the
florist's shop, which she remembered as being somewhere between
the station and the old house by the river for which they were bound.
It proved to be on the other side of the road, and catching sight of it
she halted abruptly and called to Meg, who had gone striding on,
"Just a moment. I must get a few flowers for your aunt." Whereupon
Meg laughed and inquired, "And what, darling, becomes of your
determination not to encourage these 'dreadful' prices?"

"1 o: this occasion," said her mother, "I am prepared to make hay
of it. This is an 'occasion' and Pen must have some flowers, whatever
the price."

Now that grandfather Malling is no longer here to get them for
her, thought Meg. She had been fond of her grandfather, though he
was very old, of course, and everybody knew that the coming of the
war and the death of his wife soon afterwards had, as they say, broken
his heart. He wasn't really their grandfather, of course, but her
mother's, just as "Aunt" Pen was her aunt and so their great-aunt.
But in this large and rambling family of her mother's all relationships
were simplified and Christian names among the older generation in

[3]

general use. And this, in Meg's view, was just as well, since she found the business of sorting them all out distinctly confusing. It was Fryn who liked that job, who had made what she called a genealogical table of these numerous outcroppings of the Malling and Gaywood trees, though Meg did not find it of much help; but even Fryn followed the conversational habit of omitting such qualifying words as "great" and "second". All living members of the family were just plain aunts, uncles, cousins, or grandparents, whenever you addressed them or spoke of them. Only when they were dead did they achieve the dignity of exact relationship—and by then, Meg considered, it didn't matter anyway.

The sisters knew why their mother called this day an "occasion", for their Aunt Pen (who was really Mrs. Lowe—Mrs. James Barrowby Lowe—and a widow) was a novelist and wrote under her maiden name of L. P. Malling, the initials standing for Laura Penelope —names which to Meg seemed as old-fashioned as her own little-used Margaret. She wished she had been called by her sister's name, Diana, quite the wrong name for anyone as retiring as Fryn, as somebody must early have recognised, since she was always called by a shortening of her second name, Frynford, which had been the maiden name of her father's mother, who had died just before she was born. Meg rather fancied herself as Diana, for it made her think of Diana of the Uplands, that lovely girl standing back against the wind and holding two large dogs on a leash, though she herself had never had a dog; and of Meredith's *Diana of the Crossways*, to which book she had been attracted by the title but had, alas! found rather heavy going.

For Meg, her Aunt Pen was the real celebrity of a family she considered, with no small satisfaction, to be very distinguished. For even as a schoolgirl in Buenos Aires she had seen an odd copy or so of L. P. Malling's latest novel in the bookshop in the Casa Tow, where she and Fryn went so often with their mother, who'd discovered it was an English girl who was in charge, and liked to talk to her about English books, of which, she said, there were far too few to be seen in the city. And arriving in England, first at school and now in the Wrens, she found herself basking in a reflected glory. ("L. P. Malling? Your *aunt? Really?* We all *love* her books . . .")

But in addition to Aunt Pen there was also, of course, another writer—her father, Ninian Malling ("your grandfather Malling"), who had died back in the winter, and her artist brother, Laurence ("your Uncle Larry"), any one of whose pictures Aunt Pen said were worth all the novels she had ever written, or was ever likely to write. However, artists in the family were less productive of reflected glory, Meg had found, in her circle, than novelists, though it had been satisfactory to be asked by First Officer White last year, when she came back from leave, if "the Laurence Malling who has two landscape pictures in the Academy this year" was any relation. "Yes —he's my uncle," she'd said in that casual tone she'd learnt to adopt on such occasions, to hide the immense gratification she felt in the family achievements. This was one of the occasions when the simplification of the family relationships seemed especially satisfactory.

As for her grandfather's work, "highbrow" was not a word Meg used, but perhaps it sat in her mind when she had essayed some of his books—slim volumes of essays, mostly on literary topics, slender collections of short stories that had seemed to her so old-fashioned (but after all some of them had been written in the seventies, when he was a very young man, long before Aunt Pen had been born) and the oddly unbulky novels which one could read almost at a sitting. Moreover, they all dealt with a day that she could only think of as "dead and gone", and since she did not reflect that to-day is rooted in yesterday, they seemed to her too remote to be interesting. But her aunt's novels were a very different matter. She wrote of ordinary people—people so real to Meg that she always expected to meet them coming round the next corner. They belonged to her own social class and lived their lives against a background of the contemporary world with which she had so little fault to find, war or no war. Meg Hampton was not given to overmuch consideration of the state of the world, of its woes, ancient or modern, or of the political ideologies which wracked it, though Aunt Pen made some of her characters discuss these things entertainingly enough. Just eighteen, of a buoyant and hopeful disposition, and born with a will to happiness, Meg was not to be numbered among the introverts, young or old, who "dig beneath the cypress tree".

"Right you are, darling," she said now to her mother, as the three waited for a break in the traffic before crossing the road, while Lydia reflected, not for the first time, that Meg did tend to overwork that charming term of endearment—darling. Darling: little dear. Absurd, applied to herself, thirty-eight, five foot six and broadshouldered at that. However, Meg had mercifully not adopted the horrors of "O.K." and its variants, so perhaps one shouldn't grumble.

Save for the flowers, the shop proved to be empty, and they were left for several minutes to look around before anyone appeared to serve them.

"I should have some of the pink roses," advised Meg, "and some

[5]

of the spring flowers, perhaps—there are never many to pick in Aunt Pen's garden because of that old willow tree."

"I *like* the willow," said Fryn, with gentle emphasis, and speaking for the first time since they had left the station. She was no great talker, sharing Larry Malling's habit of speaking only when she had something to say. Lydia thought it a good habit, though sometimes she thought also that Fryn overdid it. But she was a little shy, of course—a quality which was surprising, and rather pleasing, her mother considered, in a member of a generation that seemed not to include the word in its vocabulary. She did not suspect that Fryn's non-loquacity had something to do with her deep love of words. If she had ever heard the cynical view that speech was given to us to hide our thoughts she certainly wouldn't have agreed with it. But the accurate expression of what she thought was something she found very difficult of accomplishment, and while she was seeking the right word the conversation was apt to run ahead and leave her far behind.

Meg said, "*I* like the willow, too—but you can't say it doesn't prevent everything else from growing within half a mile of it."

Fryn said nothing to this. She stood there just gazing wide-eyed at the wealth of loveliness about her, and taking her by the arm, Lydia said, "What do you think, Fryn? The spring flowers, the pink roses, or some of the daffs?"

Fryn said, "I should have the white lilac and the long branches of wild cherry. They'd look lovely against Aunt Pen's pale green walls."

"Yes, so they would," agreed her mother. "Very well. The white lilac, the wild cherry and a few of the pink roses for her dressing-table, don't you think?"

"Yes, modom?"

Their presence had been discovered and the assistant was hovering —ready, Lydia felt, to hear the usual question (which she was probably so very tired of answering)—"How much are . . .?" But Lydia had no intention of asking it. She would buy what she wanted, since she was minded to be extravagant, without any such tiresome prelude to the transaction. So she asked for the lilac and wild cherry, and when they were assembled and held up for her inspection, she said, "And a few roses, perhaps. . . . Buds, I think."

"The roses are two shillings each, modom," said the assistant, hesitating.

"Very well. Half a dozen, please," said Lydia, with a nonchalance Meg found wholly admirable.

Fryn stood enraptured as the selection was made and approved;

[6]

but as the girl began to wrap the flowers in the soft white paper that did duty nowadays for the lovely crinkly kind nobody had seen for so long, she wondered that anyone could fold away so much love-liness and sweetness with so casual an air. In the same way, she thought, she would wrap up the planet Venus if she could claw it from the sky. How amused Meg would be if she could know what she was thinking! ("Why, she's wrapping up flowers every day, silly—it's just a job like any other".) But Meg was far from con-cerning herself with Fryn's thoughts. Her own, and her brightly observant eyes, were on the assistant's elaborately "permed" blonde head. Really, quite marvellous!—the front hair scooped up high above the face, and the back left to hang upon her shoulders, stiff and solid as a wig. Meg, whose own hair, soft and dark, curled natur-ally around her face and into her neck and so left her nothing to do with it, was immensely interested in the efforts of other people with theirs. She thought it a great pity Fryn's hair was straight, for it was a lovely colour, even brighter than her mother's. Between them they made the blonde head of the assistant quite tow-like, Meg felt. Taking a quick glance at her sister, she noted again how beautifully her hair grew back from her temples and how amazingly thick it was—right to the very ends. She greatly admired her sister's looks, and constantly marvelled at Fryn's indifference to them. Even at sixteen and a half (Fryn's age now) she herself (and long before) had known her own good points—her pretty hair, her large dark eyes and brilliant colouring, and had been much flattered when she heard that she was like Cousin Andrea, who had been an Edwardian beauty and known all the celebrities of her day. All the same, she would rather have looked like Fryn . . .

"Thirty-two-and-six, if you please, modom," said the assistant, handing over the flowers to Fryn's eager hands, while Lydia, without blenching, produced and tendered two pound notes.

"Very fine hay, darling," said Meg as they came out into the street, to which her mother replied firmly, "Money well spent."

"But Gaby is certain to have brought Aunt Pen a *bouquet* . . . and Mr. Anstruther, too, I dare say."

"So much the better," said Lydia calmly, but Fryn, who had had the same thought about Gaby (Aunt Pen's niece, who acted as her secretary and whose beautiful name, Gabrielle, everyone so deplor-ably shortened), wished that Meg had not put hers into words. She hoped that Gaby's would be a more modest offering than Meg's choice of noun, and her emphasis upon it, would suggest, so that her mother's extravagance should not look even a little unnecessary. For

[7]

Fryn, like her mother, needed to have her extravagances backed with a well-founded excuse, if not a good reason.

But Lydia thought only that it was a lovely morning, even if the wind did blow a little coldly, and that there had been no rocket-bombs on London for twelve days—and not a siren, so far, had been heard this morning. That thought of itself, she supposed, would have been sufficient to lift the heart and raise the poor old *morale*, even if the papers did not continue to give good accounts of the invasion of Europe—her own that morning announcing the fall of Hanover.

"I wonder if Doreen will be in to lunch?" Meg said. "Last time we came she lunched out." (Doubtless not by herself, she thought, but did not say. Aunt Pen said it was a concession to the wartime larder, but not as if she really believed it.)

"It won't break my heart," said Lydia, "if she's as considerate this time."

Meg laughed. It was no secret that nobody liked the girl Cousin Dwight had married four years ago. They all thought her stupid and empty-headed, concerned with little beyond her appearance, and to that verdict Meg had added the mental one of "common". She couldn't even pronounce her own name properly, calling it "Dawreen". Aunt Pen said that it was language, a tone of voice, which divided the classes, not birth, and certainly not intelligence—there were stupid people in all walks of life. This, as Meg knew, was her aunt's way of saying that Doreen would be much more acceptable if she never opened her mouth. But Fryn did not think that that, so far as she was concerned, would have done much for Doreen; to her everything about Dwight's wife was wrong because of her indifference to her small son, Barry. Fryn loved children, but Doreen did not seem to care for them at all, even when they were good, and Barry, she held, was seldom that. He was a sensitive, highly strung little boy, which Doreen took as a personal affront—he certainly didn't get that from her, she said. And, in any case, she'd rather he'd been a girl whom she could have dressed up, Fryn thought, and treated like a doll.

Half the pleasure Fryn took in these visits to her aunt's old house by the river was derived from the delight of seeing the children. Not only Doreen's Barry, though perhaps he was her favourite, but Serena and Becky, the little daughters of Cousin Fenella, Aunt Pen's elder daughter. The house was very full, these days, for not only did it shelter Dwight and his wife and son, but Fenella and her daughters; for her husband was in the army, and they had set up no home of their own. It could only be in her study, Fryn thought, that her aunt found any peace at all, though as she spent a good deal of her time there perhaps that did not matter. Nevertheless, she had liked it better when there were fewer people in the house, specially as nowadays her mother objected to her habit of browsing along her aunt's bookshelves, and then burying herself in the particular volume she had selected, instead of joining in the general conversation. And Bridget, Aunt Pen's younger daughter, the one who was fond of books, was never to be seen, these days, for she had a job in the War Office which did not grant leave for any "occasion" of the sort she and her mother and sister had come to honour.

However, as the day was fine perhaps they would go for a walk in the Park after lunch, which would be better, especially as an expedition of this nature would not include Doreen, who walked nowhere except to the nearest bus stop and considered Richmond, as Meg said, the last word in backwoodsdom, and no safer than London, where she would so much rather have gone on living.

So Fryn walked along in silence, her mind running back along the years since her father had brought them all to England from South America because he was sure war was coming and wanted to "do his bit".

You'd have thought one war would have been enough for him, her mother had protested, and that this time he was too old to fight; to which he had replied that he was an experienced engineer and could be of use in other ways. So to England they had come. And the war machine had swallowed him up.

At the time of their arrival she had been on the threshold of her eleventh birthday and the strange thing was that after nearly six years in England the life she had lived in South America had begun to seem quite unreal. The wide, tree-shaded streets of Buenos Aires, the mixture of races you encountered upon them, the tall buildings and bright sunshine, the contrast her mother's coloured clothes made with the almost habitual black of the other women of the city (very odd, she'd always thought, in so bright a place—as if they were in perpetual mourning); all these things she remembered clearly enough, but they roused in her no emotion whatsoever, no single thread of nostalgia. The friends of her parents, the girls she had known at school, were now all much less real to her than the people she had met here in England, the members of this large family of her mother's —even those whom she had never seen, who had died before she had been born or before her arrival in their country. They were all far more than mere names in her genealogical tree. Some of those who had been alive when she arrived she had not had time to get to know very well, like her Uncle Richie, or her rather distant cousin, Maurice Romaine, of whom indeed she remembered nothing save his beautiful piano-playing. But she well remembered his grandmother, her own even more distant cousin, Andra, who had died in an Air Raid on London in '44, and whom everyone said Meg was so much like. She had been a jolly person, even in her old age, and had been very entertaining about the life she had lived as a girl and young woman—in a world, so said her grandfather, which had not been "saved for freedom" by two wars. The most showy of his three Buds of May, he called her, which had been his name for his three nieces, Cathy, Andra and Emmy, the children of his sister Laura Gaywood, who'd become Lady Corrie, and died when Fryn was a baby.

Fryn never tired of these scraps of family history. They gave her a most delightful sense of "belonging", of having roots, which she had never had in South America, where they had a lot of friends and acquaintances, though she did not remember any of them very well, and no relatives at all. She wished her parents would stay on in England when the war was over, but she knew they had every intention of going home—they could call it that!—as soon as they possibly could. She knew also that her father was anxious to get back to the business in which he was a partner, and that the years in England, for him as for her mother, were labelled "War Interlude". She had often heard her mother say that in England she felt "shut in"; though she'd added that that was probably due to the black-out. Fryn had long ago decided that only she and her young brother, Jeremy, left out of to-day's expedition because of a cold (not entirely to his disappointment, for he was an unsociable boy and would enjoy himself at home in his own way), had really wanted to come to this country she thought of now as her own. Meg hadn't cared either way—perhaps because she knew she would be able to enjoy herself as much in England as she had in Buenos Aires; which proved to be the case. And her mother had not wanted to be uprooted; but where her husband went, there too went she—and her children. But oh dear! thought Fryn, how much, how very much I wish we didn't have to go! How she would hate leaving this country where she felt so much at home, not minding that it was shabby; not minding, either, the black-out or any of the wartime restrictions. And above all, she'd hate leaving this large family which interested her so much. Not even her mother, she was afraid, would quite understand these things, if she put them into words. She, too, was fond of England and of her family; but just as she had left it and them behind twenty years ago to journey with her father to the other side of the world, which now she thought of, as did her father, as her home, so she would do again. Never would there be any idea of leaving her children behind. Fryn was in no doubt about that, after what had happened over Jeremy.

Her grandmother had suggested that he should remain in England when the war ended and go to school at Harrow. Everyone knew, she said, that there were no good public schools in South America (she called it "S.A.") and most English people, she understood, sent their boys "home" to be educated. Jeremy really ought to have a good school at his back. But none of her arguments, Fryn was sure, had made any impression at all upon her parents.

It had seemed to her very puzzling that her grandmother, whom she found rather alarming, and who was given to talking about the "privileged" and "under-privileged" and about "equality of opportunity", should be so anxious that her grandson should have a better education than most other boys. But her mother and father had obviously been much amused about it. Her father had said, "They're all alike, these people who want to turn the world upside down. They all want their sons to go to the crack schools. Look at so-and-so, and so-and-so," and he had named several of their Socialist acquaintances who'd entered their sons for this, that or the other "first-class" school in England when they were infants in arms.

Her mother had said that it didn't make sense. If you thought the world needed to be turned topsy-turvy, why send your boys to the kind of school which would be least likely to uphold such a point of view?

And her father had laughed and said, "Ask me another," and Fryn knew that their minds were quite made up. But perhaps, she thought, Jeremy might *like* to stay here and go to Harrow. Nobody had asked him that, any more than they would ask her wishes. But Fryn had sensed the conflict between her mother and grandmother, for all, as she knew, they were very fond of each other. And she understood how this could be, because it was how she herself felt about her grandmother.

Her mother's thoughts had, she felt, been travelling along the same road, for she suddenly exclaimed, "Oh, dear, I've forgotten to let your grandmother know about her tea-party on Friday. Now one of you remind me to telephone immediately after lunch."

"If you're not going," said Meg, "you'd better let me do the ringing, darling. I'm much more 'putting-off' with grandmother than you are. . . . Or *are* you going, perhaps?"

"I haven't made up my mind—except about the speaking." (*That* I can't do, of course, she thought.) "I'm sure it will be a very interesting afternoon."

"For them as likes it!" said Meg. "I'm sure I should be bored stiff."

Lydia smiled. Her elder daughter was not to be drawn into her grandmother's activities, and had never made any bones about allowing that fact to be known. Meg was to be numbered among those who found the world as it was too interesting to be very concerned with other people's schemes for altering it. Besides, as she had shrewdly observed, alterations were so seldom improvements.

None the less, her mother's monthly "Teas", planned to keep alive in people's minds, and to improve their knowledge of, "the things for which we are fighting", seldom failed, Lydia felt, of their purpose. She herself had always taken away from her occasional attendances a quite disturbing amount of information, for Caro Bradfield knew a number of people who were authorities, in varying degree, on some special aspect of the war or the countries engaged in it, and seemed willing enough to help enlighten the less well-informed. Her mistake—as old as Lydia's knowledge of her—was in thinking that she could ever be numbered among them. There were times even now, after twenty years of marriage, when she felt a girl of sixteen again, and her lively, clever, indomitable mother was discovering what a hopelessly wrong kind of daughter she had—one who "couldn't think on her feet", and unable, so she steadfastly maintained, to make a speech "to save her life".

To her mother, brought up in a home where the younger generation was encouraged to air its views on all topics and taught to take contradictions and opposition laughter in good part, this business of saying what you thought clearly and without fumbling was second nature. Also, she belonged to that generation of women which was to take the first practical steps towards the redressing of the balance of the sexes, while her early marriage to her cousin, a rising young Liberal politician, had given her just the milieu, Lydia thought, that she needed. It had been her own home all over again, with the accent this time more strongly upon political matters than literary. The sun had shone very brightly for them both until the first World War had come—the war which, as Lydia had heard, her father had accepted as inevitable and her mother had raged against as a superlative folly which could and should have been avoided. But if she had not buckled on her warrior's sword, she had allowed him to do it without any attempt at dissuasion, for in those days she thought people must act as they believed to be right. And to-day? Lydia shrewdly suspected that there were brands of opinion she would like to prevent anyone from holding. And that was strange because, through the years, her own had repeatedly suffered re-orientation.

When her father had been killed Lydia had been a little girl of nine. She hardly remembered him. His death, it was held in the family, had changed her mother very much and was responsible for her untiring labours to promote the cause of Peace in a progressively quarrelsome world, and to bring about what Lydia for many years had called (though not to her mother) the Brotherhood of Man. To this cause, however, Lydia had been able to contribute nothing more showy than good secretarial work. She had early applied herself to the mastery of Pitmanic shorthand and for two years had taken down her mother's letters and made neat and accurate transcripts of them, kept files and a card-index, made appointments for her mother and interviewed people she had not wanted to see. All without reconciling her to the fact that she had a daughter with intelligence and no single outstanding gift. It wasn't what she had expected and it had taken her some time to accept the idea, much less the fact, and by then Gilbert Hampton had appeared upon the scene. When her mother had had time to notice him and to realise the implications of his frequent appearances at their house in North Street, she had behaved very well about it, which redounded, Lydia felt, all the more to her credit because although her son, Lydia's schoolboy brother, Richie, had obviously inherited the family brains, it must, as early as all that, have occurred to her that nothing was less likely than that he would use them in the cause of the Brotherhood of Man, his interest in which was precisely nil.

When Richie was killed in the Battle of Britain everyone but Lydia had expected it to break her mother up. For Lydia remembered, as a child, how she had taken the bitter news of her father's death. Nobody, so the family said, had ever seen her shed a tear—and certainly Lydia hadn't. (It was her first knowledge of the fact that grief could lie too deep for tears.) Later she had come to know that, for her mother, her father had died for a chimera—in a war that was to end war for ever. (And who, Lydia had thought during the last five years, would say that she was wrong?) But she knew her mother did not believe that her son had died, like his father, in vain, for this, she told them, was a different war altogether. Richie had perished not merely to help save Britain from invasion, but to help destroy the tyrannies of Fascism and Nazism, which, it seemed, her mother had come to hate even more fiercely than she hated war. She, who

[13]

had devoted so many years of her life to discrediting war, had arrived at acquiescence in the greatest war in history (and her son's part and death in it) because she believed that by no other means could these twin tyrannies be finally crushed.

But was the war really going to do that? Lydia wondered, hurrying through the bright day. Wasn't it true, as Pen affirmed, that Fascism was an idea in men's minds? Did one crush *ideas* by force of arms? Or only put their manifestations temporarily out of commission? Fascism, Nazism, or Communism, Pen hated them all, since each, as she said, was prepared to dragoon the world in the name of Progress.

Untroubled, however, by doubts, or by her sister's scepticism, her mother had taken her arduous way through the war years, fortified perhaps by the comradeship of her new marriage at the beginning of them, sparing herself nothing, convinced that this hard road of total war was the only road to the haven of peace and democracy. It was this conviction, Lydia knew, which drove her, which more even than the wartime diet had taken the flesh from her bones. It had filled her with a demoniac energy when others were falling by the wayside. She had even taken Russia back into favour, dislodged therefrom by her pact with Germany in the August of '39, by her war on Finland, her grabbing of the Baltic States, and her invasion of Poland, when she, too, came into the war. That you fought Germany and the Nazis was all she asked of anyone. All but the most strong-minded of the "useful" people who crossed her path were swept into her net. Nobody went unchallenged. Why even now, thought Lydia, this morning, she'd hound me on to a public platform if I'd let her! To her, it's so childishly simple. I've lived in South America for twelve years. I knew a lot of people there. A lot of Spaniards. I learnt to speak their language. Ergo, I must know all about the Spanish form of Fascism. I went around. I'm neither deaf nor a moron —ergo, I must know a good deal about the Farrell Government, about the Nazi activities and Colonel Perón. And could, if I would, get up and talk entertainingly and informatively about them all for twenty minutes or half an hour! ("Oh, not a *speech*, Lydia! Just a chatty, informal fireside talk. Surely, my child, in my drawing-room . . .") It amused her to think that even at this time of day she'd feel considerably safer with the South Atlantic rolling between her mother and herself.

Not that they were not very good friends or that she was lacking in affection toward her mother. On the contrary. She had too an unbounded admiration for her talents, her public spirit, her indomitable courage and energy. But where she, Lydia, was concerned, these things added up to an alarming total, apt to be oppressive. Clever as she was, there were some things her mother would never learn.

Fryn, walking silently and thoughtfully along, would have shown the greatest sympathy with her mother had she been uttering her thoughts aloud. She quite understood how she felt about Friday's "Tea". For it was terrible what a lot grandmother expected of you. She didn't seem in the least to understand that people were all different, and few of them as clever as herself. She just thought that if you were what she called an "intelligent person", then you could do just anything you chose. That was it—a mere matter of choosing or not choosing. She had a troubling trick of making you sound (and feel) just disobliging. But that wasn't it at all. Anyone could tell who knew her that her mother was not the sort of "public" person grandmother was, and Fryn, for one, would have suffered agonies of apprehension if she'd been present when she had attempted to make a speech. "Fryn's much too quiet and reserved," her grandmother had once said, in her kind and pleasant voice that made you feel she wished nothing but your good, even while trying to change you into a different sort of person altogether. "We must see what we can do about finding a cure for that." So now she lived under the constant threat of her attempting one. If you came to think of it, the one drawback—yes, she was sure, the *only* one—to remaining in England after the rest of the family had gone home was the fact that her grandmother would be there too, keeping an eye upon her, trying to re-make her to another pattern. Not that at times it wouldn't be rather nice to be someone other than yourself, to be an entirely different sort of person. But you had to go on being yourself. . . .

When her grandmother had first come out to South America to see them Fryn had been too young to remember her. Even on the second occasion she had been only seven and what she remembered of her visit was her constant remark—"This little girl has lost her tongue again." Somehow, to find upon their arrival in England that she had just married again had made her seem almost a stranger. Perhaps because she was no longer "Your Grandmother Gaywood", but "Your Grandmother Bradfield"—at least until Grandmother Malling's death had made the distinction no longer necessary, and she became just "Your Grandmother". But that, somehow, had not made her any the less alarming.

At this point in her reflections her mother roused from hers to say, "Well, here's Buccleuch House—we're nearly there, and in good time." And, oh dear, thought Fryn, I did mean to suggest we went along the tow-path and in by the garden gate. To arrive that way always made her feel not in the least like a visitor, which was how she liked to feel in her aunt's house. Being shown in, even when it used to be by old Mrs. Winfarthing, who had been housekeeper for Aunt Pen ever since Cousin Fenella was a very little girl and Cousin Bridget not yet born, was so formal. But Winny had died in her sleep six months ago and, said her Aunt Pen, had left them all the poorer. Nowadays, you never knew who would open the door to you, for sometimes Aunt Pen had a housekeeper, but more often only what she called an Obliger. But none of them ever looked at all pleased to see you. And of course they weren't. You were just extra work. You meant more potatoes to peel, more bread-and-marge to cut, more plates to wash up.

But Gaby always smiled upon you and looked (and was) delighted to see you. It seemed especially dreadful to Fryn that anyone so good and kind should have been so unfortunate; not only had her baby daughter died, but her husband had been a prisoner in Japanese hands for a very long time, and there had been no news of him. No wonder, she thought, that her face so often looked sad. Meg said that Uncle Richie had been in love with her and she with him and that they ought to have married. Then why, Fryn wondered, as they walked up to the front door, hadn't they?—and why had she married Uncle Richie's friend, Ward Findon, so soon after his death? A kind, rather silent person, very different from Uncle Richie, who had laughed so much and seemed to enjoy everything, even his part in the war. . . .

The door opened and there stood Gaby, smiling at them all, and saying, "How *very* nice of you to bring such a lovely day!"

Chapter Two

AS PEN LOWE walked across the hall to her study her daughter-in-law came slowly down the staircase. She was dressed for the street, but after the fashion of her generation wore no hat. This was her first appearance this morning, for since Pen had made it clear that she preferred people in her house to come to the breakfast-table properly dressed (and this without uttering a word) she had taken to coming down to the kitchen, collecting what she wanted on a tray and eating it in her own room, leaving Fenella and Gaby to deal with the business of giving Barry his breakfast and keeping him out of harm's way until she was ready to take him out. An arrangement, Pen thought, which suited everyone very well.

So now she looked up and said good morning, to which Doreen said only, "I must scram. I've a hair-do and manicure at a quarter to ten."

"Then you'll certainly need to hurry," said Pen, understanding why Fenella had taken Barry out with Serena and Becky. She might have explained why, but she didn't. Dwight's son was so often on her hands that comment and explanation were alike superfluous. "Will you be in to lunch?"

"Yes—but I don't know about on the dot."

"Well, please make an effort to be punctual, as we have guests. . . . And you'll find it rather cold in spite of the sun. You'd be well advised to put on a hat or to take a scarf, unless you don't mind a cold."

Doreen came on down the stairs as if she had not heard this piece of advice. At the door she remarked, "So long!" The door opened and shut, not too quietly. She was gone.

Pen went on into her study, to be greeted by the sweet scent of lilies of the valley, standing in a glass bowl upon her desk. She stood there for a moment gazing at them without thinking of them at all, but only of that empty-headed piece of prettiness Dwight had given her as a daughter-in-law. If only, in addition to being stupid and vain and lazy, she had been ill-natured or bad-tempered, she thought she could the better have borne it, for then she could have disliked her heartily. But you couldn't dislike Doreen; you could only be bored by her. I wish, thought Pen, sitting down at her desk, that I were among those who suffer fools gladly.

Then she really saw the lilies and knew that it was Gaby who had put them there. She must have slipped out early to buy them, hurried back and arranged them so that she should find them there when she came into the room after she had finished reading her letters and glancing through the morning paper. Kind Gaby! How right the glass bowl was for them, adding to their beauty by revealing their delicate pale green stems. And now she'd gone back to the shops, doubtless to stand in queues to get whatever was needed to supplement the chickens which yesterday she had somehow contrived to acquire in honour of the "occasion" and Lydia's visit. And presently she and Fenella between them would cook the lunch (for this was an "Obliger" period and Obligers do not cook) and turn her promptly out of the kitchen if she dared show her face inside it, though she had done a deal of cooking in her time and enjoyed it. Everything that was necessary to the success of Lydia's visit they would do, between them, while that lazy slut, without a qualm, sat in that scented room having herself beautified!

Not that Gaby or Fenella would have said as much as a thank you for Doreen's assistance, even had she remained behind to offer it; and neither of them would make hard-going of the job. Unruffled, looking fresh and groomed, they would sit down to table as if they'd had no hand in preparing the meal but had merely presented themselves, as of old, in answer to the ringing of the luncheon bell. Just as if her dear Winny were still with them. She thought for a moment of Winny, her devoted Grace Winfarthing, and of the comfort and peace she had meant, for so many years, to them all; of the skill with which she had kept the worst manifestations of Austerity at bay and served up even the most uninteresting of the food it yielded as she would have served a princely repast. But there were no more Grace Winfarthings; the mould was broken. Such service as hers was now voted demeaning. She had been an anachronism when she had come to her in nineteen-nineteen, prepared to take them all under her wing, as her father had once taken her Aunt Laura and all her family, including herself and her sister and brothers when they were children, and constant visitors at her house in Lowndes Square.

With a small sigh she reluctantly drew towards her the little pile of copies of her new book which Gaby had put there for her to sign, and which afterwards she would make into neat parcels and take to the post. But she did not begin to sign them. Resting her arms on the

[18]

books, her eyes wandered back to the lilies, and she remembered how first Bar and then her father had always seen to it that there were flowers on her desk every morning of "publication day." In Bar's time, it had been a charming attention, warming the heart, and followed by a dinner in town and often a play; but neither her father, after Bar's death, nor now Gaby would ever concede that such days had long since ceased to be occasions and become merely the date of the finishing of another job of work, interesting enough in itself, but one from which she was always glad to be free. Of the making of books there is no end; but how willingly, she thought, I would cease from adding to them, if only money grew on trees; if Bar had not died, if there had not been this war and the housing problem it has brought about. The eternal dredging after ideas, a theme, situation, characters!—was there any harder job? But what with income-tax at its present figure, and no hope of relief, the rationing of paper, which, for authors at least, had negatived the boom in books, the slowness of production, to say nothing of the loss (for all but a lucky two per cent of writers) of the American market, she needed to work harder than ever. She often felt, as the Red Queen told Alice, that it took all the running she could do to remain in the same place. The cottage in the country of her dreams, where, her children settled, and assured of their comfort and welfare, she could write at least some of the more ambitious books she had been longing for years to write, and take as long as she chose over them, seemed as far away as ever. If eventually they did get written they would be old-fashioned, for the mode was already changing. Frustration, violence and man's inhumanity to man were now the more favoured themes of the novelist, themes which sprang naturally from the soil of the harsh century in which we were all doomed to live. Whether they were as favoured by the readers as by the writers she could not judge, and anyway they were foreign to her pen, which must continue to earn a living for her by tracing the history of more ordinary lives. The investments her father had left her were mostly in industrials scheduled for nationalisation, and from his copyrights she could expect nothing, since his books were all out of print and likely so to remain; and he had written nothing since the death of her mother in the early days of the war. The reading world, he said, had forgotten Ninian Malling—he had been at the game too long.

Whether this were so or not, she knew that he was content to be forgotten. The war and her mother's death had broken his heart long before the death of the young men of the family, the death of her Cousin Andra and those of his younger contemporaries, had brought him to the conviction that he had lived too long.

But these were gloomy thoughts for so bright a morning, that carried still further assurance that in Europe, at least, the war was coming to an end. Much better remember that for a couple of months she could take a holiday from her desk, and if this blessed reprieve from V's 1 and 2 was maintained, go to see some plays with Gaby or Fenella and freshen up her mind. The minds of Gaby and Fenella did not seem to be in need of freshening up.

Taking up her pen she signed the books and, that done, walked out into the garden, upon which the sun lay like a blessing made manifest. Before Lydia and the girls arrived she would have time to do a little weeding—for jobbing gardeners, like most of the other amenities which once had made her life so pleasant, had gone down the bitter wind of the war, and the weeds affronted her eyes whenever she walked in the garden. Helpful and willing as Fenella was, gardening, even on its lowest levels, was for her a penance, while she and Gaby, who both liked it, had seldom time to spare for it.

She walked across the lawn to the river gate, past the willow, wearing already its spring veil of golden lace, saluting the scattered clumps of daffodils, crocuses and muscari which stood bravely against the wind, and remembering that once—how long ago!—she had meant to make a real garden here and how the willow had always prevented her. There, at least, James, her father-in-law, had been right. But having to choose between tree and flower-garden it was a foregone conclusion that the tree must win, for it was so essentially a part of the charm of this old river-side house she could never bring herself to order its destruction. And much as she loved a garden, to have had one, these days, would only have meant another thing with which to wrestle.

The keen wind was ruffling the river this morning and their old boat, *Plain Jane the Third*—now hardly ever used—bobbed up and down in the wash of the heavily-laden barges and freighters that were ploughing their way against the tide. To such, to-day, the river was almost entirely given up. Gone was all the gay and noisy traffic of pre-war days, the steamers with their happy throngs, their bands and mouth-organs, the sounds of gramophones and wireless in rowing-boats and punts, the laughter and chatter, and perhaps it was because of this silence that lay now over the river that she noticed the roar of the traffic across the bridge. In the old days one had simply never remembered the bridge was there, unless one looked across at its five lovely arches.

River and bridge and traffic, however, did not detain her long this morning, for it was cold at the gate and she needed a scarf, if she was not to catch the cold against which she had warned Doreen. And if any weeding was to be done she must get started. As she walked back across the lawn she thought the old house looked even more attractive than usual this wind-swept spring morning, bright with April sunshine. Gracious, dignified, taking on fresh beauty with the years. It seemed strangely satisfying to remember how long she had lived there. Over a quarter of a century, ever since that first spring after the cessation of World War One—when Fenella, now in her twenty-seventh year, was only a few months old. A bad spring it had been that year, holding up their renovations, and with snow at the end of March and a deplorably low temperature. And summer bursting in mid-April upon a frozen and astounded world and staying for ten days or so before the weather had returned, as Bar said, to normal. "Thames Valley weather", James had called it—as if it weren't as bad everywhere else, with the storms breaking all around London and snow in the Fens. But by the time they moved in, at the end of May, summer had really arrived . . .

She remembered all the arguments James had piled up against Bar's decision to buy the house. As an architect he considered it a bad proposition and had declared that it was "a good house once". Much better let him buy for them that little house in Chart when waste their own money on this one. But she and Bar had fallen in love with it and she had never forgotten the surge of delight which had assailed her when Bar, contrary to his custom, had not given in to his father. In the face of his coldly polite disapproval Bar had bought the house and they had proceeded to spend money upon it; to argue about its age, to decide finally that it was just, but only just, a Regency house, and to play with the idea of giving it a name. But Number Four Paradise Walk had seemed the perfect address, and the old house had never had a name save the one James had so unkindly bestowed upon it, Tumbling House. After their initial outlay it had served them well, and did not in the least deserve James's label. Only on the very eve of the present war had she had to deal with another crack. No, it was not her lovely old house which had fallen into ruin, but all the civilised world . . .

After Bar had died, so quietly, without even time to say good-bye to her, though she sat at his side, she'd wondered how she was going to bear living on here without him; but before long what she wondered about was how she could ever have thought for a minute of leaving it. For all the happiness of those thirteen years of life with

Bar was garnered in it; to have left it would have been to have cut out the very heart of her existence. Nevertheless, at intervals James, grown old and bitter down there in his pretty Kent house, had continued to tell her that she was a fool to stay there. If this war that everyone was so sure was on the way did actually come, and the bombs began to fall, it wouldn't stand an earthly. . . . But he did not suggest where she should live instead, nor any longer talk of a house at Chart. That all belonged to the days when he had wanted Bar on his doorstep, and was willing to put up with her and the children to get him there.

James. He would live for ever, she thought, as she went indoors and up to her room to find the scarf for her head. Yet he had out-lived life and its pleasures—even the pleasure of baiting her. For though she had once told herself that she would never enter his house again, when the war came she had repented, and defying the hazards and miseries of the journey, had gone down to Greystones, standing plumb in the path of bombers and robots; from which nobody had been able to detach him. Though his attitude to her did not alter, she came to believe that he appreciated her visits, though perhaps that was too strong a word; but at least he had grudgingly admitted she had pluck, which had made her smile, for it took far more pluck to go and see James than the idea of being killed in the process had required. But after all he was Bar's father and during his lifetime he had hidden his intense resentment of her very existence beneath that velvet suavity which deceived everyone but her; and she had learned, not easily, how to hold her own and at the same time to keep her temper—for which achievement James had scored a heavy point against her. So now, during these war years, hiding her own anxieties, she had continued not only to visit but to keep on terms with him, forgetting that summer day when he'd heaped upon her the insults he must have been storing up for years. For even then she had miraculously kept her temper (and, she felt, her dignity) and though in the taxi which took her to the station she had dis-covered the tears running down her face, it had been her triumph and not James's. In the end he had looked deflated and cheated—he had not expected the bulwark she had run up against his barbs, almost from her first meeting with him, to stand against this last outrageous attack. It was pity which she had suddenly and sur-prisingly felt for him. And perhaps he was aware of it, she'd thought. But it had not been in her to know him old, lonely and unhappy, hugging his grievances and resentments, down there in the path of appalling danger, and not care. . . . The bombs, however, had not

[22]

fallen on Greystones and its master. And now it looked—it really did look—as if there would be no more of them. For through the extending of their lines northwards the Canadians had cut off the German bombing sites, and so brought timely relief . . .

It was the act of putting the scarf over her head that sent her thoughts back to Doreen. . . . Nothing had ever surprised her quite so much as Dwight's choice of a wife. In the October of 1940 he had been shot through the foot in an air battle over the Channel and had been in hospital for three months, where Doreen Jerrard was doing war work. The first time he brought her to Paradise Walk she had the shock of her life. Thinking of her as a nurse, she had expected someone so entirely different that her disappointment was the more acute. At the end of the visit she could do nothing but wonder how such a person ever came to choose nursing, even as a temporary profession.

As to that, Bridget had given her the answer. Clear-eyed, keen-minded and amazingly knowledgeable about that section of her own sex for which she kept a quiet scorn, this younger daughter of hers had looked at Doreen to some purpose. Nursing, she'd observed drily, and entirely without malice, was as good a way as any other of catching a husband, and the uniform was becoming to girls of Doreen's type of good looks. The remark had stuck in Pen's mind. She did not question the soundness of Bridget's observation, but it had never occurred to her that Dwight could be a victim of the husband-hunter. For she saw that he meant to marry his Doreen. And so, early in the new year, he had. No, nothing, she thought again this morning, had ever surprised her quite as much as Dwight's choice of a wife—not even Fenella's choice of a husband, or the metamorphosis of that young woman which followed upon it.

She finished with the scarf and went downstairs, where in the hall the Obliger was flicking dust from one place to another and humming blithely to herself. Pen said good morning and hurried by. Collecting her weeding implements from the "potting" shed, in which nothing, alas! was ever potted, she began her tussle with the weeds, reflecting on the strange fact that although the willow discouraged the flowers it did nothing to dismay the weeds. However, weeding was one of the jobs which did show results, and after an hour's work she straightened her back and decided to run the mower "just once" over the lawn. It was not a job she often tackled, for lawn-mowing was popular with the elusive folk who were persuaded from time to time to do a day's work in the garden, and weeding was not.

It was a task her father had hated to see her do; but she did not find it distasteful. With her sedentary life, relieved only by walks in what she thought of nowadays as the "war-infested Park", she needed more exercise, she'd told him. As she ran the noisy machine up and down she thought of the afternoon in late August last year when he had sat beneath the willow for the last time and told her that the mower was much too heavy for her, and she'd realised, even as she laughed at him, how frail he looked, how fast the sands of time were running out for him. But she had known, when six weeks later he had died, that he was not sorry to go. He'd lived, he contended, far too long, and she knew it had distressed him to know so many strong young men of the family dead in the wars and himself "still cumbering the earth". Even the deaths, at ripe old ages, of Francis Wingham and Arthur Merrow, whom he remembered only as the two fine young men who'd carried off the two elder of his sister Laura's daughters, Cathy and Andra, in their extreme youth, had distressed him considerably. To live into the nineties was outrageous, he'd said, and she knew that he'd meant without her mother, who had been nearly ten years his junior and therefore had no business to have thought of dying, for all she was in her eighty-first year when she had gone from them. The long life they had had together —nearly sixty years of it—had never quenched the flame that had sprung up between them almost from the first time they had met, when her father's first wife was still alive, and which had caused so much dismay to her aunt, his devoted sister Laura. And he'd grieved about Andra's fate in 'forty-four and been exacerbated by it, too. If Arthur had lived he'd have kept her down there in safety in Devon. He'd not have let her come back to town, he'd complained. "Arthur was the only person who could manage Andra. . . . She was always headstrong."

Well, thought Pen, pushing the mower, she was seventy-three when she'd died, poor darling, though that, she supposed, was almost young to her father, at ninety-two. But she, too, had grieved for Andra, who hadn't wanted in the very least to die. For her the rout of life, everlastingly interesting, was far from over. She hadn't expected the bright lights to go out at seventy-three. Left to herself, she would willingly have gone on to be a hundred.

The thing after her mother's death—and the only thing, she thought—which had given him real pleasure was that Gilbert and Lydia, who were looking for a house at the very moment when the one in Hereford Square, which had been his home for over fifty years, had become unbearable, had been only too delighted to take

[24]

the lease off his hands, which left him free to come to her and Gaby at Paradise Walk. With Dwight and Fenella in the services, there was plenty of room; and though his creative faculty had died with her mother, his interest in other people's still, happily, survived. All her life she had been so used to discussing books, plays, ideas and world events with him that to have him beneath her own roof at a time when she sorely needed distraction from her anxiety about Dwight (and, too, about Fenella, newly received into the F.A.N.Y.'s) had been something for which she was profoundly grateful. And she had rejoiced with him that the house in Hereford Square was not to be given over to strangers, and so shut to them for ever. But now, she thought, with the war drawing to its end and Gilbert talking already of his plans for "going home", the strangers would most certainly come. And she would go there no more. She'd gone there to live as a small girl of three, and long after she and her sister and brothers had left for homes of their own her parents had continued to live there, keeping open house, as ever. She thought of the many distinguished people who had come there throughout the years to see her father, of the happy life she'd spent there with her brothers and sister before that bright world of their youth had vanished overnight.

Wheeling the mower back to its shed the familiar longing assailed her that the house might stay in the family, and she regretted, not for the first time, that Dwight could not take over from Gilbert when he and Lydia went. But quite apart from the fact that Dwight couldn't afford it, it was a family house, and nothing was clearer than that Doreen had in Barry all the family she meant to have. And just as well, perhaps. . . . In any case, she could not even begin to imagine Doreen in charge of such a house, especially when servants, good or bad, were so seldom to be had. She thought, not without a little inward shudder, of the London flat, ill-kept and sunless, from which, at Dwight's earnest request, she had detached Doreen in the spring of 'forty-one when, depressed by six months' pain and incapacitation, he had gone back to hospital to see what could be done for his foot. London just then was being heavily bombed at night, but all the same it had been no easy matter to persuade Doreen to leave, for she liked living in town and had no enthusiasm for existence in the "suburban wilds" with her "in-laws". The news that Dwight's foot was to be amputated did not improve her state of mind, since life with a cripple had been no part of her idea of marriage. And now, after four years of Doreen as a house-mate, Pen had no illusions about her as a home-maker. She did not like to think of Barry and Dwight in the kind of home she would make for them, when they had one of their own again; and certainly the home of her own childhood was no place for Doreen. Even the Obligers of to-day would despise her, for she was a natural slut in the house, for all she took such elaborate pains and care with her personal appearance.

Fenella and Glen? They certainly would be wanting a good-sized house when the war was over, for here in the spring of 'forty-five it was clear that Fenella regarded her two little daughters as the nucleus of the family she meant to have. But at the moment Fenella and Glen were out of it, and she mentally crossed her fingers, for Glen was helping in the invasion of Europe. She was aware that Fenella thought she worried too much about him. "He'll be all right," she said. "After all, he survived Dunkirk." Well, one had to go on believing that one's own would somehow be immune. She had believed it of Dwight. And she had believed it, all those years ago, when Bar had been in the fighting around Loos, and her beloved brother, David, in Belgium; and had gone on believing it though Caro's Gordon had been killed early on in the war. But Bar had come home so ill from phosgene poisoning that his life was despaired of, and David had been drowned in the mud and blood of Passchendaele. . . . Dunkirk. Didn't Fenella know that you could try the gods too high? Her calmness was like a gauntlet thrown down to Fate. Impossible to think of her as the moody, restless young creature she had been in those last few years before the war began, trailing her retinue of middle-aged admirers and talking so much romantic nonsense about the last of them; from whom the war had mercifully delivered them all. But she had been badly frightened that time. She had not felt easy, either, about Fenella's entry into the F.A.N.Y.'s, knowing that she had taken that step with such precipitancy because she wanted to get away from the scene of her folly. Fenella had lost considerable face, and she'd get over it better, of course, if she had strangers about her who knew nothing of it. But the Women's Services seemed to have their own dangers and when she first heard the name of Glen Westcott her fears had revived. How old was he? had been her first question, and Fenella had laughed—a good sign, she'd thought. "Nearly six years older than I am," she'd been told. That made him twenty-seven, and she had felt a sense of relief. "You'll like him," Fenella had remarked. "He's just your sort." Was he? Pen had wondered. Had she a "sort"? She had asked what he did when he wasn't soldiering and was told, "He's a poster artist—a good one. . . . Can I ask him here?"

He had come to tea—and she *had* liked him. And whether he was

[26]

her "sort" or not, she recognised in him the high qualities of common sense and integrity, which was reassuring. Also, he was clearly a young man who knew his own mind and as clearly was no philanderer. His way with Fenella, she thought, was admirable. He told her that he was a director of the firm which handled his work— a great deal of it, before the war, done for the Underground and Railway Companies. "I paint that greener green, that bluer blue, that never were on sea or land," he said, with his attractive laugh. He also said that it was seeing a sketch of Fenny's which had brought about their introduction. He thought she had considerable talent but was bone-lazy—a statement Fenny, amazingly, had taken lying down. "If you'll trust her to me, Mrs. Lowe, I'll undertake to see she improves." This had a little taken her breath away. Was he asking her approval of an engagement? Only a short one, Glen said; they wanted to get married. Quite confounded, she had not been able to find words and Glen had said, "You do like me a little, I hope?" She replied that at least she had formed a good opinion of him and had added, laughing, "And I'm very grateful to you."

That had amused him.

"For taking Fenny off your hands?"

"No, for not being forty-five and slightly bald on top. . . . You see, I've always been so afraid that was the sort of son-in-law Fenny would one day wish on me."

"You needn't bother, darling—he knows all about my infant idiocies. I've spilled all the horrid beans," Fenella had remarked calmly, and once again she had been bereft of words.

After this meeting things had happened very quickly. Glen had brought his parents to tea and mutual liking and approval had resulted. The usual announcement in *The Times* followed and the wedding within a month, in case, said Glen, all this intensive training he was getting meant his going abroad again shortly. But it didn't. The training went on, taking him all over the country—to the Surrey commons, to Wales, to the Lake District, up and down the coastline of Britain, while Fenella stayed on at Paradise Walk and began to draw again while awaiting the birth of her first child, who made her appearance in September, was called Serena and early showed that she was most amiably disposed to justify her name. Probably because her mother had made so normal a business, Pen thought, of producing her. ("Aren't you scared to death?" Doreen had asked her. "*I* should be," and Fenella had said, "Why? Some woman somewhere is having a baby every minute of the day.")

Early summer had brought Dwight home, not entirely free from

[27]

pain and wrestling valiantly with the business of getting accustomed to his artificial foot. But out of the war, thought Pen, for ever. Out of *all* their wars. . . . She was pleased, for his sake, when Doreen, temporarily fortified maybe by Fenella's example, had embarked along the road to motherhood, though without her young sister-in-law's common-sense approach. Aware that she had eventually entirely lost patience with her, Pen felt she tended to put too much of the blame upon Doreen's shoulders for her son's highly-strung temperament and tantrums. But she had been accommodating about his names, having no ideas of her own on the subject, and he had been called Gordon Barrowby, after Caro's first husband who had been killed in 1915 and Pen's own who had died in 1932. But it was Doreen, who had decided that his first name should be ignored and his fine second one reduced to Barry, not Bar. If Pen knew that she referred to him sometimes, with a little laugh, as "the widow's son", she did not bear her any grudge for that. Tantrums and nerves or not, he was a charming little boy, and as they had grown older he and Serena had become fast friends. That little person, so sedate and even-tempered, was, by common consent, very good for him.

Time had moved on, bringing larger and better bombs and presently the V's 1 and 2. But still, though he had taken his commission, Glen stayed on in England, coming out to Richmond when on leave, to prove himself a veritable Admirable Crichton, or carrying Fenella off to his parents in Berkshire. "They're saving me for the big job," he told her, but not as if the prospect dismayed him. Nor, apparently, Fenella, who when Serena was a year old cheerfully embarked upon the business of providing her with a brother. Nor did she seem disturbed when the project miscarried and Serena found herself with a sister.

It had long been clear that in Glen Westcott Fenella had found what she wanted in life. He understood her and knew how to manage her. It was rather like her father's tale of the young Andra and Arthur Merrow all over again; and his six years' seniority was all to the good. Marriage and motherhood fitted Fenella like a glove. It wasn't Fenella she needed, these days, to worry about.

These thoughts had brought her to the side door of the house, and as she pulled off her scarf she heard the telephone ringing. Gaby came out of her study door as she reached it.

"Charles Anstruther," she said, standing aside for Pen to enter the room, then shut the door behind her and retreated.

Pen sat down at her desk, hesitating a moment before picking up the receiver. She hoped he wouldn't ask her the usual question.

[28]

Because the answer must be the same. Then she said, "Good morning, Charles . . ."

"Good morning, my dear. How are you?"

"Quite well, thank you, Charles."

"I expect you'd say that if you were dying."

She laughed.

"But I'm very far from dying."

"Excellent! Have you seen the *Guardian* this morning?"

"No, but I see that Gaby has brought it in and put it on my desk. Open at the book page—with a blue-lead cross against what I suppose is a review. . . . Is it a very bad one?"

After all these years she could quail at the idea of a bad review from a quarter that mattered. The others she had long ceased to mind and nowadays never saw, anyway, since she no longer contributed to a Press Cutting Agency.

"On the contrary. It's excellent. I rang you to offer my congratulations. Did you get the flowers?"

"There are roses on my table which were not there when I went out to do some gardening—and I see Gaby has put your card on my blotting-pad."

Charles's voice said mildly, "Then those are doubtless the ones I ordered."

"They're beautiful—they must have cost the earth. I wish you wouldn't."

"I don't believe you. When can we lunch?"

"I'm free for ever as far as I know."

"Then let's make it Friday. The Ivy, twelve sharp. That all right?"

"Perfectly. But it still makes me feel as if I'm going out to breakfast."

Charles laughed. "Are you in a hurry?"

"Do I sound that way? Well, I've been gardening—and I've some 'family' coming to lunch and must go and make myself look respectable. Do forgive me. Good-bye until Friday."

"Good-bye, my dear . . . bless you."

She put the receiver quietly back into its groove, and picked up the card. "With love and best wishes," it said. "Charles."

Charles Anstruther. She'd known him for nearly thirty years. For nearly twenty-five of them he'd been her publisher and for twenty her friend as well. But never had he sent her flowers until after his wife's death, over two years ago. Six years ago James—on that horrible afternoon when he had hurled his insults at her—had

2*

declared he was in love with her, and she with him. . . . She'd been outraged. But during the last three years she had reason to wonder if, so far as Charles was concerned, James had been right. And herself? No, she was very fond of Charles, but she was not "in love" and never would be again. But that was not her reason for refusing him; nor because she still felt that, for her, a second marriage was unthinkable, as she had done for so many years after Bar's death. He had repeated his offer of marriage so many times since her first refusal that she had (almost) made a joke of it, until she had realised the real reason why she must still say "No". Quite simply, it was because she could not forget James's insinuations. If she married Charles he would assume—and declare!—that they'd been well-grounded. Ergo, she could not possibly marry Charles while James was alive; and as James meant to live for ever. . . .

She laughed, bent her head for a moment over Charles's roses, then tore his card into very small pieces and put them in the wastepaper basket. Gaby would have read what had been written upon it; but then, Gaby was in the secret.

As she crossed the hall to wash her hands she wondered if she could go on saying "No" to Charles much longer without telling him why she did it. She had used up her stock of excuses.

Not that all of them were correctly so labelled. The chief one—that she wasn't free—was certainly not. Until the war ended she felt her first duty lay still with Fenella, Dwight and Bridget. She must for some time to come continue to live at Number Four, and nothing would induce her to leave Gaby (even if she would agree to be left, which Pen doubted) and Fenny to run the house for Bridget and for Dwight and that lazy slut he had married. But this was a situation which would ultimately resolve itself—and then?

If she told Charles about James he'd only laugh. But here, for once, her sense of humour failed her. How very odd! she thought, watching the grime slip out of her hands, beneath the gentle coaxing of Gumption. Why should she mind so very much that James should be supplied with what he would joyfully seize upon as evidence of his base insinuations? Well, she did, and that was all there was to it. She and Bar had been ideally partnered. It had been a marriage of true minds. Charles had been Bar's friend as well as hers—and the friend also of the children, who had been fond of him, called him "Uncle Charles", and looked eagerly forward to his occasional visits to Richmond. It had never occurred to her, or, she was sure, to Bar, that Charles entertained any feelings toward her other than those of friendship. Neither, in spite of James, did she quite believe that he had. But since his wife's death and those of his two sons in the war, he was lonely and believed, as she did, when she allowed herself to be honest on the subject, that they could live happily together. Love and the state of being "in love" did not come into it, she thought, for her. But she must continue to say "No".

However, perhaps on Friday Charles would omit to smile at her in the middle of their lunch-table talk and take advantage of a pause to say, "Well, when are you going to marry me?" Perhaps not.

Instead they'd probably talk about the approaching end of the war in Europe, where at least people would soon stop killing and torturing each other. But she realised that the idea of peace did not fill her with the high hopes which had belonged to the cessation of the war of her youth. She no longer expected, as she had done in November, 1918, while waiting for Fenella to be born, that the noble ideals which had echoed down the war years would be carried into effect; for she had seen how much easier it was to win a war than to deal with war's aftermath. And to the problems the present conflict had produced she saw no answer; for here was the ruin of half the world. The war had destroyed Nazi Germany—but would it also have destroyed the spirit of Nazism, the dictators of all colours? She did not believe it. Charles, she knew, expected much of Europe to turn to Communism, and how much better, he asked, would the world be for that? Fascism, Communism were ideas in men's minds. The ideological factor ruled the world, pitiless and beyond reason. . . .

Thoughtfully she dried her hands, hung the towel back in its place, looked at her watch and hurried upstairs. Time's winged chariot!—she seemed always to be hurrying from the clangour it made at her heels.

Chapter Three

IT WAS very difficult, Fryn found, as she watched Gaby standing in the hall chatting with them all, to remember how many things she had to be unhappy about. Not only the death of her baby and the uncertainty about the fate of her husband, but anxiety about her French mother, who was deeply involved in the Resistance movement. Perhaps, though, Gaby had very little time to worry about her own affairs because she always had so many of other people's upon her hands, for all she managed to look as though she hadn't.

She found her face quite fascinating to watch, with its lightning changes from grave to gay, contrasting so oddly with the quietness of her bearing. But perhaps "gay" was not the right word; it was rather a sunshine of the mind that seemed to move across her face. She admired this second cousin of hers as much as she liked and approved of her, and so, she knew, did everyone at Paradise Walk, with the exception of Doreen, who did not seem to like anyone very much, though her dislikes were more passive than active, for she was too lazy-minded to allow any strong emotion about anything or anyone to disturb her. It was no secret in the family that Uncle Richie (whether Meg was right or not about his wanting to marry her) had liked Gaby very much, and she remembered how he had teased Aunt Pen by speaking of her as "your miserable slave". But Gaby was not in the least miserable, though now, perhaps, she had good reason to be; and certainly she was nobody's slave, though her devotion to Aunt Pen was undeniable.

At this moment the sight of Pen hurrying down the stairs to greet her guests recalled her thoughts, always so prone to go roaming, and she moved forward to hand over the bouquet.

"We've brought you a few flowers," said Lydia, and Pen turned her large dark eyes upon her with an expression of mingled delight and consternation as she said, "A few! *Lydia!*—you must have spent a fortune!"

"Not at all!" said Lydia calmly.

Carrying the bouquet against her shoulder, a delighted Pen preceded them up the stairs to that large airy room which fronted the gleaming river, with its little balcony, the door to which stood wide open to the bright day. Fryn stepped out and stood there sending her long observant glances across garden and river, allowing them to rest upon the golden willow and the passers-by on the towing-path who so often stopped to look across at the old house and were so free with their remarks. "I'd have that tree down if it was me," was the one most commonly to be heard, and which made her angry and, too, a little sorry for the speaker. Not to realise how long the old tree had stood there, with its feet in the river . . . not to see how lovely it was at all seasons of the year! Demos, her grandfather Malling had said, hated trees and cut them down whenever he could. Demos. The people. Democracy. Fryn thought he didn't care for it very much. However, Demos was not much abroad to-day; there were few passers-by; and the cold wind, which ruffled the river, did not persuade any of them to linger by the gate and express their views.

"Come in and tidy up," called Lydia, and Fryn moved back into the room, drew off her hat and combed her soft lovely hair back from her face, deciding that she need not re-plait it. Moving across the room she opened what looked like a cupboard door, flat to the wall, but which was actually a deep recess into which had been built hand-basin and taps. As she washed her hands she remembered that years ago, before she was born or thought of, Pen and the uncle she had never known had discovered these two hitherto unsuspected deep-set recesses which, when the house was built, had been designed as powder-closets, and had had them converted into these modern conveniences. "They spoil the look of a room, though," Pen had said. "It's very nice to be able to shut ours away." Drying her hands, Fryn thought, like her aunt before her, of the women of long ago who had powdered their hair here and troubled far less, perhaps, about washing their hands.

She emerged from the centuries to see her aunt lifting out the flowers from their wrapping and to hear her exclaiming with delight at their beauty.

"Fryn, fill the glass vase with water for your aunt, there's a good child. We thought you'd like the rose-buds for your dressing-table, Pen."

It was her mother who spoke, and back into the centuries Fryn moved, to emerge again with the glass filled to within a half-inch of its brim. How surprised the hair-powdering ladies must be, she thought, if their ghosts are hovering. She watched Pen split the stalks of the roses and drop them into the vase, where at once they fell sweetly into grace, as beneath Pen's hands flowers seemed always to do.

[33]

Picking up the cherry branches and white lilac, she stood with them in the crook of her arm, as she waited for her guests to be done with their titivations. So, thought Fryn, she should always stand. . . .

Meg had finished combing her short curls before the glass and was powdering her face, though her sister could not see that it needed the attention. But Lydia's eyes were on Pen, and she thought how easily she wore her years, in spite of all the work she had done, or, perhaps, because of it. Those large dark eyes of hers, too big for her face, as people used to say, seemed to have lost little of their brightness, and she still did not need to wear glasses, even for her work. Her springing hair, still short, was as thick as ever, and had retained much of its brightness, which was accentuated by the wing of grey, which Lydia thought becoming. It was as if Time had just touched her and withdrawn. . . .

Pen asked after Jeremy's cold, and Lydia said, "Oh, it's running its course, poor child. Too bad in the holidays! He gets everything that's going, but the girls seem to be germ-proof." She looked at them with a smile, as if she were grateful to them. Actually, she was thinking how nice it was to have a sixteen-year-old daughter who seemed never to have heard of the word "cosmetics", and was content to leave her face for the present as it was; a little envying Meg her untroublesome hair, and her unfailing ability to look soignée at all times and in all weathers—even in this morning's wind and in a uniform which, of all things, on young women, she detested.

"If we're all ready. . . ." said Penn, and they went downstairs to the room in which Gaby had set out the sherry decanter and glasses. Fryn thought the sherry was a lovely colour, but she did not drink it. "Drink" was another of the things she did not yet recognise, Lydia reflected, wondering if by now perhaps she ought to be doing so. All the women of her family had been taught to appreciate good wine—the reproach of liking only "sweet stuff" which men despised lay upon none of them. But there was little wine about for slender purses, these days, and she'd not had sherry as good as this for a very long while. Sherry, indeed, of any quality, had been for years on the ever-lengthening list of "luxuries". When she voiced her appreciation, Pen said, "You have to thank Gaby. She says we're 'under-the-counterites' because we're so well-known after all these years to the tradespeople." She made a little moue, then added with a smile, "But I will not hide from you that at times I suspect her of an intrigue at least with the wine-merchant." But as she turned to put the finishing touches to the vase an instant's memory of the excellent sherry James used to give them when they went down to Chart caused her a little pang. Not because of James or his sherry but because Bar had been there, learning at last to withstand his father's blandishments; and because they were young and in love.

The door opened and Fenella came hurrying in to greet the visitors and to drink her glass of sherry. Prettier than ever, Fryn thought her, with her red-gold hair twisted loosely in her neck, her large hazel eyes and translucent skin. Since Doreen's arrival in the household Fenella's make-up had been reduced to the minimum, no more than a light dusting of powder, and a severe rationing of lipstick. She remembered, with a little start, that Fenella had a husband fighting in Normandy and that her Aunt Pen had marvelled at her calm acceptance of the fact. Fryn thought that this must be because she was quite unable to imagine a world in which Glen Westcott no longer lived. It was much easier for her to think of him as surviving all the hazards of his situation. So Chesterton had said it was easier to believe in God than not to believe in Him. She was thus magically released from the continual nagging anxiety which would otherwise have been hers. Somehow Glen had made her believe, as he perhaps believed himself, that he bore a charmed life. And oh, how she hoped he was right, for she thought Glen Westcott was a wonderful person. She liked him almost as much as her Cousin Dwight. And she didn't have to be sorry for him, as she did for Dwight. Because of losing his foot and because—because of Doreen. Though that was presumptuous of her, for it was obvious that he was very fond of her. . . .

It was Pen who sometimes wondered what would happen if Glen proved to be wrong, if all the time the Fates were laughing up their sleeves. . . . But she didn't think this often; she was so thankful to have this well-poised, reliable daughter, since she offset the son who once had been these things and was so no longer. Strange how brother and sister had changed roles! Once it had been Fenella she worried about: now it was Dwight. Dwight who had married this boring young woman who, she was sure, made him unhappy and gave him so little; would end by making him even unhappier and giving him nothing at all. What a marriage! How much longer could it possibly last? And *how* she hated the idea of a divorce! It wasn't a thing they went in for as a family, though her Cousin Cathy's son Danny had made no bones about divorcing his ex-chorus-girl, who now graced the peerage. The family, he'd said, would prefer the divorce to the continuance of Roxane's presence among them. And so on the whole they did, especially Cathy, who wanted a daughter-in-law who would produce an heir for Bourne Manor, which had

[35]

been no part of Roxane's idea of marriage. But in her wildest dreams she had not thought her son capable of his second successful entry in the matrimonial stakes. Olivia had been the answer to all Cathy's prayers. . . .

At that moment, she saw Doreen walking up the garden path, and a few minutes later she came into the room, very set-up, it was obvious, with the results of the labours, not her own, of the morning. Pen thought she looked like any other pretty young woman you might meet in the street—and that indeed had been her aim and object. Not to have her hair "styled", her face carefully made-up, her finger-nails encarnadined, would have given her an inferiority complex. So long as she "looked right", no sense of inferiority would oppress her. And it was clear that she did this morning feel that she looked very "right" indeed. Her blonde hair was marvellously curled around her face and hung in induced immaculate waves upon her shoulders. (No wonder Fenella had thought it time to put hers up!) Her eyelashes had been lengthened and darkened, her eyebrows plucked to vanishing point, her face creamed and tinted, while her mouth had been painted to a curve which Nature had entirely omitted to bestow upon it. She must have spent a small fortune upon herself, Pen thought; thought also that it was cheap at the price, since it had induced in her a mood when she would not feel slighted. And she was grateful to her for being punctual.

The sound of the luncheon bell interrupted the interchange of greetings and Pen said, "Better take your sherry with you, Doreen." They trooped into the dining-room, where the children were already seated in their high chairs and Gaby busy at the sideboard. Fryn, who had carried in Gaby's glass of sherry, put it at her place at table and went to speak to the children. But they were too intent upon the business in hand and had little to say to her, so she moved over to Gaby and asked if she could help.

"No, darling. Sit down and be a guest. Fenny will buttle. Sit down, all of you, and be guests!" Nothing was worse, her tone implied, than having everybody getting up and down, fetching and carrying. And nothing suited Doreen better than that she should be required to do neither. She sat down in her place at once and upon her face there came the same eagerly expectant look that the faces of the children wore, her pointed tongue, as the tongues of the children did not, wetting her lips. There had been a time when Dwight had teased her about this and called her Miss Greedy, but nowadays he teased her about nothing.

Pen watched her take a tentative sip at her glass of sherry, which she did not like and would probably leave. Doreen did not "drink", never having acquired this aid to modern life so characteristic of her generation. She had, indeed, no vices. It was still, Pen reflected, her vanity and silliness which she held so unremittingly against her. Waste of mental energy, Bridget would have told her. People are what they are. . . .

She looked away from her daughter-in-law to the children, who were watching the passing of plates with immense interest but in unbroken silence. At table Barry was still a somewhat uncertain quantity, though less likely nowadays to exclaim, "Me too! Me too!" in that agony of impatience which used so often to be the prelude to meals *en famille*. To-day he was as well behaved as Serena and Becky, neither of whom expected to have any notice taken of them until the visitors were served. They would be no trouble to anyone. They had been brought there to eat and eat they would when given the chance. They were both, as Glen expressed it, very good feeders, by which he meant that they had very few fads and seldom quarrelled with what was put in front of them, and were mightily entertained when Barry would still sometimes inquire, "Will this do me any harm?" Doreen gave it as her considered opinion that he could be sick whenever he chose, that it was his revenge on you for making him eat something he disliked. But Pen, who did not think it unreasonable of children to have likes and dislikes, and had had as a child, and still did have, many dislikes of her own, sympathised with Barry over his queasy stomach; an attitude which had occasionally aroused in his mother that mild annoyance that in Doreen passed for strong feeling. So she was relieved to-day to see that Barry was pleased with his roast chicken. Remembering the good things she had eaten as a child, she often felt sorry for the dull food children ate these days, and mentally promised her little grandchildren lovely things one day. This generation, she sometimes thought, would grow up without any palate at all.

When carver and butler had taken their seats and the meal was well under way Pen and Lydia began for a time to talk "family", which bored Doreen considerably, or would have done had her lunch not usurped the greater part of her attention. In the early days of her ripening acquaintance with Dwight she had been intrigued, as she had expressed it to Milly Burke, her particular friend at the hospital, by what she learned, little by little, of the family to which he belonged. "A mixed grill" he'd called it, and had laughed at her when she'd said it sounded exciting. But how dull, in the result, it had all been! She had met very few of her new relatives and when Dwight said that was because of the war, with everyone out of London, she had not demurred but had nevertheless kept her own private opinion that had she had a "real" wedding, instead of the "hole and corner" affair at a Registrar's office Dwight had insisted upon because of his foot, many of the people she had wanted to meet would have come to it. After five years of marriage, most of the people to whom she was now related were still little more than names to her. Dwight could not see why she minded this, nor why she took it as a sort of personal slight, and had tended to treat the whole thing as a joke. So now, when Lydia and Pen talked of "Cathy", she pricked up her ears, for this, she knew, was Pen's ancient cousin, Lady Wingham, who lived down in Dorset, not any longer at the Manor House, for her husband had died soon after she and Dwight were married, and it was her son, Daniel—Danny to the family—who lived there, with his rich American wife. Sir Daniel was reputed to have been a gay dog in his youth, but of course he was now in his fifties. It would be interesting to meet him, she thought, for he sounded so much less stuffy than the rest of his family, and she liked middle-aged men. But he never came to Richmond; her mother-in-law and he, so Dwight had told her, did not like each other very much. She had hoped to meet him one day when she was at his sister Rose's house in Chelsea, but she had had no luck. Rose had married her mother-in-law's artist brother, Laurence Malling, and she liked her quite the best of the few of her in-laws she had met. She was always amiable and said pleasant things, even if, as Dwight said, she didn't always mean them; and she liked to be friends with everyone. Dwight called her the Family Chatterbox— an Agreeable Rattle, whatever that meant, but half the time she didn't know the meaning of the phrases Dwight and his mother and the rest of them threw about. "We all know our Rosie," Dwight had laughingly assured her. He'd sounded somehow condescending and yet affectionate, like the rest of them when they talked of Rose Malling. But Rose, of course, was not an outsider, as *she was*, just someone who had married into the family. She'd always been part of the family, anyway, for she and her husband were second cousins.

Larry Malling, however, had been a bitter disappointment. Knowing that he was an artist, she had expected a very different kind of person altogether, since it was well-known that artists were jolly people who lived in studios, where they gave gay parties and had a lot of models about. But Larry wasn't at all jolly—in fact, he hardly ever opened his mouth. He lived in a large house in Chelsea, not in a studio, and wouldn't, she was sure, give a party to save his life. (She thought Rose must have a very dull time of it.) And it soon appeared that he didn't use models, either, for he painted nothing but scenery! With the gathering of this piece of knowledge had perished her brief dream of seeing her portrait in the Academy!

Lydia was saying, "Cathy wants very much to see the children, you know, Pen."

"Too long a journey," said Pen. "Barry's inclined to be sick in the train. We must wait until this war's over and there's some petrol again for the old bone-shaker, if it still holds together."

It was clear she had quite made up her mind; but then, of course, she could go to see the old lady whenever she liked; she didn't have to wait for invitations. She had been down once or twice, Doreen reflected, since she had come to Richmond, but she had not been asked to accompany her. Not that she wanted to go. She'd be very bored in the country, except for the off-chance of meeting the reformed family rake. But it would be nice to say she had been, when next she saw Milly, from whom she was always careful to hide the fact that she felt an outsider in this stuck-up family of her husband's. However disappointing her marriage, it was still a consolation to use it as a means of impressing her erstwhile colleagues. First by reason of her role as a lady of leisure, smartly turned-out, and then by easy casual talk of the more exalted of her in-laws, with particular reference to the old lady in Dorset and her son, always here referred to as "Sir Daniel". It was true that that queer little creature, Fryn Hampton, always said that he was not really Dwight's cousin, but his second cousin once—or was it twice?—removed. She had explained it all with much care but it was altogether too involved to remember, and what did it matter? One needn't be as particular as all that, and "cousin" was a very useful word.

She was aware that Milly was sorry for her about having to live with her in-laws, which was why she always stressed the few advantages it had, like saving her the drudgery of housekeeping, the boredom of queues. Not for worlds would she have allowed her to think that she was disappointed in her fine marriage, though indeed she was. Apart from the fact that it had released her from the bondage of having to earn a living, it had given her none of the things she had expected it to yield. Dwight's utter incapacitation over his injured foot, and the long months of semi-invalidism which it had occasioned, had had a sadly and early disenchanting effect. She hadn't bargained for a disabled man for a husband and even now, when he was sufficiently used to his artificial foot to be able to get to and from his office, things were not much better. Dwight was a very different young man from the one she had met and bewitched at the hospital. Nowadays, once home from the office he did not often want to go out again—not even to the pictures, where he'd have nothing to do but sit still. He came home tired and after the evening meal preferred staying downstairs talking to his mother and sister and Gaby. Or, if he stayed upstairs in their own sitting-room, he sat and read or listened to some of the dullest items on the wireless or worked over plans he had brought home, so that she sat yawning her head off and thinking how mean a trick Fate had played her and even wishing herself back in the Bloomsbury flat. After all, she had by-passed a good many of the queues by the simple expedient of eating out at midday, and as for the housework, she did not let that bother her unduly. She didn't in the least mind dust and general untidiness—after the routine of that beastly hospital it was a positive joy to be as casual and untidy as she chose; and Dwight, though he'd been critical at first, had got acclimatised. Anyway, he didn't grumble much; she'd say that for him. But here he was being spoiled, like Barry, and neither of them would fit so easily into the old scheme when they got a home of their own again, if ever they did, which didn't look very likely.

She knew that her mother-in-law, for all she was always pleasant enough to her, really disliked her, and thought her a very bad wife for her son. She'd have chosen somebody brainy for him, she supposed, but with so many women around him with brains that stuck out a mile, perhaps he'd fancied a change. Or perhaps it was because she knew she didn't love him, which was true enough. She didn't believe—much—in love, except on the screen, and life wasn't like that. She'd married Dwight for reasons of her own which had seemed to her sound enough and were the reasons why most women married the men they did. A lot of fine nonsense was talked about love. She wasn't the "soppy" sort about men, she supposed, though it had seemed natural enough that Dwight should "fall" for her. And she didn't mind marriage. On the contrary. . . . And even if she wasn't in love with Dwight, she wasn't with anyone else, nor expected to be, and it was, in a way, satisfactory that he should still be in love with her. Except for this business of wanting another child. She had no intention of obliging him. Having Barry had nearly killed her. She couldn't go through all that again. . . . And that was another thing her mother-in-law held against her. She was like Fenella and thought childbirth an everyday affair. Well, perhaps it was for them. They thought too much fuss was made about it, too much written about it; so that it had become with some women what they called a "neurosis", whatever that was. She hated the whole business anyway—that first hospital they'd sent her to had properly put her off, and having Barry had quite finished her. Besides, she didn't care much for children, so it didn't seem worth it!

She emerged from these rambling thoughts to hear Lydia say that she must remember after lunch to telephone to her mother about Friday's tea, and especially about her suggestion that she should give the company a Talk after it—an idea which seemed to amuse them all very much. Lydia Hampton didn't appear to be one of the clever ones and seemed to be a bit of a disappointment to her mother, who was. Caro Bradfield. Her mother-in-law's sister. There was a woman for you!—brains sticking out all over her, always talking politics and going to meetings about this, that or something else. She called herself a Socialist, and was married to one, but she was a snob all the same—as bad as that daughter of Andra's, the one who had married the rich Jew, Paul Romaine. She might be the carpet under their feet, for all the notice they ever took of her. (It never occurred to her that, whatever was the case with Ray Romaine, Caro's attitude was prompted not in the least by snobbery but simply and solely by the fact that she considered her a fool—and Caro, like Pen, did not suffer fools gladly.) The odd thing to Doreen was that though her mother-in-law was devoted to her sister and her daughter fond of her, they hardly ever spoke of her without laughing and being "clever" about her enthusiasms and ideas. Quite good-humouredly, of course, though. They were a funny lot!

These somewhat gloomy reflections did not, however, impair her appetite for lunch. Gaby could cook—that, she supposed, was because she was half-French—though why she should be cooking food and acting as her aunt's housekeeper and secretary when everyone knew she was so well-off, was beyond her. Odd that her cousin, Richard Gaywood—Mrs. Bradfield's son by her first marriage—should have left her all that money. He must have been in love with her! Quite a lot of money, too, seemingly, which had been left in trust for him by his father, who'd been killed in the other war. He'd been a small boy then, and it had been accumulating all those years until he was twenty-one. They'd been rich, the Gaywoods, private bankers. A long while ago that must have been, before the private banks had been absorbed, or whatever it was Dwight had called it. But Gaby didn't seem to care much about money, or nice clothes, and she didn't seem exactly heart-broken about her missing husband, either.

[41]

A dark horse, if you asked her, which nobody did, or was ever likely to do. Nobody in this family ever talked about any other member of it to her. She wasn't really one of them at all. Everything they said, everything they didn't say and everything they did, had made that clear to her long ago, though Dwight wouldn't agree with her, of course. Affable, oh, yes!—and always polite. But kind of ignoring, all the same, just dragging her into things at the last moment, as if they'd just remembered she was there. A lot of snobs. And all so highbrow, too, with their talk of the things happening in the world, the speeches politicians made. As if it mattered, anyway, since nobody could do a thing about it all. And then their way of talking as if authors, even dead and gone ones, were their personal friends—or even members of the family. Well, some of the live ones were, she supposed; but it all came of the fact that her mother-in-law and her father before her belonged to the tribe.

From her mother-in-law's profession Doreen took none of the satisfaction Meg derived from it, for none of her friends was much given to reading, and, in any case, remembered, if they remembered anything of what they read, the title of a book rather than the name of its author. What did stick in their minds were the names of their favourite screen actors and actresses, in whom none of her in-laws seemed interested. It was all theatre with them, and they were "choosy" about the few films they did see—always the ones she was careful to avoid. And of course it was just swank going to all these French films the way they did, just because they understood the language. She found this impersonal conversation both boring and vexatious, for she was convinced they talked that way on purpose when she was there; that at other times they'd go all human and discuss members of the family and pull them to pieces in that funny good-natured way they had. But this, of course, was just another of their ways of keeping her outside.

As to this she was not, perhaps, entirely off the mark. Certainly it was not until Fenella's return from taking Serena and Becky upstairs for their afternoon sleep forced her to make a move to perform the same office for Barry, that Pen remarked, "Larry tells me that Audrey intends to stay on in the services when the war ends. She has hopes, eventually, of getting to Germany."

It was Lydia who said, "What does Rose think of the idea?"

"At the risk of qualifying for a saucer of milk," said Fenella, "I'm sure Rose is simply delighted. She's very chagrined that the war has not yielded her a son-in-law."

[42]

Pen glanced quickly at her daughter, whose voice had uttered this remark in the most matter-of-fact tone. All the same, it was no secret that there was little love lost between Fenella and Audrey. And small wonder! thought Pen, who did not herself care much for her niece, with her managing ways and air of putting everybody neatly in the wrong. She said, with a little laugh, "Well, I agree that Rose is uncommonly disappointed to have reached mid-fifties without having become a grandmother. Really, I do think that one of them might have obliged her."

"Well, darling," said Fenella, "as far as Audrey is concerned, a husband would seem to be a necessary preliminary. And there Audrey, poor dear, has had no luck."

Pen remembered how Andra had once said, "Who would marry a girl with a tongue like an adder's?" It was true that Audrey was a natural "debunker"; but that mattered less perhaps (for one had long ago grown used to that habit in the clever young) than her slightly malicious tongue. Men, she fancied, found it rather "putting-off".

"Well, David might have found a daughter-in-law for her, don't you think?"

"Darling, David's a freak. He never looks at a girl. I don't think he knows there are any in the world. He takes after Uncle Larry, who, so you've often told us, never looked at any girl save Rose."

"Well, Larry certainly isn't a freak," Pen defended her brother.

Privately, she was of the opinion that, fond as he was of Rose, it was Art with which he was really in love and always had been. When Rose, in her very early youth, had married another and gone off to Ireland to live, he had not behaved in the least as young men do on such occasions; and when she came home, a young and wealthy widow, everyone believed it was Rose who'd made all the running. Nevertheless, she had proved a good wife from every point of view. She'd taken the burden of ways and means from his shoulders and left him free to do the work that was, she was sure, of more importance to him than anything else in the world. She wondered sometimes if, in her heart, Rose knew this and had looked to her children to make up. But children were a lottery, and however fond you were of them there was no use whatever in depending upon them for your happiness. No use, for that matter, in depending upon anyone for that. You had to make it for yourself. Your husband, your children might add to it—or subtract from it—but to depend upon personal relationships for it, she had long been convinced, was a cardinal mistake. This large family to which she belonged offered her outstanding proof of this belief.

[43]

Fryn, delving as usual among the books that in their Minty cases lined one side of her Aunt's delightful room, found her attention divided between what she read and what she heard. She didn't very much like Audrey Malling, but she wasn't a very near relation and she did not often come to Richmond or to Hereford Square, so that it didn't seem to matter very much. But vaguely she understood why Audrey's mother wanted her to marry and have children. The family —your own part of it, especially—had to go on. Terrible to think that it might not, that it would be as if you had never lived. Fryn loved being alive so much she already understood that children, the continuance of the family, was the only immortality of which she could be certain, though she was not yet aware that she understood it. She looked down at the slim volume she held in her hand, a novel which she had not found before of her grandfather's, which was dedicated to "My three nieces, Cathy, Andra and Emmy, from an admiring and affectionate uncle." The date was October, 1887, and by then, Cathy, the eldest of the three, had been married to Francis Wingham for six months and had gone to live in Chelsea; but Andra and Emmy were still living in the house in the far corner of Lowndes Square, which had been bombed and now stood battered and out of shape and desolate for all to see, the steps broken away, the windows out, the roof gone. In 1887 Cathy was just eighteen, and now she was an old lady of seventy-six with an American daughter-in-law and a grandson of four. Andra must have been seventeen, heart-whole, still regarding her Uncle Ninian as her *beau ideal* in men; and Emmy had recently passed the Cambridge Senior examination, with honours in maths, and had started as a student at Bedford College. That achievement in maths caused an involuntary pang of envy in Fryn's breast, when first she had heard of it; for it was a subject at which she knew herself a duffer. She had only once met Emmy, at Rose's house, soon after they had all arrived in England, and she had taken away a memory of unlikely hair, a smooth rouged face and sharp green eyes that seemed to snap at rather than rest upon whomever she looked at. But her grandfather had told her that when she was young she was lovely, that Life had pushed her out of shape, and she'd cut herself quite adrift from her family. Of those who had spoken kindly of her and had sought her out, like Andra and her husband and her grandfather, all had gone save Rose. Rose and her daughter Audrey. But Audrey, Fryn thought, with quite dismaying clear-sightedness, only went to see Emmy, because she liked to hear all the horrid things she was supposed to feel about her family, and especially about Aunt Pen, put into words.

[44]

Meg, who could be quite amazingly eloquent upon the business of growing old gracefully, had declared Emmy's henna'd hair and rouged countenance "just awful". But Fryn had thought that if your hair had once been such a lovely colour as everyone agreed Emmy's had, it must be difficult to get resigned to living with it when all the colour had faded; and her face, after all, was hardly wrinkled at all, though it had begun a little to look as if it were moulded in wax and the edges beginning to run. . . .

There was some love-story, too, connected with Emmy, but when Meg, all agog, had sought information on the point from their mother, she had said, "Don't ask me. It all happened long before I was born or thought of." (How *ancient* that made Emmy sound!) Meg said it was queer she shouldn't be interested because, after all, grandfather Malling. . . . Their mother had told them all she considered it necessary for them to know about that ancient piece of family history. How that their great-grandfather had met the governess of his sister's children, "the buds of May", while his dipsomaniac wife was still living, and how eventually they had gone away together, and then the wife, poor thing, had died, and they were able to get married. But that, of course, was quite another story, Lydia said. From Emmy's, she meant. "Nobody," she'd told them, "is the least interested in *that* old story. Unless it's you, Fryn."

Lydia had looked keenly at her young daughter. She saw that to her this large and rambling family was like a story. She was always tracking down threads of narrative, odds and ends of character, anecdotes and dates. And she'd met practically every surviving member of it. Even the redoubtable Emmy. She hoped that line of country, however, would not be too closely explored. Nobody wanted the re-entry of Emmy Gaywood into the family, thank you very much.

Fryn was indeed extremely interested in Emmy's story, scrappy though it was, for nothing that concerned any member of this family to which she belonged came amiss to her. Nothing about them could ever be anything but interesting. But clearly the theme of Emmy bored everyone at Richmond, and it was obvious enough that her aunt was very far from agreeing with her father's estimate of Emmy, or with his belief that life had been unduly harsh to her. For her, Emmy was a self-deceiver who lived on the romantic picture she made of herself and of the things which had once happened to her. Emmy's failure in life, she said, was a failure in character. Born too early? Maybe. But so were they all. Did anyone, she asked, suppose that *she* wouldn't have preferred to miss this machine age if she had had any choice in the matter? It was clear the theme of Emmy bored her profoundly, and when Rose came to tea and talked of "poor Emmy" nobody could be less encouraging. Even Fenella, much given to light and casual comment on what she called The Clan, shied away from the theme of Emmy, if you introduced it. And Bridget looked blank. Neither was there any copy of her books upon her aunt's shelves; and if there'd ever been one among her grandfather's someone had removed it. When she'd asked her aunt about this she had said, "I expect they got sent to the hospitals, darling. We had a great clearance when your grandfather died."

Her eyes dropped to the book on her lap, still open at the dedication page. 1887. What an age ago! A different world, her grandfather had told her, and he'd sounded as if he wished that it could have lasted his time, or at least the good things which belonged to it. Its leisure and what he called its "comparative peace", and the freedom to wander about in it at your pleasure, with nothing to do but pack your bags and buy your ticket. He'd liked going off to France at a moment's notice; he liked the French way of life, the kind of food you could eat there, the wines you could drink. Chambertin, Musigny, Romanée. Château-Lafitte, Margaux and Haut Brion. Though she had tasted none of them their names lived sweetly in her mind. And that of the golden Montrachet—the best of all white wines, her grandfather had said, adding that he had two bottles of it stored away against the lifting of the black-out. But the black-out still preluded the dark, the Montrachet remained uncorked, and her grandfather was in his grave. . . .

"Fryn, put away that book which, clearly, you aren't reading and come and be sociable," said Lydia.

Fryn closed the book and put it back in its proper place on her aunt's shelves, thinking what a pity it was she had not kept even one of Emmy's books. It might tell her more about that fantastic old lady than she had yet been able to learn, which wasn't much more than what she had recorded in her genealogical table—that she was the youngest of the three daughters of her great-aunt, Laura Gaywood, by her first marriage, and that she had remained single. She was aware that she was prepared to like Emmy a little if for no better reason than that nobody else seemed to like her at all.

As she joined the circle round the fire the telephone bell rang and Meg jumped up to answer it. But Doreen, coming downstairs, had reached the instrument first. A bored voice inquired if Mrs. Lowe was there and in her best manner Doreen said, "This is Mrs. *Dwight* Lowe . . ." and was told, "Oh, well, never mind—I've just been on to Hereford Square and been told Mrs. Hampton is lunching at

Richmond. Perhaps you'll give her a message? Tell her that Leah is coming home on Monday for a few days and would like to see her and the girls. And also Pen, if she could spare the time. I suggest tea on Tuesday. If that isn't convenient perhaps one of them would give me a ring? No, that's all, thank you. Good-bye."

Dark fury seethed in Doreen's heart as she hung up and gave the message to Meg to transmit. Ray Romaine. Mrs. Paul Romaine, of Park Lane. Rolling in money, stuck up and bored. Never once had she taken the least notice of her, she thought bitterly, as she retreated upstairs to get over her chagrin. She couldn't even ask her, the prize snob, to a measly tea-party!

Meg watched her go with considerable sympathy. Really, Ray *might* have included her, as she had answered the call! Not that the omission was deliberate, though you couldn't expect Doreen to believe that. Ray simply hadn't thought. Since Maurice was killed and she had lost Leah to the Settlement in East London where her youngest sister, Vicky, had worked for so long, she really didn't think much about anybody but herself. Poor Doreen!—and poor Ray, for that matter, for she was as bored with her life as Doreen with hers. Oh, well, there was nothing anyone could do about it. Doreen would get over it, and meantime she might as well get through to her grandmother and deliver her mother's message about Friday. Tea with pleasure, thank you, but no talk afterwards. No, *really* none. Her grandmother, she thought, as she replaced the receiver, must have been in a hurry, for she had taken this decision without comment.

Her mother and Fryn were delighted at the prospect of seeing Leah again, for they were both very fond of her, but her Aunt Pen said, "Oh, Tuesday—I don't know . . . Well, we'll see." And they all knew that she was weighing against the pleasure of seeing Leah the awful boredom of spending a couple of hours in her mother's company.

BOOK TWO

August, 1945—December, 1946

Chapter One

THE END of the European war was a matter of history when Pen and Gaby, coming in on August Bank holiday from a late afternoon walk in the Park, turned on the wireless just in time to hear a solemn voice announcing the dropping of an atomic bomb on Hiroshima. Clearly, from the highest motives. But how, Pen wondered, sitting there on the arm of her chair, feeling cold and shaken, could human beings take upon themselves such frightful decisions?

"How appalling!" she said.

From the low window-seat Gaby said quietly, "More appalling, do you think, than the continuation of the war with Japan?"

Pen looked at her young niece, and her mind moved, as it was so wont to do, from world to personal affairs. But Gaby did not add anything to her question. Perhaps all she realised at the moment was that that war too was over, that soon she might have news of her husband. It was a very long time since the arrival of that terse card announcing him a prisoner but well. Pen had approved Ward Findon and Gaby's marriage to him, though she knew that she had married him only because she believed that a child needed two parents, a background and security. Perhaps if Richie hadn't been killed in the September of 1940 she would at last have given in and married him; and for the same reason. But Richie was dead and there was the devoted Ward, waiting so patiently, so deeply in love that Gaby's relationship with Richie had made no difference to him. The war had broken down Gaby's defences against Richie—the war which had shut her up with him in England where she must meet him continually, when she had wanted to escape to France. It had not surprised her that they had become lovers; the feeling between them was too strong to stand against the quickening of emotional impulses of that hazardous chapter in the war. And of this relationship Gaby had said only, "It's what Richie *really* wanted, you know, Aunt Pen, not marriage," and so, when he died, she must have comforted herself with that belief. But Pen was not so sure. Gaby was probably right in believing Richie no fit candidate for marriage, but she thought that for all his easy cynicism over the state he *had* wanted to marry Gaby, and if he had known about the coming of Elide would

[51]

have carried the situation. But he hadn't known—there hadn't been time. He'd been dead a whole month before Gaby herself had suspected. Even now Pen couldn't decide whether she'd intended it or not; whether, believing that Richie would not survive the holocaust, she had made up her mind that he must live on in his child. Or had Elide been no more than an accident? Gaby, who told her most things, had there been silent. Anyway, there was Ward, a faithful Dobbin if ever there was one, and her marriage to him, following so soon upon Richie's death, disposed of the family belief (which his mother had not shared) that she and Richie had been more than cousinly-fond of each other. And if Caro had changed her opinion when Richie's will was read and it was found that he had left his not inconsiderable fortune to his little cousin, even Pen did not know, and Gaby's marriage to Ward had made further speculation unrewarding.

All the same, Pen had sometimes wondered if she would have married him if she could have known that Elide would die when she was six months old. But Gaby was not of those who marry in haste and repent as quickly—her whole attitude to the *affaire* Richie was proof of that. Did she regret the stand she had taken? At times, perhaps, but probably not often, for Gaby's was a sound commonsense attitude to life, and to love and marriage—an attitude which had its root in her French heritage and which, crossed by the more romantic British attitude though it was, yet prevented Pen from worrying unduly about her, save at the time of Elide's death, when she had said, with an infinity of sadness in her voice, "Now it's all over." Pen had known what she had meant and how deeply it had grieved her—that now it was as if Richie, that vital attractive creature! had never lived.

She had frequently reproached herself for acquiescing in Gaby's plea, after Elide's death, to be allowed to stay on at Paradise Walk. It had been fatally easy, having regard to her own position as breadwinner, for Gaby to get exemption from war service; and she knew that in her interview with Authority she had been able to make out a good case; and although she couldn't imagine what she would have done without her, she still believed Gaby would have benefited from a wider life. But at the time she had been ill and very unhappy, and Pen had had no heart to urge her to seek a new life for herself elsewhere.

Now, however, with the war over, she longed for her to escape, for Ward to return safely and to carry her off to a life of such happiness and serenity as existence in this unfortunate interval of Time permitted. It's time she got away from me, she thought, with sudden mingled impatience and regret. But oh! how she would miss her when she went!

Departure would soon be much in the air. Gilbert and Lydia would go back to South America, where all their roots were laid, and Meg's too, she fancied, whatever was the case with Jerry and Fryn. Glen and Fenella would go hurrying into the house they vacated, and Doreen would bustle Dwight and Barry into the first flat that offered. All very right and proper, of course. Best face the fact that soon she would find the busy canvas of her life looking decidedly empty, as if it were not a canvas at all but a *tempera* painting from which, slowly but surely, the hand of Time was obliterating all the chief figures and all the detail. Well, there was always her ambition of writing less and living in a country cottage; but there was also a housing shortage; even country cottages stood at a premium.

"You're very thoughtful, Aunt Pen," Gaby interrupted her musings to say.

"Yes, I was wondering what it will be like when you have all gone."

"That won't be just yet, surely? Where can we all go? I know Fenny talks so gaily about stepping into the Hereford Square house when Lydia and Gilbert go, but Gilbert has to get out of the army first. And Glen too. It will be months, perhaps years, before you're free of us."

"Well, when it happens, it will be queer living on here alone."

"Why do it? . . . You don't have to live anywhere alone, you know."

"I don't know what you mean exactly, but I don't know that I should mind living alone, once I'd got used to the idea."

"You do know what I mean, Aunt Pen . . . I mean, you could marry Charles Anstruther."

"At my age, I feel it's rather absurd to marry anyone."

"Charles Anstruther isn't just anyone. And he's been asking you for years."

"What makes you think so?"

"Well, hasn't he? I do think you ought to say 'yes'. But I know why you won't . . . It's James, isn't it? I can't *think* why you should mind what he says about it—or thinks, rather. There can't be many people we know to whom he can say anything, anyhow, for no one goes to see him. Except Rose—and you. And Rose wouldn't believe any scandal about you."

"I'd hate him to say . . . that particular thing, all the same. Or to think it."

"He thinks it now—or thinks he thinks it. What does it matter?"

"Probably not at all—except that that is the one thing I couldn't endure to have said of me. Or to have said of Charles either, bless him."

"I should stop troubling about James and think seriously about the idea of marrying Charles the next time he asks you. One can say 'No' too often."

Pen looked thoughtfully at her niece as she said, "But supposing I did say 'Yes' to Charles, I couldn't leave you all here to cope."

"Why not? We rather like coping and do it rather well too, I think. And if it's Doreen you're worrying about, don't. She's not your responsibility, and Fenella and I are equal to her worst transports. And we'd look after Barry, I promise you."

"You sound quite anxious to get rid of me."

"In a way I should be glad—for your sake. You've slaved long enough."

Well, here was a turning of the tables! But—*had* she slaved? She'd enjoyed writing, though she regretted having to write so much—the mind of the novelist needed to lie fallow. And novel-writing was now much less fun—the boundaries of her familiar world had narrowed considerably during the war years, and now the class of which she wrote was suffering a sea-change. It was out of fashion and might soon very well be out of existence. People no longer mattered; for all the politicians talked so much of them. But it was people *en masse*, not individuals; and political ideologies lay thickly upon everything everywhere. She found it depressing. I was born too late, she thought. As a writer I'd have been happier in the '90's. They, surely, were the novelist's Paradise. Well, now that The Family was standing on its own feet, even, she felt, about to take wing, her need to constitute herself the breadwinner was diminishing. Maybe she could write less and enjoy the business more. The hungry generations were on her track all right, treading down her and her generation of writers. The clever young of to-day sniffed at the gods of yesterday, and to most of those newly-elevated she seldom felt disposed to bow the knee.

Gaby went on, "I'd rent this house from you and make myself responsible for overheads—I can well afford it, you know. Fenella and Dwight and Doreen—and Glen too, when he comes back—can stay on here until they can find homes of their own."

[54]

"You *have* got it nicely fixed up. And supposing Ward comes back?"

"He wouldn't mind. He quite liked The Family, you know. Look, Aunt Pen. You know as well as I do that you'll say 'Yes' to poor Charles some day, so it's just as well to think things out. And whatever happens—about Ward, I mean—I'd hate to live anywhere but here, you know. It's been my home for so long."

The sharp ringing of the telephone bell prevented Pen from making any rejoinder to this, and Gaby rose and hurried out to answer it. She came back very quickly, to say, "It's Charles. Now don't you dare to say 'No' again."

But this time Charles forebore to ask her the question he'd been asking her so long, though he began with his usual inquiry, "How are you, my dear?"

"A trifle low, I think."

"Hiroshima?"

"Possibly."

"Can you find time to have lunch with me on Wednesday—or does the book enchain you?"

"On the contrary. I'd like to come on Wednesday. What time?"

"Could you manage twelve?—at the usual place. I've an appointment out of town in the early afternoon and if the weather's fine I thought you might like to drive out with me. I'll get you home in good time for dinner."

"It wouldn't matter, anyway. Gaby and Fenella do the coping. And the evening meal is no longer graced by the name of dinner, you know."

"Then you'll come?"

"Thank you, I'd like it very much."

It was a briefer conversation than usual and an impersonal one. As she put on the receiver Pen wore a thoughtful air.

"Well," said Gaby when she rejoined her. "Did you say 'Yes'?"

"To a different question," said Pen, feeling oddly as if she had been reprieved.

"Lunch?"

"And a drive out of town afterwards."

Gaby looked thoughtful.

"Don't let me be late—the lunch is for twelve."

"I'll make a note of it," said Gaby, the perfect secretary. She saw that Pen wasn't going to add anything to these remarks, without realising that this was because she had nothing to add. But that Pen should go driving with Charles Anstruther into the country was

[55]

certainly something new. Though they had been close friends for so long and had seen much more of each other since the death of Charles's wife, and though he came frequently to Richmond, Pen had never committed herself to anything but a lunch or dinner in town and an occasional theatre. We're getting on, thought Gaby, watching Pen as she picked up her hat and walked to the door. All the same, I wish he'd asked her the usual question. . . . She might not have said "Yes", but I don't believe, this time, that she'd have given him a forthright "No". Or is this Invitation to the Drive another way of asking it?

Pen, at any rate, asked no questions during the lunch as to what was to follow. Neither did Charles refer to it. They talked of the recent election, of the "new democracy", the book world and similar impersonal themes. They were, as ever, very comfortable and at home in each other's company. They found the same things amusing, exasperating and worth while. They were fervent Jane Austenites. They jointly hated the spread of industrialism, the spoiling of the country to serve the town and deplored the tendency, in film and novel, to deal with violence, ugliness and morbidity. Spivs, racketeers, murderers and their female retinue, together with casual adulterers of both sexes were, they agreed, heroes and heroines as depressing as they were boring. It had become entirely démodé, Pen said, to write of ordinary pleasant people. "Violence is the common currency. Not to help circulate it writes you down 'old fogy'. Well, I suppose I am. Anyway, I've been at the game too long."

"There's a man called Eden Phillpotts," Charles suggested with a smile. "He can still show the youngsters a thing or two."

"He seems able to let the political ideologies go hang," said Pen. "But I hate—and so cannot altogether ignore—them. Like father, like daughter."

"Don't you believe it. You're a born novelist, which your father, though when he liked he could write like an angel, was not. But you've driven your talent hard. If you took two years off you'd feel fresh again."

She did not say, "How can I?" for she knew what was in his mind. She thought, How heavenly it would be not to feel I *must* write! Once nothing could keep me from my desk. Now I have to drag myself to it. Perhaps writing for a living is what's wrong.

"Two wars in a lifetime are very hampering to the novelist," she said. "*My* sort of novelist, anyway."

"Our Jane's war didn't hamper her unduly, I fancy."

"No, but the misery and ruin of it wasn't hammered out on the wireless several times a day. No one had thought of the bombing aeroplane. Jane's war stayed a long way off."

"But the consequences reached home. Jane had a capacity for ignoring in her novels everything not germane to her chosen scheme."

"I know. As a novelist she could ignore the burning of Moscow, the banishing of Napoleon to St. Elba, his escape and Waterloo . . . All the world-shattering events of her day, in fact. And yet she never produced the effect of setting her characters in a vacuum—which is the fate of modern writers if they ignore the background of life to-day."

This topic lasted them until the waiter brought the bill. But it was not until Charles was nosing the car through the Piccadilly traffic that Pen inquired what time his appointment was.

"Oh, any time this side of tea," he told her.

"And where does it take us?"

"To the neighbourhood of Petersfield. Do you know it?"

"I think not."

"It's a pleasant spot, with a market-place and some interesting old houses. And a statue, for some reason, to Dutch William. It has certain literary associations and no interest whatever for the tourist, thank heaven. It has a hill of its own—Butser, the highest point, I believe, in Hampshire—as well as several pleasantly wooded slopes. And not very far away is Broad Halfpenny Down, where the men of Hambledon, old John Nyren and his pals, were playing cricket when we were losing the American colonies. And there's enchanting country all around that you'll like, I think, very much."

"Shall we have time to see much of it?"

"All the time in the world, I hope," said Charles, somewhat enigmatically, as he edged the car into the King's Road at Sloane Square.

The pleasantness of the Portsmouth Road, the Surrey heights, and Hindhead in particular, despite the disfiguring radar masts, were a revelation to Pen, who had done so little rambling around, either in the car she and Bar had once owned, or by what Dwight as a little boy had called "on feets". Definite journeys they had made—to Chart so often to see James and occasionally on to the Kentish coast; to Sherborne to see Cathy—these were the routes by road with which she was acquainted. For years there had been no car until Dwight spilled his gratuity out on another bone-shaker, to get himself to and from the station when his convalescence was at last complete. This country on London's doorstep, snatched from the greedy grasp of the builder by the National Trust, was worth more than the hasty glance of the passing motorist, and she was glad when Charles suggested they left the car by the roadside and walked to the summit of Hindhead to look at the view and the stone direction and distance disc someone had thoughtfully placed there. She was ultimately detached from this spot, not without difficulty, and promised another fine view, time permitting, nearer Petersfield, from South Harting Down. There was another from Petersfield's own hill, Butser; but that must be walked up and so must wait for a later occasion. But two fine views, one in Surrey and the other in Sussex, within twelve miles of each other, would be overflowingly good measure to Pen, for one day.

But in between them, said Charles, came the house . . .

"The house?"

"Yes—the one I've brought you out here to see."

"And your appointment? Is that a myth?"

"No—it's with the house."

Pen felt the colour run up warm into her face, but she said as casually as she could manage, "Well, I like looking at houses," and nothing further was said on the point as they travelled smartly along the Portsmouth Road, which now offered a view ahead of the Downs, rising over the steeple of a church which Charles told her was in Sheet, with the giant Butser Hill blocking the sky to the south, and wooded slopes and green fields climbing steeply between them. The afternoon, Pen felt, had somehow become adventurous; the years flying from her shoulders like a discarded coat in the wind.

"Where are we now? In Hampshire or Surrey?"

"Hampshire—with Sussex very close at hand. Surrey-Sussex, Surrey-Hampshire. Border country. I've a particular liking for it."

The house, when they came to it, lay beneath the very lee of Butser, and stood well back from the quiet road. Its gate had been opened and secured, as if they were expected, and as they drove through she saw the name neatly painted upon it, Wyngates. Her mind explored the name. Should it or should it not have an apostrophe? Who or what were "wyn" gates, or was Wyngate the name of the owner of some previous building on the site? If so, definitely the apostrophe.

It was a low white-washed house, with a beautiful dark-brown roof and leaded bay downstairs-windows, one of which was set to the corner instead of in a line with its fellows, producing an un-symmetrical effect which gave an odd charm to the house, though

Charles said it had been done to catch the sun from morning to late afternoon and that the charm was accidental—and a little surprising. There was a porch of heavy oak timbers; a wide oak front door, with shallow circular steps leading up from a paved formal front garden. This much Pen's sharp eyes, trained to absorb a scene quickly and accurately, took in at once; but gazing closer, standing on the steps and looking up above the porch to the panels beneath an up-stairs window, she saw that they were of herring-bone brickwork, contrasting in colour most delightfully with the dark-brown of the roof, the grey oak, the whitewashed bricks of the wall.

Standing there on the steps she saw that the downstairs rooms, save for a few odd pieces of furniture set against the walls, were empty; but she made no comment. At her side, Charles said, "How do you like it?"

"I think it's very good-looking indeed. Quite modern, despite the oak."

"*Except* for the oak. It was built just before the war began. I think you've lived long enough in an old house."

Again she was conscious of the warmth of her face, but she did not otherwise show that she had noticed this second twist to the personal, and Charles, putting his hand on her arm, said, "Come and look inside."

"You have a key?"

He took it calmly out of his pocket.

"Certainly," he said, "since the house belongs to me."

"You've *bought* it? Recently?"

"A month ago, to be precise, but the late owners only moved out on Monday."

"Strange, in these times, to leave a good house like this."

"They're going to the other side of the world. They think England's finished and have a son in New Zealand."

Stranger still, Pen thought, walking up the steps at Charles's side. How did one turn one's back on one's own country for ever? Much as she'd enjoyed her trips abroad, she had always been glad to come back. Austerity or not, she could not live anywhere but in England.

It was not a large house. It had four upstairs rooms and three downstairs, in addition to kitchen quarters. All were well-planned, light and of a sensible size, and Butser seemed to be keeping guard over them all. No house could have been more strongly in contrast with her old house by the river, and yet, in its way, its charm was as potent. It was the same sort of charm that was possessed by her father-in-law's house at Chart, which he had designed so long ago for himself; he might, almost, she thought, have designed this, though at some of the modern gadgets he would have sniffed. James. The fly in the balm . . . but she owed him a visit. She sighed as she made a mental note of that. She neither liked nor loved him; but he was old and alone. And bitter and resentful and ready with his barbs as ever, doubtless. No matter . . .

"Well?" said Charles at her elbow. "Could you bear, do you think, to live here?"

"Oh yes—anybody could bear that."

"With me, I meant."

"Oh, Charles!—are you presenting me with a *fait accompli*?"

"Not entirely. I can't carry you over the threshold and lock you up until you say 'Yes'. I wish I could. But I confess I did hope to tempt you."

"I didn't need a house to tempt me."

"Yet you've never said 'Yes' to my question. And you evade it now."

She was silent.

"Shall I tell you why? Because of James. James's spleen. James's tongue . . . You hide it with talk of The Family but it's James and only James really. Gaby can take the old house over from you—I know that she'd be glad to. The place would be run well without you and you know it. You're not the sort of woman who never realises her children are grown up. Since Gaby is willing to house everybody until they can find homes of their own, even that problem doesn't arise. So it must be James still. And James only."

She sat down on a window-seat and said, "Yes, I suppose it is."

"Well, that admission is a step forward. If there were no James— or if he were a reasonable person—I take it that you would have married me long ago?"

"I don't know . . . I couldn't, while the war was on and Dwight so ill, have left Richmond."

"But you'd marry me now?"

"Yes—if . . . if James, as you say, were different."

"And as he isn't different you'll let me live in my nice house alone?"

"You're making it very difficult."

"I'd like to make it impossible. Say 'Yes', Pen—and leave your father-in-law to me. I can deal with him."

"I can deal with him, too, Charles."

"Not on this point. You care so much for your good name—and for mine?—you'd sacrifice the rest of your life to preserving it from James's tongue."

[60]

Gaby, she thought, had been talking to Charles, as well as he to her. She said, "No—he would never *say* what he pretends he thinks; at least to anyone but me. James isn't crude. Even now. But I can't give him the satisfaction of believing that he has proof of what he once asserted—that years ago, when Bar was alive, I knew you were in love with me . . . and encouraged you by 'gallivanting about Europe' with you."

No point in hiding that from him now. But she smiled to remember James's description of that professional visit of hers to Vienna, and of the perfectly *comme il faut* Tyrolean trip, with Charles and two other people, with which it had ended.

"But it was true, my dear, as far as I was concerned. I've always been a little bit in love with you, I think; and the Austrian meeting deepened the state. If you never suspected it I must have behaved even better than I'd hoped. But you're not the sort of woman . . . you weren't the sort of girl . . . who imagines every man who likes her, and likes her company, must be in love with her."

Pen's large eyes had widened in dismay as this little speech proceeded. When it stopped she looked oddly deflated. Even now, on the edge of being labelled "elderly" and "old fogy", it dismayed her to have James proclaimed right. "Clear as daylight," James had said. "Don't tell me you didn't know it too."

"But Charles, I never did suspect . . . I hadn't the faintest notion. When, years later, long after Bar's death, James asserted it I was dumbfounded."

"I'm ready to believe that. If you had you'd not have gone on with the friendship—or if you'd felt the least bit toward me as I toward you. I know that about you—just as I knew that when Bar was alive there was no other man for you. Do I get a good mark for that?"

"Several good marks, Charles."

"And it is true, isn't it, that but for the . . . hindrance, which you call The Family and which we both know to be James, you'd have married me any time during the last three years?"

"I don't know . . . I don't think so—the last year perhaps . . . Only—there *was* James. There still is."

"I insist that James can be dealt with."

"I'd rather he wasn't."

"Why not leave him, then, to his bitterness and spite? It cannot harm us. What does it matter what he says? Or thinks? *We that have free souls*, you know."

"It ought to console me, but it doesn't. I should hate to hand James his case against me—against you—on a platter."

"I can understand why you feel like that. But it's quite quixotic, all the same. For consider, my dear. Why, if we were what James thinks we were, or thinks he thinks we were, didn't we get married directly I was free? Can you answer that? What explanation do you imagine James put upon the fact that we didn't?"

"Either that we were tired of each other, or having dispensed with the ceremony for so long, decided there was no need to bother so late in the day. Or that I hesitate to provide him with 'proof' of his base insinuations."

"Which is, in fact, the fact?"

"Which is, as you say, the fact."

"But Pen, I begin to wonder. Is it? I'm not at all sure that these aren't bogeys you're putting up because the idea of marrying again at this time of day makes you feel a little ridiculous."

She stared at him, then began to laugh, a little to Charles's surprise, even to her own.

"Well, so it does—so it did. But that doesn't eliminate James. On the contrary, it brings him even more emphatically upon the scene with the pointing finger of scorn. Nothing eliminates James. Nothing ever will."

"Oh, cheer up, my dear. I suggest you emulate Jane's Mr. Bennett and look on the bright side. James will leave this earthly scene in due course, like the rest of us. I suggest again that we eliminate him by ignoring him. Or at least, his unworthy suspicions. Or, even far better, by *not* ignoring him. In short, by announcing our forthcoming marriage in *The Times*."

"Will you live here—alone—if I ignore all these ingenious suggestions of yours?"

"Yes. . . . The lease of my flat is running out. I don't want to commit myself to another London tenancy of seven years, at a postwar rental too."

"But won't you find it a long journey every day?"

"There's a good electric train service—and you can drive me to the station . . . that is, you *could*. I propose to go to the office four days a week only. Murrayfield's out of the army now and he's a capable chap. I'm sixty-three and want a little home life before I die."

"You talk as though you've never had any."

"I haven't. I had a great deal of social life—too much. And a great deal of a good many other things—some of them very jolly. But not home life."

That, Pen felt, was probably true. She had only once met Dorothea, Charles's beautiful and socially-exalted wife—that spring in Vienna, where she used to go each year for the opera. She had been interested (and then but faintly) in only the most renowned of Ffoliott authors, which did not include me, she thought. And quite properly. And as for my friendship with her husband, I was one of many. His capacity for friendship with his women authors is legendary. She reflected that this was the first time she had ever heard Charles utter a word of even the most oblique criticism of his wife or marriage.

"Except," he went on, "when I came to Richmond—particularly in Bar's day, when the children were small and used to call me 'Uncle Charles'."

She was touched by that. She said, "Give me a few days—until the end of the week. You shall have a definite answer on Saturday evening, if you'll ring me after the News."

He smiled at her gently, but said, "No. Three more days of 'thinking' will have no more effect upon you than that of the last three years. You'll say 'Yes' or 'No' before you leave here, and if it's 'No' I'll take it as final, my dear. I'll not ask you again, though that's no argument against you telling me if you change your mind. Now come and see the garden. It may prove more eloquent than either the house or I. The recent owners had a good man and luckily he's willing to stay on."

"No," she said, surprising herself, "I won't look at the garden. I won't look at anything else. Take me home, Charles, please."

"I'll take you to have some tea. It'll do us both good," he said.

Pen was silent as they got into the car and drove in search of tea. She was angry with herself and angry with Charles—though for exactly what she didn't know. For springing this . . . this *temptation* upon her, for arguing with her about the unarguable . . . the intuitive; for being so understanding and so certain of her feelings; for having realised that James was the real stumbling-block and for being so understanding about that. If only someone could laugh her out of her complex about James. . . . That had been Bar's word for it, and she'd never admitted it was the right one; but she saw suddenly that it was. James's resentment and unfairness touched her pride, gave her an exalted idea of her integrity, which Bar, she fancied, had seen, which was probably why James and her feeling about him had never come between them to disturb their relationship. In her youth perhaps it was easier to understand, and justify, her reactions to the possessive attitude of her father-in-law to his son, his resentment of her appearance upon the scene; but now in her late fifties she was, she felt, made slightly ridiculous by their persistence. And without meaning to do so—probably without being even slightly aware of it—Charles had brought her face to face with that unflattering conclusion.

And besides, he had been too guarded, too considerate. He hadn't once used the word "love", only the phrase "in love" —and that a qualified description of a past state. Yet even at the early "fogy" stage something more than a warm liking, sympathy and mutual interests seemed to her to be necessary to marriage. He had gone so carefully. Having used up all his courage upon the house trick it was as if he had none left for tackling her and her complex. Himself sane and well-balanced, he could have laughed her out of her fixation if he'd set about it. But he'd walked delicately, like Agag before the Lord, had reasoned with her as if on this point she was a reasonable creature. And she wasn't. She never had been—which Bar had known. But Charles did not. . . . *We that have free souls, it touches us not. . . . Our withers are unwrung*. It was true, of course. Only her pride, her overweening sense of integrity, her anger at the injustice meted out to her, her chagrin that James would not really let her *exist*, had barred the way to seeing before how very true it was.

She sat silent at Charles's side, thinking how absurd it was that she had wanted—needed—in this matter to be rushed off her feet, but respecting him for having in the end refused her delaying tactics. The situation had, she knew, to be settled once and for all before they parted this evening. He meant what he said—he would never bother her again, even though, generous creature that he was, he had left the door open for her own approach.

And suddenly she realised another thing which lay behind her stubborn attitude. Confronted with this attractive house, she had suddenly, and for a moment, seen marriage with Charles as a means of escape from the job at which she had worked for so long. She felt stale and tired: she needed a rest and Charles was offering her a chance to take it. And something within her stood back. Was it her reluctance to forgo the independence she had maintained over so long a period? She had enjoyed the hard work she had done and there had been satisfaction in her role as breadwinner after Bar's death, and in the fact that her talent had remained unflagging for so long. But now perhaps the long strain of the war, or the general sense of anti-climax and frustration which had followed upon its conclusion—or, much more likely, and growing out of these things, the conviction that the kind of book she wrote, even the people she wrote about, were démodé, completely out of favour not only with the oracles (with which she had never unduly concerned herself or they with her) but with the average journalist cum-reviewer—had given her a sense less perhaps (though that, too) of staleness than of stalemate. It would be pleasant not to have to earn a certain amount of hard cash a year—much more difficult now, with shortage of paper and labour—and to find, perhaps, a new *venue*.

When she had talked of these things to Charles he had gone at least part of the way with her, even, she felt, accepting her self-verdict of staleness, though with a delicacy that should have pleased her more than it did. But now she thought he had realised the situation much earlier and had seen in her marriage to him a way to a new lease for her of her writing career. Charles had played his part over the years in helping to build her up as a Ffoliott author, and would be concerned in this matter. It surprised her that this view of the situation had not before occurred to her, though might it not have been the unconscious impulse behind her refusal to marry him? If so, Charles was right in thinking that James was only the bogy which her pride had set up in the path, blocking out all else. (She began to think Charles knew her better than she knew herself.) And the bogy had blocked out not only the realisation of the real reason for her long-continued refusal to marry Charles but something which, surely, had been very clearly to be seen for a long while—that her responsibilities as a breadwinner had for some time now been considerably less onerous, since Gaby had said she was willing to take over the house in Paradise Walk and was financially capable of maintaining it in good order. And, as she had recently made plain to her, the constitution of the present household would cause her no shrinking of the spirit.

There remained, then, only two obstacles in the way of her re-marriage. Her pride in her long career as a breadwinner, and James. And if Charles was right, only one—her pride.

It was this view of the situation in which she was immersed as they drove through the quiet countryside.

And then, surprising her, she saw (and for the first time) something else which Charles was offering her. Not only an easier way of life, an opportunity to refresh and re-trim her writing talent—but the deep affection of long standing. It shamed her now to reflect that that was something she had always taken for granted, without seeing it for what it was. But now, suddenly, she saw it as a kind of fragrance down the years, like a bush of honeysuckle everlastingly in bloom beneath her window. She found herself remembering Edna Vincent Millay's poem about love offered as children brought you "cowslips in a hat swung from the hand", and felt as if, carelessly, unseeing, she had knocked it to the ground. But he had behaved as if he had not

[65]

noticed the gesture. She sat silent, watching his long thin hands on the steering wheel.

After tea he drove her home. A friendly, easy-mannered Charles, who showed no sign whatsoever of disappointment or hurt pride, or the knowledge that his little plan had failed or his hopes withered in the dust. And for very shame Pen could not, she found, re-open the subject. Swung over from her uncertainties and reservations to a perception of something so deep-lying, so modest, that for years she had not seen it for what it was and had taken what she did see for granted, she was now left without words, without any knowledge of the way back to the old path of easy familiarity which together they had trod for so long. And because she was afraid of saying the wrong thing, and because she felt ashamed and suddenly a little shy, she said nothing, and was wracked with dismay because for Charles it must, she felt, be evidence that the mood which had caused her to refuse to look at the garden of the house and to ask to be taken home still persisted. What he said was kindly, tactful, and as utterly impersonal as it had been over tea. My poor Charles, how shabbily I've treated you, she thought now, and felt very small and thin. Bar, she thought also, would have known how to deal with me. He'd always known she had a phobia about James, and besides, it wasn't love as a woodland bouquet he'd offered her, that they'd offered each other. Swinging together, how many years ago? down that wide street in Rome, love had flowed abruptly between them, while he'd looked down upon her from his superior height and talked all the while of the medieval palaces he'd brought her there to see, and which, as a budding architect, he'd found so fascinating. Well, that sort of love happened once in a lifetime—and in one's youth. And frequently the flame died out; but not for Bar and her. Even the grave, which had snatched him so untimely from her, had not quenched it. Love of that kind was not for her again; but the thin sweet fragrance of Charles's bouquet of wild flowers was infinitely attractive to her, and she thought, They liked each other, these two. Bar would approve of our marriage and be glad—if he could know.

But still, for all the lightening of her spirit, her thoughts would not clothe themselves in words. The path back was still hidden from her. Here I sit, most idiotically, like a sulky child, she reflected, who speaks only when spoken to. . . .

"Come in," she said, when soon after seven o'clock Charles drew up quietly outside the iron gates of the old house in Paradise Walk.

The windows stood wide open, but there was no sound of wireless or voices, such as usually greeted her after a short absence. "Yes, please do. Gaby will be expecting you to take pot-luck at the evening meal."

After a brief hesitation, he followed her up the path to the front door, and taking the key from her, turned it in the lock.

The house was very quiet and cool. The door of the dining-room stood ajar and she saw that the table was laid for three. The young people were obviously not expected. Her study door was shut, but that of the sitting-room stood wide and that to the garden at the far end of the hall. And beneath the willow sat Gaby, quietly darning a sock.

"Hallo," she said. "Come and sit down. I'm all alone. Fenella's had a message from Glen—forty-eight hours' leave. So she dashed off to town to meet his train. They're eating out and doing a show. And Dwight and Doreen are in town too. I was hoping you'd both come and keep me company at supper. I hunted the salmon this morning, with some success—before I knew there'd be no one but me to eat it, unless you came in. . . . Have you had a pleasant time?"

"Very," said Charles. "It was a good day for a drive. And Pen approved the country."

"I was taken to see a house," said Pen.

"Whose is it?"

"Charles's."

Gaby didn't appear very surprised.

"Are you going to live in it, Charles?" she asked.

It was Pen who replied, and the sound of her voice saying what it did awoke a mild surprise in her. It was as if, suddenly, the path stood clear. . . .

"*We* are going to live in it—that is, if Charles still wants to marry me."

"Well, considering that he's been asking you on and off for the past two years . . ."

"I think, perhaps, he's got tired of asking me."

"I dare say. He should have knocked you on the head long ago and carried you off . . . When's the great day to be?"

Charles tucked Pen's arm beneath his own and smiled at her.

"As soon as maybe, I think. We can't, these days, keep an empty house waiting."

"Sit down and tell me about it," said Gaby.

The sharp ringing of the telephone soon cut across the conversation

[67]

and Pen, seeing Gaby hastening to disentangle herself from a sock of Dwight's and a collection of darning wools, got up to answer it.

For a second her heart stood still as she recognised the prim correct voice at the other end of the line. Mrs. Simmonds, James's housekeeper.

"Can I speak to Mrs. Lowe, please?" it said.

"Speaking," said Pen, with that little familiar throbbing of her pulses. How odd that at this moment James should be sending her a message!

I thought I'd better let you know, madam, that the master died this afternoon at four o'clock. Quite sudden. His heart, the doctor said."

Pen heard herself saying, "Oh, dear! I hope he didn't suffer?"

"No, madam. Instantaneous, Dr. Morgan said."

"Oh, I'm glad of that. I'll come down to-morrow, Mrs. Simmonds, shall I? I might be of some use."

"Just as you like, madam—but everything's in train. The funeral is to be on Saturday at two o'clock . . . Alston will meet any train, madam, if you will let us know."

"Very well. . . . Thank you for ringing me, Mrs. Simmonds," said Pen and after an instant's hesitation hung up. There was nothing she could usefully add to this conversation. For a quarter of a century Mrs. Simmonds had been in charge at Greystones and never once had she managed to thaw that icy correctness. She was, James had said, the perfect housekeeper; she was an excellent cook and she knew her place. But to Pen she was unknown and unknowable. It was as if she had sensed James's own attitude to her, which would not, she felt, have been difficult, for it was like an emanation through the house. She knows, thought Pen, sitting there at her desk, her eyes on Charles and Gaby beneath the willow, that in that house I was never welcomed, only tolerated, first as Bar's wife, then as his widow. There's nothing I can do if I go, she thought—"everything is in train"—and now there will be no James to feel aggrieved if I do not go, and unwelcoming if I do. James is dead—and that long chapter in my life is closed at last.

Then suddenly she could think of nothing save of her satisfaction in the fact that she had given Charles his answer before she knew that James was dead.

She got up and went out and stood in front of Charles and Gaby and gave them the news. And then she was moved to add, "Poor James!" and a sadness which surprised both her and her hearers spilled over into her voice and muted it.

"He was very old, my dear," said Gaby, as one excusing death. "Eighty-four, wasn't it?"

It was strange to hear that past tense, to realise that he was gone from her life for ever. She'd had over thirty years of James, and for the past fourteen, ever since Bar's death, he'd not troubled to hide his dislike of her, which formerly he'd smothered beneath that un-yielding suavity of manner, so much admired by the undiscerning Rose. And though it had angered her, she had felt sorry for him—for making such a poor thing of life, for getting, with all his posses-sions, so little enjoyment out of it; for hugging his eternal resentment against her for daring to marry his son. And though Bridget had once said, "But, mother, James *does* get enjoyment out of his way of life—at least, he would if you didn't, somehow, take the sting out of his remarks by seeming not to notice them," she had continued to feel sorry for him. And now as she thought of him dead, among all his lovely things, his summer garden flaming beyond his windows, she wished she could believe that he was re-united in some happier world with Bar, the only person he'd ever loved—and alas! so sel-fishly. She would willingly have forgone, in this moment, all her silent victories over him during the years to have been able now, just for this evening, to believe in a heaven where earthly relation-ships, which Death had snapped, were reunited. But she didn't believe it, and her inability to believe seemed now the first real unkindness she had ever done him. But doctrines and dogmas had nothing to say to her. Her response was still to the humanism which she had im-bibed in her youth, though her father had reminded her shortly before his death that it was not to-day "in credit, nor familiarly understood", and that "it bore the open reproach of powerful opponents and the more injurious reproach of its own lack of advocacy". Nevertheless, it remained for her the only torch which could light her way through the forest we call Life.

Chapter Two

WHEN JAMES'S will was read it seemed to Pen that he had not entirely done yet with this world, for apart from three small straight legacies to Fenella, Bridget and Barry, and a modest annuity to herself which she would never enjoy, since it was conditional upon her not re-marrying, he had left the whole of his possessions to Dwight, but on condition that he and Doreen went to live in his house. When old Dartford, James's solicitor, dropped this surprise into the quiet room Pen involuntarily sighed out a faint, "Oh, dear!" But this legacy too was conditional, it seemed. If they decided not to live there, or sold within ten years, two-thirds of the proceeds of the sale, and of the up-keep income that went with the gift of the house, were to be held in trust for Barry until his coming of age; or, if he died before that date, then for any son of Fenella's, or, failing her producing a male child, then to any son of Bridget's should she marry. If neither of them produced a son within the next ten years, the money was to go to some professional charity in which James was interested. He had thought of everything, Pen felt—even of the possibility that Barry might be the beginning and end of Dwight's family. . . .

Her first reaction (before the conditions were recited) had been one of dismay, for she did not want Dwight to live in James's house, even though it would be pleasant to think of him well-housed and well-provided-for. Greystones to her was an unhappy house, so alive with James's hates and bitterness that she could not believe anyone could be happy there. But she did not attempt to dissuade Dwight when he said that he was willing to try the experiment if Doreen would consent.

What Doreen thought of the proposition is best related in her letter to her friend, Milly Burke, who was just then away on holiday, and although, if she could help it, Doreen did not put pen to paper, this was an occasion when the effort would bring her what she thought of as a little "kudos". And she wrote at unusual length, but only one short extract need concern us here.

"What *do* you think my dear Dwights grandfather has died and left him a lot of money only we have to live in his house in Kent

[70]

to get it or else most of it goes to Barry—aren't people awful? So I suppose we shall have to have a shot at it but fancy me in a country house, quite a mansion too my dear but modern of course or I wouldn't dream of it—having to keep my end up with all the starchy nobs and nobesses in the place. Of course it isn't in the *depths* but I dont know—I don't fancy it much and of course its too far away from the city with that foot of Dwights really—still it would be nice to get free of this place because my revered motherinlaw is getting married again to her publisher which looks to me like good business but he is very nice really quite human—hes been coming here a lot for years and nobody seems very surprised. Theyre going to live in the country too but in a place near Petersfield ours is in Kent near Westerham isnt that where Mr. Churchill lives? When the will was read my motherinlaw said Oh dear at the bit about the house and us living in it but Dwight says that was because she never liked going there on account of the old gentleman who didnt like her it seems though I must say that on the two or three occasions when I was taken down there he was niceness itself to me kind of fatherly too— I tell you I *was* surprised after all Id gathered about him. I told Dwight I thought the Oh dear was on account of me—meaning she didnt think I should suit the place but D. said it was much more likely she thought it wouldnt suit me which seemed to be the same thing only not put so nasty. Dwight says we shant be as well off as the old gentleman supposed because of the death duties or something but there we are old thing and Ill let you know how we get on— Excuse mistakes in spelling etc, you know how I hate writing. Cheerio. Doreen.

"P.S. My motherinlaw gets married in a fortnights time quick work—I expect youll see it in *The Times* if you go to the library."

In due course Fryn made the requisite addition to the entry in her genealogical table below her aunt's name. M. (2) 1945 Charles Wingfield Anstruther, and on the following morning read the brief record of that event in *The Times*. "At Richmond, on the 31st August, Charles Wingfield Anstruther to Laura Penelope Barrowby-Lowe." Meg was bitterly disappointed. They might at least have put L. P. Malling in brackets, she complained to Lydia, who laughed. L. P. Malling, she said, had been married thirty years ago, and anyway, her aunt would tell her that it wasn't the *novelist* who was marrying Charles Anstruther.

Writing to her father, Fryn said: Uncle Charles has given Aunt Pen a puppy for a wedding present. She says she always wanted to have a dog. He's called Hamish and is a darling.

For Doreen Pen's marriage day had held, in the finish, one excitement only—that of meeting at last the family scapegoat, Danny Wingham. "My dear!" she said to Milly when next they met, "he was *fascinating*! Such a thrill! And a surprise, too, for of course my Revered hadn't invited him. He came to deputise for his mother, who wasn't well enough to make the journey. She's frightfully old, of course. If you ask me, he was glad of the excuse. At any rate, he seemed to be enjoying himself. No side about him at all!"

"Did he bring his wife?" asked Milly.

"Oh, yes . . ."

"What's she like?"

"Well, you couldn't call her pretty, of course. Dark and small. No make-up at all, as far as I could see. But beautifully turned-out."

"Young?"

"Younger than Sir Daniel, yes."

"Well, he must be a bit long in the tooth . . ."

Doreen positively recoiled from this vulgar description of the attractive Danny. She said, "Well, he's middle-aged, of course, but he's frightfully handsome."

"And bald on top?"

"No," said Doreen. "Not even thin, and no grey either."

"He sounds a perfect Adonis," was Milly's comment, to which Doreen retorted, "Well, I don't know who the gentleman was," but as Milly didn't either she laughed and said, "And when do you get an invite to the Manor?"

As that was a question to which Doreen did not know the answer, perhaps it was just as well that she hadn't heard Fenella's comment to Meg upon her encounter with the owner of the Manor.

"Angling for an invitation to Bourne. But if she doesn't stop being so *very* fascinating she'll be unlucky. Livvy, I perceive, has her eye on her!"

But Fryn, writing up her diary of the day's events and impressions, recorded that she thought Danny had been "nothing loth". She wrote: "I think he's a very *impudent* man. Not because he says impudent things (though he does) but because he *looks* them. Any other man could have said to Fenella, 'Well, my child, prettier than ever, I perceive,' without making it sound flirtatious. Fenella said calmly, 'I hope so,' which made him laugh, but left him without an answer. And I do not think somehow, that that often happens to Sir Daniel Wingham . . ."

It took some time to settle up James's estate and the spring of

[72]

'forty-six was well advanced before Dwight and Doreen moved into Greystones. It was, perhaps, unfortunate that out of that sunny April —the warmest, so the weather experts said, for thirty-five years—it should have been the very wet Friday of its first week which they had chosen for their "moving in". Not that that, of itself, was a very onerous task, since they were going to a house fully furnished and ready, as the house agents say, to walk into. But Doreen had amassed (though no one knew how, or did they? as Fenella expressed it) a truly imposing wardrobe and they drove off in the pouring rain almost smothered with suitcases, and as many strapped on behind, which put Dwight in a poor humour as a start, because, as he complained, it made him feel like a draper's traveller. He was suffering, anyway, from a riotous conflict of emotions—pleasure at getting so pleasant a house in the country, considerable doubt that Doreen shared in it, and fear that she would not be able to stay the course, though he was grateful to her for consenting to try. He knew that the idea of being mistress of a house so well-run that she would have little to do in it, and at a time when such a thing was almost unheard-of, appealed to her mightily; but would it last? Nothing lasted, with Doreen—all her new brooms swept clean, though he smiled wryly at that figure of speech applied to the lovely, beautifully-dressed creature at his side. It seemed strange to him that James should have taken to Doreen (though he must say she'd made herself pleasant enough) and had always had his knife into his mother, who, his common sense told him, was worth a dozen Doreens. Though he was in physical fetters to his wife, his mind was unclouded on that issue. He had a deep respect and affection for his mother and knew that nothing less than James's irrational hatred of her as his son's wife could have made him blind to her sanity, reasonableness and probity, and to the fact that she had made his son extremely happy. That, perhaps, was what James had found hardest to bear, that his mother and father had lived in amity and understanding too firmly built to be shattered by his animosity, cloaked indeed, but with a dagger beneath its graceful folds. That he should leave her an annuity with such a condition hanging on to it had made him angry. But not Pen. She didn't want James's money, she said: she had, he knew, always protected herself and his father from James's generosity, as conditional, as she believed, as the gifts bestowed now under his will. But as he drove along this morning he still continued to marvel at the prejudice which had blinded his grandfather alike to his mother's integrity and his wife's utter lack of it.

Neither had he forgotten his mother's involuntary "Oh dear!" as she sat at his side when the will was read. Money, even James's money, she would, he knew, have welcomed—for him, though not for herself; but this gift of his house, under the conditions imposed, or any others, was to her only a matter for regret. It was an open family secret that she had always hated Greystones and its atmosphere. Even as a child he had understood that she went reluctantly to stay there and was always glad when it was time to leave. He had been puzzled by his grandfather—all that smooth talk that seemed to mean so much that it left out, and was rather like a clever school-master's talk aimed at a difficult child—and as he'd grown up his distrust had waxed with the years. Something stubborn within him —and also, perhaps, his sense of humour—had caused him to refuse to call him James, as he required all adults, even his mother and father, to do; and he had envied Bridget the wealth of meaning she had been able to put into her use of the name. To Bridget James was a joke, and she strove to make him one for everybody else. But for some reason Bridget had never come beneath the lash of his notice, as had the rest of them at some time or other. During that term he had spent in James's office, when he still put in an almost daily appear-ance there, he had been rendered miserable and incompetent by his continual nagging and debunking. He'd not wanted to leave his Architectural School to go into the office, and still believed he'd have done better if he had refused to do so—certainly in that first year he had learnt little, save that he had none of his father's brilliant talent, which he knew before, though hearing it put into words half a dozen times a week had been distinctly debilitating. If he hadn't been so sure that war with Hitler was coming, he'd have left. But things had improved before that began, for James became too ailing to put in even an occasional visit to the office. And relieved of the incubus of his grandfather's presence and his perpetual grieving and nagging, he had found his feet, ceased himself to believe that his work was as bad as James declared, and contrived to pass his Finals before the war began. Maybe it was this good report of his progress that had softened James's heart towards him, or the fact that he had lost a foot in his country's service. And was Greystones and the money left for its upkeep his reward?

He could not forget that little intake of breath with which his mother had greeted old Dartford's smooth reading of that part of the will, which had made him feel he had been bequeathed a curse. An unhappy house, she'd called it often, despite its architectural charm, its well-tended and always attractive garden and the family parties James for years had held in it, and the holly wreath hung at

Christmas time upon its oaken door. James, she said, had stamped his personality all over it.

Well, maybe, thought Dwight now, driving through the drenching day; but then, his mother felt more strongly about his grandfather's personality than he did, as was natural, since the old man had from the first done his best to make her feel a thief and intruder, so savagely possessive had his hold been on his son. And, too, of course, she had the writer's analytical mind, which couldn't leave him alone. One could understand very well her instinct for pulling him to pieces, but it was at least conceivable that she had put him together a little wrongly. Maybe that, too, was natural. Had she not once said that as a character in a book he'd have come out all wrong —that he'd appear crude? And there was nothing whatever crude about James, she'd always held, which was the trump card in the game he'd played everlastingly against her. Always—or at least until the last few years—there'd been that deceiving air of suavity and urbanity—hiding what? . . . Dwight had never known, but it had been practised on him often enough to give him a deep sympathy with his mother's opinion of the old man. But now he was dead and it was the sane thing to accept the gift he had bequeathed without looking too closely at the terms pinned upon it. Perhaps Doreen would surprise everyone by settling down to country life, even to the modification of her present intention of "running up and down to town". The day they'd travelled down to see Mrs. Simmonds she'd gone out of her way to let her see that she had no intention of interfering with her management of the house, and had generally made herself very agreeable. Too agreeable, perhaps, he thought, remembering Mrs. Simmonds's unbending reserve, even when they were all children. He was left now with the impression that Mrs. Simmonds was the real mistress of the house; that she was being confirmed in an attitude which had belonged to the long years of service with his grandfather. Doreen had said afterwards that it was easier and more diplomatic to give the impression of knowing nothing of the domestic job you paid someone else to do; which had amused Dwight, who was under no delusions as to his wife's capabilities as a housekeeper. Anyway, here they were, all set. Nothing to do but to hope for the best.

"Mummy," said Barry, "why doesn't daddy answer my questions?"

"Daddy's busy driving—and with his poor foot he can't talk to a little boy as well. You must be content to sit quiet, like mummy."

"You're *not* sitting quiet—you've said a lot of things to daddy."

"Have I?" said Doreen sweetly. "Well, you see, I don't expect answers."

"Will it be nice in the country, mummy?"

"I expect you will think so, at any rate."

"I shan't then . . . 'cos S'rena won't be there."

"Now don't begin on Serena again, Barry, please. We've had enough trouble over that. Serena has to stay in her own house with Becky."

"And there won't be any river, either, I don't suppose."

"Wait and see."

"I *can't* see—not anything. It's raining."

"So I've noticed. . . ."

Dwight went on with his thoughts.

A few weeks later Gilbert Hampton came home on leave, rather, Lydia thought, like a cat on a gridiron; longing to get back to South America and the business he'd left behind, and unable entirely to put out of mind this idea of going out to Germany for a year. Men with his knowledge of machinery were needed, he said; and, too, having been kept in England throughout the war he saw that he wanted to go to see what state Germany and the Germans were in now that it was finished. It was a toss-up which of these desires would win, but he made it clear that if it were Germany Lydia and the children would stay behind; a point about which Lydia did not at this stage trouble to argue. A year, he said, would give Fryn and Jeremy time to pass their exams and Meg a last opportunity to secure that English husband she'd doubtless set her heart upon.

This remark amused nobody. Not Meg, because she was already very homesick and had nourished a plan of her own for going home with her father while her mother stayed on with Fryn and Jeremy and saw to the disposal of the lease of the house. And lo!—there was to be no question at the moment of his even inquiring about a passage. And Jeremy and Fryn were not amused because they knew too well what their father thought of examinations and of those who failed to pass them. Nor Lydia, because she was often worried about Jeremy's health, which had interrupted his education considerably since he'd come to England, and to Lydia his health seemed more important than any examination. There had been times when Gilbert, riding his examination horse too high, had provoked her into saying that it was a pity he'd ever taken part in the war at all if it had to be done at the expense of Jeremy's health; and that anyway Jeremy was

[76]

like her, intelligent, but no brains, while Fryn's were not of the sort that flourished in the examination room. Gilbert was only so mad on exams because he could always pass them with flying colours, like Bridget. Or like that idiotic Emmy—and much good had it done her! After which she would feel a lot better and Jeremy and Fryn would feel as if someone had taken them off a leash.

But this time she left the theme of exams severely alone, partly because she felt that Germany would be worse for Jeremy's health than England and examinations. Nor did she tell Gilbert that he reminded her of a cat on a gridiron, or that his business in Buenos Aires was probably falling into ruin and that the sooner he went back there the better. She understood that his divided mind was causing him a good deal of trouble and wishing to divert it from its problems she talked about the experiment at Greystones which interested them all, but not Gilbert apparently, or not very much. He listened to what she had to say with his customary air of wondering why this family into which he had married should all be so concerned in each other's welfare, and at the end of it opined that the conditions seemed very stupid since if the scheme didn't work there would be a general upset, and to all such he objected.

"The old boy seems to have had a down on women," was his only comment, to which Lydia said, "Intelligent women. And Pen in particular, for daring to have carried off his son. Quite apart from Doreen's not being likely to make a 'go' of living in the country, Pen believes it won't work, anyway—that James didn't mean it to work."

"How come?" asked Gilbert.

"Well, in leaving Dwight the house and *not* leaving it to him, so to speak. As if even in his grave he'd get a kick out of putting anyone belonging to Pen by the ears. It wasn't as if he particularly liked either of them—Dwight and he had always been at loggerheads when he was at the office, and he only made a show of liking Doreen because he knew she was the kind of girl Pen disliked and never would have chosen for a daughter-in-law."

All that, Gilbert said, was miles beyond him. People didn't do such things.

"James did them," said Lydia. "James was a law unto himself. But also, you know, I'm sure Pen thinks that nobody in this family, at least, could be happy at Greystones."

"You mean because *she* was always unhappy there?"

"I suppose so. Not that Pen ever allowed herself to think herself made unhappy by James. Angry, furiously angry, if you like, though she never once lost her temper with him, and seems always to have been, outwardly at least, a match for him. He wouldn't be likely to like her any the better for that. I fancy that she thinks his machinations aren't ended, yet."

"The dead hand, you mean? But Doreen won't start with that handicap. James to her was a polite and polished old gentleman. I dare say she'll enjoy it all very much. She'll have plenty of leisure and think herself a fine lady. Isn't that what she wants?"

"Some of the things she wants, yes," said Lydia.

"Well then," said Gilbert, "why all the doldrums? I don't see in the least why the idea shouldn't work. The only snag is the long distance from town for Dwight."

But after their visit to Pen and Charles at Wyngates even Gilbert was a little shaken. He admired Pen very considerably, and had never forgotten her efforts all those years ago to make her sister, Lydia's mother, reasonable about his marrying her young daughter. He had admitted her plucky fight to finish the education of her children in the years which followed Bar's early death; but never having met James or suffered from his peculiar form of possessiveness he found it extremely difficult to reconcile her distrust of the old man, dead as alive, with her usual sound sense.

"The trouble is," he said to Lydia as they drove home, "she simply will not give that old blighter credit for a single generous impulse. It isn't like her—she's usually so sane and balanced."

"I think it's because she is so sane that she saw some kind of insanity in James's attitude that the rest of us missed. For her Greystones can never somehow be free of it. Or of him, lovely as it is. And it really is a lovely house, Gil—one of the most delightful small houses I've ever been in. Even Pen agrees that, for all James designed it. For Pen, though, the whole place is poisoned with the atmosphere of hatred and malice which James breathed into it."

Gilbert could not understand that. A house was a house, anyway, and in it you made your own atmosphere. It was up to Dwight and Doreen to lay the ghost.

"I doubt if they will," said Lydia.

"Don't they get on?"

"They don't quarrel—Dwight isn't the quarrelling sort. But that's the best you can say, I think. Of course Dwight's very much in love with her, but Doreen, I'm afraid, is very disappointed in her marriage. She has had bad luck, of course. Over Dwight's injury, I mean. She's a lively young creature, and there's no doubt the amputation put an end to many of the things they used to do together. Dancing, for example—she's very fond of that."

"Well, you can't expect to spend all your life dancing," said Gilbert. "When you're married there are a few other things to think about."

"I dare say, but not all the time. The young still want a good time, at least upon occasion. And of course Doreen has few resources within herself, and so gets easily bored. Pen says she's cinema-minded, and that does, I suppose, rather define her."

"And what exactly does 'cinema-minded' mean?"

"I think what Pen means by it is that Doreen is an example of arrested adolescence—that she has an incurably romantic view of life. At the pictures she sees—I mean at the kind of pictures she likes—she'd gather that a pretty girl's face was her fortune, and assume that hers ought to have got for her if not everything she'd like, then considerably more than it has done."

"Well, I suppose it got her a husband a cut or two above her own station in life. Did she expect a duke? Never could see why Dwight had to choose a wife like her. He seems a thoughtful, intelligent chap."

"He is, but the most intelligent men make the oddest matrimonial selections, you know. But it surprises me that Dwight should have married someone so essentially stupid. She hasn't an idea in her head and is bored by other people's. I suppose she's typical of her generation in that she must be kept constantly interested and amused, and perhaps she thought her marriage was going to be the complete Success story. Certainly she didn't bargain for a husband who was going to be a semi-invalid for months and then lose a foot."

"Good God!" Gilbert exploded. "She ought to think herself lucky to have a husband who's lost no more than a foot!"

"Well, Doreen is no ministering angel. I've never seen anyone so helpless before any kind of illness—why she ever took up nursing, even wartime nursing, beats me hollow. She hated the hospital and makes no bones about saying so."

"Then I'd have thought that marriage with Dwight on any terms would have been better than what she was getting out of life on her own."

"Perhaps it is. I don't know. But it's odd how people forget what life was like on their own, as you express it. To hear Doreen you'd think her life had been roses, roses all the way before she married—that she had given up at least a successful career. And she made, Pen says, a terrible fuss when Barry was born and is too terrified to have another child. Pen, however, says she had a perfectly normal time."

"It's a pity she doesn't have half a dozen, then she might come to

[79]

her senses," said Gilbert. "What's the use of running away from life, anyway?"

"No use at all," said Lydia, "but the trouble is, Doreen would never be convinced that she's doing anything of the sort. She doesn't care for children, either, you know, so it's just as well she doesn't have any more."

"Rough on Dwight—he's fond of kids."

"If you want children you must choose your partner more carefully than Dwight chose his, I think," said Lydia, a little sadly, Gilbert thought, and on that the conversation languished and Lydia's mind moved round her own affairs and those of her children.

She wished Gilbert hadn't this bee in his bonnet about going to Germany, for she thought it was time they all got home again. They'd been away six years and that was a long time. The girls were grown up, though it was still possible to think of Fryn as a schoolgirl. Meg was quite ready to go home, and Jeremy too, she thought; he was an amenable person. But Fryn would hate leaving—she had sent down roots here in the old country. Not for the first time her heart missed a beat when she thought of Fryn; she said so little, her instinct was all for keeping her feelings to herself. But her feeling for England stuck out a mile. Perhaps it was a mistake their having come over with Gilbert; she'd have done better, perhaps, to have stayed at home with the children. It was little enough she had seen of him. But such thoughts were worse than useless. Six years without seeing Gilbert at all? No, she couldn't have borne that. Even if it had ever occurred to Gilbert to leave them all behind. On the contrary, he'd considered it an excellent opportunity for her to visit the old country and to pick up the threads of the existence from which so early he had snatched her away. And so had she. And she'd never regretted it, save through Fryn, though she'd go home without a scruple, since home, to her, was where Gilbert was. Well, she must hope that Fryn would bear the wrench with fortitude and not find life on the other side of the world as alien as she was afraid she felt it would be. And there was nothing to prevent her, when she was older, from coming back. No one, then, would stand in her way, if she wished to come. After all, Gil was quite right when he said these six years had been an interlude. On which hopeful thought she closed her eyes and ceased to think of anything whatever. So much fresh air and Pen's surprisingly good lunch was responsible for that. It had been a pleasant day. . . .

Chapter Three

WHEN BRIDGET reminded Gaby that she was week-ending with Meg and Fryn Hampton at Greystones, that young woman said she hoped she would have a pleasant time, but not in the least as if she expected she would.

"I don't see why not," said Bridget calmly. "I don't love Doreen any better than the rest of you, but I don't *mind* her. People have to be themselves, anyway."

Truth to tell, she was much interested in the prospect of the spectacle of Doreen "being a lady", as she herself had expressed it to her friend Milly. And she was curious to see how the arrangement James had brought about was working out. Her mother's idea of the dead hand at work she found tantalising, though she didn't believe her grandfather had here been actuated by any really sinister motive. After all, he'd always been nicer to Doreen than to any of them, save Rose, and he had to leave his belongings to somebody, and since his own son (for whom he had accumulated his treasures) was dead, what more natural than that they should go to his grandson? Greystones had been his pride; he'd not have liked to think of it being sold in the open market to some outsider. At the worst, she thought, he had got a certain amount of satisfaction out of the idea of inflicting Doreen upon the stuffy neighbours he had scarcely troubled to know. Bridget had not found her paternal grandfather a lovable person and quite understood why her mother in her youth had resisted his tactics, but she was in the fortunate position of somehow never having much attracted his notice and so approached the problem he represented with a more open mind than those who had.

It was now the best part of three months since Dwight and Doreen had taken up their occupation at Greystones, and no member of the family had so far made the journey to see them except her mother, who had reported unexpectedly favourably upon the situation she had found there. Doreen was clearly enjoying her position, though she complained that it was a long journey to town, without seeming to see that it was as long for Dwight, who must go there at least four or five days out of the week, whereas she went at and for her own pleasure. (Not indeed that Doreen considered his journeys necessary, since they had enough money to live on. That there was any uncertainty either as to their tenure of Greystones or their adequate income seemed not to have occurred to her, nor that Dwight might be interested in his profession. In Doreen's view one only worked if one needed the money it brought in.) However, by not interfering in the domestic machinery she had contrived that it should run smoothly, Pen said, and she had obviously found it a little amusing that Mrs. Simmonds, who had never evinced the slightest enthusiasm for herself as a young married woman, should appear to approve of Doreen. Maybe she approximated more to what she thought a wife should be; she left her home and the care of her child to those who were paid for their services, and, of course, did not demean herself by "all this writing". Besides, James's attitude to Doreen had not been lost upon Mrs. Simmonds; obviously she had been as receptive of the atmosphere which surrounded Doreen upon her visits as she had been to that which from the first James had created for herself. On the whole, so her family had deduced, Pen had been amused as well as reassured by what she had seen of the new regime. Dwight was happy and Barry well looked after. The dead hand, if it had not entirely vanished from the scene, as she had surveyed it, had at least receded. However, Pen's visits had belonged to very early days, and Gaby said that she would be much interested to hear Bridget's opinion of the situation at this later stage.

"Nothing, I'm sure, surprised your mother more than to find that the arrangement seemed to be working."

"I never really saw why it shouldn't," Bridget said. "Here's Doreen, who hates running a house and is no good at it, anyway, and the precious Simmonds taking it all off her hands, wrestling with ration books, points and what-have-you—just as you do for us, God bless you!—and leaving Doreen free to run up to town, as she expresses it, whenever she likes, with Alston on tap with the Hudson to take her to and from the station. And no trouble about petrol, James having thoughtfully built his house five miles from the nearest railway station and bequeathed it to a grandson with an artificial foot. If that's what you want, you couldn't, I should say, do better than Greystones."

"Your mother said she thought Barry was missing Serena."

"I know, and that Dwight said he had been an only child too long."

"That isn't an argument which is likely to appeal to Doreen, I fancy," said Gaby, to which Bridget said only, "Well, you never can tell. . . ."

She did not share in the general verdict against Doreen because of her lack of enthusiasm for maternity, holding that the women who didn't want children had far better not have them. But being a fair-minded young person she would have conceded that this was a matter which should be properly thrashed out between the two people concerned before marriage, which she didn't think had been done in this case. As for your duty to the State, Bridget hadn't much use for that argument. Like the State's impertinence, she thought, having killed off the young of two generations, to expect the next one to redress the balance. (She remembered the cold cynicism of Napoleon's remark as he'd looked upon the carnage after one of his victories, "One night of Paris will replace all this!") And to what end? Quite apart from the young men of her own family—victims, as she held, of the State's ineptitude—who had been wiped out in World War One, like Gaby's father and Cousin Andra's young Ronnie, and those with their health permanently wrecked, as was the case with her own father, and those who had died in World War Two, there had been many interesting and clever young men of her acquaintance who had been destroyed in it too. Perhaps the only argument which would bring Governments to their senses on this business of war was a stationary birthrate. At least, if one had children one must have them for their own sake and not for that of the State. Of all words in the language, she hated, she thought, the word "State" the most. And nowadays there was no escaping it. Before long, and from the highest possible motives, it would give us all numbers to hang round our necks. . . .

While these thoughts kept Bridget silent Gaby was quietly regarding her young cousin, of whom she was very fond. She had, she thought, many of her mother's qualities, including her integrity, but excluding what Pen's critics called her quixotry; and her attitude to life was much more detached. She gave you the impression of one holding a watching brief for life instead of being an eager participant in its pageantry, as was her mother. It surprised her that she had so few young men friends, or if she had others was not minded to display them; but the war, of course, had got in the way of any parade of young men. . . . Her thoughts at the moment were certainly stayed elsewhere, on working for the degree she would long ago have taken but for the war, and of making for herself a career, since her mother was married again and in no need of the services which, in any case as things had turned out, Gaby would still have been free to give her. And she had steadily refused the invitation of her mother and stepfather to make her home with them at Wyngates.

Who, she asked, could go up to town each day from Petersfield? But that, Gaby suspected, was not the reason. Neither was it so much that Bridget wanted her freedom, as that she wanted her mother to have hers. For close upon fourteen years, ever since her father's death, she had worked for and considered only her children, and it was time she was free of them all, she thought. And like Gaby herself, she would not have liked to leave the old house by the river.

At Charing Cross station Bridget met her cousins, as arranged, with the tickets already purchased. They were all in good spirits, Bridget because she looked forward to an interesting week-end and the sisters because neither of them had seen Greystones, for Pen was never minded to take her relatives on her scattered visits and was never encouraged to do so by James. So that to them both his house had become something of a legend. And for Fryn, at least, seeing a new corner of England was an exciting adventure. Her spirits had risen slightly with the prospect of being able to forget for a while the examination ordeal in front of her, and particularly her father's well-meant exhortations and mistaken belief in her ability to "pull it off". So much optimism over something as to which she felt so diffident had depressed her considerably. But Bridget's company was reassuring, and her air of tranquillity when Meg questioned her about her plans when she should have taken her degree caused a rag of courage to flutter across her flagging spirits. Everything sounded possible, even easy, while Bridget talked. But the fact remained that in school certificate she had failed to reach the matriculation standard required by her father, and that failure (or, rather, her father's disappointment) now clouded her outlook for the much more difficult task ahead of her.

"But this time, my child, all you have to do is to pass," Bridget told her. "As you've already got school certificate you'll then get matric. automatically."

Fryn said sadly, "But I feel in my bones that maths will floor me."

Bridget laughed at her gloom.

"In that case you'll be able to stay on in England and try again, perhaps."

Fryn managed a laugh at this and said it was the first really good argument she had heard for failing, although she was afraid that her mother, who cared less than nothing for exams and could never pass them, wouldn't be very keen on her staying behind when the rest of them went home. "If I were her I dare say I'd feel the same," she added, in her reasonable young voice.

"How do you know what you would do if you were your mother?" Bridget inquired, and to this poser, Fryn found, there was no answer, as Pen years ago had done when she had said the same thing to Bridget and had received the same reply.

"If father goes to Germany," Meg put in, "all will be well," and when Bridget asked if that idea was likely to come to anything, Meg said "Oh, he seems keen about it, and father usually does what he wants, you know, in the end."

So Fryn's spirits rose again and by the time they had arrived at their station, to find Alston awaiting them with the car, she had cast her burdens overboard and was "all set", as Meg expressed it, for a happy week-end.

To Bridget, who had known him for so long, Alston seemed unusually taciturn. In the old days one could, as her mother used to say, always rely upon getting a warm greeting from Alston, which was so very cheering since you knew you'd be frozen on your arrival at Greystones by the arctic atmosphere Mrs. Simmonds would create by the mere act of crossing the hall. But to-day Alston touched his cap, opened the door and laid the rug across their knees as respectfully as ever: but to all Bridget's chatty remarks he responded with a brevity that was stiff with politeness, and advanced none of his own. Of course he was getting on and doubtless he found he had a lot more to do now than during the last years of James's life. Doreen wouldn't keep a chauffeur and give him nothing to do. Maybe, too, he thought his long service had deserved better recognition than the fifty pounds James had left him, especially as Mrs. Simmonds had been left a hundred. (But Alston, of course, didn't do the cooking—so much more important to James, the gourmet, than being driven about in a car!) Besides, James had believed in keeping servants in their place and probably thought that to leave them more would militate against their remaining in it; and his will had clearly stated that he hoped they would both continue their service under Dwight's ownership. But it seemed to Bridget that not only had Alston nothing to say—not even asking after her mother, which was distinctly odd, for they were old and good friends—but that his very back, as he sat at the wheel, seemed somehow resentful. However, she left him to himself and she and Meg kept up a light-hearted conversation of their own while Fryn lost herself in admiration of what she had heard called the "Garden of England" through which Alston drove them as competently as ever.

Bridget had told her that she was a little too late to see it at its best; for the fruit blossom was already gone. But it seemed to Fryn

C.G.U.—4　　　　　[85]

that there was much loveliness left, that all the fields and wayside trees and gardens still wore their shining spring garments. It was as if the world was hung with blossom of every kind—chestnut, hawthorn, laburnum, syringa—even though the gentle breeze was shaking down the blossom of the white may, that fell softly, like snow, and like snow lightly covered the ground. Snow without cold. . . . The grass in the meadows was studded with daisies and buttercups, and a sea of bluebells flowed gently over the floor of the woods. The air, drifting in through the open window of the car, was soft and most sweetly scented, so that it was easy to imagine one was driving through a large, well-kept and much-loved garden.

For all her gay chatter with Meg, who accepted the country but was not lulled into silence by its beauty (nor, indeed, by anything else), Bridget was very sensible of the loveliness through which they drove and which, like a magic carpet, had removed Fryn abruptly from their company, and now she drew her back with a soft touch on her arm.

"Lovely, isn't it? . . . We're on the North Downs—that's the Weald over to the east. If you climb Brasted Chart you can see for miles—and all as lovely. And there's a rewarding steep road, too, up Ide Hill. But I'm afraid you won't have much time this week-end for exploring."

"It's beautiful," breathed Fryn, "and Cathy said it was 'just London country'."

"I know," said Bridget, laughing. "And how scornful she sounds when she says it! But she's thinking of the north-west approaches, now all suburbanised, poor things! And of the coast towns. But at its heart Kent is lovely—all foaming orchards, and woods with primroses and bluebells. At least, it is in the spring."

"I like the cottages," said Fryn, "the way the roofs come sloping down so steeply, and their colours. And I like those queer towers, with a kind of steeple on top."

"Oast-houses. Inside there are kilns for drying hops. In some parts of Kent people have converted them into country houses. No, not on account of the housing shortage—they thought of it long before that arrived to plague us. Because they're attractive, and so many of them no longer used. And also, of course, because they are old."

Fryn considered this plan for a house in silence for a moment or two, then said, "I suppose you used to walk a good deal when you used to come here so often?"

"When we were children? Oh yes. But Dwight was the real

walker among us, poor boy! I wasn't so bad, perhaps, but Fenella soon got tired of walking and wanted to sit down and sketch, and would get very annoyed when Dwight laughed at her efforts and said she couldn't draw a recognisable cottage or house. It really was true, of course, and she believes it now because Glen has told her so often and that she should never attempt to draw anything but young girls with pretty legs."

They both laughed at that and Meg, asking to be told the joke, drew them into the sort of conversation—personal gossip—that she liked best.

Arrived at Greystones, Mrs. Simmonds's welcome was precisely as Bridget remembered it, distant, correct, utterly impersonal, and to it she responded as of old, with the same degree of politeness, but with that air of placid awareness she had caught long ago from her mother. She was surprised, however, that Mrs. Simmonds did not shed a little of her formal correctness for the young strangers she had brought with her, but evidently they had already been ticketed as belonging to the invader's camp; and her surprise reached out and caught at something quite unexpected, after her mother's report—the fact that nearly three months of the reign of Dwight and Doreen had not induced in the dragon, at least superficially, a more engaging manner. However, Doreen, very smartly attired, came in from the garden, and her welcome to the sisters certainly made amends.

"Oh, here you are!" she said. "Leave your things—Alston can take them up. Do you want to titivate? I've given you the garden room, Bridget—with Meg and Fryn next door to you. Tea's just ready."

Her voice had a new note in it which Jeremy, Fryn thought, would have called "fancy". She did not think it an improvement. And as they went upstairs together Meg raised her eyebrows expressively but made no comment. How horrid we are! Fryn thought, always a little troubled by her inability to like Doreen very much. But for the "fancy" voice she really seemed much nicer than when she was at Richmond.

The titivating did not take long, and Meg having dissuaded Fryn from too lengthy a survey across the open country towards a hill she supposed audibly must be Ide, the sisters went downstairs with Bridget, who came tapping at their door.

"It's a lovely house," said Fryn, and Bridget, who had known it all her life, agreed. And all that time, she thought, and all through the war, with the bombs falling all around, one embittered old man had lived in it alone, save when, in the days before their father's death, they all came down for the longer holidays of the year. It

[87]

seemed to her that James was still there, noticing that there was no bowl of beautifully arranged flowers on the wide turn of the stairs, that the teak floors were a little less immaculately kept, that the wide window on the landing was thrown back and not secured. . . . Mrs. Simmonds was perhaps relaxing a little after those long years with the house-proud James, and Doreen wouldn't notice.

Tea had been set in the loggia, one of James's particular delights and which in their youth Fenella used to call "super", to James's disgust. When they were very small, a pergola had been built on to it as an extension, so that, wet or sunny, one could secure shelter or shade as required. Bridget saw that the roses were already heavily in bud and sniffed appreciatively at the sweet thin scent of the pinks which filled the narrow bed in which the roses were planted. Oh, how familiar it all was! she thought, though she had not been there for some years, for after the war began her mother had always gone alone, and had quite dropped her erstwhile habit of taking with her at least one loudly-protesting victim.

But to-day she felt that James still hovered around—keeping an eye on things (*his* things still) and on their new custodians. Custodians. Yes, that was what Dwight and Doreen really were, of course.

"What a lovely place!" said Meg politely to Doreen, who just then came strolling in, followed by Mrs. Simmonds carrying a tray. While she disposed tea-pots and jugs of milk, Doreen, ignoring or probably not having noticed Meg's comment, invited them all to sit down and asked Mrs. Simmonds to tell "her master" that tea was ready. Her master! thought Bridget. How very behind the times! But Mrs. Simmonds's face was expressionless, or, more correctly, held fast to its usual expression, as she said, "He's just coming, madam."

Doreen began to pour tea and Mrs. Simmonds to hand things around, and then Dwight appeared, limping rather more than usual (which showed he was feeling a little nervous, thought Bridget—though of what?) and apologising for his late arrival. He'd gone for a stroll and hadn't realised the time.

"And made yourself tired," said Doreen, her voice empty of sympathy, and also of its new "fancy" note. It sounded, indeed, quite snappy, and Fryn did not remember ever to have heard it so before. "You're limping quite badly again."

Dwight kissed his sister and cousins, Mrs. Simmonds withdrew and in an odd little silence everyone began to eat. It was Dwight who said, "Nice of you all to bring such a pleasant day. I hope it

[88]

lasts over the week-end, for we've a party to-morrow, and it makes things much harder for the staff if we all have to crowd indoors."

"I don't see why," said Doreen. "There's plenty of room, surely? It was a clever idea of James's to have these rooms opening out of the hall and the glass folding doors, so that you can make one big room of them, if you've a party. I remember saying that to him the first time I came here."

Bridget raised an eyebrow. James had as much use for a party as Jane Austen's Mr. Woodhouse. . . .

"Locals?" she inquired.

"To tea, yes. But Rose and Larry are coming down to lunch. We have got to know quite a lot of nice people in the neighbour-hood."

"That's a change," said Bridget. "Hardly anybody set foot across the threshold in James's day—except us."

"But James, of course," Doreen offered, "was quite eccentric."

"No family save Larry and Rose?"

"Well, Danny . . . perhaps."

"*Danny?* Hasn't he gone to America with Livvy?"

"Apparently not. Rose said he was in town and if he's free she'd ask him to come. I don't think he ever came here in James's day." Somehow Bridget was left with the impression that he had been there since Doreen and Dwight had taken over. Ignoring that, she said, "Danny's being the gay bachelor again, is he?"

Dwight laughed. "Oh, I thought he was a reformed character since his marriage. It's odd he didn't go with Livvy, he's so fond of America."

"I expect," Bridget said, "it's on Cathy's account. She's not very well, these days, so mother says. She's getting on, of course."

"Fryn can tell you exactly how far she's got," said Meg. "She knows all our ages and has inscribed them on her genealogical table. Horrid thing!"

"Well, Fryn?" said Dwight.

Fryn blushed and suddenly looked very shy. She knew this was not exactly a popular pastime of hers in some quarters. But Cathy was an old lady and it couldn't matter telling how old she was. So she said, "She was born in March in the year eighteen-sixty-nine." And sighed faintly, as one who had stepped back amid the dead and gone centuries. "How old does that make her?"

"Seventy-seven," said Dwight. "How do you remember all the facts you've assembled, Fryn?"

"I don't always," said Fryn, "without the table."

"Lucky for you, my girl!" said Meg.

"Do you have many week-end parties?" Bridget now inquired of Doreen.

"We've had a good many since we got properly settled. During the last six weeks we've been very busy. It's such fun. And I don't see any sense in having such a nice house if you don't ask people to come and see it."

"But it isn't, I'm afraid, very popular with the staff," commented Dwight. "Sunday's now their busiest day and of course, in grand-father's day, it was the easiest."

"That's always Dwight's argument," said Doreen, snappy again. Then, with a sweet reasonableness, "But James was an old man. They can't expect *us* to live like hermits. We're young."

Doreen, Bridget noticed, had fallen into the habit her grand-father had inculcated in the family, even in his own son, of calling him by his Christian name, though Dwight had already refused, and steadfastly spoken of him as "grandfather" and addressed him as "sir", which he'd accepted—perhaps because Dwight had worked for a time in his office. Even James, she supposed, must have realised that it would scarcely do for his young grandson (nineteen when he first went to the office) to address him by his Christian name. But certainly these week-ends could account for the gloom and despond-ency which had settled down, after a reported lifting, upon Mrs. Simmonds, and for Alston's taciturnity. She said, "Whatever do you do about food? Don't tell me you sneak the child's milk!"

"Oh, we manage," said Doreen airily. "We've an all-time helper for Mrs. Simmonds, so that gives us five adult ration books and I know how to get extra sugar and butter if we need it."

Black-marketeering! thought Bridget, thinking also, Well, of course it wouldn't occur to Doreen that in buying in the black market she's helping to create a whole new body of parasites . . . a new criminal class, which certainly won't vanish with the black market. And all those clothes she manages to parade! She ought, she felt, to have known long ago what Doreen was at.

"Well, don't announce it so brazenly," Dwight told her. "The worst of my wife," he added, with a rather forced smile, "is that she has no moral sense."

"I don't know what that means, I'm sure," said Doreen. "But of course everyone who can afford it supplements their rations."

"If true, very reprehensible," said Dwight. "But I don't think it is true."

To turn the subject Bridget said, "Mind the staff don't walk out

[90]

on you. There's a servant problem, you know! At home, since dear old Winny died, we've had a long dreary procession of itinerant domestics. Not the same thing, I assure you. On the other hand, I'd not be sorry, if I were mistress here, to say good-bye to the Dragon. None of us could ever stand her."

"Oh, I get on very well with her," said Doreen, and in Bridget's mind sprang up the picture of a bird preening itself, shaking up its feathers and not seeing the lurking cat. . . . "Of course, she wants a little managing. Those last ten years with James did rather spoil her for younger folk, there's no denying."

At this moment the telephone began to ring and in a minute or so Mrs. Simmonds opened the door to say, "Mrs. Laurence on the telephone, madam."

"Now don't tell me she and Larry aren't coming!" said Doreen to no one in particular as she got up from her seat. "That would be too bad." When she returned, with her brow a little furrowed, she announced, "Rose says they haven't enough petrol for the car and wanted to know about trains. I had to look one up for her. I can't see why she couldn't *hire* a car—with all the money she's got!"

"I don't suppose her investments are worth what they were—nobody's are," said Dwight.

"I don't see why not. I expect they're much the same as ours because I know James looked after things for her. And in any case, her income's her own. She doesn't hold it on condition, like poor Us. I think it rather mean of James to dock our income if we don't go on living in his house."

(She speaks, thought Fryn, as though he's still alive!)

Nobody offering any comment on these observations, Doreen added, "Well, I mean, we ought to be allowed to sell."

"So we can."

"Oh, Dwight, don't be so tiresome! You know what I mean. The money wouldn't be ours—it would just lie around earning more money for Barry, while we should have to live on what would be a perfectly *hopeless* income after this one."

"Well, it's up to us, my dear. No one's taking either our income or the house away from us . . . By the way, where *is* Barry?"

Doreen made a grimace of despair.

"Gone out to tea . . . Now don't say I didn't tell you!"

"I don't think you could have done, my dear, or I should have suggested that as Fryn was here you might have made an excuse."

"I certainly did tell you. It does him good to spend time with children of his own age—he's made some very nice little friends in

the neighbourhood, you know, Bridget. Really nice people . . .
I'm sure Fryn hasn't come all this way just to be bothered with a
small boy."

"Barry's never a bother," said Fryn, the colour quickening in her
small face.

"So *you* think!" said Doreen, with a small unkind laugh. "Barry,
let me tell you, can be a perfect little fiend when he likes. Miss Deans
is quite good with him, but I think it would be much better for him
to go to school. There's quite a good kindergarten in Westerham and
Alston could take him and bring him back. However, Dwight doesn't
agree with me."

Dwight saying nothing to this, there was a little silence, which
Meg broke to ask if it was true that Audrey was trying to go to
Germany. She was interested in such a project because long before
the suggestion had arisen of her father going there she had herself
played with the idea. But it had got no further than that, for she knew
her parents would never have consented, and Meg did not waste
effort on the unattainable.

"Oh, I believe that's *quite* fizzled out," said Doreen. "Actually,
there's a much stronger attraction at home, I understand." (Doreen's
lingo, Bridget thought, was that of the superior servant. She never
presumed to *know* anything. She always "understood" or "was
given to understand".) "Someone she's met in the army, I fancy—
a major, I gather, years older than she is. But married."

Into the little silence that greeted this unexpected announcement
Bridget dropped her laconic comment. She hadn't noticed, she said,
that that circumstance was an overwhelming obstacle to-day to the
"other woman".

"Of course," continued Doreen somewhat hastily, "it was told
me quite in confidence. Rose doesn't know I know about it, of course.
Not that I do know much."

"I don't think, Doreen," said Dwight mildly, "that I should
repeat what you do know, or have been told, if I were you."

"Well, it's all in the family, isn't it?" said Doreen, quite unaware
that that was the head and front of her offending. "If it's true, I do
feel very sorry for Audrey."

Dwight said, "Fryn, you've an empty cup and nothing to eat."

This was true. Fryn had been too much embarrassed by this turn
in the conversation, though interested in it as yet another scrap of
family history, to remember food and drink. She allowed Dwight to
pass her cup and took a small cake and began nibbling at it.

Emmy! thought Bridget. Audrey and Emmy were very thick, and

[92]

she'd be the one person in the family Audrey could count upon for sympathy—and support. Emmy, whom Rose had always befriended, for whom she had always made allowances, to everyone's secret annoyance! Rose, so well-meaning and "clan-minded", joining up all the loose ends of the family, explaining, apologising . . . "So-and-so has excellent qualities . . ." "Oh, I'm sure So-and-so didn't mean *that!*" "Of course, we do have to remember . . . *Poor* Emmy! Poor James!—such sad lives!"

From Rose in the role of the family peacemaker they'd all suffered, reflected Bridget. And though doubtless it was peace she desired, it was seldom peace she achieved. It was a pity, Bridget had once observed to her mother, that words didn't cost half-a-crown apiece, then perhaps Rose wouldn't be so prodigal of hers—which had made Pen laugh in that sudden way she had. For Rose's regard for her money-bags, her keen sense of business (which James had so applauded) was well-known in the family. But now, for the first time in her life, Bridget felt sorry for her irritating but always well-meaning second cousin.

Doreen pushed cigarettes in Bridget's direction. Her thought too, it seemed, had been on Rose, for she said, as she lighted a cigarette for herself, "I hope Rose doesn't let us down to-morrow. If she's bringing Danny I don't think he'll fancy the journey by train. I should have thought *he'd* have suggested hiring a car if Rose is too mean."

"My dear Doreen," remarked Dwight, "Danny isn't the one in that family who has money to burn, you know."

"Well, he always seems to have plenty," said Doreen and Bridget saw the colour come suddenly into her face and she added, somewhat hastily, "From all accounts of his doings, anyway. Well, if we've all finished, take the girls round the garden, Dwight. I've some things to see to for a bit."

"Don't come if it will make you tired," Fryn said. "We can take ourselves round."

Smiling down at his little cousin, Dwight protested that he was not in the least tired. "Come along. It's an extremely nice garden, quite worth looking at. Our grandfather was a great gardener—he thought less than nothing of our efforts at Richmond, as I expect you know. But luckily he bequeathed his gardener with all the rest."

Fryn thought the garden very ill described as "extremely nice", but Dwight, she knew, was reputed in the family to be a master of under-statement. To her it was the loveliest garden she had ever seen, and smelt divinely of pinks and lilacs—the same delicious scent which had filled the air as they had driven from the station. The scent of Kent, perhaps. The lawns were shorn, green and like velvet beneath the foot, and on one of them stood a graceful tree with downward-hanging branches holding still much of their pink and white blossoms, not unlike that of the apple tree, she thought. But Dwight could not tell her its name, nor the name of any other of the fine blossoming trees—all superbly placed for effect—with which the garden was adorned. Bridget obligingly grouped them all together for them as "prunus", which Dwight accepted willingly enough.

"Anyway, whatever they are," he said, "you ought to have seen them a fortnight ago," and was promptly told by Meg that he sounded like Ruth Draper. "I know," he agreed. "But I'm one of the people who like spring better than summer and wish it would last for ever."

Fryn smiled up at him from beneath the spreading tree and said, "I'm afraid I don't know who Ruth Draper is. I'm frightfully ignorant. But I think you must be like Richard Middleton."

"And *I* don't know who Richard Middleton is," Dwight said.

"He was a poet—he died a very long time ago, before I was born, I think. I found a volume of his poems on grandfather Malling's shelves. I always remember the one about some imaginary land, *Where summer comes not to perplex the flowers, But Spring stays ever*. I think that was how it went. But there were others, too, all lamenting the passing of spring. Is that how you feel about it? I think I do, too."

As she stood there beneath the lovely tree Dwight thought she herself looked like a part of the spring day. "I must look up Mr. Middleton," he said, as they strolled on.

Their tour of the garden brought them soon to the gate at the end of the drive, and through it came Barry and his nursery governess, Miss Deans. Barry rushed forward and flung himself upon Fryn with delight, and in a minute or two the pair of them had gone off together. Miss Deans moved on into the house, Bridget was out of sight, and Dwight, much to his disappointment, found himself left with Meg, who said how bonny Barry looked. His country existence must be doing him good.

"Fryn ought to live in the country, I think," she went on. "She's not a town-ite at all, really. Don't you think she looks very washed-out?"

Dwight said that she did look a little pale, perhaps.

"She worries too much," said Fryn's sister. "Even about growing up. She has quite a down on *that*, you know—that's what she meant, I think, about liking spring better than summer. But I think it's fun to be grown up and not to have to bother about exams. Fryn worries about everything. *Especially* about exams. If she doesn't get matric. standard this time she'll be simply wretched—and all because father will look glum and say, 'You've disappointed me very much, Fryn,' and go about for a day or two giving an excellent imitation of a man wondering why he should have such a stupid child. He doesn't expect anything of me, luckily, but Fryn's clever, and he simply can't see that it isn't examination cleverness. Nor Jeremy's either—he's pretty certain to fail school cert. first go, poor love! And the joke of it is that father doesn't really *mind*—at least, not half as much as he imagines. He likes us, more or less, as we are—he's really *quite* a lamb. But Fryn hates the idea of not being able to do something he'd like her to do. Gosh!—what eloquence! Sorry, Dwight."

"No need to apologise," said Dwight, who had found this piece of analysis of considerable interest. It put up Meg's stock with him considerably. Clever she might not be, but for all her disparagement of herself, no nit-wit. She was wise. Wise and kind. And she had the good sense to appreciate Fryn, which redounded to her credit, and the perspicacity to read her correctly. Odd that Doreen should believe she had a crony in Meg, just because she cared about clothes! . . .

Chapter Four

ON THE Sunday morning Dwight suggested at breakfast that his cousins might like to have a look round the countryside, and proposed taking out the boneshaker and cruising around for a while before lunch. Meg and Fryn were delighted with the idea but Doreen said, "You'll have to be back in time, I'm afraid, to collect Rose and party from the station. Her train's due at 12.20. I can't spare Alston."

"But that means taking the Hudson."

He looked, Fryn thought, quite alarmed at the idea.

"Well, you'll have to get used some day to driving it, you know—the boneshaker won't last much longer. It's all right, surely, if you start in good time and drive slowly. And I dare say Rose or Danny—if he comes, that is—will take the wheel for you coming back."

Glancing at her brother's face Bridget could have slain Doreen for putting him in such a position. She knew quite as well as they all did how he hated attention drawn to his artificial foot; and how hard he had found it to bring himself to drive even the old boneshaker. "But my dear," he expostulated, "it wouldn't take Alston much more than half an hour there and back."

"I'm sorry, but I really can't spare him—or I shall be in trouble with Mrs. Simmonds. Besides, it would mean his changing into uniform."

"I really don't see why he need do that."

The subject, however, as far as Doreen was concerned, was obviously closed, except that she said, "Why don't *you* drive, Bridget? You're just the type, I should have thought."

"No car," said Bridget. "Sorry, Doreen."

Dwight inquired the time of the train and said he'd take the boneshaker and drop the girls at a convenient spot for walking home and then go on to the station.

"But you can't pack Rose's party into the boneshaker!" Doreen expostulated.

"Well, that's the best I can do, I'm afraid. I won't drive the Hudson. The only alternative I can suggest, if you really can't spare Alston, is to ring the garage and ask them to meet the train."

"Very well," said Doreen, "but it seems very unnecessary to me."

She went out of the room, leaving two of her young guests looking rather limp and embarrassed. Bridget had gone very white, a sure sign that she was with difficulty controlling both her tongue and her temper.

"Let's just not go," said Meg. "Fryn and I can quite well go for a walk instead."

"Oh, I dare say the garage can oblige," Dwight assured them with a smile.

Bridget inquired if he had indeed quite given up driving the Hudson.

"Well, I haven't driven it for a month past," he told her. "I dare say I'd be all right if I persevered, but driving a car's small pleasure to me these days, and the Hudson none at all."

She knew this was all he intended to say upon the subject, but it told her all she needed to know. And at that moment the telephone began to ring, so evidently it wasn't to communicate with the garage that Doreen had gone so abruptly out of the room. The ringing ceased, and a minute or so later Doreen put her head inside the door to say, "That was Rose again. They're hiring a car after all. Why they couldn't have arranged that first I don't know."

And now she sounded amiable, which was something to the good, Bridget thought. Dwight said calmly, as one used to these storms in tea-cups, "As everything's all right, I think we'll just go for a stroll —and not bother about the boneshaker."

"Now, don't tire yourself out, darling, before our guests arrive. Bridget, do see he doesn't go too far . . . Oh, and by the way, Rose says she's bringing Emmy." As if aware of the surprise in the faces of her husband and sister-in-law, she added, "I've often said to Rose that she must bring her some time when she and Larry were coming. Well, I must fly."

The door closed behind her.

"I must get my hat," said Fryn, and obeying some instinct, Meg went with her out of the room. Left with her brother, Bridget exclaimed with a grimace, "Emmy! What a blow!"

"I could do without her, certainly," said Dwight. "Rose was bound to bring her some time, I suppose, but it's a pity she had to choose this week-end. When did you see her last?"

"Emmy? Not for ages. Somewhere in the dark backward and abysm of our childhood, when she used to come down to Richmond to take Fenny out in her car."

"Lord, yes, and we were so bucked when she made it quite clear that she didn't intend us to join the party. Fenny and she went on being friends for years. I've never understood what broke up the association."

"Mother. She found out that Emmy had been aiding and abetting Fenny in one of her sillier pashes on a middle-aged—and married— Don Juan. So she paid Emmy a call to tell her what she thought of her conduct, and ended, I believe, by calling her a 'vindictive and silly old woman'."

"How amusing! Why did I never hear of it?"

"For the same reason that I didn't—at the time. Mother and Gaby never intended we should. They were bent on saving face for Fenny. It's only since she's been safely married that they've told me anything about it. It was a bad 'do'—Fenny, I gather, was shocked into common sense. It would have been the end of Emmy, for her, even without mother's fine effort. Poor mother!—even now I feel that sometimes she can't believe her luck in escaping the bald-headed divorcé she was always convinced Fenny would inflict upon her as a son-in-law."

They both laughed, thinking of Glen Westcott's thick mop of curly hair, which even the army had barely been capable of keeping under control. Then Meg and Fryn came in and they set off for their stroll.

They took a leisurely pace up the steep road to the top of Ide Hill, where they sat down to admire the view—the little village of Toys Hill lying beneath the brow of Chart, the stretched-out pleasant Kentish countryside, with its villages, wooded valleys, its hop-gardens, pastures and oast-houses; the expanse of the Weald. There they sat and stared—and talked; and because Fryn did not feel shy with Dwight she, too, took her share in the conversation.

Dwight considered her a delightful child—it was so he thought of her still, as if she was the little girl nearing her eleventh birthday who'd arrived in England on the eve of war. Perhaps, he thought, it was because she still wore her hair in that long thick plait.

"When I heard you were born," he said to her, "I was very disgusted and pointed out, so I'm informed, that we were very short of *boy* cousins. My excuse is that I was at a very trying age."

Fryn laughed. She had a pretty laugh, soft and oddly infectious, Dwight thought.

"You weren't the only disappointed one," she said. "Mother and father had both hoped I'd be a boy. However, they've always been very nice about it."

Dwight found it very pleasing to watch her. Her face had an odd way of changing completely when she was talking, her varying emotions chasing each other across her face in a manner he found enchanting. No poker face, Fryn's, but neither had it the undeviating animation of Meg's, to see which in a static mood was to imagine, as Lydia said, that she must be sickening for something. Fryn's smile could be slow, like sunshine moving across a hill, or sudden and unexpected, like her soft laughter, but always you saw it against the habitual gravity of her young face. Odd, he thought, too, how few girls to-day had short oval faces, like Fryn's. Most feminine faces he remembered as nondescript in shape; but some were square or pointed, more often round, perhaps, like Meg's, or long and narrow —the shape he liked least. But the mould of the short oval seemed to have been discarded by nature, and Fryn's possession of it gave to her face a distinction quite apart from its look of sensitivity, its steady grey eyes and the frame of gold-chestnut hair, guiltless of wave. Her hair, Dwight thought, was an undoubted beauty, so soft and growing so charmingly from the broad brow from which it was brushed back. When she sat in the sun it was like standing corn, dead-ripe; when seen in the shade, like bracken beneath the autumn sun. Sitting there watching her, the thought ran through his mind that he could not imagine her at any other stage of her life than this at which he now saw her; could not see her middle-aged or old . . . She belonged to the faery world of the poet of whom she had talked, where spring stays ever. . . .

He found something oddly touching, too, in her love for this country which her parents had early left; her interest in the large and sprawling family to which she belonged. For the family *en masse* bored him considerably, and though he was fond of certain members of it, and admired others, he saw no reason why Doreen should have wished the egregious Emmy upon him, and perhaps Rose's unlikeable daughter, Audrey. He was aware he would prefer that Fryn should meet neither of them again, particularly not Emmy, who, object of fun though she had been to them all in their youth, now seemed to him, after Bridget's account of her last interference in family affairs, to have become a slightly sinister figure. Oh, lordy, but there were drawbacks to this inheritance from James! If it gave him a more contented wife and a well-run home it enjoined upon him these constant week-end crowds, and dull people (dull, at least, to him) to dinner once or twice a week, since Doreen did not recognise the social limitations imposed by these days of austerity. For the first time in her life she found that money did not have to be ruthlessly and endlessly considered and that was the only thing that mattered. Too much money chasing too few goods? Doreen might never have heard the phrase.

[99]

"It's beautiful here," said Fryn. "I can't believe there's such a place as Redvers Green."

"Have they allowed you to go to Redvers Green?" asked Dwight, his voice not wholly free from disapproval—or was it, perhaps, consternation? For Redvers Green was the East End slum in which Andra's younger daughter, Vicky, had worked for years as a doctor and where, in the early days of the war, she had been joined by her young niece, Leah Romaine.

"Oh yes, why not?" asked Fryn. "I want to see everything I can before I go back. When we met Cousin Vicky at Aunt Pen's wedding she asked mother to bring us—Meg and me—over. We all wanted to see Leah again, too. I thought the Clinic would be interesting, and so it was, but mother and Meg found it rather depressing."

"Mother and I are like Aunt Pen," said Meg. "Illness depresses us, especially so much of it in one place. Mother has put Redvers Green out of bounds for Fryn until after her exam, but Leah has promised to play at some 'do' of Gran'ma Bradfield's next week, and she says she may go to that. We've never heard Leah play, you know. She never would when we used to see her before she went to the Clinic."

"She doesn't play much now, either," said Bridget. "I'm surprised she didn't resist Aunt Caro's blandishments. But it seems a great waste of talent. I'm among those who think it a pity she's deserted music for good works."

"Is it true she did it because Maurice was killed?" Meg asked.

"I think it was because of the war generally—or Life with Mother during that first year of it. Ray, you know, believes Hitler was sent as her special scourge and that no one has suffered as she has through the war."

No two sisters could well have differed more, Dwight thought, than Ray and Vicky—Vicky fired with a sense of social service from her youth upwards, Ray a butterfly of the pre-war social scene, which for her had stretched across the continent, to Paris, Berlin, Vienna, Budapest. . . . But even before the war Hitler had spoilt a good deal of that for the wife of the Jew, Paul Romaine. And the war had taken her son from her, for Maurice was killed quite early, in the retreat from Greece; and then Vicky had snaffled Leah. Or so Ray held, according to his mother, who still maintained relations. Ray was one of the members of the family for whom Dwight had little patience and less affection. Her children, Maurice and Leah, were another matter. . . .

"I think it's splendid of Leah to give up everything to work in a slum," said Meg. "I mean, the Romaines are so rich—she could have such a good time."

"Leah and Vicky are alike, of course, in not wanting just 'a good time' out of life," Bridget said.

"No, but I still hold," said Dwight, "that Leah wasn't born with Vicky's passion for tidying up the universe. Nor with a social conscience in such good working order. Vicky is Aunt Caro all over again—only she goes down the road marked 'Health and Housing' and Aunt Caro down that sign-posted 'War and Peace'. But as a very young girl music was the only thing Leah really cared for—and Maurice was the same. It was the calamities which befell her father's race and his confidences in her, in lieu of her mother, who was bored by them, which made her so generally serious-minded. And then Maurice's death, I suppose, made her feel that in so shocking a world even music had ceased to matter."

"I think mother might agree with you," said Bridget. "But she thinks it a thousand pities, all the same. And she has a faintly guilty conscience because it was she who first took Leah down to the Clinic. She'd never been allowed to go. There were lots of things Leah had never been allowed to do, of course," she added for Fryn's benefit, "like riding in buses or travelling by Underground. And at that time Leah was fifteen. Actually, she had never travelled by either until the war came. For when she was twenty-one Paul gave her a car of her own."

How odd, thought Fryn, to *know* somebody who'd lived for twenty-three years before travelling in bus or Tube. This was a conversation after her own heart—a whole chapter of the family saga.

"I thought she looked very tired and rather sad," she said. "Perhaps she can't ever be really happy without her music. But perhaps she felt that music only belonged to a world that had Maurice in it . . ."

"Didn't you think she seemed happy at the Clinic?"

"No. I don't mean she was *un*happy exactly. I felt that neither happiness nor unhappiness came into it, somehow. It was as if she had just found a justification for her existence."

"That's it, I think," said Bridget. "She's been sheltered too long and suddenly she saw contact with suffering and ugliness as something she must face and endure."

"Well, I think it's very hard on Cousin Ray to have lost both her children," said Meg. "Perhaps it was really her duty to have stayed with her mother—I don't know. In any case, she's so attractive she would have got married if she hadn't buried herself in that awful place."

"Oh, but for the war, she'd have gone gallivanting all over the world with Maurice, giving concerts," said Bridget. "Ray couldn't have kept either of them at home for ever. But it's Paul who misses Leah, not Ray. Ray only misses Maurice."

"All the same, I shall go on feeling sorry for her," said Meg.

"We all feel sorry for Ray, but even sorrier for Paul," Bridget told her.

"Yes. He's nice, I think. And so handsome, but he looks so worn-out. It can't be very nice being a Jew, these days, even a rich one."

"Paul wouldn't complain on the personal score—after all, *his* side of the family had the foresight to settle in England. But he's worn himself out over the Romaines whose forbears were less long-sighted."

"I once heard Uncle Richie say," said Meg, "that much as the family liked Paul, they should never have allowed Ray to marry him."

"To which, my child," Bridget told her, "the proper reply, as mother would tell you, is 'Nonsense!—but someone should certainly have prevented Paul from marrying Ray!'"

They all laughed at that, including the speaker, who, however, soon stopped and, looking at Meg with a somewhat contemplative eye, said, "Do you see much of Paul and Ray at Hereford Square?"

"They never come to Hereford Square. But they've asked mother to dinner once or twice, and when we saw them at Aunt Pen's the last time we went down to Wyngates they asked mother to take Fryn and me next time. So she did and since then Ray has sent me quite a lot of invitations, which mother won't always let me accept. I think she doesn't want me to get ideas above my station in life!"

"Actually," said Fryn, "Ray has taken quite a fancy to Meg. I expect it's because she's so like her mother."

Bridget was not disposed to think that Ray was likely to be swayed towards friendship for any such sentimental reason, though it was true enough that Meg was very like Andra, as she remembered her. The same dark curling hair, the same parchmenty skin, taking the March winds, like Shakespeare's daffodils, with beauty, the same merry look of one who loved life. . . . But she said, "Yes, you're very like what she must have been at your age, I think."

"By which time," said Fryn, "she had been married two years and had three children."

"It sounds better, my dear, if you also mention that the first two were twins!" laughed Bridget. "Well, I'm sorry to break up this jawbation, but oughtn't we to be starting back?"

Dwight looked at his watch, and confirmed Bridget's view of the quite deplorable flight of time and they all rose, reluctantly, for it was pleasant there on the hill and the conversation had been lively and of particular interest to Fryn, to whose pursuit of family history Bridget was always very indulgent. She was a little alarmed at the idea of meeting so many strangers at tea, but lunch should be interesting, since it was all family and would afford her an excellent opportunity of getting to know a little more of the legendary Emmy. She hoped Audrey wouldn't come, now that Doreen had told them about her major! How horrid it was of her! And how horrid she had been about the car! Even Bridget, who always gave you the impression of having no emotion of any sort to waste upon her sister-in-law, had gone quite white when she had refused to accept Dwight's decision about driving the Hudson. She herself so disliked Doreen she felt she was always ready to be unfair to her, but if Bridget concurred in her verdict, even by no more than the sudden blanching of her face, she felt her own indignation was justified. Besides, had not the tolerant Meg taken her arm for a moment as they had gone upstairs together, and whispered, "Wasn't she *awful*? I was ready to sink through the floor!"

It had not yet occurred to her that she so much disliked Doreen on these occasions because it made her feel sorry for Dwight. For the moment that truth was hidden from her by his own imperturbability and by the quiet way in which he upheld his own decisions.

Back at Greystones, the presence of the hired car drawn up to the side of the drive announced the arrival of the luncheon party, which fact drove Bridget straight to her room; but hearing voices in Doreen's she as hurriedly descended, for she did not feel in the mood to hear Doreen playing up, as she mentally phrased it, to Rose. She hurried through the drawing-room into the loggia, hoping to find Larry and Dwight there, but encountered instead Danny, gallantly escorting Emmy from a tour of the garden. Unmistakably Emmy, over-dressed, her hair shrieking henna above her elaborately made-up face. She stopped in her tracks, waiting for them to come up to her, perfectly well aware that good manners dictated she should hurry forward with a greeting as effusive as it would be false. And she thought: Now why did Doreen inform us so carefully that Rose was bringing Emmy but as carefully refrain from confirming that she was bringing Danny?

[103]

"Here's a surprise for you, Bridget," said that gentleman, with a smile that still retained its old remembered deliberate charm; but not otherwise greeting her.

"Not at all," said Bridget. "It's you who are the surprise. Doreen told us Emmy was coming, but you were only a rather vague 'perhaps'."

"*Really?*" Impudence mingled with the charm of smile and voice, as their owner occupied himself with the business of detaching Emmy and settling her in a chair, carefully plumping up the cushion at her back and inquiring attentively if she would be sufficiently out of the sun. Somehow by his attentions he made Emmy seem a hundred and himself not a day beyond thirty. Which was absurd.

"Well, Bridget," said Emmy, looking up at her young relative with a smile which revealed teeth that were obviously genuine and the one beauty left to her bedizened countenance. "It's a long time since we met."

"A very long time indeed, Cousin Emmy," agreed Bridget, thinking, in some other world, and also that Emmy's make-up was a mistake of the first magnitude and that people of her age, perhaps, would be well-advised if not to refrain, at least to put on their spectacles before beginning the operation.

"Yes," said Emmy. "But as Audrey had an engagement and couldn't come I thought it would be a good opportunity to take advantage of Doreen's standing invitation. I don't run a car, these days—so very expensive!"

Bridget smiled, reflecting that expense, even in these days, was hardly a theme that Emmy need dilate upon.

"When Rose told me she was going by train because of petrol shortage I said I'd rather leave it until another time. But then Danny decided to hire."

She turned a much too sprightly eye in Danny's direction, but her cavalier had slipped away.

"Doreen suggested that course to Rose," said Bridget, not without malice, "but she thought it quite pauperising, I gather."

"Oh, we're all paupers, these days," said Emmy. "Danny tells me that Bourne simply *eats* money."

"His or Livvy's?"

"Oh, well, Livvy's a very good business woman, I hear. She isn't an American for nothing, of course."

It was as if she'd said, "Poor Danny!"

"Well, it was just as well Danny came up to scratch—since Doreen wanted Alston to help Mrs. Simmonds. Though I can't help thinking that Alston would rather be doing his own job than messing around in the house."

"I dare say. But it's marvellous how Doreen—from all I hear—manages the staff." (For one, said her tone, who has never been used to servants.) "Not that I ever considered Mrs. Simmonds a patch upon the servants mamma had when I was a girl at home. But you never knew Merrick, of course. He was with mamma practically all his adult life and quite devoted to us all."

"We had his daughter at Richmond, you know. She came to mother two years before I was born. I gather she was very much a chip of the old block."

"Yes, indeed. A most worthy daughter of her father. But times, alas! have changed."

(Nothing Emmy had wanted so much, when she was young, so the family legend recorded, as that things should "change".)

"Well, I hope Doreen won't overdo the 'managing'," said Bridget. "Alston strikes me as distinctly disgruntled. And Mrs. Simmonds is clearly 'quite devoted' to nobody."

"She was devoted to James, of course . . ."

Not willing to follow that conversational lead, Bridget said, "Are you writing anything now, Cousin Emmy?"

"Good gracious, no, my child! I know when to stop."

Ignoring this gambit, Bridget lighted a cigarette and offered one to Emmy, who said she had quite given up smoking—*such* an extravagance, these days. "What do you intend to do with yourself when you've got your degree?"

Bridget said she hoped to get a job—preferably in some publishing house.

Emmy said, "Ah yes, doubtless you'll find Mr. Anstruther of assistance to you there . . . *So* lucky for you."

Bridget felt it would be quite useless to expect Emmy to believe that she had neither thought of her step-father as an "influence" nor intended to enlist his help. She looked around for some relief from this unrewarding conversation in the approach of Meg or Fryn, and thought how much more she would have enjoyed her week-end if she'd spent it at home. Only curiosity, she knew, had brought her to accept Doreen's invitation and she hoped it would see her through the day. As for the invitation, she felt that Doreen would have been just as pleased if she'd refused it, having a shrewd suspicion that she made up her invitation lists on the principle of Mrs. Podsnap, who cheerfully ticked off the name of a refuser with the remark, "Asked and got rid of." However, she answered Emmy's questions without

[105]

impatience, holding that Emmy was as entitled to her curiosity as she to hers. How did she feel about her degree? English, wasn't it? A pity she had had to leave her Finals so late . . . Yes, her war work, of course . . . Any young men friends? Not any *special* one? Had she met Audrey's major? Unfortunately . . . But that was *quite* a secret. Dear Rose would have it that there was nothing in it —and that Audrey would be very annoyed if it was suggested that there was. But of course mothers didn't always hear everything. And Emmy smiled a small secret smile.

Relief came at last in the appearance of the rest of the company and Mrs. Simmonds's "help" with glasses of sherry.

Fryn, who had wanted so much to meet Emmy again, now found herself so intimidated by her appearance that she blushed and was tongue-tied. She looked so much worse than she remembered her, and she could not believe that this fantastic old woman, with the incredible hair and over-rouged face, was the legendary Emmy about whom she had woven such a romantic and interesting life-story. But perhaps she was better than she looked—she could hardly be worse . . . "Quite incredible," whispered Meg, as Doreen came up to the startling apparition and began fussing around her. "I do believe she's had her face lifted since we last saw her— you can always tell by the eyes. I can't look at her without doing a sum in mental arithmetic . . . She must be lots over seventy."

"Seventy-four—nearly," Fryn whispered back. That was easy to remember. The three daughters of Laura Gaywood—Uncle Ninian's original "Buds of May"—had gone down the years almost in steps. Cathy, 1869; Andra, 1870; Emmy, 1872.

Bridget hovered in the background with Dwight, who said, "Patience—all things come to an end," and Bridget whispered back, "I simply can't believe she was ever clever as a young woman, because she's so incredibly silly as an old one."

"An unsound argument," Dwight replied.

Before lunch was finished Bridget thought she knew why Doreen was cultivating Emmy. For she flattered her out of hand, commending everything—the lunch, the flowers and her own appearance. (*Belinda's praised for labours not her own*, thought Bridget.) And though Doreen certainly did not lack admirers, it was clear that she got a "kick" out of approval from the member of the family who once had been something of a celebrity, even a scandal. And her passport to Emmy's good offices, it was equally clear, was the fact that she was not approved by, and did not like, what Emmy called "my precious family".

But clearly, Bridget thought, following Danny's glances at his hostess, it wasn't only *Emmy's* approval Doreen was after. Danny and she gave the impression, rather oddly, of knowing each other quite well. Maybe they'd met often at Rose's, for not even Livvy could keep Danny playing Squire to Bourne all the time, and he was fond of his sister and doubtless not infrequently accepted her hospitality when playing truant. It was Rose who interrupted her thoughts by saying, "Isn't it nice for us to have Danny for a while? Livvy had to go off in rather a hurry, you know—her father's not at all well and her mother's last letter worried her so much. *Dear* Livvy!—she's so devoted to her parents. And, of course, she's an only child."

"So you took pity on the poor deserted husband?" said Bridget, glancing across the table at her cousin's handsome head bent towards Doreen, who was chatting with unwonted animation. Hearing his name he cocked an expressive eyebrow before turning back to Doreen, and Rose said, "Oh, I don't think that's at all a good description of Danny, Bridget. He loves an odd week in town and there's always room with us, as you know. More than ever, these days, for Audrey has made so many friends in the services, and she's frequently away staying with them. Larry and I miss her terribly, of course, but after those dreary years in the army we don't grudge her a little pleasure, poor child!"

Her eyes on her uncle, who was listening with his usual air of abstraction to something Emmy was saying to him, Bridget wondered not only if the years in the army had been as stagnant for Audrey as her mother believed, but if her father really grieved at her absences from home. Larry had always had an odd detached attitude to his children, even when young, and privately, like her mother, Bridget considered Audrey more of an affliction than a daughter.

"What on earth would you have done, Rose, if she'd decided to try to go to Germany?" asked Emmy, who had apparently finished what she had been saying to Larry.

"Oh, she was never very serious about that," Rose assured her, and again across Emmy's bedizened face there came that small secret smile, which Bridget found decidedly intriguing. If Doreen's tale of the friendship with the major who'd had the shortsightedness to take a wife before meeting Audrey were true, here, of course, was a situation after Emmy's own heart. Dished of her own romance (as she appeared to believe, by the machinations of family interferers) it was romance she had lived on ever since. . . . Even if

Doreen's story were true, what could be done about it? Audrey was no youthful Fenella, to be rescued by a determined parent. She was a mature woman well into her thirties. And as hard as nuts. Take what you can get—and don't pay for it, she thought, amending the Spanish proverb, was Audrey's motto. In the matrimonial stakes anything rather than being left at the post.

These reflections kept Bridget almost as silent as Larry during the meal. Heavy-going, Doreen would think them both, for she expected her visitors to be bright and chatty. Still, all the others, except perhaps Fryn (obviously well settled-in as observer and listener), were being obliging enough. So why worry?

She wondered why Emmy should buttonhole her so determinedly when lunch was over and they'd adjourned to the loggia for coffee. Dwight had walked off with Larry and Rose, and Danny with Meg. Fryn had vanished and Bridget was soon grateful even for the appearance of Doreen, who came over and asked Emmy if she was sure she was comfortable where she was or whether she would prefer to have her coffee indoors.

Emmy said she was very comfortable indeed where she was, and then, as Doreen took a seat, "That child of Lydia's—the younger one, Fryn isn't her name?—seems very shy, I thought. Quite gauche."

"Fryn never talks very much," said Bridget. "She's a born listener."

"Her mind's on this examination of hers, I suppose," Doreen commented.

"Rose tells me she's convinced she will fail because of her maths," said Emmy, "and suggested that as that was always my favourite subject, I ought to be able to help her. But I don't know—I'm very stale, I'm afraid. I deserted figures years ago, of course, for figures of speech."

She gave a little titter at the small joke and added, "Besides, I very much doubt if I should have the patience."

"I'm sure it would be far too much for you, Cousin Emmy," Bridget said firmly. "And I'm sure Lydia would never dream of imposing upon you. Rose is always so . . . so enterprising in her suggestions."

"She only meant to be helpful, I'm sure. And I'd be willing to do anything I could, of course, as I told her."

"If Fryn really needs a coach her father can quite well arrange for her to have one," said Bridget, thinking, Oh no, Emmy, you don't get your talons in Fryn—don't you think it! And she wandered off down the garden with an air of nonchalance, though she felt as if someone had taken off her a chain.

"Bring them all back, Bridget," Doreen called after her. "Coffee should be here any moment."

Doreen lighted herself a cigarette and belatedly offered one to Emmy, who refused. She'd never cared very much for smoking, and now she'd given it up altogether. "*So* expensive, nowadays!" The way the well-off people in this family harp on about expense! thought Doreen, as she said, "Yes—terribly, but I simply can't give it up! . . ." Her eyes on Bridget's lithe young figure moving down the garden path, she inquired, "What do you make of that young woman?"

"Bridget? Oh, she's her mother, at her age, all over again," Emmy told her. "But she's less inclined to blurt things out than Pen was, which is something in her favour. Don't you agree?"

"I suppose so," said Doreen, reflecting, however, that whatever she might have done in her youth her mother-in-law wasn't much given to "blurting" now. She'd have liked her better if she was. It was her habit of seeming so controlled when you knew she was "hating your guts" that had got Doreen down. "She isn't particularly like her mother to look at, except for the eyes" (which privately she much admired). "But you never know what she's thinking. She and Dwight are a pair, there. He's much fonder of Bridget than of Fenella. It was his idea I asked her down with Lydia's girls. One has to work the family off somehow."

"Personally, I wouldn't bother," Emmy said. "I always liked Larry and Rose. Larry leaves you alone—and Rose couldn't if she tried. She always had to have her nose in every family quarrel."

"Quarrels? Don't tell me this family ever had quarrels?"

"Oh, well, disagreements . . . And feuds occasionally. Mine, for instance. But that's a very old story now."

"I should love to hear it some day. Now that you've broken the ice I do hope you'll come again."

"Thank you, my dear," said Emmy. Her voice was benevolence itself, her claws velvet-sheathed. "It's very kind of you to bother with an old woman. And you must feel free to look in upon me when you are in town, and care to do so. . . . You have lunch with Danny sometimes, don't you? I know he likes to be seen with a pretty girl. I must tell him to bring you in to tea one afternoon."

"Thank you. That would be lovely," Doreen murmured, wondering how she knew that when Danny was in town she often met him for lunch. But Emmy, so the family tradition ran, always knew things, and was altogether too fond of getting her finger in everybody's business. However. . . .

"I suppose you've been to Wyngates?"

"Only once. Dwight and I went down to lunch. My revered mother-in-law looked flourishing but thought we ought to have taken Barry. But he's always sick in the car—I s'pose he'll grow out of it. I think it's just excitement. He's terribly highly-strung, you know. Quite the last sort of child I'd have expected to have."

"Am I not to see him?"

"Miss Deans will bring him down after tea. She seems able to manage him, which is more than I can do."

"Only children seem to be rather difficult," Emmy offered. Then, archly, "Don't you intend to give him a little brother or sister?"

"Not if I can help it, though Dwight of course would like half a dozen, but then he doesn't have to go through the horrid business of having them."

"In one of her books," remarked Emmy, "your mother-in-law, I remember, says women to-day talk of having a baby as if it were a major operation instead of a natural process. So vulgar, I thought."

"I don't read her books," said Doreen grandly, "but I know that's her point of view. She often takes a knock at me. But she's one of the fortunate ones. . . . Oh, dear, where *is* that coffee? The kitchen seems to have gone to sleep. . . . Oh, here you are, Elizabeth—I thought you'd all forgotten us. And now of course the party's missing. Just see if you can round them up, will you?"

The party, however, now came streaming back of its own accord and the girl retired. Emmy said to Fryn, "Come and sit by me, child. . . . I should like to talk to you."

"Your garden's looking lovely, Doreen," Rose said. "It must be a great satisfaction to you."

"So long as Groom continues to look after it," said Doreen. "Most of our neighbours have been left in the lurch and have to wrestle themselves. But I'm no daughter of Adam, you know, and Dwight, of course, would never have time. I hope Groom doesn't let us down."

"He seems contented enough at the moment," Dwight said, handing sugar to Emmy and Fryn. The one really contented person among his staff, he considered, probably because no one interfered with him, expected him to do anything but his own job or to do double work on Sundays.

"You look tired," Dwight said to Rose.

"Do I? . . . I think I *am* a little tired lately. I'm getting old, I suppose." (She will be fifty-six this year, thought Fryn.) "Or perhaps everybody's tired, these days."

It was so unlike Rose to admit any failing of her vitality that Bridget looked at her in surprise. She wouldn't have said that she looked tired—but, rather, a little worried. And that, too, was unusual for Rose, for whom life moved in very pleasant places, and on oiled wheels. Even, it seemed, in these post-war days. Maybe she wasn't so easy in her mind about the major as Doreen had suggested.

"Larry and I think of going to Switzerland next month," Rose went on. "Though Larry would prefer Holland—even to-day! I can't help thinking we'd do better to go to Switzerland."

"More food, of course," said Larry, feeling that some comment was expected of him.

"And plenty of scenery for you to paint," said Rose, laughing, but as to this Larry made no observation. He'll find something to paint wherever he goes, thought Bridget. Even after this second World War which had destroyed many of the places he had known and loved and painted in his youth. For Larry painted the skies, the rivers, the trees that grew beside them. Rain on a long stretch of road, sunlight on a hill, across a valley, over a London street. But she could understand his longing to paint again in Holland—it must be a Paradise for the landscape painter, with its watery sunshine, its far flat distances and enchanting reflections, its windmills and canals, wide skies and piled clouds. What appealed to him was the permanence of nature in a world of shifting values and senseless destruction. But Rose, when she thought of Holland, saw none of these things. Their earlier trips to that country had elicited from her the verdict of "So delightfully clean—quite the cleanest country I ever was in—but rather dull, I thought. Too flat for me."

"What's wrong with *your* going to Switzerland and Larry roughing it in Holland?" asked Emmy.

"Now how could I go to Switzerland without Larry? It was different when David and Audrey were younger—we often went away on our own and left Larry to go where he liked. But now, of course, they have their own interests and friends. They don't want to go holiday-making with old fogys. If Larry decides on Holland, then Holland it will be."

"Spoken like a dutiful wife, my dear sister," said Danny, getting up to light Doreen's cigarette for her. A simple act, yet not so simple in this instance, Bridget felt. If it was possible for two people to make eyes at each other while one of them was lighting a cigarette and the other holding the lighter for the operation, then Doreen and Danny were doing it.

Elizabeth came in and collected the coffee tray, and after she had disappeared Dwight said, "Why *don't* you leave Larry to go his own way, Rose, and go off to Switzerland yourself—taking Doreen with you? She's never been out of England—and Switzerland would be very much up her street. What do you say, Doreen?"

"Well, darling, it would be lovely, of course, especially with Rose, but I don't see how I could possibly, just now."

"Why not? Present conditions seem to me most favourable. Everything here will go on just the same. Mrs. Simmonds and Elizabeth to look after me. Miss Deans to look after Barry. What more could you want?"

"Darling! how you do spring things! As if one could decide a thing like this in a moment!"

"The only way to decide anything, these days."

"You're not serious, are you?"

"Of course I'm serious. You'd enjoy Switzerland no end, and it would do you a world of good."

"But Dwight, you can't force my company on Rose like this."

"Rose would like it, I'm sure."

"She'd be too polite to say so if she wouldn't."

"Well, she could take Danny to keep you both in countenance," went on Dwight.

"And Livvy?" said Danny, smiling. "I expect her back shortly, you know."

"Oh, yes, I'd forgotten Livvy," said Dwight, also smiling. "Sorry, Danny. I still find it hard to think of you as a married man."

Rose said, a trifle too quickly, "It's very kind of you, Dwight, to offer to spare Doreen—it would be very pleasant, of course. But as I have said, I shall go to Switzerland or Holland, whichever Larry decides on. And equally of course we mayn't go abroad at all. 'Abroad' seems so very far away, these days. We haven't decided on anything. It was only an idea. . . . Nowadays everything's so difficult to arrange. Perhaps it would be simpler to go to Ireland. . . . There'd be heaps of scenes for Larry to paint there—in Connemara, for instance."

The sound of car wheels heralding the first afternoon arrivals, to greet whom Doreen now hurried out, put an end to her somewhat rambling remarks and relieved the slight general sense of embarrassment which Dwight's suggestion had produced, from which, however, Emmy, to judge by the little half-smile upon her painted

[112]

mouth, was immune. She thought Dwight's suggestion a little odd, to say the least, and Doreen, for all her level tones, had flushed and looked a little disconcerted. Yes, distinctly odd. . . .

Bridget could have found another word for it, for she had not been unaware of Emmy interrupting her obviously unrewarding conversation with Fryn to give her attention to this much more interesting one. What on earth had possessed Dwight? she wondered. He must, she supposed, have noticed that little bit of by-play over the cigarette lighting and had a twinge of jealousy. Yet surely he hadn't just discovered that Doreen couldn't help making eyes at any man who pleased and flattered her with his glances? Why, she'd done it with all the young men with whom Fenella had filled the house at Richmond in the early days of the war before the advent of Glen Westcott had swept them out of it like a gigantic broom. Maybe he'd only thought it would be rather pleasant to get rid of Doreen for a while? Or perhaps there was no reason for it at all, it was nothing but a piece of harmless teasing. But curiously unlike Dwight. . . .

"Bridget, let me introduce Mr. . . ."

Doreen's voice at her elbow, her face smiling and beguiling and no longer discomfited, banished Bridget's attempts at explaining Dwight's *diablerie*, for that doubtless was what it really was. Not natural to Dwight, perhaps, but those who lived with Doreen would suffer, she felt, a sea change.

"A near neighbour of ours, Bridget, whose perfectly *ravishing* wife has her eye on you both. You have been warned!"

Much pleased with her witticism Doreen moved off.

Chapter Five

ON A fine warm morning towards the middle of July Gaby looked up
from the letter she was reading at the breakfast table to say to
Bridget, who was wondering if a third piece of toast would mean
losing her train or exhaust her rightful share of the fat ration,
"Fenny and Glen will be home on Saturday—in time for the evening
meal, which Fenny, I notice, still refers to grandiloquently as
'dinner'."

"Which term," said Bridget, risking the piece of toast, "the
evening meals you provide, my dear Gaby, invariably deserve."

To this compliment Gaby said only, "How low our standard
must have fallen! Well, it will be very nice to have them home, I
must say!" And to the little girls at the table she added, "Mummy
and daddy are coming home the day after to-morrow. Won't that
be lovely?"

Becky, busy over the business in hand, merely nodded assent, but
Serena, her elder sister—a remarkably placid-looking little girl, with
hair as dark as her mother's was fair, and quite straight—turned an
equally remarkably quick smile upon the speaker. Her smile (like
her rare scowl) always came before her words, even when her mouth
didn't happen to be full of bread and margarine, thickly spread with
the marmalade to make which earlier in the year Gaby had chased the
elusive Seville orange with a pertinacity worthy, so Fenella said, of a
better cause. But then, Fenella didn't like marmalade and Serena did.

"Yes, oh yes," said that young person, whose habit it was at this
stage of her existence so to emphasise her affirmatives and negatives.
She had enjoyed the company of the large robust person referred to
as "daddy", when he had recently arrived upon the scene, and
although her "No, oh no!" had been frequent and, for Serena, quite
shatteringly passionate, when he tossed her ceiling-high and held
her there, she had soon learnt to bear the indignity, which her sister
so much enjoyed, with the calm she opposed to most of the more
alarming manifestations of existence. Then he had gone away again,
taking mummy with him. And now he was coming back. . . . As
one used to the vagaries of grown-ups she dismissed these facts and
returned to the pleasures of breakfast.

Bridget had been a little indignant at the calm way in which her sister had gone off on her second honeymoon, not so much because she had left Serena and Becky behind as because of the matter-of-fact way in which she had done it, taking Gaby's presence and her willingness to shoulder fresh duties for granted. But then, they all did the same—and almost without realising it. Only her mother, Bridget thought, was patently aware of Gaby's unselfish devotion—to herself first, and then, because of her, to them all.

"I often wonder, you know, Gaby, why you were in such a hurry to marry mother off to Charles. I don't believe she'd ever have said 'yes', much as she wanted to, if you hadn't made everything so easy for her."

But she didn't really wonder. It was all part of the same thing. For Gaby there was nobody like her Aunt Pen, and she had thought, quite simply, that it was time she stopped thinking so much about her family and their war-time or war-introduced problems and had a little life of her own. It pleased her to think that she was now doing this, at least to some degree. She had ceased to slave at her desk—but had she ceased worrying? About Dwight and his marriage, for instance?

"You must have known that it would mean the end of all the things you'd shared for so long—and an awful gap in the more interesting of your activities," Bridget told her. "Not that you're looking for a job—you've too many. But you must miss all the secretarial and other work you did for mother for so long."

Gaby laughed.

"Of course I realised it," she said. "I must have a really beautiful nature, I suppose. . . . Aren't you going to read Fenny's letter?"

"I don't think so. She never writes more than half a dozen lines and they'll last until I get back this evening." Gaby had given her the only item of useful information in it—the day and time of their arrival, and it was a quite generous gesture of Fenella's to write at all, when she could have sent a wire or spent money on a long-distance call. It was Glen, she knew, who'd planked her down with pen and paper and stood over her, most likely, and said, "Write, minion, write!" "Heavens, I must fly! 'Bye, Gaby . . .'bye, children. . . ."

The door shut behind her, then opened an inch again and Bridget's voice said, "Oh, Gaby, I forgot to say I'm going to the theatre this evening. I'll be having a meal first, so don't leave me anything—and *don't* wait up . . .!" I'm like all the rest, she thought, I take Gaby for granted and never think of her being here alone all day, now that Fenny's away, save for that gowk of a girl in the kitchen. I could just as well have seen the play next week after Fenny's back. But imperturbably Gaby said, "Have a good time. I'll leave you some sandwiches and coffee, in case you're hungry." As she would be, of course, with the theatres still starting so early, and meals out what they were. . . .

"Serena and Becky! Would you like some more bread and butter and marmalade?"

"I'm full," said Becky, but Serena, it seemed, was not.

"Yes, oh yes!" she said.

Spreading the marmalade for the little girl Gaby permitted herself to wonder if Bridget was going alone to her play. It was a habit of hers, for she had a critical mind and was always careful to take it to the theatre with her; and during the intervals preferred to commune with it rather than to chat with a companion. Bridget was just past her twenty-fifth birthday: she had few close friends of her own sex and none nowadays of the opposite. The Cat that Walked Alone, Fenella called her. However, thought Gaby, one might be permitted to wonder. . . .

Waiting for Serena to finish her breakfast, she picked up Fenny's letter and re-read it, which was not in the least necessary but somehow made up for Bridget's not reading it at all. It was very short and fulfilled exactly Fenella's conception of the purposes of a letter, to give you any specific items of information it was necessary you should have and to add a few others that might or might not interest you—that you were well and happy, for example, or not, perhaps. But this time, she thought, Fenny had bettered the model. She had begun by writing down the day and time of her arrival home and then had added, "The weather has been behaving well, on the whole. We like the hotel and the food might be worse (Glen says it couldn't be; but he's army-pampered). He's doing a lot of sketching (with me as the principal victim) and when he isn't sketching we're walking. This, Glen says, is good for me, which means *he* enjoys it. I hope Becky is not getting into mischief and Serena as good as she invariably looks. (Glen, looking over my shoulder, says I mean 'almost invariably'—and that 'invariably' means 'always' not 'sometimes'. I dare say he's right.) Love from us both, Fenella."

Despite Bridget's scorn, Gaby considered that was not at all a bad letter to get. It was a happy letter, and it was quite touching in this world, she thought, to know someone who was as happy as all that. It was difficult to believe Fenny had once been a source of continual worry to them all; a mass of sentimentalism and romance coated over with that quality of "hard-boiled"-ness which was so very

[116]

wearisome. Pen had always maintained that beneath it she had plenty of sound sense if one could only get at it. Nobody ever had—and even the war hadn't been conspicuously successful—until Glen had appeared upon the scene. Glen, said Pen, was a gift from heaven; and had laughed at Bridget's suggestion that he was a civilised Petruchio.

Gaby, perceiving that Serena had finished her meal, got up and put the letter on the mantelpiece. Unpinning the children's bibs she left them to their own devices while she permitted herself five minutes with the morning paper. As usual, this was depressing, posing problems it seemed beyond the wit of man to solve, so that it was a relief to turn to anything as simple and everyday as clearing a breakfast table and carrying the tray out into the kitchen, where the recently installed Berta was still at her meal. Though distinctly a rough diamond, she was good-natured and willing, qualities so outstanding, in Gaby's recent domestic experience, that they automatically cancelled out all natural disabilities. Leaving her to finish her meal, she set Serena and Becky to play in the garden, assuring herself that the river gate was locked and the key in safe custody, and the garden doors of the house standing wide. There they would remain, with Berta's casual eye upon them, until she returned from the shops, from which she meant to wrest something for the Saturday evening meal which Fenella so optimistically called "dinner".

She was well-known at the local shops, for she had added these raids for food to her other duties many years ago, when the task had proved too much for their adored but ageing Winfarthing. She was a good marketeer, even in these days of austerity and the new bread-rationing, and minus the boon of the extra ration books, now that Doreen and Dwight had left; and for the last three weeks minus also those of Fenella and Glen. No use to tell a young woman with French blood in her veins that it was no more easy to feed a large family than a small one. She set off this morning in what Fenella called her "booted and spurred" mood, aware that Fenella was right when she said Glen was "army-pampered". Pleasant creature that he was, he had not so far grasped in the least the limitations of the ration book; much less, so far as she was concerned to-day, of no ration book for him and Fenella at all; or that the shops in July 1946 were not exactly bulging with unrationed food. Returning soldiers, poor things, had a lot to learn.

Perhaps it was these reflections which shifted her thoughts to her still-missing husband. It was strange, she thought, that close upon a year after she and Pen had sat and listened to the wireless report of the terrible Hiroshima bombing, she should have heard neither from him nor of him. She was astonished and dismayed by the calmness with which she considered that fact, for though it wasn't Ward she had loved, she had affection for him and gratitude for the love he had borne her. (Why did she always think of him in the past tense?) In their few months together as husband and wife she had grown fonder of him than she had believed possible; so that she had sometimes felt that if there had never been any Richie she might have loved him. But now he appeared to have become only a faint pleasant memory in her mind, and she felt that she had done him a great wrong in marrying him, even though it was for Elide's sake she had yielded to his persuasions, not to save her good name or to save herself from the scorn of her Aunt Caro, Richie's mother. For though it was true that Caro would not have approved of her marriage to Richie (having, since she did it herself, acquired strong views about the marrying of first cousins) she would have disapproved even more if she had known that she had refused to marry him; outraged that any girl could turn down her darling. So civilised elsewhere, Caro Bradfield was entirely uncivilised where her son had been concerned, as primitive as any peasant woman, and knew little about him save that he *was* her son, not even that she had spoiled and indulged him.

But perhaps, she'd often thought, Richie would have been what he was even if Caro had not been so adoring and foolish. For though he had lost his father in World War One, as she hers, when she was too young to remember much about him, life had fallen to him in very pleasant places. At twenty-one he'd been a rich young man, inheriting not only money from his father but from his paternal grandfather. He was rather like Cathy's Danny as seen by Pen, who held that he was a throw-back to the gay and reckless family of his great-grandmother, who'd been Georgiana Iden and thought the Gaywood family into which her only daughter had married, a stuffy crowd. Not that Gaby ever thought of Richie as a Regency "buck", but there was altogether too much of the roving eye and philandering male about Richie to make her accept him as a husband, though he'd clearly considered that the part of her that was French should cause her to turn a blind eye to that side of his nature. But Richie forgot —or perhaps did not know—that the Frenchman has a respect for his wife and for his home, whatever he does outside it, and she did not believe Richie would have had the one and was most unlikely ever to have acquired the other.

Poor Richie! why did she still analyse him in this fashion? He'd been so long in his grave, and though he'd been a satisfying lover and his death had killed passion in her for any other man, she could never deceive herself into believing that she would have been happy with him as his wife. She sometimes wondered if he'd minded that she would not marry him—apart from the jolt to his self-esteem. She could never tell; and certainly he had readily accepted, in the summer of 1940, the relationship she had accorded him because she believed, so despairingly, that he would be killed. Perhaps he knew it, too, and like so many others of their generation had lost interest in the more permanent things like marriage, if indeed he'd ever had much in the state, which she could never believe. As a lover he held all the cards; as a husband not one. And it was as a lover she remembered him. . . .

Yet when he had died the world had looked most frighteningly empty, even with Ward standing there like a sentinel. In the end this illusion would have been corrected, she felt, without her acceptance of Ward's so often repeated offer of marriage. But the knowledge, soon after Richie's death, that she was to have a child had altered everything, for children, she held, wanted the security and background of the normal married state. But Richie's child, like Richie, had been taken from her and for a time the pulse of her life had ceased to beat. Ward, already on the other side of the world, scarcely existed for her, and she was torn with contempt of herself because she had not found enough courage to marry Richie. But he could no longer be hurt by her cowardice (if ever he was) nor Elide benefited by the father she had provided for her. And in that knowledge her life had seemed to fall to pieces. But gradually, under the spur of the tasks, so many and unceasing, that lay to her hand; beneath the understanding sympathy of her Aunt Pen, life had taken shape again, a new shape, drawing its sustenance from the lives of those around her whom she loved, and who loved her, and even from the rare letters she had from her husband before silence, like a curtain, fell between them. It lifted once, to let out the fact that he was a prisoner and well, and then dropped again. If only, she had thought sometimes, he had not been sent to the Far East! She might by now have made something of her life, compensated him for what she had made of his. She had just passed her thirtieth birthday and the French side of her nature, dismissing romantic love, sometimes yearned for a settled life of her own; and children. If Ward came home—unless his experiences had entirely changed him, which she thought un-likely—she did not doubt that they could pick up again the threads of their brief life together and be happy. Perhaps, for herself, she meant happy *enough*. The unqualified mood belonged to her unlegalised

[119]

union with Richie. She did not expect—and did not desire?—that kind of happiness again. Most people, she reflected, got on very well without it.

She gave herself a mental shake and began to think of other things —of her courageous mother, newly restored to her family from the hazards of the Resistance Movement in France, and fired with an unusual approval of the British for their stand against Hitler; of her beloved aunt in her new home, so obviously happy and content and no longer harassed by the need to write so many thousand words a day; of Dwight and Doreen and the small Barry in James's pretty house; of Fenella and Glen now at the close of their second honeymoon; of Bridget so quietly competent and self-confident, taking the interruptions the war had made in her plans so calmly, taking life in her stride, as her mother had done, but less inclined, she thought, to be as grateful as she for life on any terms. . . .

Well, they'd all be glad to have the honeymooners back. Glen was a pleasant creature to have about the house and that he had improved Fenella out of all knowledge had added to the laurels he had earned in the family. She'd be having another baby, too, doubtless—and the house would once more be full of excitement and the murmur of the busy stream of life. Nothing could be better, she thought, as she walked into the first shop on her list and announced that she wanted a tender chicken for roasting. It was part of her marketing technique to ask for things as if she was shopping in a normal world; one frequently went empty away, but it was as well to behave as though you believed things were moving towards normality, even though you knew they weren't. So now she announced her desire not merely for a chicken but for one that could be roasted in a civilised manner and not boiled to string in the faint false hope of ultimately achieving tenderness. But on second thoughts she added, "I need to feed five people, so perhaps it had better be *two* tender chickens."

The assistant, to whom she was well-known, agreed that it had.

"They won't, I expect, be as plump as I should like, but you will see that they are really properly dressed?" said Gaby, who was not half-French for nothing. If she had to pay through the nose for chickens, then she would; but she had no intention of doing it for birds that were tough or uncarvable. She had a way with shopkeepers, even in this bleak period of austerity, and usually secured a fair share of what politeness there was to be had in the shops. Pen envied but could never emulate her technique. Rudeness from shopkeepers to Pen (who had outfaced James's worst sallies) was so deflating that the household, she'd declared, would starve to death if it had relied upon her to find food. Luckily Charles had been able to take an old and valued servant along with him to Wyngates. "Between you, Winny and Lottie," she'd said to Gaby, "I've been spoiled!" Spoiled! Gaby thought now, counting her change. As if she hadn't for years worked harder than any of them. If there was anything worse than sitting at a desk dredging for ideas and dealing with them when they came up, Gaby couldn't imagine what it was. She ticked off "chickens" from her list and went along to see what kind of vegetables were to be had. Already she felt a different person. Food was a vastly important and interesting subject and even at its worst there was always one thing you could say for the business of tracking it down—that it took your mind off lesser things. This morning it had successfully arrested hers in its favourite trick of running back and considering past mistakes and tragedies and sorrows, or, even worse, running forward and pushing her across bridges not yet built and maybe never to be built.

It was a month later when she received the official notice that Ward Findon, long posted as missing, must now be presumed dead. It had been ascertained that he was among the twenty-four hundred prisoners, British and Australian, whom the Japanese had driven into the interior at the end of 'forty-four—a tragic death march from which there had been few survivors, and Ward's name not among them. . . .

She put the notice with the postcard announcing that he was a prisoner and the few letters she had had from him, and knew that it was this for which she had been waiting—the official closing of the chapter. For in her heart she had long known he was dead. Her silent, tearless grief was not for herself, but for him, and for all the integrity and simple goodness that had died with him, and which the world could ill spare. For weeks that thought was a sharp spear in her heart, then the pain lessened and life at the old house by the river went on as before.

Chapter Six

IT SURPRISED no one at Richmond when Pen, paying them a visit towards the close of the summer, announced that Alston and Mrs. Simmonds had given notice and were leaving at the end of the month; that Doreen was already in touch with a married couple and did not seem unduly depressed, reporting that James's old retainers had been so very tiresome of late that she would be quite glad to see the back of them.

However, the married couple stayed exactly a month and then left, forfeiting their wages rather than remain. By the end of September Doreen was reduced to the services of daily workers, who could not cook and did not work at the week-end. Then came the news that she had secured "a perfect gem", who was a good cook, did not mind what she did and positively "adored" company. It was true, Pen said, that there had been some rather queer happenings, as when the potatoes came to table sweet as saccharine and the coffee salt as brine. Doreen had been shaken but not dismayed, averring that accidents of that kind might happen even in the kitchens of Buckingham Palace. On the one occasion that Pen had gone down to Greystones during the "gem's" term of office, she had, however, arrived at the unwelcome conclusion that such accidents—and worse —were likely to be recurrent, and advised Doreen to get rid of her; advice which was neither well taken nor acted upon. But Pen had maintained that she would rather do all the drudgery of a house herself than live with the company of Mrs. Loder. Not so Doreen, however, who must have time for her trips to town, to do what nobody seemed to know, unless it was to support the boredom of all the other days spent "in the wilds".

But when a few weeks later the "gem" was found hanging in one of the kitchen cupboards she rushed, more or less, shrieking from the house, which was odd since it was Barry, not Doreen, who had found her. But Barry, of course, his mother declared, had no right to be in the kitchen at all, much less opening cupboards, and if Miss Deans had done her job properly he wouldn't have been. Doreen was too scared to pay much attention to any effects the horrible discovery might have had upon Barry—she had a comfortable theory

[122]

that children "soon forget". But she declared that nothing would induce her to live any longer at Greystones—her terror would have driven her to insistence that they should go back to town quite apart from the fact of the discomfort that now fell about her, left with no one to run the house, even the local "dailies" fighting shy of it, and Miss Deans hastily, much too hastily, dismissed as "incompetent".

However, it did not take long to get rid of the house: and the new owners seemed quite unmoved by the story of the suicide, of which they soon heard. The cupboard, they said, could be blocked-up—there were cupboards and to spare. And they were well enough aware that they'd got the house at a bargain price. For what, asked Doreen, did it matter *what* they sold it at, since they wouldn't benefit? All she cared about was getting out of it.

"To go where?" asked Dwight; and Doreen said, Richmond, until they could find a flat. And to Richmond they went—to nobody's satisfaction save Barry's, whose reunion with Serena was probably, Pen thought, the best thing that could happen to him. Nevertheless, even that did not prevent him from waking at night, shaken with terror and rousing the household with his screams. And since Doreen considered that he was not to be encouraged and should be left to go to sleep again with the friendly company of a night-light, it usually fell to Gaby to carry him off to her own bed and ultimately to have a bed put up for him in her room, an arrangement in which Doreen acquiesced willingly enough, quite undisturbed by Dwight's uncomfortable conscience. After all, Dwight had to rise betimes to get himself to the office by nine-thirty, whilst Gaby, her tone implied, had all day in which to repair the ravages of the night. And anyway, left to himself, Barry would go to sleep again. If Gaby *must* interfere she must put up with the consequences.

Gaby, however, had no complaints to make. With the old house full again she was happy, or too busy to indulge either in criticism of Doreen or her own sorrow or sense of frustration. Doreen, indeed, had become to her no more than a mild irritant; criticism was futile applied to anyone so febrile and self-centred; and as she took herself off to town several days in the week Gaby found it easy enough to forget her. With no household cares, no difficulty about leaving Barry, and no vestige of the conscience that troubled Dwight, Doreen found life pleasant enough under the new conditions. Amiable, decorative, entirely unself-critical, she came and went, keeping her own counsel, spreading about herself an air of social busyness that, if not convincing, was certainly impressive. Gaby found she preferred this Doreen to the earlier one who had so obviously been bored to death. Whatever nowadays she found to do with her time at least it had the merit of making her if not a more interesting person at least a less irritating one.

It was Fenella who was moved to criticism of Doreen and her ways—not to Gaby, who would not have troubled to listen, or to Bridget, who would have been bored, but to Glen, who was seldom bored and always interested, in his odd fashion, in most people and most things.

"It's the way she puts upon Gaby that infuriates me," she exclaimed one morning when she was sitting to Glen for a pencil sketch and Doreen had just left the house for an engagement in town.

"Well, what about you and me and even the detached Bridget? We all put upon her shamelessly and intend to go on doing it, I suspect."

"Glen!" Fenella's voice rocked with indignation. "We do no such thing!—at least, not the way Doreen does. We do pull our weight—we don't behave as if we were paying guests. But Doreen just expects to be waited on hand and foot, to behave as though Barry doesn't exist. I do think Dwight ought to pull her up. Since the Greystones interval she's a lot worse, though for some reason Gaby and Bridget don't agree with me. I can't imagine what she *does* in town. It can't be the shops—she's got no more coupons than the rest of us, though Bridget says she knows where to get others."

"Keep your head up! Rationing suits you, my girl. Prevents you from putting on fat. I warn you I shall leave you if you ever get a double chin. . . . But take that Mona Lisa smile off your face—it doesn't suit you to look mysterious. And anyway, you aren't."

"Of all the people to try to carry on a conversation with! Don't you ever wonder what Doreen finds to do in town?"

"Good lord, no! Does it matter?"

"I don't suppose so. But it *is* interesting. If it isn't the shops it can't be family visits—she hasn't any family. That's the nicest thing about her, not having any relations. We might have to know them else. She was brought up by an aunt, who died soon after the war began. You know, Glen, I'll bet you anything you like she goes to see Emmy. They got very friendly during the Greystones era."

"Do you mind?"

"In a way. Emmy has a tongue, you know, and I'm sure she wags it about us."

"Do you mean about you?"

[124]

"Do I? . . . Not altogether, anyway. But she and Audrey are a debunking pair."

"Why bother?"

"I don't know—I just hate to think of Doreen lapping it all up."

"Secrets of the prison house, eh?"

"Oh, I wouldn't mind Emmy telling that old story about me, if she didn't make it a fine high romance."

"You let her think it so once, my girl."

"Did I? I don't know. . . . I was a frightful idiot at that time. I got romantic about the most absurd people. But over that business with Claude Widmer I don't believe I'd have been so silly if Emmy hadn't taken such an interest in it. In a way she pushed me much farther than I wanted to go, though I didn't see that at the time, poor mutt that I was. I see now that in a way she was revenging herself for something that went all the way back to mother's girlhood. Emmy's like the elephant—she never forgets."

She fell silent, thinking how this realisation had frightened her into a sense of her own folly over her middle-aged Lothario, and though she could never bring herself to believe that it was the coming of the war which had saved her, there had been dreadful moments when she wondered what would have happened if the war hadn't come to send Claude scurrying off to America. He'd certainly have found some other way of getting out of the logical consequences of his philandering. For Emmy had pushed *him* a bit, too. . . . How he must have thanked God for the war! Remembering the letter he had written her and delayed sending until he was actually on the way to America, she felt as humiliated as if she had just read it. Of *course* Emmy wouldn't miss the chance of pouring out her version of it all to Doreen.

"Could you manage to look a little less as if you were going to be hanged at dawn?" asked Glen. "Thank you—that's a lot better."

"Oh, Glen, wouldn't it have been *awful* if I'd gone off with him —and missed you!"

"Perfectly appalling. And now if we may re-bury your horrid past, I've some news for you. I rather fancy Doreen and her doings will soon cease to trouble us. Or you, rather. She's far from troubling me, I assure you."

"And doesn't she *hate* it! You know, Glen, she's so pretty I often wonder you've never wanted to use her face for your sketches."

"Not on your life! . . . Well, here's my news. I've got good reason to believe that Dwight is in the running for a flat. Somebody is pulling a few strings for him."

5*

"A flat? *Where?*"

"Facing Battersea Park, I believe."

"Gosh! Doreen won't care for Battersea as an address."

"Oh, she'll not mind all that much. Battersea's such a good jumping-off ground for 'town'."

"Yes, so it is. . . . And it'll be near enough to Hereford Square for Fryn to go and take Barry out sometimes."

"I thought Fryn was still up to her eyes in examination prep?"

"Yes, but she can't work all the time. If only she had passed that silly examination last year to Gilbert's satisfaction, they'd all have gone home a month ago, and we'd be installed in their house by now. If she had he'd not be going to Germany. He wants her to get matric. and he doesn't want to leave her behind to do it."

"We shall have a lot of time to live in the house."

"Not *enough* time—there's never enough time. If I weren't so fond of Fryn I should owe her a grudge for keeping me waiting. She'll hate going back."

"She's a nice kid—and a much better sitter than you, my girl. For one thing she doesn't let her nice face fall to pieces while she considers her mis-spent youth." He surveyed his drawing, with both eyes apparently shut, for a while and then put it aside.

"That'll do for this morning, minion. Run along and amuse yourself."

"I shall take Serena and Barry into the Park. See you at lunch-time."

"By the way, when do you propose to finish that lettering for me?"

" This week some time . . . perhaps."

"Lazy slut, aren't you?"

She grinned at him and went away. It was pleasant to be married to a man who didn't *every* morning have to rush off to catch a train but could do his work at home two or three days a week. She felt a little guilty over the lettering, but she'd clean forgotten it. She no longer cherished any illusions about her talent, but it pleased her that Glen encouraged her to improve it. He couldn't bear, he said, to see any talent wasted—she'd neglected hers too long. That was true, anyway. What a hopeless dilettante young creature she had been! No wonder, she thought, mother used to feel so hopeless about me! How queer that of all the young men she'd known—and what a retinue there'd been of them!—Glen was the first man to make her feel that she was a mess. And how surprised, she thought, putting the knitted bonnet over Serena's sleek little head, Glen would be to know that he'd done anything of the sort!

[126]

Dwight signed the lease of the flat a week or so later.

Neither Fenella nor Bridget pretended to be sorry about the imminent departure of their sister-in-law, but Gaby was deeply concerned for Barry, and Pen for both Barry and Dwight. Pen, indeed, remembering the dirty neglected flat from which she had with so much difficulty detached Doreen in the early days of the war, was filled with gloom, for she could not but feel that the life Doreen had since lived, both at Richmond and Greystones, was scarcely calculated to have improved her capacity for running a house. And neither she nor Gaby liked to think of Barry shorn first of the comforts of Richmond and then of the delights of the Greystones menage —the garden, the care and attention of Miss Deans, who, for all her ultimate lapse (not entirely her fault, perhaps, thought Pen, remembering Barry's quicksilver moods and actions), had been very competent and conscientious. He'd miss, too, the companionship of Serena. Moreover, neither of them considered a flat the place for a child (though a good many people seemed to think otherwise) and Gaby putting this point, rather nervously, to Dwight, so withdrawn and elusive, these days, found him adamant; talking of a "home of their own", the "shouldering of their own responsibilities", and the easier daily journey to town for himself. (And for Doreen, Gaby had mentally added, giving up the argument.) But she knew that she would rather have put up for ever at Richmond with the boredom of the casual, untidy and selfish Doreen, than hand Barry over to her charge. Always a rather difficult highly-strung little boy, and still suffering from the effects of that ghastly discovery of the suicide, she could not bear to think of the impatience, the impercipience Doreen would oppose to his disturbed nights, the resultant edgy days. . . . But you couldn't, Doreen said, make a profession of motherhood—children had to fit in—that was one of the things she *did* agree with her mother-in-law about.

Gaby had marvelled that the same phrase used by two people could mean two such very different things.

Doreen's reactions to the flat were much as they had all expected. The flat itself she considered "not bad", but it was a pity it wasn't on the other side of the Park. It was clear she considered Battersea somewhat low, though improved by the addition of the word "Park", which green space the flat overlooked. The address, however, was carried off lightly when she had an afternoon in town with her friend Milly Burke. "Battersea, my dear—I *ask* you!" But of course it was very convenient, really—one could get anywhere in town very easily, and after the depths of the country and this awful suburban strap-hanging that was a lot. Reminded that there would be the bus queues, she said, "Oh, but there are taxis! Of course I wish it were farther in—Kensington, say—but you can't choose where you live, these days, can you? I mean, you're lucky to find anything at all possible . . ."

"You won't like starting on housekeeping again, will you? Not after having everything done for you for so long."

Doreen said that in a neighbourhood like Battersea there ought to be plenty of daily labour to be had.

"Oh, I wouldn't be too sure. Those are the only people with any money, these days," said Milly, who was apt to be bored by Doreen's suggestion of her own unlimited means when everyone knew the middle classes were broke.

"Well, I must hope for the best. But I know one thing. I'll be glad to get away from Richmond—and glad we'll be gone before Fenella has her baby. Of course no one's told me she's going to have another—but I'm sure she is. She means to have a proper family, I'm sure. You know, I'd never have thought Fenella'd have fallen for a man the way she'd done for Glen Westcott. When she was in the F.A.N.Y.'s she always had a crowd of young men in the house when she was home on leave—a regular honeypot. But you'd have said she couldn't have cared less. Of course Emmy—Miss Gaywood, a sort of cousin she is—says she was in love with some married man she used to meet at her house just before the war, only he went off to America to dodge the bombs, and that she never liked *young* men. Anyway, she fell for Glen Westcott all right."

"Fenella. That's the pretty one, isn't it?"

"That's right. Hazel eyes and bronze gold hair. And a nice figure, too. I don't care for her much, but I'll give her her due. She's got what it takes."

"I s'pose they'll be going off on their own as soon as they can find a house?"

"They're going to take the house in Hereford Square as soon as the Hamptons go home to South America. *He's* just gone off to Germany—volunteered for the Allied Commission, or whatever they call it. Something to do with the blitzed cities, I fancy. He knows about buildings, I suppose, being a civil engineer."

"What's going to happen to the Richmond house?"

"Oh, I suppose Mrs. Findon and Bridget will go on living there. Gaby—Mrs. Findon—rents the house from my mother-in-law—but she's rich enough to buy it if she wants."

[128]

However, Milly wasn't very interested in this side of the family. She said, "What about the baronet? Seen him lately?"

"He's in America with his wife. They're expected back soon, though. He doesn't come to Richmond, you know. When he's in town he stays with his sister in Chelsea. At Richmond he's not what my highbrow sister-in-law Bridget calls personagrater—which seems to mean welcome."

"Well, Chelsea will be nice and near for you, won't it, when you get to Battersea? I suppose Barry'll be going to school now there's no nursery governess?"

"Yes—as soon as we get settled in the flat. He'd have gone before if I'd had my way, then he wouldn't have been mixed up in that business of Mrs. Loder."

"It must have been a nasty shock for the poor little chap."

"Yes, but children soon forget, you know. At least, if they're not coddled and encouraged to remember. I had a bit of a shock myself, if it comes to that. He came running up to me and said, 'Mummy, Lody's hanging up in the cupboard.' Just like that—he always called her 'Lody'. He didn't sound frightened. Just looked a bit white—he might have been telling me anything. I'd no idea what he meant."

"Quite dead, I suppose?"

"Lord, yes. Must have been there for hours. She was supposed to be out—it was her afternoon off."

"Didn't you ever suspect she was that sort? You can usually tell."

"No, she seemed all right. Good-tempered. And didn't drink, like the woman I had before her. And liked company. Of course there were one or two funny accidents . . . they *would* happen when my mother-in-law was with us, and of course she said I ought to get rid of her—that she was sure she was 'queer', but I didn't take the incidents as seriously as all that. After all, these novelists are always looking for 'situations'."

"Bit unfortunate she was right, though."

"Very," agreed Doreen, whose deepest regret over the horrid occurrence was that she *had* been. "But how was I to know? I had good references with her—it's terrible how dishonest women are about giving references. Afraid of slander proceedings, I suppose. . . . Anyway, if people are once put in lunatic asylums they ought to stay there, if you ask me."

"I dare say you're right. Well, I must be getting back to the treadmill. Thanks for tea and the flicks. . . . Let me know how you get on."

Chapter Seven

WALKING IN Kensington Gardens one morning towards the end of October Fryn caught sight of Doreen Lowe pacing slowly past and re-past the statue of Physical Energy. Very smartly dressed, in a red suit, her head as usual uncovered, she made with her fair hair, piled in curls upon the top of her head, a bright splurge of colour against the autumn landscape. For a few seconds Fryn hesitated, aware that she would prefer not to encounter her cousin's wife, but feeling that she might herself already have been seen, she continued her way.

"Good morning," she greeted her, and saw at once that her instinct to make a detour had been a right one, for Doreen turned in her pacing with well-simulated surprise and the over-bright smile which Fryn had come to recognise as something she kept for people upon whom she would much rather frown, but before whom appearances must be preserved.

"Hallo," she said. "Why aren't you at school?" And her tone added, Where you ought to be, instead of wandering about Kensington Gardens at inconvenient moments.

Fryn felt her face grow warm, as one caught in some tiresome misdemeanour.

"I don't go every day now," she said. "I work at home. But mother insists that I take a walk when it's fine."

"I see. . . . Isn't it cold?"

Fryn didn't feel in the least cold, but then she had been walking sharply through the gardens, not lingering by the statue of Physical Energy. She agreed, however, that the wind was rather keen, and inquired how Doreen was liking the flat.

"Oh, all right. It's a bit cramped after Greystones, but it's very convenient, of course."

"Don't you miss the country?"

"I never miss the country. I loathe it. Give me bricks and mortar every time."

Not knowing the correct reply to this, Fryn inquired after Dwight and Barry.

"They're all right," said Doreen, and her tone asked, "Why

shouldn't they be?" After a little pause, she added, "Barry goes to school now in the mornings and likes it very much."

"Is he all right now?"

"All right? Oh, you mean the Lody business. Yes, he's forgotten all about that. And he gets on very well with Mrs. Mann, my morning woman, thank goodness."

Fryn's heart momentarily ached for the little boy so much given over to the company of "daily" women and she could think of nothing to say. With an impatient gesture Doreen turned up her wrist to look at her watch. Clearly, whoever it was she was meeting was late, a privilege Doreen accorded to none but herself. The bright smile quite faded; she looked slightly put out and even—Fryn hunted for the right word—flustered. It was not one which she would have connected with a young woman who took so easy a way through life, but it did this morning seem the only word with which to describe her state. Confronted with this fact, with the gesture with the wrist and sensible of Doreen's complete disinterestedness in the scrappy conversation they were having, Fryn felt suddenly embarrassed and said that she must be going.

"Oh, good-bye," said Doreen, the bright brief smile appearing again on her carefully made-up face, her one sensation obviously relief, her thoughts already elsewhere.

Fryn walked quickly away towards the Palace Gate and there, swinging into the gardens at a fine pace, Danny Wingham almost collided with her. He swept off his hat with an elaborate gesture, rather, Fryn thought, as if he were laughing at her, and stopped.

"Hello, young woman," he said. "Whither away?"

"Home," said Fryn, thinking that though she didn't very much like Danny Wingham he was very handsome, with his hair just greying, and his gay smile.

"No school to-day?"

"No. Are you staying in town?"

"For a couple of days, my child. Just a spot or two of business."

"Are you staying with Rose?"

"To let you into a secret, my child, I'm not. Of course it's always delightful to see the Family Chatterbox, but not always . . . possible. So keep my guilty secret."

"Of course. I've just been talking to Doreen. She's waiting for a friend over there by the statue of Energy."

"The devil you have! Somebody daring to keep her ladyship waiting?"

"I'm afraid so."

"Well, I must be off. Good-bye, my child. I'm glad to see you're keeping that schoolgirl complexion—and the plait."

She knew he thought her no more than a schoolgirl, though she had just had her eighteenth birthday, but she took his leave of her with less of a flourish than that with which he had greeted her, as if he had suddenly decided she was not a child to be laughed at and teased, but a properly grown-up young person.

As she walked on Fryn wondered why Doreen should be so patently annoyed at their encounter, so anxious to be rid of her. Perhaps she thought she would mention the meeting at home, but why should she? It was of no importance to anyone where Doreen went or how she spent her day. Nobody expected her to stay in her own home. Perhaps it had ruffled her pride to be discovered waiting about for whoever it was she was meeting. It was, of course, the sort of thing that *would* annoy Doreen. But perhaps, thought Fryn, it was only that she doesn't like me, though she felt no slight at that, not only because she herself did not find it easy to like Doreen, but because she knew that Doreen really liked no member of this family into which she had married, unless it were Emmy, who, by common tacit consent, no longer really belonged to it. Emmy, to Fryn, had been a great disappointment, so much so that she very much wished they had never met, since now it was impossible to think of her as that fine figure of romance and pioneer work she had once conceived her to be. There seemed nothing of that early Emmy left and what she had become Fryn did not care for at all. Thinking of Emmy, her thoughts entirely forsook Doreen and their uneasy encounter by the statue of Physical Energy.

That young woman had her back to the hastening Danny as he came across the grass towards her and was, indeed, in the act of consulting her watch again, when he took her lightly by the arm and halted her in her pacing.

"Sorry," he said. "Circumstances over which . . ."

But Doreen was not so easily placated. She could conceive of no circumstances in which a gentleman kept a girl waiting in public and was not disposed to cheapen herself by allowing even Danny to suppose that he could do it with impunity. But Danny merely laughed.

"Take that frown off your face, my dear. It doesn't suit you. . . . *That's* better."

He took her by the elbow and turned her in the right direction, remarking with extreme casualness, "I've just seen Fryn."

"I guessed she'd run into you. I hope she didn't put two and two together."

"If she did the answer wouldn't be four—maths, I understand, is not Fryn's subject. She was looking very charming, I thought."

"She ought to put up her hair or have it cut short and permed. That plait's absurd."

"Oh, that would be a great pity. She's not a fashionable type, you know. She's like the girl in a picture in the National Gallery. One of Rossetti's, I think. The girl in the left-hand corner of the central figure, whose eyes seem to follow you round the room."

"I wouldn't know," said Doreen.

"No—well, I'll take you in one day to have a look at it. But Rossetti and Burne-Jones faces are out of fashion to-day. Where shall we lunch?"

"I don't mind. I like it where we went last time. I'm terribly hungry."

He looked at her and laughed. It was a pleasure to take out this wife of Dwight's—she was so frank about her appetite. She loved food and never politely pretended that what she ate and where she went to eat it were matters of little importance beside the overwhelming pleasure of your company. And not only did she like food, she expected to be taken to such places as could still provide, even in these days of austerity, food that was attractive and properly served. She didn't know one wine from another, and had no palate for wine, anyway, which was a great blessing, as there was no necessity to waste money on the stuff they charged the earth for these days. A cocktail she considered a necessary preliminary to a meal but wanted nothing stronger than cider to follow, which was kind to his by-no-means deep purse and left him free to order himself a humble Bass.

He found this young woman Dwight had picked up and surprisingly married good company. He liked her particular brand of silliness, and appreciated less her fashionably pretty and carefully adorned face than the attention it always attracted in public. She had other attributes, too. On the whole, he considered her cheap at the price. He'd known many pretty girls far more expensive to entertain who had yielded him much less satisfaction. But they had all belonged to his wild youth, which he regretted only because it was over. Married to Livvy he had settled down quite surprisingly, he thought, living for the greater part of the year at Bourne, which, but for the War to End War, he would never have inherited. But he had never wanted the place and on his father's death would have tried to break the entail and have sold out if he had not met and fallen in love with

Livvy; or, rather, if Livvy had not fallen in love with Bourne and was prepared to pour out money on its upkeep. However, she did not expect him to be chained there for ever, and as she retained a deep affection for her own country and for her parents, they spent several months in the year in America, which, as Doreen would say, made a nice change. For the rest, Livvy and his young son gave him an unexpected interest in a way of life which at one time he had found difficult to contemplate with equanimity. Bourne, like all such places, he considered doomed; but if Livvy wanted to enjoy its last phases, then she should, bless her!

Nevertheless, such breakaways as presented themselves from the life of a country squire were more than welcome, and meeting Doreen at Pen's wedding, he had wondered if his reformation was quite as thorough as he had come to believe. Livvy's long and frequent absences since that event, owing to her father's health, had given him unexpected opportunities of putting the matter to the test. A young and pretty woman, he'd found, was a young and pretty woman to him still, though, happily married to his dear Livvy as he was, she could of course be nothing more. But pretty women who smiled upon him and liked his company subtly restored his old vanity and self-complacency. They restored, too, his youth, which did not lie entirely quiescent beneath the mounting years. It was immensely to his taste to be smiled upon by young and pretty women; he liked to feel that he could still attract them; it was delightful to be seen about with them. Doreen, it was clear, was bored to death by that stick of a husband of hers, Pen's son, and glad enough to amuse herself when the opportunity offered. Not that she had not been entirely circumspect in all their encounters, though one could hardly be anything else when eating in public; but he was tempted to wonder if she would be at all accommodating if the circumstances of their meetings should ever lend themselves to a little harmless philandering. It would be very interesting to find out. . . . He believed that she was fundamentally a-moral and sensuous. The type was not new to him, nor obnoxious. Far from it. He had known many such young women, and in his unregenerate days had taken what pleasure was to be had from association with them. He had even gone as far as marrying one of them. . . .

He thought of that adventure with amused detachment now. Roxane had been a peach and as common as dirt. He found it as amusing to think of her as the wife of a belted earl as he'd once found it to inflict her upon his upper middle-class family as his wife, when she'd made it clear that her favours depended upon marriage. With two good lives between him and the succession to Bourne, his titled connections had sadly misled her, poor dear, as they had, he fancied, Dwight's wife. However, he'd not expected the marriage to survive many years. Neither had it, and much of it had been fun. . . .

Listening to Doreen's polite babblings, he remembered that evening he'd taken his show-girl to his grandmother's party, just after he'd announced his engagement. He'd got the old girl to send her an invitation. *Sir Ralph and Lady Corrie request the pleasure of the company of Miss Roxane Loveday.* . . . He'd forgotten what the party was for, but it had been arranged months earlier and nobody had expected that the event would take place on the very eve of war. It was a family affair; everybody was there. Even Emmy, who'd not been near her mother for years, had staged a come-back, and taken considerable pains about it—you'd never have guessed she wouldn't see forty again. She'd looked marvellous. . . . Pen's young man, Bar Lowe, was there; and her brother, David, had brought that little French wife he'd just married in Paris to be introduced to the family. (A smiling and sweet-voiced little creature. Who'd have thought she'd have turned out as she did, hounding David into a war of which he so strongly disapproved as a diplomatic mess—and how right he'd been!—and in World War Two taking part in the underground fight against the Nazis?

That evening in August, nineteen-fourteen, when he'd introduced Roxane upon the scene, it was the war they'd all been talking about. Until Roxane had been announced by old Merrick. Gosh! she'd looked stunning! He could see her now in the red frock that outlined the lovely body she paraded every evening at the theatre. She'd knocked them all flat!—even Emmy, who'd said "Roxane Loveday? Who is *she*, pray?"—as if the picture postcards of her weren't flooding all the shop windows in the Strand! Oh yes, Roxane had been a beauty all right, with her large dark eyes, that lovely skin and her soft gold hair. Old Sir Ralph had been quite overcome—had spouted poetry. *She walks in beauty like the night.* And Emmy—the cat!—had capped it. "And not much else," she'd said. . . . Oh well, gentlemen prefer blondes. *He* did, certainly. Pity they didn't wear better! The last time he'd seen Roxane, sailing into some film première, her hair was distinctly brassy, and she'd grown more than a shade plump. . . . He'd done a sum in mental arithmetic and made it forty-nine. But that wasn't the whole story. Small and dark and slight, Livvy beside her looked an aristocrat, and perhaps she was, product of an old Boston family and Bryn Mawr.

"What time," he asked Doreen, "must you be home?"

"The usual time, not later than six. My woman goes then."

"Time then for tea at the flat."

Emmy's flat, as she knew, where he was staying and from which he had telephoned her yesterday to arrange this meeting.

"But Emmy, you said, was away."

"So she is. Finding herself without even a daily maid and only a woman to come in from nine till twelve, she fled to the hotel she patronises occasionally at Brighton."

"Poor old thing! She's too old to live alone."

"I don't think she'd mind that if she could turn a handle and find the housework done and meals appear. All the same it's a pity she never resolved her quarrel with her dear Phoebe Lane, who'd have seen to that side of things. Emmy didn't foresee War Two, of course, when she was so high-hat over Phoebe, nor this charming aftermath. I'd recommend hotel life in perpetuity to her except that I do find the flat so extremely convenient these days."

Doreen was silent. She had often been to tea at the flat, once or twice in Danny's company, and without incurring surprise or comment from Emmy. But she wasn't sure that she wanted to go there with Danny in her absence, and she was a little affronted that he should take it for granted that she would. Besides, she found him, with his impudent smile and tongue and his look of distinction, altogether too attractive. No sense in running the risk of making a fool of herself.

"Well, what about it?" he asked.

"Emmy might not like it."

"Oh, Emmy's a wise old bird. She never asks awkward questions."

"What a thing to say! You *are* awful!"

"Don't you believe it! I'm a reformed character. Have been for years. I believe you're afraid to come!"

"What an idea!"

"Truth in it?"

"Of course not."

There was, all the same. Her fear, however, was less of Danny than of herself—really, he was altogether *too* attractive. She preferred middle-aged men to young ones: they had more money to spend, for one thing, and it was flattering to be admired by men of experience, and Danny was certainly that. He'd been about a lot: he'd known all sorts of girls. She'd heard from Emmy all about that youthful marriage to a "show" girl, who'd become the Countess of something or other. But he was still married and she didn't specialise in married men friends—never had. Not from scruples but because such associations were apt to have complications. She didn't want to be *involved* in anything. A girl had to watch out for herself.

"Say you'll come. I promise to be on my best behaviour."

"You'd better be."

He laughed. A threat? Or a promise? he wondered, squeezing her hand.

"Here we are," he said, as the taxi pulled up. "Come and satisfy that hunger of yours."

Doreen reached home in time to see her daily woman preparing to depart. She had bathed and put Barry to bed and had stayed on, she explained, because he was so upset at the idea of being left in the flat alone. Doreen trotted out an easy explanation of her lateness and, having dispatched Mrs. Mann, went along to take off her hat and coat and reassure Barry. She did not want a noisy evening with that young man.

"I thought you were never coming," he complained. "Mrs. Mann kept saying she must go."

"Mummy was kept. There were so many other people also trying to get home, you see. Have you had your orange juice?"

"I've had *every*thing," Barry assured her.

"Then you must go off to sleep. I have to see about daddy's dinner."

"Where have you been?"

"I told you where I was going, Barry. Out to lunch with Cousin Danny."

"Oh, I know you did. But lunch was a long time ago—and I didn't say 'who with'—but *where*."

"To a nice place for lunch. And then we had some tea."

"Where did you have it?"

"Oh, at another nice place . . ."

"Oh. . . . I remember Cousin Danny. He used to come to Greystones. Once he gave me half a crown for my money-box. But Lody took it."

"Lody? . . . Oh, nonsense, of course she didn't take it."

"She did then."

"Well, we don't want to talk about Lody ever again, do we?"

She was a little disturbed to think that he still remembered her. It was a long while ago now since he'd mentioned her. Children soon forget. It was annoying to have one's most reassuring theories upset.

"Would you like a chocolate?"

[137]

"Yes, but I've brushed my teeth, so I can't."

"It won't hurt you for once."

She brought him the chocolate, tucked him up and told him she wanted to hear nothing more of him until to-morrow.

"But I don't feel sleepy," he objected.

"You will, if you lie still. Count sheep jumping over a stile."

"Why does it have to be sheep?"

"It doesn't. It can be lions if you like."

"I shouldn't like lions. Besides, they don't jump over stiles, do they? Lions are in forests . . . or in the Zoo."

"That's right. Now, no more argument. If dinner isn't ready by the time your daddy comes in I don't know what he'll say."

"I do—that you ought to have come home earlier."

That amused Doreen, so unused was she to a Dwight who complained, and, irrationally, it sometimes annoyed her that he didn't. It gave her a feeling that he didn't care enough to bother, as if he'd given up expecting her to behave like those paragons at Richmond. Just as well, though.

"Good-night, Barry. And don't call me along again because I can't come. Just lie still and go to sleep."

"But you won't go out again, will you?"

"Of course not. I shall be cooking the dinner. . . . Don't be a baby. You're a big boy now."

"You've forgotten the night-light."

"No—I'm just going to get it."

"Don't be long."

"It isn't really dark yet."

"It's nearly dark, and that's worse than *really* dark. Don't shut the door."

"Very well . . ."

She went away, leaving him in the semi-dark, and had no faintest inkling that, for all the unclosed door, she had shut him in with terror, hearing her steps going irrevocably away from him. She suddenly remembered that yesterday she had used the last night-light in the old box, and it took her some time to find the new one she had asked Mrs. Mann to bring in that morning: she always put things in the wrong place and out of sight. However, it was eventually unearthed, and the little light was prepared and carried along to Barry's room.

"It's *awful* in the dark," he told her.

"But you weren't *in* the dark and I was only at the other end of the passage, in the kitchen. Well, there's your light. Now off to sleep with you," she said in the bright detached voice she seemed to keep for her small son as a counteracting measure to all the Richmond night fuss.

Barry looked with love upon the little light, making a bright glow upon the ceiling, and said only, "Thank you," until his mother was out of the room and pulling up the door, when he remarked plaintively, "I wish S'rena was here."

"Well, she isn't. Serena has to be in her own home," she said, not pushing back the door and looking in at him, but just standing there outside, waiting for silence and wanting to be gone.

"Can't I have a sister of my own instead, then?"

"I'm afraid not."

"Why not?"

"No more questions to-night. . . . Go to sleep."

She was gone. Again he lay listening to her footsteps retreating to the remote region of the kitchen, the flat grown suddenly huge and full of emptiness and silence. He lay there, his eyes on the kind and friendly light until sleep swept down upon him.

In the kitchen Doreen made a hasty search in the larder for something for dinner. Dwight's dinner. She had been very well fed and had little appetite for the sort of meal she would serve to Dwight. She had asked Mrs. Mann to see what she could find that morning on her way to the flat, but had forgotten to ask if she'd remembered, and if so what it was. If she'd not remembered or had failed to find anything, it meant a meal at the Good Intent, and that wouldn't please Dwight, for he objected to Barry being left alone in the flat, and if she offered to stay he was always argumentative, though to-night, as he knew she had been going to lunch with Danny, he might believe her when she said she didn't mind and wasn't really hungry. However, the larder yielded fish. The everlasting fish. And cod, she thought, at that, remembering the lobster she had eaten at lunch. Thank heaven for the good lunch and her not inconsiderable tea. The fish could be baked. It was easy—she'd adopted the recipe which appeared so often in the newspapers these days, for it gave the least trouble, and Dwight never raised any objection to the method, though he ate fish cooked that way, he felt, far too often. The second course was the trouble. There were a few apples on a dish keeping company with two oranges; and there was an inch of cheese; but "fruit and cheese" was not, she had learned, a very popular alternative for a sweet unless the fruit dish were considerably more varied and the cheese less dry and mousetrap. But she'd had no time for the shops to-day; their rations were nearly what she called "non-est", and she'd have to dash out first thing to-morrow. Still, all that didn't solve the sweet question. Rummaging around, she found the remains of a semolina pudding Mrs. Mann had made for Barry's lunch. It was quite stiff, of course, and would have been even if it hadn't been put in the refrigerator—that woman always put in too much semolina. Ah well, she reflected, without rancour, when I make one I put in too little and that wouldn't be much use to-night. If she turned Mrs. Mann's version out into what Madame Gaby called "individual" small glasses and put some jam on top it would do. Having settled the menu she set to work, bored to the soul and thinking of a woman in a recent novel she'd read, who'd been everlastingly cooking, eternally stirring sauces and what not—and all as a hobby! Where she got the ingredients from defeated her—but as they lived in Soho perhaps it was easier. Those little shops didn't bother so much, perhaps, about points, and they had all those continental things, of course. Oh, well, baked fish and semolina shape would have to do. No time to do potatoes, she decided, which meant that Mrs. Mann had forgotten to peel them and she wasn't going to do it because of staining her hands. They'd been freshly manicured and the stuff that took the stains off also removed the varnish. So it would have to be toast. . . .

Dwight came in at seven and ate his dull meal without protest, though the fish was sadly over-cooked. Until he'd gone to stay at Richmond he'd really believed this kind of meal was the best that could nowadays be managed in one's own home, and having learned better there he'd accepted Doreen's efforts as the best of which she was capable; and realising that complaint was useless, took the precaution of having a good lunch in the City and so arriving home with a less urgent hunger. All the same, he did wish she would learn to make coffee. That commodity, at least, wasn't rationed. . . .

Over the thin light brown concoction that Doreen placed before him after she had stacked up the crockery to await Mrs. Mann's attention in the morning, he inquired after her day. Had she had a good lunch? "Lovely!" said Doreen, like a delighted child. A perfectly heavenly soup and then lobster mayonnaise and pancakes to follow—the sort Mrs. Simmonds used to make when she felt good-tempered. French, she used to call them.

Dwight, who wished it had occurred to her to find out how they were made, said, "Good! And how was Danny?"

"He seemed all right," Doreen said, grateful to him for not asking what time she had got back. Had he done so she would have had to tell the truth, for she had been caught out before now by Barry's

[140]

passion for that tiresome virtue. But her voice had gone flat, as if her host had inspired in her far less enthusiasm than the food he'd bought for her, which was not the case since the host was Danny. "He's always good company," she said.

"Livvy, I take it, is in Boston again?"

"Yes. I can't imagine why Danny doesn't go too. He's so fond of American life."

"Boston," said Dwight, "isn't New York. And to Danny America is New York, not Boston."

"What's wrong with Boston?"

"For Danny? Too much culture and high-thinking, perhaps. By the way, I've had mother on the telephone this morning. She asks us to Wyngates for the week-end. She thinks this fine warm weather won't last and we'd better take advantage of it."

"I s'pose you've accepted?"

"Yes. I thought you'd be glad of a respite from your Mann-less week-end."

It took her a second to realise that he meant without Mrs. Mann, suspecting some covert allusion to the fact that at week-ends her outings were temporarily suspended. Then she said, "I wish I could find someone who'd come at week-ends."

"You won't. Hang on to Mrs. Mann. She's the best you're likely to get. I've told mother we'll catch an early morning train. I can manage the morning off from the office. There's one about ten-thirty, I think. Charles or mother will meet it with the car."

Doreen resigned herself to boredom with a good grace.

"Don't tell your mother that I've seen Danny, please. He says his visit is 'unofficial'."

"What does that mean exactly?"

"Well, he usually stays with Rose, as you know. But this time Emmy's lent him her flat. She's away—fed up with domesticity, with only a morning woman."

She hadn't meant to tell him this, but doubtless he'd heard from his mother, or would do at the week-end. She never kept anything from Dwight that it was obvious he would come to hear and so had established for herself with him a reputation for frankness to which she was by no means entitled. He had not yet learned that Doreen was never so frank as when she had most to hide. He said only, "I didn't know Rose was as possessive as all that about her brother."

"Well, you know how strong her family feeling is. Danny's very fond of her, of course, but he does hate a family fuss, so when Emmy

[141]

offered him the use of her flat while she's away I suppose he preferred to be on his own."

He didn't ask where Emmy had gone. She knew he couldn't care less. She said, "I met Fryn this morning. She asked after you."

"Did she? Did you ask her to come and see us?"

"No, I didn't think of it. She's busy cramming. I suppose when she's done with this exam, she'll do something about her hair."

"Why should she?"

"Well, she can't wear it that way for the rest of her life."

"No, but it seems a pity."

"You admire her, don't you?"

"I have a distinct liking for pre-Raphaelite faces, though they're not fashionable any longer."

"Danny said something like that. About her being like some girl in someone's picture. I forget whose."

"Rossetti. *The Well-Beloved*, I expect," said Dwight.

"I must go and have a look at it some time. Danny was quite poetic—said her eyes seemed to follow you round the room."

"That's true, too," said Dwight. "I didn't think Danny was so discerning. Bad taste, though, to take out one pretty girl and praise another."

"Oh, *I* don't mind," said Doreen. "I found it very interesting. I must admit Fryn isn't the type that appeals to me. What's it mean—this pre-whatever it is?"

"The chap you want is Larry."

"But Larry doesn't do portraits."

"Try Glen Westcott the next time you see him."

Doreen laughed as if she considered that rather a joke. She wondered what Fenella's husband would say if she did ask him. Nothing that she'd understand, anyway. He talked what she thought of as "funny stuff", and she never knew whether he was being sarcastic or not. He made her feel either a fool or as if she didn't really exist. Which was odd, because he was always what Milly would call "studiously polite".

Her laughter ended in a yawn. And now she'd yawn for the rest of the evening. Dwight had picked up a book and would probably not utter a word until ten o'clock nor hear anything she might say. And would look resigned if she suggested turning on the wireless. If anyone had told me, six years ago, she thought, that we'd sit here like this, evening after evening, just bored to the soul, I'd have laughed. But she remembered the young man who'd fallen so violently in love with her with something less than regret. Flattering, of course,

[142]

but she'd never been in love with him. She'd never been in love with anyone and Dwight she had seen as deliverance from a dull world in which she earned a precarious living. But in this post-war world there was no such thing as deliverance. There was no fun any more and getting married and having a baby and being expected to have others was just a tiresome and frightening business. She had no idea what she wanted in its place—certainly not to go back to the hospital or to do any of the silly jobs she'd had before she'd taken up war-work. But she still believed in Romance; it just happened that she had missed it. But if she'd been asked to define Romance, even with a capital letter, she couldn't have done it.

So she sat there yawning her head off until Dwight looked up from his book and suggested politely that she went to bed.

She did not make any move to go, but said, smothering another yawn, "Lord, what a dull existence!"

"Dull?" Dwight raised his eyes again from his book, "I thought you'd had a pleasant day."

"So I have, but this evening is a dreary anti-climax. You know, Dwight, I never thought marrying you would be like this."

"No? Did you imagine it would be one long round of hectic pleasure? Dining and wining and dancing till all hours? That world's finished, my dear. These are the days of austerity and though I'd hate to depress you any further it's my opinion that they will grow considerably grimmer."

"It's this Labour Government."

"They'd be grim whatever rulers we had."

"Well, other people seem to be able to amuse themselves. They go to parties and dances . . ."

"You forget I can no longer dance. Why not go to some of the hospital dances?"

"Without a partner?"

"You'd soon have half a dozen."

She made a little grimace. She didn't see herself arriving man-less at any dance, particularly those given by her old hospital. She said, "Well, surely a party now and then? Or you might bring some of your business acquaintances home, the way you did at Greystones."

"We had a competent staff then. What should we do now with guests to dinner or lunch?"

She chose to read a reproof in this remark. It was as if he said, "We had a competent staff till you antagonised it." She knew he'd always blamed her for Mrs. Simmonds's departure. But she'd been spoiled by James. Lazy, that's what she was. Looking for a good excuse for retiring on her pension and James's legacy. What was the sense in having a properly-run house if nobody ever came to see you? She'd got to know some "nice" people at Greystones, but Dwight, for all his politeness when they came visiting, had seemed quite willing to drop them all. He was nothing but a recluse—he just didn't want visitors. He'd be just as happy on a desert island.

"Well, we might throw an evening party occasionally. We're not exactly paupers, even if we have lost most of the money that went with Greystones."

"Money no longer buys things. It won't get you servants, unless you happen to be the King of England or a film star, and there are distinct limits to the amount of food it will buy, much less party drinks, outside the black market, which, as good citizens, of course, we don't patronise."

She made no reply. As usual he had knocked the bottom out of her arguments. For much as she would love "having people", the difficulties of preparing and catering for them were self-evident. Moreover, she knew it was not the lack of "parties" which was wholly responsible for this gloom and dullness which overspread the hours she and Dwight now spent together. The trouble between them had really started when she had refused his argument that at Greystones they had the perfect background for the bringing up of a young family. She did not want a young family; she would not even concede his right to ask her to have another child—everyone knew the last word on this subject was with the woman. He simply didn't see her point of view at all, and to her it had seemed silly to harp so much upon the need for Barry to have the company of other children. For he had made lots of little friends in the neighbourhood at Greystones, much nearer his own age than a brother or sister could now be. And Dwight had quite forgotten what she'd been through when Barry was born—of course he'd listened to his mother, who thought she and her generation were "neurotic" about childbirth. And, of course, *she* liked children, and would have gone through hell to get them. But, neurotic or not, the idea of having another child did terrify her and when she made it clear that nothing would induce her to do so she realised that it had closed for them one side of marriage completely. She had found his overwhelming physical passion for her flattering and had raised no objection to his satisfying it; but it humiliated her to think that either it had ceased or that he would not indulge it upon her terms. Nevertheless his attitude had automatically put an end to an argument at which he, as in most arguments, was considerably cleverer than she. So she solaced her pride by calling him a Puritan, though this did not alter the fact that he had withdrawn the basis upon which their marriage had rested, as she had supposed all marriages to do. She would not have expressed it so, but dimly she realised that it was the fact. Her marriage now was no more than the dull business of running a home (or seeing that someone else did it) and looking after a highly-strung and difficult child. She laboured under an acute sense of injustice, for she was twenty-five, very attractive and unable to support an existence in which these facts were not recognised.

All the same, she realised that if the Greystones experiment had not failed, Dwight's attitude toward her would have mattered far less; for there she had not been bored. She had had plenty of acquaintances and social life; and freedom to go and come as she chose without dependence upon some wretched daily woman. She knew that Dwight blamed her for the Greystones failure, remembering how he had tried to dissuade her from upsetting that dragon, Mrs. Simmonds. But what had she done except see that she did the job she was well paid to do? Perhaps he'd hated his mother's idiotic prophecy coming true—or her thinking it had. For of course it was all nonsense. It was just that her mother-in-law had hated poor James and couldn't be fair to him even when he was dead. *She'd* liked James and he'd always been "perfectly sweet" to her, and if he'd never liked her precious mother-in-law, well, ten to one it was her own fault. Highbrow, cock-sure, know-all—and so clever at talking! Though God knows all the family were that! But it wasn't *only* leaving Greystones, it was that business over the wretched Mrs. Loder. She knew he blamed her for Barry's fright, though it would never have happened if he'd been obedient and kept out of the servants' quarters, and if that woman they'd paid to look after him had seen that he did. Or if he'd gone to school, as she'd wanted. It was most unjust to blame *her*. But then Dwight *was* unjust. Unjust and self-righteous. He saw nobody's point of view but his own, and thought being polite and never raising his voice made up. She'd have preferred he should have shouted at her, because at least she could have shouted back, which would have been a relief. What she hated was being sent to Coventry. Anyway, there it was. As a wife she did not exist and perhaps Dwight wasn't really interested in wives, only in mothers. Unknowingly, she had here touched upon a profundity; but, true of many men, it wasn't true of Dwight. He wanted children because he loved them and also because he believed that Doreen needed to acquire a sense of stability and responsibility. He had seen it work with Fenella, who once had waved about like the grasses in every wind; and he made the mistake of believing it would work with Doreen. He was a poor psychologist, and he knew nothing about women, not having really noticed (apart from his own sisters) any woman until he met Doreen.

Tired of her thoughts and utterly bored, she got up at last and said good night, and Dwight rose from his chair and opened the door for her. His good manners irrationally annoyed her, for somehow they put her subtly in the wrong. She didn't know, even after nearly six years of marriage, that accepting a situation which he could neither avoid nor alter was one of Dwight's characteristics. He did not fight or assert himself when he was convinced that no good was to be achieved by it. He did not believe people could be altered, except perhaps by life. It was an attitude which had kept him from open conflict with his grandfather, and that old tyrant, he was convinced, had given him less trouble than had been his mother's lot, though she had her own way of dealing with him, which had certainly at least deflated him. But what he did not know—and Doreen, for all her stupidity, knew in her bones—was that the attitude he had adopted to her, polite, formal, detached, made their marriage impossible; that by it he was sowing the seeds of its dissolution. Was that, she wondered, as she brushed out her hair, what he wanted?—to force her to leave him? Well, she'd do it to-morrow if for her there was anyone else on the horizon, she told herself, staring at her reflection in the mirror with her usual appreciation. But unhappily there wasn't. At least, nobody who was eligible. . . .

Her thoughts ran back suddenly to Danny. Nobody had to tell her that Danny Wingham was an experienced flirt, and knew how to get a girl interested. In him or herself? Both perhaps. She was perfectly well aware that this afternoon at the flat he'd wanted to kiss her, but he'd behaved very well about her refusal. After all, a girl couldn't make herself cheap. . . . But he certainly didn't seem to find her a dull companion, to whom it was too much trouble to talk. . . . Danny was an amusing, if rather naughty, talker, and they'd got on famously. He'd seemed at Emmy's flat to find *her* amusing too, judging by the way he'd laughed. He'd sent her stock up considerably with herself, and she felt a lot better for the hours she'd spent in his company. She wondered what Dwight would have said if she'd told him that after their lunch together she had gone back with him to Emmy's flat? She'd resisted the suggestion at first but what harm was there in it? Danny had "behaved" all right (she had seen to that!) but all the same she meant to go carefully. She didn't want any complications that might put an end to so pleasant a friendship just when circumstances seemed so favourable to its continuance. Begun in the early Greystones days, it had always followed a strictly circumspect course, which, however, had not prevented her from finding it exciting. But Danny was not often in town, and she knew it was only Livvy's recent long absences from England which had made their meetings so frequent. But she was not unaware that this afternoon the friendship had moved a pace ahead; and so far as she was concerned the word she would now apply to it was not "exciting", though it was still that. She took the new word out of her mind and looked at it. Dangerous. Dangerous because she was undeniably attracted to a man who was married and reputed in love with his wife.

She wondered. . . . Livvy, of course, had all the money, but if she was so marvellous, why then did he look at *her*? No, she couldn't count on that. She was aware that she could have an "affair" with Danny to-morrow, if she chose. But she didn't intend to. A girl had to be careful. Not that it wouldn't serve Dwight right. . . . But "affairs" were not at all up her street.

Oh, why did he have to be married?

Chapter Eight

DOREEN ENJOYED her week-end at Wyngates considerably more than she had expected, and this was due chiefly to Charles's efforts to entertain her. These were made not because she was a pretty woman, for he was oddly impervious to the stereotyped appeal of the conventional blonde, but because he felt that she was so hopelessly bored by the company into which her marriage had dragged her and, above all, by her husband, whom Charles would like to have shaken. It did not very much surprise him that this marriage was so obviously unsuccessful, but he felt that Dwight's attitude of icy politeness precluded any improvement in their relationship. It was so like an insult. He had once heard a young poet who had married, as they used to say, "beneath him" tell his young wife to "shut up", when she had ventured to express an opinion in company; and she had laughed and not minded at all. But it was clear that Doreen minded Dwight's ostentatious politeness very much indeed, because she was helpless before it and knew it for the barrier it was. Told to "shut up" she would have reacted sharply and precipitated a quarrel, maybe; but that might at least have cleared the air and given them a chance. As it was, she was merely bored and resentful. Whatever the urge that had hurried Dwight into his marriage it was at an end, and if he wanted her to walk out on him he could not, surely, have adopted a more helpful attitude? And Doreen, he thought, did the right man, which meant any man eligible and willing, come along, was perfectly capable, he felt, in her present mood, of doing it. At the moment his sympathy was almost entirely with her, since whatever her shortcomings Dwight's attitude was indefensible. So, faced with Charles's undeviating attention and consideration, Doreen felt her stock had risen, and reacted accordingly.

On the Sunday Lydia and her children came down for lunch and after it Dwight took Fryn off for a walk. Even Pen, whose sympathy was quite evidently with Dwight, considered this an error of judgment, and that he should at least have asked Meg and Jeremy if they'd like to accompany them. Jeremy, for once free from colds and any of the lesser indispositions to which he was prone, had, however, no desire to walk. He was not, to Gilbert's dismay, a very energetic youngster, and he found a stroll around the place, poking about here and there, quite sufficient to wile away the gap between lunch and dinner. And Meg announced that she didn't feel like walking either; but her mother was well aware this was because she knew she wanted her out of the way while she talked to her aunt about this young man she'd been meeting at Ray and Paul Romaine's house. She knew that her mother was a little upset about it and that her father would disapprove, because he'd probably disapprove of any young man for years to come who wanted to marry her. Neither was she sure that she wanted to marry him, but she had found it oddly exciting to be asked and not at all embarrassing, which must mean, she thought, that she liked him at least enough to want time to think about it. But her mother said that at nineteen she was too young to know her own mind, which was rather good, she considered, coming from her mother, who'd made up her mind about her father's proposal when she was nearly a year younger. Her mother's real reason was a very different one and she knew what it was—because it played, she felt, some small part at least in her own indecision.

Getting rid of Meg for a quarter of an hour by asking her to take some letters to the post, Pen presently made it possible for Lydia to have a brief chat about all this with her. The young man's name was Lenham—George Lenham—and he'd been recently freed from the army and Paul had taken him into his business. He had a fair share of good looks, pleasant manners—and, obviously, excellent prospects. How old? Oh, about thirty, she thought—much too old for the nineteen-year-old Meg, said Lydia, who'd forgotten perhaps that there was the same difference between her own age and Gilbert's and that she had once thought it quite absurd for her mother not indeed to put it forward as a reason for her objection to an engagement, but to pretend there was no young man who wanted such a state.

"English?" asked Pen and Lydia said, "Oh, you mean is he a Jew? Well, there was, I believe, a great-great-grandmother who was a Jewess. Not, of course, that I've any objection on that score, nor will Gilbert have, either, I should say, but I fancy Meg minds it a bit, oddly enough."

"Then what *is* the objection?" Pen asked.

"Apart from Meg's age, the fact that I feel she doesn't know her own mind. No, she admitted it. She's been quite frank. She told me he'd proposed to her and that she'd put him off—that she'd promised to give him an answer before we go back home. But of course if she decides to marry him maybe she won't *go* back."

"And that's the real trouble, as far as you're concerned, isn't it?"

"I suppose it is. I wouldn't mind, though, if she were older and was very much in love. But, quite clearly, she isn't. He's attractive, he's been very attentive and it's her first proposal. I'm perfectly certain Gil will never give his consent until she's of age."

"And if you go home next year you think she may, before her coming of age, have forgotten all about him or found somebody else on the other side? So you'd keep her with you, after all. What does Meg say to these arguments?"

"Oh, she sees them all right. She's a highly reasonable young creature. But she's fond of a good time . . . and I don't think the idea of marriage altogether appeals to her at the moment. It's too much like settling down. Besides, you know, Meg's a bit homesick. She hasn't taken root here the way Fryn has."

"And Ray? What does she say about it?"

"What you would suppose. She thinks it's the twenty-fifth part Jewish blood which is really the trouble. So very silly, that argument —especially as I happen to know she was so afraid at one time Leah might fall in love with that young Austrian cousin—Kurt wasn't his name?—who was over here after the Anschluss. . . . She didn't want her daughter to marry a Jew, she said. Things were different when her own parents said the same thing. Poor Ray!—she's written Ichabod over everything. However, over this business of Meg's she'd welcome the marriage because she's taken a fancy to Meg, as you know, and has had her at the house quite a lot. She makes up, I fancy, for her loss to Good Works, of Leah. She'd like something—this marriage for instance—to keep her permanently here."

"Well, I shouldn't worry. Meg's a level-headed young person. She won't be rushed off her feet . . . and she won't be twenty-one for another sixteen months. Anything may happen before then. And before Gil's term in Germany is up."

"I don't think I shall tell Gil anything about it, for the moment. It isn't as if Meg had made up her mind—and I think she'd prefer it that way. That he would leave a daughter behind in this fashion was no part of Gil's plan for coming over here when war was threatened."

"Why should it have been? Meg was then six months short of her thirteenth birthday and Fryn not quite eleven. The war lasted longer than we ever thought possible and the aftermath's going to be at least as long, I fear."

This conversation came to an abrupt end with Meg's reappearance on the scene. If she guessed that her mother had been "talking" she gave no indication of it, and Lydia said innocently, "By the way,

Pen, mother suggested the other day that perhaps Dwight would help Fryn with her maths. . . . What do you think?"

"Well, why not ask him? I'm sure he'd be glad to help if he could."

"I will then. Of course it's all nonsense, this examination craze of Gil's. Though mother doesn't agree. She thinks, as Gil does, that matriculation's important because it's the Open Sesame to so much. But if you ask me, it spoils a lot of girls' lives."

"Oh, there's a lot of life left for them when exams are over and done with, you know."

"The walkers back yet?" said Meg. "Walking's in the air to-day. I saw Charles and Doreen strolling over the hill with Hamish. I don't believe anyone has ever got Doreen to take a walk before."

"She wears the wrong sort of shoes for walking," said Lydia laughing. "But a walk would have done you good, Meg. You'll get fat."

"No fear, darling, while rationing lasts."

Pen, glancing at her, thought that she looked, as ever, quite untroubled by life. No, she certainly wasn't in love with that young man—yet, though there was plenty of time for that to happen, of course. You could slip into love, gently, hardly knowing it was happening, quite as easily as falling headlong into it. But so far there was no sense of urgency about Meg. Life was certainly not revolving around George Lenham at the moment. Physically like Andra, had she also her trick of making life eat out of her hand? Ah yes, but it had snapped at her more than once and, in the end, had had her by the throat. . . .

It was on the homeward journey that Lydia mentioned her mother's suggestion to Dwight, who said, after a little pause, while his heart jumped out of his breast and back again, that he would be delighted to do anything he could, adding that he didn't think Fryn needed coaching so much as, on this subject, to be given a little confidence in herself.

"Where exams are concerned she would tell you she wants her hand held all round," Lydia said with a little laugh, "don't you, Fryn?"

The faint colour in Fryn's face deepened and she smiled, but said nothing. The idea of having Dwight's assistance had two sharp edges to it. The pleasure of being in his company and the misery of his seeing what a duffer she could be at a subject upon which he was so good.

"You must arrange times best suited to yourself," Lydia said. "Fryn can come to you, of course, if you prefer, but if Doreen would spare you to us sometimes for our evening meal, you could come straight on from the office."

"Of course," said Doreen, very affably. She'd had an unexpectedly pleasing week-end and was really in the mood to be accommodating and did not overlook the fact that it would be pleasant to be free of Dwight's company for a couple of evenings a week, even, upon occasion, convenient.

"That's very good of you, Doreen," Lydia said. "And of you too, Dwight."

"Not at all," Dwight murmured politely, wondering what Lydia would say if she knew what a service she was doing him—presenting him with a sound excuse for escaping for two evenings from the boredom of Doreen's company *solus*, and with opportunities for seeing more of Fryn, in whose companionship he found peace and consolation. Neither was he disturbed by Lydia's next remark, "Of course, Doreen, we shall be pleased to see you too, any evening you feel like coming along . . ." For he knew that Doreen, though she smiled and thanked Lydia and said she would love to come sometimes, would never go. . . .

At Wyngates over supper that evening Pen and Charles discussed visit and visitors. "I thought you behaved nobly," Pen said. "You deserve all my commiseration—and gratitude. This must be the first time Doreen has ever enjoyed a visit here."

"Did she say she had enjoyed it?"

"Yes—quite graciously, too. What made you take her for a walk? Dwight had asked her to go with him and Fryn and she'd refused. She's no walker."

"Well, did you happen to notice *how* he asked her?"

"Very politely, I thought."

"Too politely altogether. If ever an invitation said, 'I don't want you,' that one did."

"Really, Charles, you're not suggesting that Dwight wanted a walk alone with Fryn?"

"Perhaps he did, but that wasn't what I meant—he certainly didn't want to go walking with Doreen, Fryn or no Fryn. You know, Pen, I'm really very sorry for Doreen."

"Was she so very confidential?"

"She wasn't confidential at all, but all the same I felt once or twice that there was something she'd like to have said if she'd known how. Has it ever occurred to you, my dear, how very bored she must be?"

"By Dwight or by us?"

"By us, certainly—and by Dwight, too, I should think, if his behaviour this week-end was any criterion."

"What was wrong with it? . . . If you think Doreen is bored, *I* think Dwight's boredom must be colossal."

"Yes, he made that very obvious. I know they can't have much in common but so far as my recollection goes Dwight never used to exhibit the fact."

"Well, he's no longer infatuated by her. That had to come some time. Only a *very* foolish man goes handcuffed to infatuation for ever. I confess I could wish he'd worked his off in the ordinary way instead of letting it drag him into marriage."

"An affair? Do you think Doreen is the sort of girl who'd have had an affair?"

"Probably not. Quite certainly not with Dwight, whom she saw as a deliverer from the dreary business of earning a living, and also, I fancy, as a way of mounting several steps of the social ladder. I'm sorry if that sounds snobbish. Well, now she's convinced she's thrown herself away, of course. She thinks she got a very poor bargain. But so did Dwight. So did we all."

"But I think, you know, Pen, that there's something else aggravating the situation between them. They've been married now how long?—nearly six years? and it hasn't taken all that time for them to find out they'd made a mistake. This manner of Dwight's toward her is something new. It suggests that he's entirely out of love with her. And more—that he positively dislikes her. To me, this week-end, that was manifest in every single polite syllable he uttered to her. It was like a studied insult. And he never once, or so it seemed to me, addressed her unless it was quite unavoidable."

Not being an idolatrous mother unable to stomach criticism of her son, Pen considered this point in silence for a moment, then said, "Yes, I did notice his silence, but it seemed to me a logical enough development of the situation. His feeling for her couldn't possibly last, and every unsuitably matched married couple becomes in time, I suppose, a Veneering couple."

"I dare say. But, as I've said, I felt once or twice on our walk that Doreen was on the point of giving me a confidence. But it never came."

"I think I can tell you what it was. You see, Dwight wants children and Doreen won't even consider having another child."

"I see. That is certainly a situation. But does he make it any better by adopting this attitude?"

"No, but I rather gathered—not that Dwight has said so, it's what

[153]

he refrains from saying that I always seem to hear—that this decision of Doreen's has put an end to their marital life. It's odd, with the infatuation at an end, so that he sees now, I mean, what his marriage really is, that he should want it to continue for this express purpose. After all, nothing could be clearer than that Doreen is entirely lacking in the maternal instinct. There's no sense in such a woman having children, though it's a point which should be considered before, rather than after, marriage."

"And Dwight despises her for her attitude?"

"Perhaps—I don't know. But that's senseless, too, since, as Bridget constantly reminds us, people are what they are and can't be changed. In any case Dwight should have known what to expect after Barry's birth. It was clear during the months before his arrival that she was scared to death of the whole business. Nevertheless, she had a perfectly normal time—Dwight had this from her doctor. But I think she'd rather die than go through it all again."

"That does seem rather final. But if Dwight really feels as he seems to do about the situation wouldn't it be better to do something about it?"

"Divorce, you mean? Well, you need other grounds for that, don't you? Oh, I know he could leave her and she could get a divorce for desertion. But I can't see Dwight doing that, somehow. And as for collusion, well—that would depend upon both parties being of the same mind and I very much doubt if Doreen wants a divorce. I think she'd rather endure whatever it is exactly she does endure with Dwight than face again the prospect of earning an honest living."

"She's extremely attractive, you know. She'd soon find another husband."

"You have a poor opinion of your own sex, Charles. Do you really think it's only a pretty face, an alluring form, which wins a husband?"

"I fear it's a very strong factor, however much we may deplore it."

"I don't agree, you know, Charles. *Think* of all the extremely plain and unattractive wives you meet every day. Good looks and shapely bodies didn't do the trick for *them*."

"There are men, of course," said Charles, "who prefer women no other man is likely to look at with a desiring eye."

"Worse and worse," laughed Pen. "I don't know the answer to that."

"There isn't one, I'm afraid, my dear."

"Well, I wouldn't wish Doreen on to any decent normal man,"

said Pen firmly. "But this is not a subject upon which I could presume to offer Dwight advice. Nor upon any other, for that matter. I always felt that when he met and proposed to Doreen he was in no fit state to choose a wife. All he saw was a pretty girl in a nurse's uniform, a symbol of tenderness and sympathy. How was he to know that she was really the bored and boring young woman with whom he has lived for the best part of six years? If you'd hinted at such a thing he wouldn't have believed you."

After a little pause Charles said, "Even so, and at the risk of rousing your scorn, my dear, I repeat, I really am very sorry for her."

"I feel sorry for her myself, in a way. Sorry for all the Doreens of the world. They deny life at its foundations and don't know that nothing can ever make up for that. And now, haven't we discussed this tiresome young woman enough for one evening?"

"Forgive me, my dear, if I seem to harp, but there's one other aspect of the situation that ought not to be overlooked. Doreen's type of good looks may not be to your taste—I don't know that it's much to mine, either, but according to modern day standards she is very attractive indeed. Certainly to men. You say she doesn't want a divorce—that she'd rather put up with anything than attempt to be self-supporting. But there's a very old way, you know, of providing, if one is a young and attractive woman, for one's needs, quite apart from either marriage or hard work. Don't you think there's a danger that Doreen may be offered—and take—such an alternative?"

"Has she so many men friends? I know that's the legend, but I don't accept it. Of course there's always the chance that she may meet someone who will convince her that she is cut out for a mistress rather than a wife."

"Do you think Dwight realises that, or is, even, quite prepared for it?"

"I can't tell you. Dwight doesn't discuss Doreen or his life with her with me, and as I've said, and as you know perfectly well, I shouldn't dream of giving him advice upon such a subject. All I know is that he does realise his marriage was a great mistake, and, for Barry's sake, I think, is doing his best about it, even if it mayn't look very good to you—or to me. Dwight's no actor. When he's bored or disgusted, well, he just is. All the same, I think that here he really is doing what he can to make the best of a hopeless situation."

"By sending her, very politely, to Coventry?"

"Well, things may improve. Meantime, Doreen is free to go her own way if she chooses. Dwight has never attempted to restrict her goings and comings."

After a longer pause than any which had preceded it, Charles said, "I think that a mistake, you know. . . . Are you aware, my dear, that during Livvy's absence in America Doreen has been a good deal in Danny Wingham's company?"

The wind was temporarily taken out of Pen's sails.

"Danny? *Oh?* Well, that doesn't matter much, surely? Dwight's not likely to misunderstand that. He's quite aware that they meet for lunch or a matinée occasionally when Danny's a grass widower."

"I gathered that. But it was Doreen I was thinking of. Suppose Doreen—misunderstood?"

"She must be a bigger fool than I take her for if she does. Nobody could mistake Danny's intentions, which are to make himself as pleasant and entertaining as possible in return for the same efforts on the part of his companion. Danny's a very old hand at that game. None of his partners will ever be allowed to forget the rules of the game with a married man."

"All the same, I think it a pity Dwight should be so complacent about the association."

"My dear Charles! We all know Danny Wingham. And if there's one thing we know better than another it's that his marriage to Livvy is for keeps. He may or may not be faithful to her, but he has no intention of letting any of his philanderings upset his marriage. And Cathy said in her letter to me a day or so ago that Livvy was expected home next week."

"Yes, so Doreen told me."

"And she sees her little ray of sunshine fading away? I shouldn't let that worry you."

"Danny, even in his late fifties, is an attractive creature, you know, Pen."

"I could never see the attraction, even in his youth. He's actually a year younger than I am, you know. The word my elders used about him was 'dashing', I remember, and Fenny, when a very small girl, was immensely taken with him. But Danny and I never cared for each other. I often wonder how he persuaded the delightful Livvy to marry him. She's worlds and away too good for him, 'reformed' or not. . . . By the way, I wonder whether Dwight will agree to Lydia's proposal about his acting as coach to Fryn in maths?"

Seeing that Pen had neatly guillotined the conversation about Doreen, Charles inquired, "Does she really need one?"

"Not so much as Lydia thinks, perhaps. But she's determined to leave no stone unturned to have Fryn quite free to go back home with her in the spring."

"Fryn and Dwight get on very well together, I think."

"Of course. But anybody could get on with Fryn. A more natural and delightful child it would be hard to find."

"And not such a child, either. Wasn't she eighteen a week or so ago?"

"Yes, but no one would believe it to look at her. It's rare to find a girl of eighteen so completely unspoiled. At heart she's still the schoolgirl she looks."

"I wonder!" murmured Charles.

"Now what do you mean by that?" asked Pen laughing. "You're in a very inquisitorial mood this evening. Come along and have coffee in the other room round the fire. We shall be just in time for the News. And much good it will do us!"

A few weeks later Pen sat down soon after breakfast to telephone to Paradise Walk. She wanted to speak to Fenella, whose twenty-eighth birthday would fall on the morrow, and to suggest that if Glen was not at the office he might be able to find enough petrol to drive her and the children down for lunch. To her surprise it was Bridget's voice which travelled along the wires to her saying that she'd been at home for a week with a mild attack of 'flu. Fenella, unfortunately, was out, but Bridget knew that she and Glen and the children were spending the birthday with the in-laws, and instead proposed herself for a visit on the Sunday.

"A man I know, who has a car, has to make a business call at Milford and has offered to drive me on to Petersfield. In view of the recently-departed 'flu I've accepted. . . . I'll have a bit of news for you, too, which I *think* you'll like. Oh, no, nothing like that, darling. . . . Just a business acquaintance but as he's in publishing I expect Charles will vouch for him—Robert Dereham his name is. He's an admirer of yours, by the way."

"Oh?" said Pen, which was what she always replied to this remark, then added, "Well, start early—you oughtn't to be out late after the 'flu. Are you sure you feel well enough to come?"

Bridget said she was so much better that by Sunday she would almost certainly be out of danger, and was her mother sure she could find enough food for two extra, or should they eat on the way down?

Pen said there would be plenty to eat, using the word, of course, in its modern sense, and added, "What about Gaby? Would it be indiscreet to suggest bringing her?"

"You mean does she think two's company? I don't know—perhaps, but if so, she's quite wrong. I repeat—nothing like that. And anyway, Gaby says she has an engagement of her own for Sunday."

"I'm glad to hear it. Does she know Mr. Dereham?"

"No. Why should she? I don't take my business acquaintances home, you know, mother. As for the Sunday engagement, I fancy it's mythical. Gaby is altogether too self-effacing."

"Well, try to get her to change her mind. By the way, how's Fenny?"

"Fit, as usual. Likewise the children and Glen. I managed very cleverly to keep my 'flu to myself. . . . Well, see you on Sunday. Love to Charles. . . . Good-bye," and Bridget rang off.

Pen went away, found Charles, and said, "Do you know a young man in the publishing world called Dereham? Robert Dereham?"

"Oh, yes. He's with Mavins. Said to have a flair for books."

"War?"

"Demobbed about a year ago, I think."

"Young, then . . ."

"Thirty-ish, I should say. Why all this interest?"

"Well, he's driving Bridget down on Sunday for lunch."

"Good!" said Charles in the way he always greeted the news that somebody was coming to eat with them. He disliked immensely the way in which austerity produced the mental impression that they lived in a beleaguered city. "Excellent, in fact. By the way, Dereham is an admirer of your books."

"So," said Pen, "Bridget has been kind enough to tell me."

"What you're wondering, I suppose, is if he is also an admirer of your daughter. Or if she has any special interest in him."

"She very carefully stressed the fact that he was a business friend who happened to have a car which he wouldn't be entirely opposed to driving as far as Wyngates on Sunday morning."

"Well, let's hope they have a fine day. November has begun so well I heartily distrust it. Did you speak to Fenella?"

Pen gave him the news of that young woman and he asked, "When's the event due?"

"At the end of January."

"Three children in—how many years? Five and a bit, isn't it? Well, people must, on balance, I suppose, get more happiness than unhappiness out of life on this sorry planet since they're so keen to introduce others to it."

"Of course they do. . . . Don't you?"

"I suppose I do. . . . Still, it *is* a sorry world, my dear, and I don't believe if I were young again I'd have any children."

[158]

She knew he was thinking of those two fine sons who, babies when the War to End War began, were killed in their twenties in the next one. And of how, doing his bit in the first, he had always felt he'd missed the best part of fatherhood.

She said, "The race has to go on."

"I often wonder why. It's so stupid. It has learned little save how to move about the earth quickly and how to destroy itself most effectively. I often wonder if Tom and John would have thanked me for my part in bringing them into the world if they'd foreseen their fate."

"I think they would, you know. They enjoyed their lives."

"Such short ones. And death so swift and horrible. You had more courage than I, my dear."

"I've had so little to bear . . ."

But she knew he meant over her children—two of whom were born during the War of her youth; Dwight while Bar was out in the fighting, Fenella two days before it came to an end. Only Bridget had made her appearance in the years of peace. And in 1921 it did begin to look a little like the real thing, though she had forgotten why. Perhaps because at that time nobody had heard of Adolf Hitler, though Mussolini had arisen in Italy. She remembered how Caro had come to see the new baby and had told her that the counter-Revolution in Russia was over, the White Generals dead or fled the country; and had told her also that she had no right to have had Bridget. She did not believe peace had really come, or was even on the way. What they had was only a breathing-space between the wars. And how right she'd been! But even if I'd known, she thought, it wouldn't have stopped me. I could never understand that there were people who didn't enjoy being alive as much as I did, whatever befell. And personal relationships mattered to me so much—and how heartless Caro used to think me to be so much taken up with them, when the seeds of another war were, as she firmly believed, even then being sown. Fenella takes after me. I understand perfectly what induced her to produce those two children while Glen was still in England. No time to waste. . . . No time to waste. . . .

"Did you know Bridget knew Mr. Dereham?" she asked presently.

"No—but it's some time since I saw him. However, since publishers do have a little social intercourse, it's not surprising. She has a departmental job and so has he. And the same sort. Children's books."

"I see," she said, and thought that certainly sounded reasonable.

Nevertheless, Sunday would be an "occasion", for this was the first time Bridget had ever got as far as introducing a young man to her family. In her girlhood it was not Bridget who filled the old house at Richmond with young men, who, indeed, seemed to exist for her only as squires to a play or partners at a dance. During the war years she appeared to have met no young men at all, or if she had they were not allowed to interfere with her avowed intention of working for her degree in what she called her "spare" time, and taking her finals within a year of the war's cessation. This ambition she had achieved, and shortly afterwards had secured the hoped-for appointment in a publisher's office, where she had been enjoying herself very much. Well, thought Pen, business acquaintance Mr. Dereham might be, but she found it impossible not to feel—to hope? —that he might be, even at this early stage, a little more. She found herself looking eagerly forward to making Robert Dereham's acquaintance, well enough aware that Charles saw this and, in his sober fashion, was distinctly amused by it.

When Sunday and the visitors arrived she was a little dashed to discover that they called each other "Miss Lowe" and "Mr. Dereham", though their acquaintance appeared to have the warmth of a cordial and well-established friendship, and so worth a somewhat less formal front, she thought. Mr. Dereham, she found, with his stimulating talk on books and ideas, was a distinct asset to the gathering, and although the opinion he expressed of her own work was very pleasant to hear, she felt she would have continued to approve of him even if he had not mentioned it at all or had done so in a way which made her wish he had not, as was much more often the case. When Charles remarked that the book she was writing at the moment was a complete breakaway from anything she had done before she stopped him by a faint raising of her eyebrows and said that it would probably cost her her public.

"Or gain you a new additional one," said Robert Dereham.

But Pen, who always found it difficult to discuss a book "on the stocks" with anyone, said only, "Thank you. I hope you're a good prophet," and then turned the conversation from herself by saying "Bridget promised me a piece of news which she thought would please me. May we not hear it?"

"Of course," said Bridget, but she left Robert Dereham to relate it. Bridget, it seemed, had written a children's book and Fenny had done the illustrations. They hoped it would be in the bookshops for Christmas but there had been a little delay over the illustrations. . . .

Pen laughed and said that did not in the least surprise her.

"They'd never have been finished, I'm sure," said Bridget, "if Glen hadn't butted in. But you know what Fenny is at the best of times . . ."

(Which means, thought Pen, when she isn't going to have a baby.)

"She has two children, of course," said Robert, as one putting forward an insuperable excuse for the delay.

"Who give her no trouble at all," Bridget commented. "Fenny would rather be occupied with them than get on with her drawing. Her husband calls her a 'lazy slut', which, believe it or not, she takes as a compliment. But it does, for some odd reason, move her to spasmodic effort."

Pen gathered that Mr. Dereham and his firm were delighted with the book and with the illustrations. It was, he thought, something fresh in children's books. A good deal of it came under the heading of Nonsense and that, he thought, was good for children. . . . He criticised juvenile literature, not merely that of the present day. Look at the appalling endings to some of the fairy tales—the Wicked Queen who had to put on red-hot shoes and dance in them; and how when she cut off her feet they went on dancing on their own in the red-hot shoes! Enough to give any child a nightmare.

"I agree entirely," said Bridget. "All the same, I'm bound to admit that the only child I've ever known who hated cruel stories is my small nephew, Barry. For him all stories must end happily and nobody must be cruel to anybody or to any animal."

Pen was delighted about the book. She had always wished one of her children would want to write, but though Bridget used to make up rhymes as a child, chiefly levelled at Fenella, it had never occurred to her that this was anything more than Bridget's love of nonsense in a different guise; a facile trick, at which one smiled but did not take seriously. She felt now that this had been rather stupid of her—and very clever and discerning of Mr. Dereham to realise that Bridget had a distinct talent which should be taken seriously and developed. She thought he must be a little like Glen Westcott, who became really angry at wasted talent. But Mr. Dereham didn't sound in the least angry, and when she asked him what had made him think Bridget could write for children, either in rhyme or prose, he said, "Oh, just a remark she made one day when she was in the office, when I showed her proofs of a new child's book on our list. She laughed at me, of course, when I said she should try her hand at it, but the idea took root, and a few months ago she brought me the manuscript. Just like that!"

"When you'd forgotten all about it," said Bridget laughing

"However, don't expect too much, mother. I'm no 'E. Nesbit' or Beatrix Potter."

"Don't you worry!" said Mr. Dereham. "You fill a gap, believe me."

"And may even make a little fortune," said Charles.

"Bless you," said Bridget, kissing her finger-tips in his direction.

That evening, after Bridget and Mr. Dereham had driven away into the gathering gloom of the November evening, Pen wondered if his interest in Bridget and hers in him, for that matter, were centred wholly in the book, or if, like some other authors and publishers, they were destined to have a closer relationship. But certainly she had seen nothing—not the very slightest sign—that there was between them anything but this particular interest.

When a few weeks later a copy of the book arrived at Wyngates she had only time to look at the illustrations before Charles bore down upon her and went off with it. But she had had time to see that Fenella's drawing, under Glen's influence, had improved out of all knowledge. She had clearly used her own small daughters for her models, and, lacking a son, had fallen back upon Barry. The names of the three children appeared very fittingly upon the dedication page. *For Serena, Rebecca and Barry, with love from their devoted Aunt.*

"Quite a family affair," commented Charles. "*The Cherry Tree and Other Stories*, by Bridget Lowe. Illustrated by Fenella Westcott. Now why didn't this book come to us?"

"To Ffoliot's? That's simple, my dear. It never occurred to either of us that we had such a very clever pair of daughters. As authors, I fear they're lost to Ffoliot's for ever."

A little stricken by this blithe statement, Charles was comforted by the suggestion that Bridget and Fenella were his daughters. He had known them for a good many years, and when they were very small he had thought how pleasant it would be to have a little daughter of his own. But Dorothea had wanted sons, and had had her wish. But if, he thought now, they had been daughters, I might have them still. . . .

"Well," Pen went on, "I liked Mr. Dereham, didn't you? He has a lively, interested and interesting mind and he's a very good talker. And oh! how very pleasant it was to meet a young man who doesn't say 'yep' when he means 'yes'."

"But you'd scarcely expect Bridget to smile upon a young man who murdered the King's English."

"You think she does smile upon him?"

"To the extent of introducing him to us, yes."

"You wouldn't put it higher than that?"

"Not at this stage. Would you?"

"I don't know. In this matter there are no antecedents. Bridget is a law unto herself."

"I can't answer for Bridget, but I rather fancied, you know, that Dereham was distinctly attracted—to put it mildly."

"But aren't you, perhaps, confusing two things—the personal and the impersonal? What attracts Dereham, perhaps, is Bridget's ability to do something he very much wanted to find somebody to do. And, of course, she's very capable in other directions. She must be a god-send from that point of view. And I dare say he finds her attractive. She is, in her own way, though as a child Fenella rather obscured the fact. She has, I think, a thoughtful, intelligent face . . ."

Charles laughed.

"I never met a woman who was so given to under-statement over her children's looks. Bridget, my dear, though she hasn't Fenella's poster-prettiness, is an extremely good-looking young woman. She has a delightful heart-shaped face, intelligent, as you allow, soft dark hair she has the sense not to torture into the fashionable coiffure, and her mother's astonishing eyes."

Pen smiled.

"Well, the intelligent face used to wear a puckish expression, I remember, in the old days, which I don't seem to have seen for a long time. And rather miss. I've often thought that something happened to Bridget during the war we didn't know about . . . or perhaps it was just the war."

"But the puckish mood, my dear, is very much the point of these stories, if I'm not mistaken. Sit down with them this evening and see if I am."

This she did, and when she put the little volume aside she felt as if it had restored to her the little girl she had once known, so much at home in the world, so reasonable even when her little face wore an aggrieved expression. So very reasonable indeed that Pen used to wonder if she got it from James, whose reasonableness hid so much that was nothing of the sort. But luckily this quality of Bridget's hid nothing and, in her, James's loathed suavity came out as no more than a pleasing tone of voice and suggestion of self-possession. These little stories did show a remarkable understanding, she thought, of the child mind; in them Bridget had remembered, and with quite startling exactness, what it was like to be a child. It would be a thousand pities if she did not marry and have children of her own. She was twenty-five. Had there really been nobody?

When she next came down to Wyngates early in December she came alone, very calm and self-possessed, not in the least like a non-sense-loving little girl. About the book she was, as perhaps befitted a member of the publishing fraternity, very businesslike. Of course, these days, any decently produced book for children sold, though she had to admit the reviewers had been very pleasant so far. Mavins seemed pleased. Mavins. Not Mr. Dereham, who was the book's 'onlie begetter'. When Charles inquired after him, she said he seemed to be bearing up commendably. "We've had speech together over the telephone but haven't run across each other lately." A little deflated, Pen said she hoped she would allow him to drive her down again some day—they had both liked him so much. To which Bridget said only, "Well, there's always the petrol difficulty, of course, and in this weather I prefer the train to a car."

It was as if, having dismissed Mr. Dereham's car, she had dismissed him also, but she added, "Maybe the weather will change, since that's what the English weather is famous for doing."

Well, thought Pen, if Mr. Dereham's visits were to be dependent upon the English weather and the state of the wintry roads, in addition to finding a good and sufficient reason for being abroad in a car at all, it would be some time before they saw him again; for the winter had barely started and general conditions and expert opinion did not offer much hope of its being a mild one. If Charles was right in his view that he was attracted by Bridget, it wouldn't appear that she was giving him much encouragement. Nor, it seemed, were her hopes of getting Bridget to Wyngates for Christmas any brighter, for she and Gaby hoped to go to Paris. Aunt Yvette, it seemed, had suddenly remembered that she had a half-English daughter and had written asking her to come over for the holiday. Bridget had no idea why she also had been invited. But it would be pleasant to see Paris again and to look up their Passy friends, if there were any of them left.

"So it would," her mother agreed. "And I dare say Yvette will be interesting on the theme of her Resistance activities. But what is happening to Fenny and Glen? Fenny ought not to be coping with an austerity Christmas just now."

"She won't be. They're all off to her in-laws. Nothing would have induced either Gaby or me to accept Aunt Yvette's invitation if it had meant leaving Fenny to cope. The in-laws asked them some time ago, but Glen said they'd leave it a little later to see how Fenny was. But directly she heard about the Paris invitation she said she was quite fit to go."

"And is she?"

"She seems all right. But it's a bit near, of course, and she says she's only fit for a *very* intimate eye. She's convinced she's going to have twins and asked me to warn you. . . . Glen teases her and says if she could only make it 'quads' they'd be all set up for life."

This made Pen laugh.

"Have you seen anything of Dwight lately?"

"Not at Richmond. I've looked in on him once or twice, but he's very taken up with Fryn and her maths, of course. However, her exam's next week, so that will come to an end."

"How does Fryn feel about it?"

"Well, you know what she is. Self-confidence isn't her strong point. But Dwight says that as far as maths is concerned, she's reasonably safe. Lydia's delighted. By the way, she's off to Germany for Christmas, taking Jeremy. The girls are going to Ray's. Fryn's funking it, rather, but Meg's in the seventh heaven. Or at any rate, the sixth."

"You *are* full of news," said Pen, whose marriage had a little detached her from her "monstrous family" so that she was always behind-hand with news of it, save when Rose, still the Family Chatterbox, came down or rang up. "Perhaps we might ask Dwight and Doreen down for Christmas. Doreen seems to have enjoyed her last visit a little, but I'm bound to say the credit belongs entirely to Charles. Could you repeat your kind offices, do you think, my dear?"

"Certainly," said Charles, nobly suppressing expression of his hope that for once he and Pen might spend Christmas alone.

"No use, I'm afraid," said Bridget. "Dwight has fixed up to go to Brighton. Doreen adores it and he thinks Barry needs a little sea air."

"I hope to goodness the weather's kind then," said Pen. "Anyway, that is rather that . . ."

Secretly, however, she was relieved, for even with Charles playing cavalier she found her daughter-in-law a little heavy going, and it was no way, poor lamb, for him to spend his Christmas. If the weather was kind Hamish could take them both for some familiar walks, and for the rest they could sit by the fire and make up some of their arrears of reading.

Which is precisely what they did, and enjoyed it very much. Half at least of Charles's pleasure was in having so successfully detached Pen's mind from the affairs of her children. Not that he was not fond of them, but they were all, he considered, well able to look after themselves. Even Dwight, who'd so obviously married in haste and was repenting at leisure. At least he had discovered a technique for his dissatisfactions and did not parade his disillusions, so that unless you could get beneath the technique you'd never suspect how bitterly he regretted his marriage. It was useless to worry about future developments though he knew Pen did quite considerably. He was grateful to Bridget for her casual reference to that menage and to Dwight for taking wife and child off to the sea. Barry, perhaps, was the really unfortunate member of that trio, but he wasn't old enough yet to realise it, and as at the moment he was probably enjoying the excitement of being for the first time in his life at the sea, it was a little superfluous to worry about his future. As for Bridget, nobody need bother. Whatever happened to Bridget she'd be captain of her soul, and this, he was sure, Pen knew. But the knowledge did not prevent her, as he also knew, from desiring for this talented and attractive young creature the kind of life she herself had been living at her age—happily married, with three charming and accommodating youngsters, time in which to do the work that had stood her all her life in such good stead, and a delightful home most capably run. But this was a very different world and delightful well-run homes were far to seek; moreover, he had a shrewd suspicion that Bridget would resolve her own problems, whatever they were, for she was her mother's daughter. Perhaps it had been a mistake on his part to suggest that Dereham liked her rather more than somewhat, for if he were wrong, or nothing came of it if he were right, Pen would feel disappointed. However, at the moment she was content with her daughter's debut as a writer and with the knowledge that Dereham evidently considered her a "find". A pity, all the same, she hadn't shown the book to him, but maybe as Dereham had put the idea of writing it into her mind she felt he was entitled to its first refusal. "Lost to Ffoliots for ever," Pen had said. And had seemed amused. As if already she had Bridget married to her publisher. But he wasn't so sure. He'd be inclined to wager that Bridget would give him as long a run for his money as Pen had given him. And not get her, in the end, if you asked him. . . .

BOOK THREE

January—July, 1947

Chapter One

ONE WARM and sunny afternoon that came at the end of a patch of unexpectedly fine weather between the snow, fog, cold winds and rains of January, 1947, Fryn walked across the bridge to Battersea to announce to Dwight that she had passed her exam. She found him at home helping Barry to build up a puzzle; Doreen had betaken herself, she was told, to a cinema. When she inquired what picture she had gone to see, Dwight said, "I don't know. Neither, I expect, does—or did—Doreen. She never goes to see 'a picture.' She goes 'to the pictures'."

"It's a lovely day," Fryn said after a little rather awkward pause. "Wouldn't you like to leave the puzzle for a bit, Barry, and come and trundle your hoop in the Park instead? Or is the puzzle more interesting?"

"It *is* interesting but I can do it when I come back," said Barry, always ready to leave any indoor occupation for the joy of rolling a hoop in the Park. "It's going to be a·cathedral—the belfry's the hard bit. . . . Daddy's awfully good at it. I 'spect you are too."

"I don't think I would be, you know," Fryn said. "Perhaps being an architect helps."

"Daddy doesn't build *cathedrals*!" said Barry. "Do you, daddy?"

"Rather not," Dwight told him, "nor anything else, I'm afraid, these days. If we're going out we ought to go at once. Fryn's lovely day won't last much longer, you know. So run and change your shoes, sonny, and wash your hands if they need it."

"As if any small boy ever thought his hands needed washing!" he commented to Fryn as Barry ran off, and then, "Getting your matric, you know, Fryn, means that you are a fit and proper person to go on to a university."

"But not that I shall go, unfortunately. It was only to satisfy father that I'm not a complete nitwit I was so anxious to pass properly, though I should never have managed it but for you."

"You know what I think of that argument. . . . Can you come back to tea? I'd suggest having it out somewhere, except that Doreen will be back in time for it."

Fryn was afraid she couldn't.

"Quite sure?"

"Quite. We're going to the theatre to-night, and you know how early the theatres start."

He did not inquire what she was going to see. He made that queer little sound which reminded her of Jean Cadell, and excusing himself, went out. He was back in a few minutes clad for the street, with Barry at his heels, well wrapped up and duly equipped with hoop.

It was delightful out of doors. There was a joy in the winter sunshine that lay lightly upon the drab houses and upon the streets through which they walked quickly, gilding even the steely river running so swiftly beneath the bridge. But it would soon be gone. Fryn, most annoyingly to many people, had enjoyed the snow, and Dwight said that her odd liking, according to weather experts, would be further indulged and that the last few days were but an interlude.

As he walked along at her side he felt more keenly than ever before that this rewarding intimacy with his young cousin was also an interlude and one which, now that the exam, which had brought it about, was safely at an end, would shortly also come to an end. He had missed her regular appearances since the lessons had ceased, the quiet walks after them back to Hereford Square, the sound of her gentle voice that had so pretty a lilt in it. He had never at the time allowed himself to acknowledge how much he had enjoyed her company, what a bright thread it had woven in the drab pattern of his life with Doreen. And when that young woman had said one day, "You know, Dwight, you ought to have married someone like Fryn. Pity she was such a kid when she arrived—she's just your sort," he had been annoyed. He had always thought of Fryn as a child, twelve years his junior, and in any case he was married to Doreen— a bond he had no intention of breaking, even now, when it was already broken in spirit. But bereft of the visits, and of that beguiling voice uttering her gentle always slightly uncertain observations, and all the pleasure of her presence, the memory of them had lived in him with a tenderness he had known for nothing and no one since the days when he had first met Doreen and believed she was as kind as then she had looked. Or seemed. . . . Which was it? He didn't know and in any case she had long ago lost the look and he knew that kindness did not dwell with her. Bad-tempered? No, she was not that, but her good-humour was rooted in indifference, in a mild unconsidering toleration, in her personal satisfactions and vanities. In her outings, a new dress, a fresh lipstick. . . . When she was out he did not miss her, except with a sigh of satisfaction, and he had purged himself of her physical attraction for him and had done it so thoroughly that desire no longer lived in him.

Since Fryn's regular visits had ceased he had been aware of more than he'd cared to admit. Too often his thoughts had strayed to the picture of her bright head bent over her text-book, to the look of earnestness upon the little face she turned up to him and which sat so incongruously upon its youth; the little frown of concentration upon the low wide brow. Remembered, too, those walks home to Hereford Square, her comments, always so shyly made, the small sound of her (always somehow unexpected) laughter.

His heart had jumped when he'd opened the door this afternoon and seen her standing there. It seemed a very long while since he'd seen her, and soon he would see her no more. Six months and she would be gone. The spring and the early summer were all that was left to him. His heart contracted with pain at the thought. It would be years before they met again—perhaps never. It was Meg who was likely to stay in England, not Fryn. If only Fryn, he'd once thought, had found someone to fall in love with here. But this afternoon he thought only how painful it would be to have her here as someone's wife; that he would rather lose her to South America than to another man.

Looking at her face as they walked along by the river wall his leaping thoughts were subdued by the sight of its unawareness. That she liked him, he knew; that she was happy in his company. But that was all. She was asleep, sex had not found her out. Every thing else in the world interested her, but not sex. She had never had even the faintest suggestion, he was sure, of a love affair. It was Meg who attracted the men; Meg, so ready with her smiles, her sprightly comments and bright glances. And Fryn accepted that. She would have been extremely embarrassed, he felt, if any man had paid her the compliments Meg must have received during the past two or three years.

It was of Meg she was speaking now. At Ray's fine house over Christmas and the New Year, she had danced a great deal with Mr. Lenham, who was a beautiful dancer and had even, Fryn said, once or twice put up with her, who was not at all good. She thought Meg really did like him very much and meant to marry him. It was characteristic of her that she did not use the word 'love'.

"The thing that holds her back is that she will have to live in England. And she's terribly homesick. She will have to arrange matters as Livvy and Danny have done and spend a certain time each year in South America. Only as Mr. Lenham's a business man perhaps

[171]

it won't be so easy. Danny's a country squire and free to go where he chooses."

He moved, not without gratitude, along the path she had taken. Danny and Livvy, he said, would soon be home again.

"Is her father better then?"

"I don't think so, but like Charles II he's an unconscionable time a-dying."

"Is he really dying?"

"He has an incurable and inoperable disease. Livvy is very much attached to him."

"Meg says she will be much richer when he dies than she is even now. Meg always knows that sort of thing."

"I dare say she's right. He is a very wealthy man and Livvy's an only child. It must be very pleasant to have so much money and to be immune from our crippling income-tax, most of which, I feel, Livvy considers is spent on supporting or bringing about all the things she most distrusts and dislikes."

"Doesn't Livvy have to pay income-tax?"

"Not here. Although married to an Englishman she remains an American citizen. . . . I suppose," he said, after a little pause, Fryn having apparently found nothing to say to this piece of information, "that you'll be putting your hair up now?"

"I suppose I ought to have done it before. But I could hardly go to school with my hair up!"

"I wish you need never put it up."

"Why ever not?"

"It will make you look so grown-up."

"But I *am* grown-up."

"You say that as if it makes you sad to acknowledge it. As sad as it makes me."

"But why should you feel sad?"

Since he could not say, "I don't want to think of you as a grown-up young lady but only as the little girl cousin I've known for so long," he said nothing. And suddenly he realised that all his safety lay in *not* thinking of her as grown-up.

She said, "No, the idea of being really grown-up doesn't make me sad at all—but I find it rather alarming because I'm afraid I shall make such a failure of being grown-up."

"Why?"

"Oh, because I shall have to think of the future . . . and what I intend to make of my life—to do with it. And I don't know. Except that I'd like to go and study English at one of the universities. Yester-

[172]

day and Now are simply crammed full of things, but To-morrow's only a void."

"Even when it's full of South America?"

"*Because* it's full of South America, I think. To me it's just like going to a new country instead of somewhere where I belong. I suppose that seems very odd to you."

"No, not very. I can understand it."

"Nobody else does. Even mother, who was born here and lived here for nearly twenty years, thinks of South America as her home. None of them understands my feeling that way about England."

"Is the idea of the university quite out of the question?"

"Yes, I'm afraid so."

"But if you went to the university, it would only be for three years."

"Father would never believe that. Mother says he's convinced that if I don't go back with them at the end of the summer I shall not go back at all."

"But why?"

"Perhaps he thinks I should get a job here. A good one, which I shouldn't want to leave. If only I could! But I can't think what it could possibly be."

Don't encourage her. Let her go, said Dwight's common sense. But he said, "By the time you'd taken your degree you'd be old enough to please yourself where you live."

"I can't believe that father has overlooked that point. It isn't, you know, the university he objects to—he has quite sound ideas about women's education—it's a university *over here*. I gather from mother that he quite smiled upon the idea of the one at Montevideo, just as he does upon the idea of Jeremy going to the Argentine Public School—out at Quilmé. Montevideo's in Uruguay—the most modern of the South American States, so mother says, where women lead much more independent lives than in the Argentine, which, as you know, she considers a man's country."

"I'd heard it before—from your revered grandmother. As my Aunt Caro she acquainted us all with that discovery when she came back from her first visit."

"She says she can never understand how any daughter of hers could live in such a place. Pre-Victorian she calls it. But of course it isn't that at all. It's just the Spanish tradition."

"What sort of a house did you live in at Buenos Aires?"

"Not in a house at all, really. In an apartment, though it was like

[173]

living in a very large house. It didn't look a bit like flats do here. I remember a handsome iron gateway and a little courtyard; a door with a lot of glass, a tessellated hall and a lift. And large lofty rooms. Father used to say nobody but mother could have made anything so un-English look like a cross-section of Waring & Gillows. But he liked it that way, all the same—it was so comfortable. I don't remember very much of Buenos Aires itself—I'd get lost in it now. I'm not sure I could even find Parera—that was the name of the street we lived on. A very grand one. I feel I know London much better."

"It's a pity you never saw London at its best."

"Oh, I had all those months before the bombing started. I remember perfectly what the Temple looked like—and the tulips that grew against one of the old walls . . . and the Master's lovely house. Perhaps when I come back they'll have rebuilt some of it."

"You're so sure you'll come back?"

"Of course I shall come back. I shall soon be twenty-one and shall be able, as you've just said, to live where I like. And if Meg marries Mr. Lenham, we shall have to come over to see her."

"I thought you were arranging that Meg and her husband should come to see you."

A little taken aback, as though he had stripped away her finest argument, she laughed and said, "Well, I hope it will be both. With a sister living in England I shall have a really *good* excuse for coming back."

Apropos of nothing or of too much, he said, "How much of your Spanish do you remember?"

"Oh, quite a bit. After all, it was as much my language as English when I was at school there. One can't forget one's language, can one?"

"Spanish is a useful language. What about giving me some lessons?"

"I'm not much good at teaching, I'm afraid. But I'd like to try, if you really want to learn—to make up for your having pushed me so successfully across my asses' bridge."

"When shall we begin?"

"Do we have to decide that now? . . . I shall have to mention it to mother—and then there's Doreen."

"Doreen won't mind. Why should she? She'll just be amused."

It seemed to amuse Fryn too.

"At the idea of my teaching anybody anything?"

"At the idea of anybody wanting to learn anything."

[174]

Though he laughed, he was angry with himself. This was an absurd proposition. He hoped Lydia would pour cold water on it, for the less he saw of Fryn the better. But oh, too, so much the worse! He wrenched the conversation into a safer channel by asking her if her mother had enjoyed her short stay in Germany.

"She enjoyed being with father, but not being in Germany. She found it very depressing. When grandmother came along to collect her 'impressions' and to try to urge her to come and talk about them at her Friday afternoons, she said she hadn't any—that she'd gone to Germany to spend Christmas with father, not to study the state of Germany. But grandmother said she should have been glad of the opportunity and made the most of it. And in any case she must have received *some* impression. Mother said Yes—one of complete hopelessness everywhere. And grandmother, of course, said, 'Well, there you are! Come along and tell us why you feel that way about it.' When mother said she didn't know, but that father blamed some of it on to Russia and said that the more hopeless any country was the better pleased Russia was, she gave her up as hopeless. Everyone knew, she said, that we'd make a mess of our zone and look what Russia had done with hers!"

"Did your mother find an answer to that?"

"Several, but she didn't mention them to grandmother, because she'd have said, 'Well, there you are!—there's your theme . . .'"

Germany, Russia and his Aunt Caro were safe impersonal topics of conversation and Dwight kept to them for the rest of the walk. Caro had long been a joke to him, so passionate were her advocacies, so complete her changes of front. Even over Russia—particularly over Russia. Her dream of that country as an earthly Paradise had been rudely shattered by the purges of 'thirty-six, when the Revolution devoured its own children, liquidating its "fifth column", which seemed to be nearly all the people who had made the Revolution; she had seethed with indignation when Russia had signed her compact with Germany and called the war an "imperialistic" one in which no good Communist should become embroiled, and then helped the Germans! She had approved M. Blum for putting his Communists in prison and would have put ours there too if she could. When Russia had seized the Baltic ports and fought recalcitrant Finland her stock had fallen very low indeed and Caro had resigned from the Society for the Promotion of Cultural Relations with Russia, calling it a "Society for Understanding the Un-understandable". Then Germany had attacked Russia—and she had seen these acts in a more forgiving light. Russia had merely had the sense to lock her back door. . . . When she began to push the Germans back and the opening of the Second Front was still delayed, Caro talked as if no one else but Russia was doing anything whatsoever to win the war and, when it was won, as if she had won it single-handed. Luckily the phase passed, but, convinced that if England always won her wars she could always be relied upon to lose the peace, she turned (and still did) a but half-responsive ear to the allegations of Russian un-co-operativeness in Germany. To the coming Conference at Moscow in the spring she pinned all her hopes, scornfully dismissing such doubting Thomases as her Socialist and strongly anti-Communist husband, the anti-Socialist Charles and her un-politically-minded sister.

Dwight could understand that if she didn't make you laugh she would make you very angry. The only person who could really deflate Caro Bradfield was his mother; and that was odd, for nobody hated the political side of life more than she did. Politics and politicians, she asserted, had become the curse of the modern world, as religion and its bigots had been of an earlier day.

Fryn interrupted these reflections by glancing at her watch and announcing that she must go home and that she thought she ought to take a taxi. So Dwight, accepting the inevitable, whistled up Barry, who had galloped along in front of them all this time with very few interruptions, and they made for the gate at the foot of the bridge, where a taxi almost at once came along. Fryn got into it and was driven away and Dwight walked thoughtfully home with a Barry inclined to resent Fryn's hurried departure and to think his father's explanation highly inadequate.

Doreen had not reached home when they got in, so he prepared Barry's tea and sat down with his evening paper, to which, however, he gave a somewhat divided attention and from which Doreen's arrival presently detached him. She'd encountered Emmy, she told him, at the cinema, and they'd had tea together. Something in the over-casual tone of her voice caused him to wonder if the meeting was quite as casual as she wished him to believe. Of all Doreen's odd friendships this with Emmy was the only one to which he took exception, for Emmy was a mischief-maker, though how much so he had not realised until that story of Bridget's about her encouragement of Fenella's youthful encounter with her married Lothario. She expressed surprise that he should have waited tea for her instead of having it with Barry, but she made fresh tea for him without further comment, and set it before him on a tray and cleared away the debris of Barry's repast. That young man promptly returned to his interrupted puzzle, his grievance apparently forgotten, and Dwight gave her an account of their afternoon.

"Oh, she's passed, has she?" He fancied she sounded a little crestfallen. Only why? "What's she going to do now?"

"Nothing, I gather, save wait for the summer and the return to South America."

"I can't see, in that case, why the exam mattered so much, why she had to get matric. standard, or whatever it is."

"Her father has a phobia about exams."

"A what?"

"A phobia—what you'd call 'a thing'."

"Oh, I see. Well, you'll miss her."

"So shall I," said Barry. "Why does she have to go?"

"Because South America's where she really lives," said Dwight. "How's the puzzle going?"

"I *can't* do the belfry."

"You can put it all away for to-night, Barry," Doreen told him.

"Must I, daddy?"

"It's after bedtime."

"Do help me with the belfry."

"It's too late. You must go to bed," said Doreen.

"Please, daddy."

"I'll see what I can do for you to-morrow, sonny. Better go to bed now."

The child frowned and sat staring at his puzzle.

"Come along now, Barry," said his mother.

"No," said the child. "No . . ."

"Do as I say, Barry. Put the puzzle away."

"It'll spoil it all . . . and I'll have to start all over again to-morrow."

"That won't hurt you—it'll keep you amused."

"It won't then."

"Do as I say, Barry. Clear it away at once."

"I won't."

Doreen leaned across the table, and with one casual sweep of her hand knocked the puzzle to pieces. Barry screamed at her, his little face contorted with rage.

"I hate you," he screamed. "I hate you!"

Doreen pulled him away from the table and shook him, not with any force but with the helpless exasperation that always seized upon her when Barry had what she called one of his "fits". And the child screamed with more vehemence and determination and sat down

[177]

upon the floor, the tears of rage falling faster and faster down his little face.

"Go away!" he yelled, "go away. . . . Go out with your friends. . . . I don't want you!"

Dwight rose from his seat and picked up his demented son.

"Come along, old chap. . . . It's all right. We'll do the puzzle again to-morrow morning—and the belfry, too. . . . But to-night it's bed."

Barry stopped his noise and allowed himself to be led out of the room. Doreen shrugged her shoulders, lighted a cigarette and sat down with the evening paper. She was still busy with it when Dwight came back and she looked up to say, "Well? Is the storm over?"

"Oh yes—Barry's storms are brief. And they needn't start if only you'd have a little more patience, my dear."

"Patience? I like that. When he's in one of his tantrums he's a little fiend."

"But if you'd shown a little interest in his puzzle . . . if you had not smashed up all his afternoon's work."

"Well, he must learn to do as he's told. I can't be bossed by a child."

"Barry wants handling. He's a very highly-strung and sensitive child."

"Highly-strung? I'd say he is. Well, anyone can have these sensitive children for me. When I hear women boasting about theirs I wish they had mine to deal with. And he's always worse after Fryn's been here—she's as bad as you are, and as silly about him."

"Fryn's very fond of him—and very good with him, too."

"I'm sure she is," said Doreen darkly. "By the way, I heard from Emmy that Audrey's gone off with her major. No question of a divorce at the moment—the wife doesn't think it will last. She's still quite friendly with her husband and Emmy says this is annoying Audrey quite a bit."

"It would do. It makes her story of an unhappy marriage look a little silly."

"All the same, I don't know that *I'd* want him back. I should divorce you, you know, if there was another woman."

"You don't have to worry."

"No?" She looked at him over the top of the paper and said, "You'd divorce me, wouldn't you, if you found out I was unfaithful to you?"

"Have you been?"

"*I* was asking the question. But you couldn't very well complain

[178]

if I had been, could you?—seeing the way you treat me. But supposing I *had* been, would you divorce me?"

"Not necessarily."

"What does that mean?"

"If the other man wanted to marry you, yes."

"Or if you . . . wanted to marry someone else?"

"That takes us a little too far, I think, but as both cases are hypothetical we needn't discuss either perhaps."

"Hypo-whatever-it-is. . . . Does that mean they're not real?"

"Not actual, yes. Just something assumed as the ground for a reasoned argument."

She made a little grimace and put the paper aside.

"Emmy also says Danny's sailing home next week."

"Without Livvy?"

"So I gathered. Danny might as well not have a wife."

"He could remain in Boston if he chose."

"Yes. Yes, I suppose he could. Perhaps there's another attraction nearer home. By the way, do you know anything about Bridget's young man?"

"I didn't know she had one."

"Emmy says she's seen her several times in town with the same young man. At the theatre and at some Book Exhibition and once, last week I think it was, at Scott's."

"Emmy would seem to get about, for such an old woman."

"Yes. She goes all over the place. She's interested in everything—theatres, films, pictures. . . . I mean *your* sort, galleries and exhibitions . . . and in good food. She'll go anywhere to get that. She's quite a character. And awfully amusing."

"Yes. She's the sort of woman you hope will always leave a gathering before you do."

Doreen laughed.

"Oh, yes, she's a bit scandalous, I agree. But I find her a scream. . . . I'm a bit curious, though, about Bridget, aren't you?"

"No. At least, not very."

"Perhaps you know something?"

Pen had certainly mentioned that she had taken her publisher down to Wyngates just before Christmas. But that didn't mean anything. At least, not necessarily. When he'd laughingly asked his mother if there was anything in it, she'd said, "Bridget says not." But he had seen no reason to mention this to Doreen, nor did he now. It would only be handed on to Emmy, and no one, on his side of the family, ever fed that fire of gossip and innuendo. So he said that Bridget was old enough to do as she chose and that it was no affair of Emmy's—or of theirs—how often Bridget went out with the same young man.

"Still, one can make a remark, I suppose," said Doreen. But she did not sound as if she'd minded the reproof. She was in too good a mood, anyway, if Dwight had but known it—a mood induced by the news that Danny was coming back without the encumbrance of a wife. She had missed him considerably, for life had been the duller for his absence. She lighted another cigarette and lapsed into silence, her thoughts on Danny Wingham, remembering their last meeting. Exciting. Dangerous. But she'd kept her head, thank goodness. . . . She wished she found him less fascinating, that she liked him less. If only she knew where she was with him. . . . She couldn't afford to make a fool of herself. But he was coming home alone. Perhaps he'd arranged that, meant to do it. . . . Perhaps he'd come to town soon . . . ring her up, suggest lunch, a film. . . . With Emmy back in town it would be safer. . . . At this thought regret struggled with relief. Well, anyway, she must get something to wear, get hold of some coupons somehow. And have a new hair-do. Danny always noticed what she wore—how she looked—and was ready with his compliments. Life with his return would be interesting, exciting again. But supposing he didn't come to town?—didn't ring up? No, she was a fool to suppose such things. By keeping men off you keep them on. . . . All the same. . . .

Dwight's voice saved her from further pursuit of this confusing line of thought. It said, "I've asked Fryn to give me some Spanish lessons. . . ."

Chapter Two

IF PEN'S mind had emptied itself of family and family concerns over Christmas, January had not yet quite run its course when they came crowding into it once more. First, there was the news of the safe arrival of Fenella's son, who had chosen to make his appearance when the weather was so bad that even his grandmother accepted the fact that she must wait awhile to make his acquaintance. And following upon the heels of Fenella's news there arrived a letter from Rose, who, it was clear, had turned to pen and paper for the same reason which kept the recipient at Wyngates when she would so much rather have been at Richmond. For though Rose wrote good letters, being content to put down her thoughts as she would have spoken them, the epistolary art was not one she cared for. And from this one her horror sprang full-fledged. For it announced that Audrey's major was asking his wife for a divorce and that when that was accomplished they were to be married.

"Of course," she wrote, clearly looking for what crumbs of comfort the miserable situation held, "if the wife has any sense she won't be so obliging. After all, she has been married for nearly twenty-five years and there are two grown-up children. The situation's preposterous, and I am ashamed to say that it really does look as if Audrey has been making most of the running. Emmy, I grieve to say, is on Audrey's side and talks of 'love' and 'romance' and hints at all sorts of short-comings on the wife's part, for which I'm sure she has no evidence whatever, save what Audrey has put about—and that can hardly count. This silly idea that men only make fools of themselves over another woman because of short-comings in their wives! Even if I *believed* in divorce I should still think that a marriage which has lasted as long as this one ought not to be dissolved. Larry says the Chinese would agree with me, though that doesn't seem to help much.

"Larry, of course, is *no* comfort to me at all. He says it's always been obvious that Audrey never intended to die an old maid if she could help it, and as the young men didn't fancy her she's made good use of the opportunities the war afforded her to hook one in the 'silly fifties'. Of course he and Audrey, since she grew up, have never got on (a great grief to me, as you know), but all the same, his attitude is *most* hurtful to me. I know that he hasn't any *religious* beliefs, but I think that he ought to have some moral objections—I mean, he ought to *mind* about this awful business, but he doesn't seem to. It isn't that he approves—how *could* he? But he says Audrey is old enough to know what she is doing, and although if she'd been in her 'teens or early twenties he'd have felt it his duty to intervene, that course with a woman of thirty-four would be ridiculous. Audrey herself is quite shameless. When I told her that divorce or no divorce I should never consider her married, if she goes on with the dreadful business, she laughed and said, 'Don't be ridiculous, mother. In the eyes of the law I shall be married, whatever *you* think!' And yet I brought her up in the true faith. Larry says she's admitted to him that she hasn't been to church since the affair began, and added that she'd said she thought that ought to earn her a good mark with me, for at least she hasn't been a hypocrite! When I told her that, wicked though she has been, she has only to give up the association and make confession of her wrong-doing to get absolution, she said she didn't want it. She wanted to be married to this man and when Larry said, 'Why this belated regard for the marriage ceremony?' she said, 'I've always wanted to be married and to have children . . . being a man's mistress isn't at all the same thing.' When I said that it was wicked to break up a marriage she said, 'Well, she's had Geoff for twenty-five years and she's fifty now. Marriage can't mean a thing to her any longer! Besides, why should she want to hang on to a man who's tired of her? I'm sure I shouldn't want to.'

"You can judge, my dear Pen, how terrible all this is to me. I know you won't agree with me but I was driven to say to Larry that if he had shared my faith perhaps Audrey would have grown up differently, and perhaps I was being punished for marrying an unbeliever. But Larry only said it was a little late in the day to think of that . . . but he never says much, as you know, on any subject, and on this he seems to think it would be best to say nothing.

"Do you think I could possibly do any good by going to see the wife? Larry says not and that I should only make myself ridiculous, though I shouldn't mind that if I thought it would help. I'm not saying anything to mother—she would be so upset—and luckily Danny has changed his mind about coming back yet awhile and cancelled his sailing. I must say that at the moment I find that a relief—you know how hard it always is to keep anything from Danny. I didn't see much of him when he was in town last time—Emmy was in Brighton and had lent him her flat. But she's back now—and to my mind Audrey sees far too much of her. I feel that Emmy—and you *know* how I've always defended her!—has become old and silly.

"I expect you've heard that David goes to Canada in the spring. Of course I quite see that he ought to accept the post offered him—it appears to be a very good one. But all the same I feel quite stunned. It hardly seems worth while to have children . . ."

This was the longest letter Pen ever remembered having received from Rose, and she did not think she would be able to write anything very comforting in reply. But the memory of Fenella's romantic dallyings made her feel deeply sympathetic to Rose's situation, though she would not for one moment allow that the young Fenella could ever have behaved as Audrey was doing. She took up the letter, and after her habit, these days, took the problem to Charles, who listened while the letter was read aloud to him and then said, "Of course your brother's right. There's nothing to be done. A woman of Audrey's age is not to be restrained. Do you imagine she's in love with this man?"

"I dare say she'd call it that—they all do. But it all boils down to the fact that, as Larry says, she's determined to find a husband at all costs."

"And the man?"

"Don't ask me. I've never seen him. He wouldn't have a chance with a girl like Audrey. She's both ruthless and unscrupulous. Probably he was an ordinary decent husband and father until the war loosened the bonds and threw the hungry Audrey across his path. A case, I should say, of Larry's 'silly fifties', plus the pursuing and relentless Audrey. The worst part of it—though Rose doesn't mention this—is that the wife has shown her so many kindnesses. Had her there for week-ends and all the rest of it, under the impression, doubtless, that she was the helpful colleague of her husband, and anxious to be kind to the daughter of Laurence Malling, R.A. Uprooted from a good home. Rather lonely, perhaps . . ."

"And all the time she nourished a viper in her breast. . . . Well, he must be a poor sort of creature to allow his wife to show hospitality to the woman who was his mistress. He deserves what's coming to him for that."

"It's strange, you know, what even a decent man is capable of in the hands of an unscrupulous woman."

"And now she slanders the wife who treated her with so much kindness and generosity."

"Yes. He mayn't know that, of course. It would serve them both

[183]

right if the wife stood firm. As I'd certainly do in her case. There ought to be a law which gives a wife the right to sue the interloper for alienation of her husband's affections, as there is in America."

"Well, there's certainly no law that can force a wife to divorce a husband if she doesn't choose to."

"Not yet," said Pen. "Maybe we shall come to it. Marriage is already heavily discounted and the law of the land compels us to do most things to-day. The totalitarian state in Russia made marriage look pretty silly."

"But it had to go back on its tracks. Even a totalitarian state would prefer legitimate to illegitimate children."

"Well," said Pen presently, "I think the most hopeful thing I can say to Rose is that the husband may change his mind and get out while the going's good. After all, at fifty a man does prefer the familiar and settled and may be a little alarmed (at least in the dark watches of the night) at the idea of starting life all over again with a wife young enough to produce offspring and clearly minded to do it."

"Then why contemplate asking his wife for a divorce?"

"You reckon without your Audrey. Trifling with her young affections . . . the gentle art of seduction . . . restitution and what have you. (No man, of course, would like to admit that *he's* been seduced!) However, what will happen if there's no divorce?"

"Clearly an alternative to your picture—which is, none the less, the same picture. Man in the fifties saddled with woman *not* his wife but minded none the less, as you say, to produce progeny. . . . By the way, it never struck me that Audrey was the maternal type."

"She isn't. But if the production of a child is a way of catching a man it's also a way of holding him. A man who's left one woman may leave another, you know."

"You think there's really a chance that the major may back out?"

"I don't know. It's just my guess. But I fancy he'd like to. However, I hesitate to raise poor Rose's hopes too high."

"That's a new adjective for Rose, isn't it?"

"Poor? Why yes, I suppose it is. Rose has always been so cushioned with comfort and happiness. Even during her first unsatisfactory marriage one never thought her an object of pity. Obviously her lamentable Edward was soon going to die—and Rose had a lot of time left. Not that any of us imputed that view of it to Rose. She earned the admiration of everyone for her behaviour. But for the last thirty years she's been the member of the family Fortune smiled upon most warmly. She was the little beaver that had warmly lined her nest, the little lizard sunning itself on a warm and sunny wall. You might occasionally feel annoyed enough with her to want to push her off it. But you never stopped being fond—and even a little envious—of her."

"And now she's just 'poor Rose!'"

"No, not really. She's terribly out of her depth after so many years of happiness. If she weren't a Catholic I feel she'd be less unhappy, even though she'd still disapprove—but she'd probably do what so many others do. Rely on eventual marriage making everything right . . . and upon other scandals for the gossips, and upon Time. But these are the consolations of those outside her Church."

"It's a pity, just now, that David is taking this job in Canada."

"But Canada, like most other places nowadays, lies almost on one's doorstep. When we're allowed to get ourselves about the world again without let or hindrance she'll be able to visit him. And I expect he'll find a nice Canadian girl to marry who'll give her the grandchildren she wants, who will all have arrived in the right way. I'm a good prophet in this department—witness Danny and his Livvy. . . ."

She went away and wrote as consolingly and as hopefully as possible to Rose, but as she folded up her letter it was not of Rose and her problem that she thought, but of Fenella now happily recovering from the birth of her son. Impossible to believe that she had ever indulged in romantic posturings over a married man, from which the war had rescued them all! If only Audrey's major were the same kind of romantic philanderer! But nothing in Rose's letter had suggested that. Larry's phrase, "the silly fifties", probably correctly described him. And how *very* silly they could be!

And as for Emmy, I'd like to wring her neck, she thought, remembering her aiding and abetting of the young romantic Fenella and the pleasing interview she'd had with her when she'd had the exquisite satisfaction of saying what she had always wanted to say to her. To do this to Rose, who at all times, in season and out, had defended Emmy from the family critics!

Chapter Three

THE WEATHER in February was so bad that Charles made his three days at the office run consecutively and stayed at his club, coming down on the Friday evening. Left alone Pen wrote steadily at the last chapters of her book and felt that she was really living in Charles's beleaguered city, so cut off did she feel from him and the busy hub of life. But though her writing profited, she was glad when toward the end of the month the temperature rose a few degrees, and when the next day dawned warm and sunny after a night unvisited by frost —the first for over a fortnight—she put away her work and telephoned to her brother's house in Chelsea. Her promised visit to Rose was a duty still to be performed, and though she did not look forward to the occasion she well understood how hardly she was taking Audrey's departure to her irregular new life, and her assertion that she must have someone to talk to about it, and that Larry was worse than useless.

She did indeed feel sorry for Rose, though she could not go down with her to the uttermost deeps of despair, agreeing as she did with Charles and Larry that Audrey was a young woman approaching middle-age and that one could not for so long take responsibility for one's children. This was an unhappy situation which could not be helped, and must be faced and endured with what courage one could muster. But she was acutely aware that Rose did not believe she would be taking this attitude if Audrey were her daughter. Having no hope—and indeed no way—of convincing her to the contrary, Pen felt that, on the whole, she would be of little more comfort to Rose than was Larry.

However, her visit, she decided, feeling an arrant coward, need not be of long duration. It was Thursday, and after lunch at Chelsea she proposed to go on to Richmond, where she hoped to make the acquaintance of her new grandson and hear Gaby's account of her visit at Christmas to her mother's. She would spend the night at Richmond, go up in time the next morning for some shopping and lunch with Charles and with him catch the first possible train back home.

Having arranged this time-table on the telephone she set out, and arriving at Chelsea found her sister-in-law at exactly the spot at which she had been in her letter on the matter—blaming herself for Audrey's behaviour and still convinced that she was suffering for her marriage to an unbeliever—and the persistence of this attitude, it was clear, was not exactly helping the situation, since the word-chary Larry was moved to protest at this extension of the theory of punishment and rewards. Carefully refraining from taking her brother's side, she felt that it was unthinkable that Audrey's bad behaviour should have the effect of disintegrating a marriage which, for all Rose said about it now, had been a very happy one. Larry could at least find relief in his work, but Rose had no such avenue of escape. Her whole life had been her marriage and motherhood and both were failing her. Even David's forthcoming departure to Canada, she clearly felt, was but part of her punishment.

Conscious of her helplessness before this unarguable state of mind, Pen contrived at last to detach Rose from her theme, and presently was moved to suggest that she should go out to Richmond with her. It might do her good, she thought, to see the small Harry. But Rose could not bring herself to make the effort. And Pen did not press it. For all her sympathy with Rose she was, beyond doubt, heavy going, and she was not sorry to say good-bye. Apart from her desire to see Harry and her mother, and to hear the family news, she was aware that she wanted a private chat with Bridget. For when at last Rose had ceased to speak of her woe, she had briefly become again the Family Chatterbox and said that at Christmas, when she was still on terms with Emmy, that Snake in the Grass—as she now thought of her—had looked in upon them and announced that she had seen Bridget two or three times in the company of the same young man. On the last occasion face to face in the Kensington High Street, and Bridget had had, of course, to introduce him. Rose couldn't remember the name but she thought it began with a D.

"Mr. Dercham, perhaps," Pen suggested.

"Yes, that was it. Have you met him?"

"Bridget brought him down to see us one Sunday—her own version was that he offered to run her down in his car, as he admired my poor works and wanted to meet me. Charles and I liked him very much. He is a junior partner in the firm which published her book."

At this Rose appeared to grow quite her old self and said, "Oh!" in a very meaning way, to which Pen rejoined that a friendship between a woman author and her publisher did not always—in fact, very seldom—mean what Rose seemed to suppose. She added that

Charles had thought him attracted to Bridget, but that neither of them had any evidence at all that Bridget thought of him otherwise than as her publisher.

Rose said that the Snake in the Grass had said he was a very pleasant and personable young man, and with this Pen readily agreed. Whereupon Rose's brief return to normal petered out.

As she made her way to Richmond Pen decided to try to find out how far this friendship had progressed, if at all. But she did not expect Bridget to be very forthcoming on the subject—she would probably laugh and tell her she was grown sentimental in her old age; and perhaps she was. All the same, she must know whatever there was to know, since Rose and the precious Emmy appeared to know so much more.

Gaby, who opened the door of the old house to her, said that she would find Fenella upstairs with the baby—Serena and Rebecca had gone to a party. They went upstairs together and Gaby opened the door of the nursery, put her head inside to say, "Here's our visitor, Fenny," and departed. Fenella was seated in a low chair beside the fire, with a sketching book on her knee and her son in his cradle on the rug. A charming interior, Pen thought. Bundling the sketching block on to the table, Fenella rose, kissed her mother and said had she had a frightful journey and that she must be frozen. It did not take long for Pen to decide that the new arrival was all that a baby should be at so early a stage of his existence and that his mother had made her usual quick and complete recovery. Fenella, indeed, proved to be in excellent spirits, very pleased with her son, with herself, and considerably less depressed by the weather and the turbulent world than most other people Pen knew. "What's the use?" she asked. "We can't do anything about it—we might as well enjoy our lives as much as we can as long as we can." And to this Pen could find no cavilling reply, since for all she worried considerably now about the parlous state of the world and had done so for many years, she remembered how at Fenella's age she had felt about it much as she did, though the interest she had taken in international affairs was sharp and keen.

"Glen grumbles, of course, about the state of trade," Fenella went on, opening the Cozy stove and ensconcing her mother in the low chair before it, "and about the shortage of paper and about income-tax and the Government and all the rest of it. But then people always do grumble about all governments and Glen's really rather bored by politics and seems to feel about politicians much as you do, darling.

All the same, he doesn't get unduly bothered. Too busy, perhaps. And there's still a lot of life that politics don't touch."

Warming her hands at the Cozy, of grateful memory, Pen said, "Oh?" and that she hadn't noticed it; that the political finger seemed to be in every pie at the moment. However, it wasn't to discuss the political situation or the state of the world that she had risked limb if not life to get to Richmond. So she steered the conversation along the domestic and family channel which presently brought her past the little girls at their party and the elusive Gaby to Bridget.

Fenella said, "Oh, Brid's all right—why?" Mr. Dereham? Oh yes, he came to Richmond sometimes—not lately, though, because of the weather. She supposed Brid saw him in town a good deal, professionally anyway. Yes, they did go out together sometimes she knew. Again, why? Oh, *Rose!*—well, she always knew a good deal more about everything than there really was to know. She didn't think there was anything in it, though it wasn't easy to tell with Brid. "She gets kind of distant if you suggest the slightest thing. You know her way of removing herself about a thousand miles by the simple act of uttering a couple of words."

Yes, Pen did. She said, as she had said to Rose and to herself many times, "Charles and I rather liked him when Bridget brought him down in the autumn. Or rather, according to Bridget, when *he* brought *her*. We were sorry, whichever way it was, that it didn't happen again. Charles, of course, has met him occasionally in the course of business, but he was glad to improve the acquaintance. And if I may mention something I've been very careful not to suggest to Bridget, Charles rather thought he liked her 'more than somewhat' as I expect you'd express it."

Fenella laughed and said, "He may do—at least, he may have done once. I'm not in their confidence—I only go by what I see and hear. He's been here a few times . . . and he doesn't strike me as the sort of young man who'll for long cast his pearls before swine, so to speak. And I shouldn't say that Brid is the sort of girl to keep a man hanging around if she doesn't mean to have him."

"But those meetings in town?"

"Well, you should know, darling—you used to make quite a habit of lunching and dining with *your* publisher, if you remember. Rose and the rest remarked it, of course—but you'd have been mightily indignant, wouldn't you, if anyone had checked up on you and suggested there was 'anything in it!' And, in any case, where Brid's concerned, I don't suppose there've been anything like as many occasions as Emmy has made out to Rose. What an incubus she is for any family to have to put up with! Though if it weren't for Rose—and Doreen—I don't suppose we'd ever hear what she says."

Pen was of the same opinion. The conversation shifted away from Bridget and also from the family. Fenella's world, these days, had narrowed remarkably and yet was full of so much more than of old. Pen suspected that it contained, actually, only her husband and children, though the gates opened occasionally to take in briefly herself and Charles, Bridget and Dwight. Gaby was an inmate too, but one Fenella took for granted. She'd miss her if she went, and probably be less comfortable, but the gates would close again; her world would stand. Without Glen and the children it would fall to pieces. Pen regretted this but could do nothing about it. Luckily, she reflected, it was an attitude Glen did his best to correct. Nobody but Glen would have detached her sufficiently from the delightful business of being Mrs. Glen Westcott, and the mother of Serena, Rebecca and Harry, to participate in Bridget's literary experiments. From nobody else would she have taken so much correction, as an artist, or derived so much benefit. No one else would have dared to call her, where her drawing was concerned, a 'lazy slut'. From Glen she took it as the most delightful of compliments. . . .

"Who is fetching the children from the party?" Pen inquired. "Gaby?"

"*No*, darling, our faithful retainer, Berta. She's very good with them and it isn't far—they've gone to the Rowledges, new since your departure. They've a perfectly enormous family and pots of money, apparently, judging by the number of parties they give. Becky isn't really old enough for parties—at least, I don't think so (said Becky's mother, who used to think that one was never too young for a party!). But she loves them, and Serena, if she were anybody *but* Serena, would howl with fury if Becky wasn't allowed to go with her. They're an inseparable pair. A conspiracy, so Glen says. However, to the party they have gone and on account of Becky's extreme youth Berta will collect them both at five o'clock precisely. So, if you want a *tête-à-tête* with Gaby—and I'm sure you do—I suggest you go and rescue her now from the kitchen. It's my turn to do nursery-maid this evening . . . so I'll get Berta to bring me up a cup of tea and see you after I've got the children to bed. Meantime, you can have a heart-to-heart talk with Gaby."

That young woman was run to earth, as Fenella had suggested, in the kitchen, wrestling with the recalcitrant boiler which, fed on everything it liked least (like its owners, perhaps!), only consented to survive at all if it was raked free of dust every half hour, thus devolving an unpleasant duty upon the race of domestic "helps" and "dailies" which they preferred not to remember. Even the "faithful retainer" did not here, it seemed, come up to scratch. It smote Pen's sense of the ridiculous that Gaby, who even in these impoverished days was a very comfortably-off young woman, should be found at this menial job; still more it tore at her heart-strings to consider to what her affection for them all had brought her. Ever since she was eighteen and through school and matriculation, she thought, Gaby has been slaving in this house; in the first place, after Bar's death, in my dear Winfarthing's day, more pleasurably it's true, as my secretary; but with the coming of the war and Winny's death, as nothing less than a general factotum. She knew Gaby would remind her that Fenella, regenerated by her marriage, had more than done her share; but there had been years of the lazy sluttish Doreen, and even when she had gone there had been quite a family to cater for— Fenny, Glen and their children and Bridget. Gaby was still considerably on her conscience. It seemed to her she had had no life at all. If only Ward Findon had returned from the war and dragged her off to a home of her own. . . . If only she'd fallen in love and married again. . . . Anything rather than this!

But Gaby laughed at her face of horror. Since electricity was "off" for so many hours a day, she said equably, the stove must be encouraged to work with the appalling fuel that was all the home consumer apparently was likely to get.

"If they send this unscreened stuff abroad," she said, "our credit must be pretty low."

"Well, leave it to its own devices," Pen told her, "and come and sit down. It's ages since I saw you. I want a chat with you. Now don't tell me you have to lay tea or cut bread and marge or something."

Gaby laughed and said it was all done and led the way to the sitting-room, where a fire was burning, well banked up with logs, and with the electric kettle, its bronze face very bright and welcoming, standing at the side of the wide hearth awaiting the moment when the electricity would be restored to a long-suffering public. The room looked charming, Pen thought, and well-kept, the furniture, with which she had lived for so many years, well polished, flowers as ever in the wall vase, chairs and settee drawn hospitably to the fire, and the set tea-table offering its silent eternally-consoling welcome.

Pen walked to the french window and stood for a moment looking out at the snowy garden, at the naked willow and beyond to the river, moving slowly past, like molten steel. How cold and dismal it looks, she thought, and found herself for some reason remembering that January night—how many years ago?—when Charles had taken her to see the first "talkie" and Bar had been dining out with his father and brought him back, as usual on such occasions, for the night, which was a bitterly cold one. She had gone to the door when she heard the car arrive and had watched James coming up to the house, his shoulders hunched against the Arctic wind. He had followed her into the house and as she turned now from the window she could see him coming into the room, rubbing his gloved hands together, his handsome face blue with the cold. And he'd told her about some other equally Arctic winter of which she remembered nothing, for when it raged she'd been a little girl of seven. Happy, indulged, carefree.

"Let's shut it all out, shall we?" she said to Gaby. "I must be getting old, for I begin to dislike the cold—or perhaps it's only the cold in this horrid austerity world. And I used to think I could never live without seeing the river whenever I looked out of the window. But now I begin to feel that way about Butser and the climbing fields between the wooded slopes of Stoner and Wheatham, and I don't miss the river at all."

Gaby looked back at her as she stood drawing the curtains, and thought how lightly the years lay upon her. "Sit down and get warm," she said. "You must have been frozen on the journey. How do you think Fenny looks?"

"As one who lives in Paradise, not in this cruel untidy world at all. Having a baby seems to improve her looks. And I thought Harry rather a successful effort, too."

"So do we all. It's very endearing of Fenny to give us such good-tempered babies. Harry's as amiable as his sisters."

"Yes, that's a great help. I'm sorry the girls aren't coming down to tea. Fenny says she's nursery-maid to-day."

"It's only because she thinks we want a *tête-à-tête*."

"So we do. So do I, certainly. But I hope Berta will bring the children in to see me when they come from the party."

"Yes, I've arranged that. I expect Fenny's given you all the news."

"Not a great deal. She seemed to think what I needed was a chat with you. And so I do. It's ages since we met. With Fenny's business and the weather it was inevitable, I suppose."

"It wasn't Fenny—her nurse was admirable and Fenny was so obliging as to have no complications at all. But with this weather, Petersfield might as well have been the Antipodes."

"It let up for Christmas, but you were in Paris. Did you have a good time? I want to hear all the news."

"Mother's news, chiefly. We lived in a very political atmosphere, as you may guess. Mother really does seem to have been intrepid during the war. I wonder she's alive to tell the tale. And now she's a de Gaullist. She says de Gaulle's the only person who can save France from the Communists."

"I dare say. I wish I knew what could save Europe from them." Gaby laughed.

"I expect mother could tell you. She thinks we're all much too tolerant of them here. She'd suppress them vigorously—all in the interests of freedom, of course."

"I'm not sure she wouldn't be right, since they abuse freedom in order to have power to deprive everyone else of theirs. However, we won't go down that road. These political ideologies are a curse. I want to know what's been happening to you. Did your family try to persuade you to go back?"

"Oh, no, they've given me up. Even though the stock of the British rose considerably with mother during the war, she can still not understand why I should prefer to live in England." She glanced at the clock and switched on the electric kettle. "Four o'clock. Thank goodness!—now we can have some tea."

"I sometimes wish you *didn't* like to live here," said Pen, looking at her niece as she sat back upon her heels before the fire, and thinking how like her mother she was, as she remembered her when Gaby was a little girl and she was telling them all so angrily that they were too kind to their late mutual enemy and that in the next war they'd be on her side, maybe. . . . And yet, though Gaby had Yvette's small neat face and pale skin and the same long dark eyes, she had none of her French vivacity; her hands lay quiescent upon her lap when she talked, guiltless of Yvette's dismissing and deprecating movements with hers. She had her father's English ways and his way of speaking. She could hear again his amused voice talking about "Latin excitability" which "meant nothing". David, who'd loved France and married a daughter of France and in the end had died for her. . . .

"What makes you wish that?" Gaby asked her now.

"Because I begin to think your mother's right and that we've taken up altogether too much of your life here. I often wish you'd been able, as you wanted, to get back to Paris on the eve of the war."

A little cloud came over Gaby's serenity of expression. She said, "It wasn't any of you I wanted to get away from."

"I know, but it would have meant that, too—and that would

[193]

have been a good thing for you. You'd have had some life of your own then."

Gaby smiled.

"But I shouldn't have liked Paris so much, you know, with the Germans tramping all over it. And I was glad—afterwards—that I had to stay here. It would have been cowardly to have run away. . . . And you're quite wrong to say I've had no life of my own here."

That brief time with Richie, the birth (and death) of her child. . . .

"But *since*! . . . Ever since Ward went to the Far East you've slaved here for me and my family."

"How you do exaggerate, Aunt Pen!"

"No. It's true. . . . You ought to have left us and had a home of your own. And children. I hate to see you using up all your maternal energy on other people's children, even when they're my own."

"But this *is* my home. What's more, my offer to buy the house from you when you like still holds."

"It would be a poor bargain, I'm afraid. James was sure it would fall down upon us years ago—do you remember his name for it? —Tumbling House—but by some miracle it still stands."

"It could be made to last my lifetime if certain things were done to it. I've made all inquiries and I could afford it."

Pen laughed.

"By the time you got permission to do them you'd be grey-headed. Besides, you couldn't live here alone, when Glen and Fenny go off to Hereford Square. Even with a couple of maids, which you could never get anyway, you'd find it rather a warren."

"You forget Bridget."

"Supposing she wants to live in town, or . . . gets married?"

There was a little pause before Gaby said, "She says she doesn't mean to marry."

"She can't be serious."

"She assures me she is."

"We must await Mr. Right. I must say I did hope his name was Dereham. . . . Charles, I'm sure, was of the opinion that Mr. Dereham hoped so, too. He thought he was very much attracted."

"Oh yes, he was. Very much so. But Bridget, I gather, refused him."

"But Fenny says he still comes here."

"He did before the winter got going. He's a very sensible person."

"Sensible? I don't call that at all sensible."

"Isn't it sensible not to cut off your nose to spite your face? Even if Bridget won't marry him she still meets him in the way of business, and she's still an author of his—his own special 'find'. There's a new book under way, you know, only at the moment Fenny's too occupied to be very co-operative."

"You mean, Mr. Dereham has given up entirely?"

"If he hasn't he hides it very successfully. I told you he's sensible—and no sensible man bludgeons a woman into accepting him."

A little colour stained the clear pallor of Gaby's face as she spoke. She switched off the kettle and made the tea. Was she thinking of Richie? Pen wondered. For herself, she thought he should have knocked her over the head and carried her off to church or the registrar's office. But, always *laissez-faire*, he didn't, and but for the war her refusal might have stood; but given the war, only a fool, or somebody like Richie, whose forte was clearly not marriage, could have allowed it to do so. Without the war Gaby would have withstood him, as she withstood marriage; but, with Richie engaged in so hazardous a section of it, in a world of war, she never had a chance against him. Dead though he was, Pen still held that a little to his discredit. Even though he'd died too soon, before he knew about the child. She said, "I don't think anyone could make Bridget do anything she'd made up her mind she wouldn't do." She could understand well enough that she might not care enough for Robert Dereham to want to marry him. Such matters were beyond argument. But that she should have set her face against marrying *anyone* did a little defeat her. "Do you think Bridget's unhappy?" she asked.

"No." Gaby hesitated. "But the war, of course, altered Bridget."

"It must have altered a lot of people. In what way do you think it altered Bridget?"

"I don't know exactly," said Gaby, stirring her tea. "She was only seventeen when it began, of course. She seemed then to take it for granted, as most of us did, and she was disappointed at having to come back from France. But that wasn't it. . . . It began later, after she'd given up her work at London University and gone to the War Office. Perhaps something happened to upset her. I don't know. She never said anything, but I think she hated the war from then on . . . or, rather, not *the* war but just War. That's only my guess, though."

"Well, we *all* hate war. . . . What has that to do with Bridget's ban on marriage? Do you think there was someone she was fond of who was killed?"

"I've no idea. I may be all wrong. . . . Do eat something."

As she thoughtfully took a scone, Pen said, "You know, Gaby,

Bridget worked very hard during the war, carrying on her university course as well as doing a job. If she hated it—more and differently, I mean, than the rest of us—it didn't appear."

"No. But then, even if you hate war you may still think that it must be won, once started. Particularly this war, which most of us believe our politicians could have prevented. After all, as you said at the time, much as one hates war one hates slavery more. I'm sure Bridget felt that way too."

"Well," said Pen, "I've heard this suggestion before, from Charles, but it didn't lead him as far as it seems to have led you. And I'm sorry about Mr. Dereham, even if I can't take this business of Bridget never marrying very seriously. Apart from my own approval of him I think he and Bridget have a good deal in common. It ought to have been a very suitable match."

Thoughtfully sipping her tea, Gaby said, "You say Charles thought Mr. Dereham was very attracted to Bridget. What about *her*? Did either of you think she was attracted to Mr. Dereham?"

"We couldn't judge. Bridget didn't mean us to know anything—until, as we supposed, she'd quite made up her mind. She scoffed at my curiosity when she announced that he was bringing her down one Sunday in the autumn, and gave an excellent impression of a young modern making use of an obliging young man with a car. And there was the book, of course. That made an excellent cover for all things. What impression did you get?"

"Much the same, I think."

"And where are we now?"

Gaby was silent for a moment and a little, Pen thought, embarrassed, as if she did not like to be discussing Bridget's affairs. Yet how often, in her youth, Gaby had played sleuth for her over Fenny's sentimental (but very frightening) youthful attachments. Gaby had been much more useful to her there than Bridget, who, when tactfully questioned about Fenella's latest infatuation, always said, "Don't worry, mummy. You know Fenny's *always* romantic about men."

"Or don't you know, perhaps?" Pen asked Gaby now. "The tea's delicious. Can I have another cup?"

As she poured it out, Gaby said, "Yes, tea remains a comfort, and I've managed to get some quite presentable 'blended' China, which is very useful on one's milkless days. We're very scrupulous here about not drinking the children's milk, though Becky would love us to help her out with hers. I never met a child who so disliked milk. And it's almost impossible to get her to drink it hot."

"She takes after Bridget. We had endless trouble with her about

[196]

hot milk." Having dealt with this red herring, Pen said, "Well? . . . *Do* you know what stage Bridget's affairs have arrived at?"

"I don't know any more than I've told you, I'm afraid. That Bridget says she doesn't mean to get married and that it looks as though Mr. Dereham has accepted the situation."

"But what I can't get over is that he still comes here! I should have thought that most unwise. If it's business, he doesn't need to come all the way to Richmond to see Bridget, surely?"

"No," said Gaby, the colour staining her face again, "of course not."

"Curiouser and curiouser," said Pen, stirring her tea. But she perceived that Gaby was now most certainly embarrassed by her persistence and began to talk of other matters. Poor Rose and her troubles; Audrey and her fine romance; David's departure to Canada; Danny's approaching return from America; Lydia's comments upon her stay in Germany; whether Meg would or would not marry her George, until Gaby said, "What about your book? Is it nearly finished? I hope you're going to let me type it for you?"

The tinkle of children's voices in the hall, the little laugh gaily ascending the scale that was Becky's, broke in upon their conversation. The door opened and in they came, making a gay splash of colour in their bright coats—Serena's red, Becky's green, their hands juggling with the jerking strings of balloons, packages of all kinds hugged to their small bodies and dropping from them as they came forward to greet their grandmother. Their little faces were flushed and warm, their eyes bright with the cold air and the afternoon's excitement, though Serena's habitual placidity had not entirely forsaken her. Yes, it had been a lovely party, they assured her—there'd been jellies and a large iced cake and chocolates and some funny things they couldn't remember the name of. Long things, with a skin you peeled off. Yellow—and white underneath, Serena said.

"Bananas, I expect," said Gaby. "We tried them out on you both several times when you were smaller, but you neglected them completely. Did you like them any better at the party?"

Serena shook her head. "Not very much," she said. But Becky said "they were all right, only funny . . ."

"We used to eat them, long years ago," said Pen, "with cream."

"Oh . . . what you see on the top of the milk," Becky offered. Pen laughed.

"If you're very lucky," she said, wondering if she would ever see cream again and wondering for the thousandth time what became of it.

[197]

"Gaby always shakes the bottle," Serena commented.

Pen laughed again and reflected on the odd fact that that was all her little grand-daughters should know about cream in the year of grace 1947.

"Have you seen our baby brother?" Serena inquired.

"Indeed I have. I think he's lovely."

"Too small," said Becky firmly, "and he's hardly got any hair."

"He will have plenty soon," said Pen, unable to make the usual comment to such a remark, "neither, darling, did you have at his age," for Fenella's younger daughter had been born with her red-gold hair curling in her neck, and Serena's little head had been well if less noticeably covered. "We don't have bald babies in this family," Fenella had said, laughing.

"I hope you've both behaved nicely," said Gaby, "and haven't eaten too much."

"No, oh no," said Serena, but Becky's laugh ran up the scale again and she said, "I ate an awful lot . . . I couldn't eat a single thing more. I'm full right up to here"—and she put her hand just below her little rounded chin. "Aunt Gaby, I *needn't* drink my milk to-night, need I?"

"I'm sure you don't need it, but your mother won't agree with us, I'm afraid," said Gaby.

"But I shall be sick if I have to drink it."

"You'd better not be or it'll be no more parties for you," said Gaby laughing. "Did you have some nice games?"

They proceeded to tell all about them until Gaby, pointing to the clock, said, "Well, a good time was had by all, it seems. And now I'm afraid you must run upstairs or mummy will be thinking you've not kept your word and left the party early."

"It was horrid having to come away *first*," said Becky.

"Bosh!—it ought to have made you feel like the Queen of England. Nobody may leave a party until she has left, you know."

Serena solemnly considered this piece of information but Becky said, "If *I* were the queen I should stay right to the end 'cos nobody could tell me I mustn't."

"You'd be very unpopular," said Gaby. "All the poor guests dropping with fatigue and simply longing for you to go."

Serena said to her sister, "There wouldn't *be* any end till you went, silly. I mean, if you were the Queen of England."

This was such a Bridget-like remark that Pen was instantly transported back through Time to the days of that young woman's early childhood, and when she emerged Gaby had gathered up the small packages which had been dropped on chairs and on to the floor and was exhorting the sisters to say good-night and run along upstairs.

"Will you come and see me when I'm asleep?" Becky asked Pen. "Would you like that?"

"Oh yes . . . Promise. I shall know if you don't."

Serena smiled. "How?" she asked.

"Now, don't start an argument," said Gaby. "Kiss your grandmother and run along. . . ."

This they did and the room seemed suddenly empty, and a little forlorn, shorn of their young voices and bright clothes, the little sparkling cascade of Becky's laughter.

"A terribly argumentative pair," said Gaby, laughing. "But they're very good friends. I can't remember a quarrel between them. It wouldn't, of course, be easy to quarrel with Serena. No child ever more thoroughly deserved her name. I hope Becky won't deserve hers. All Beckys, to me, are incipient baggages. Thanks to *Vanity Fair*."

"Oh, but it's a charming name," Pen said. "And amoral though Thackeray's Becky was, she was considerably better company than the exemplary Amelia."

"I dare say. But *our* Becky's an outrageous little flirt, you know. At five, if you please! She must take after Cousin Andra, who made eyes at the men before she could talk. Or so your father used to say."

"Well, we shall see," said Pen, who didn't remember her Cousin Andra as a child. Andra was seventeen and on the verge of her youthful marriage when she was born. But Andra had been a lively entertaining creature, and for all the sorrow it brought her, had enjoyed life to the end of her days.

Pen could see no change in Bridget when she came in that evening. She was delighted to see her mother and handed her a bouquet for her hardihood in making the journey in the middle of such an appalling winter; and clearly it had not occurred to her that she and her affairs had played any part in her decision to do this. If she had got as far as Chelsea, Richmond was not likely to prove an impossible objective, especially with a new grandson at journey's end. She talked with her usual ease and freedom of the work she was doing and of the new children's book which she was writing in her "lighter moments", and for which she hoped soon to be able to enlist a little interest from Fenella, much too much above herself with satisfaction at having produced a son to be able to put pencil to paper, though why, she added, she should be so set up about having produced a man child goodness alone knew.

"Well," said Fenella, "I've got two of the other sort already. When you send me some of the book I'll see what I can do for you."

Glen arrived in time to open a bottle of sherry and to sit chatting with his mother-in-law while Gaby and Fenella repaired to the kitchen to wrestle with the last stages of the evening meal, and Bridget went upstairs to change her frock. He was delighted to see her, told her he wished she came more often and, though no novel-reader, asked politely after her book.

"Here's to you!" he said, raising his glass.

"And to Harry!" she said. "How many children, if one may inquire, do you and Fenny intend to have?"

"Fen has decided upon equality in numbers as between the sexes." Pen laughed.

"That may take you a long way."

"I hope it will take us no further than four," said Glen, "though Fen's good at her special job, and doesn't make heavy weather of it."

"Yes," said Pen. "Have you quite decided upon taking over the Hereford Square house when Gilbert and Lydia go?"

"Yes, we'd both like it very much. Fen's quite set on the idea—can hardly wait until the poor Hamptons set sail. But I hope I shan't have to buy—at present prices. What will you do with this place? Gaby talks of buying it. We'd gladly take her to Hereford Square, but she's got some idea about not wanting to live anywhere else than here."

"I've told her she can't live here alone. But she says there'll be Bridget."

"For a time, yes. . . . But that young woman has some idea of removing herself to Paris as soon as things improve there. Her firm's forming some alliance with a French house—and of course she'd be just the person, talking the lingo, as she does, like a native."

"That is news to me. Gaby didn't mention it."

"She probably doesn't know. Brid mentioned it to me—all very secret—when we were discussing this house business. Don't give me away—I oughtn't to have mentioned it. I dare say she'll tell you herself."

"Gaby should certainly be told when the question of the sale of the house really comes up. She says Bridget told her she doesn't mean to get married, so I dare say she's counting on her continuing to live here with her. I really don't like the idea of her living here alone."

"Well, maybe she won't for long. After all, how old is Gaby?

[200]

Thirty-one, isn't it? Why shouldn't she get married again? I suppose there's no doubt her husband *is* dead?"

"No reasonable doubt, certainly."

"Well, there you are. She'd be a bargain for any man—attractive, a first-rate housekeeper and cook, and highly intelligent withal."

"I should very much like to see her happily married. I've as good as told her so. But she never goes anywhere to meet young men—she's just buried here. I wish she'd come to Wyngates—we do at least have a little social life, in normal weather."

Glen grinned.

"Oh, we see people occasionally, too, you know. You'd be surprised. At one time, we saw quite a lot of young Dereham. But the weather's kept him away lately—and everyone else too. You're our first visitor for weeks. You deserve a medal."

"Are you sure it's the weather which keeps him away—and not Bridget?"

"Bridget?"

"Well, I understand he asked her to marry him and she refused."

"Oh, yes . . . I believe that did take place. But it's ancient history. He's quite got over that."

"He couldn't have been very much in love."

"No—to tell you the truth, I don't think he was . . . for long," said Glen and grinned cheerfully at her again.

"I wish I could get to the bottom of this business," said Pen. "What may I ask, are you implying?"

"Nothing, oh nothing."

"I'm not to be put off, Glen."

"Well, you know, Brid's a very definite young woman. If she says 'no' she means 'no' and young Dereham's aware of it. . . . The fact is, Brid's got some bee in her bonnet about marriage and Dereham's not the man to tackle it. But one day she'll meet someone who'll sweep her off her feet, buzzing bee and all. You needn't worry."

"I'm not so much worried as mystified. All this is most unexpected from Bridget. And not in the least like her."

"Well, you'd better tackle her yourself. She may be moved to give you her confidence. We don't expect it . . . and aren't used to it, anyway."

"But Gaby knows—something."

Glen laughed.

"Yes," he said, and added again, "you'd be surprised."

For the first time in her life Pen felt exasperated by this son-in-law of hers. But clearly whatever it was he and Gaby knew, it was nothing, in Glen's opinion at least, that she need worry about. All the same, she hated mysteries and determined to get to the bottom of this one before she slept that night. It was all too ridiculous. Her exasperation, however, was short-lived, incontinently beheaded by the apparition of Berta in the doorway, neatly clad in a black dress and cap and apron, enunciating with the careful diction of the nervous, "Dinner is served . . . if you please."

Soon after eleven, having given her time to get into bed, Pen tapped at Bridget's door and was told to come in. As she had expected, she found her younger daughter reading and if she was surprised at all by this visit no sign of it appeared in her face, voice or manner, as she looked up from her book and said, "Put on the fire again. Austerity or not. I've only just turned it out, but the room's cold already."

Pen turned down the switch and seated herself in the armchair beside the glowing bar.

"I'm sorry to interrupt your reading," she said, "but I wanted a little talk with you."

"Go ahead," said Bridget obligingly, but as Pen remained silent she said, "It's about Bob Dereham, I expect, isn't it?"

"We might as well begin there, if there's anything you'd like to tell me. I don't want to bombard you with questions. But I've heard all sorts of rumours and, this afternoon, some more definite statements. I find it all a little confusing."

"It isn't really. Bob Dereham asked me to marry him toward the end of last year. I refused him."

"For the usual reason?"

"Partly. I'm not in love with him. I like him very much as a friend. We've a lot in common and I dare say we'd have made a success of it if we'd married, but, you see, I never mean to marry anyone."

"Yes, I've heard that, too."

"From Gaby?"

"And from Glen. He doesn't take it very seriously, but Gaby, I thought, did."

"I'm perfectly serious."

"Would you very much dislike telling me why?"

"Not in the least. I won't get married because I don't mean to have any children."

"But you're so fond of children."

"I know. That's why. I simply won't have children in the sort of world we have to-day, and, it would appear, are going to have for many years to come. I won't bring children into this world to be blown to pieces or maimed by the atomic bomb or to take part in World War Three. That's all there is to it."

After a little pause, Pen said, "Well, your Aunt Caro will be pleased with you. After the War to End War she was saying the same sort of thing. If I had listened to her you would never have been born. Don't you think that would have been a pity?"

"For whom, darling?"

"For me, certainly. And don't you enjoy being alive?"

"That's the sort of question I always find it so difficult to answer. No, on balance, I think I find life more interesting than enjoyable. But I don't think that has much to do with what we're talking about. It really wouldn't have mattered at all whether I was born or not. I happened because you wanted another child. I don't bear you any grudge for that—but it didn't really matter to anybody but you and father. I'm not important enough to matter one way or the other. And in any case when I was born there seemed, I fancy, to be more hope for the world than there is to-day. At any rate nobody had thought of the atomic bomb."

"Aren't you, perhaps, trying to shoulder all the misfortunes of the world? One is here, after all, for better or worse. And how do you know that it won't be for better?"

"I don't see any signs of it. Do you?"

"At the moment, no. But I am still far from embracing your creed of utter despair. If everyone took your point of view and behaved accordingly the human race would perish from the earth."

"Or call a halt, perhaps, in its headlong rush to the abyss. If it doesn't, then it deserves to perish. But you need have no fear. Everyone *won't* take my point of view. People will go on having children because they want them and even if they don't, without scruple and certainly with no thought of their fate in the world."

"You know," said Pen, "I can't help feeling that something must have happened to awaken this mood in you."

"It isn't a mood, it's a very deep conviction. But I think the bombing of Hiroshima confirmed it—that was an outrage. We're not all like Ray, needing some personal tragedy to make us realise how stupid as well as abominable war is. For me it isn't just the deaths of so many of those nice young men who used to come here so much before the war—most of them Fenny's friends but some of them Dwight's too—not even the deaths in our own family, Richie,

[203]

Ward Findon and Maurice Romaine. Though Maurice's death enraged me. All that talent thrown away!—and Leah's too, in consequence. But it's more than that. I think it's chiefly the idiocy of war and the waste of it, what it does to human life, reducing it to no more than a tale told by an idiot."

She paused, but Pen said nothing. Whatever it was that Bridget felt, she wanted to hear it, and it was unlikely she would ever again surprise her in this mood of candour and confidence. After a little she went on.

"Take a look at the world to-day, darling. National bankruptcy, the savings of the thrifty swallowed up in the cost of the war and the crippling taxes of peace. Victors and vanquished alike ruined. And everyone feeling everywhere that they have no protection against war, that even those politicians who hate it most are powerless to prevent its recurrence. The sovereign state's still with us; the national spirit rampant—fighting still in many parts of the world, ideologically inspired. Totalitarianism. Even here in England more than a touch of it, with everything controlled, incentive crushed, ambition stamped down. The lowest common denominator setting the standard. The State supreme. The State, the State, the State—how I loathe the very word! It just isn't good enough! I for one won't, in order to gratify my natural instincts, produce fodder for fresh wars. And I hear people talking calmly every day, everywhere, of the Third World War as if they were talking of the coming of Christmas! Men make the wars and expect women to redress the population balance. Why should we oblige them? I want a world of stability, in which war has been outlawed, before I'll even think of marrying and having children. The world to-day isn't fit to live in."

No, thought Pen, and yet and yet. . . . Her love of life, her ever-springing optimism would not let her take Bridget's point of view. She said, "My dear child!—has there ever been such a world? There have been wars innumerable."

"Not of our magnitude. Not mass murder from the skies. And not this perpetual threat of further wars and worse horrors to come. One of our politicians said smugly the other day that no war 'was expected before 1954.' "

"Did he say with whom or between what countries?"

"No. I dare say he meant between Russia and America. It's unlikely that even in six years' time any country in Europe will be in a position to make war on one of its neighbours. But Europe would be dragged in—that's certain. You've only to consider Russia's

European annexations and the countries in Europe she dominates politically."

"Well, perhaps the prophecy will be proved false. After all, wars aren't inevitable. Most of us believe that the last one could have been prevented."

"Well, it wasn't. And what use has it been? It hasn't even destroyed the dictators, and now the Russian instead of the German brand of ideology is making a bid for world domination. And Russia's aims are wider than those of Hitler. She means to destroy the democracies and is creating a fifth column everywhere to help her do it. And the appeasers are still with us and very vociferous."

"There are other voices, if quieter ones. And don't you overlook, perhaps, the many efforts that are being made to break the tyranny of the sovereign state, which is the real villain of the piece?"

"No, but I don't believe in miracles. The federation of Europe won't stop Russia, who is the most powerful sovereign state, with America, to-day. Far from shedding any of her prerogatives, she means to become the World State."

"I think you are altogether too pessimistic, my child."

"Do you? Well, it's how I feel about things, and I've quite made up my mind that to help in the business of carrying on the human race under present conditions is a responsibility I don't care to shoulder. You know, mother, to me that does seem reasonable."

Reasonable. Yes, Bridget was always reasonable. Her position now was logical enough, but it seemed a little de-humanised. Yet Charles had said, hadn't he? much the same thing—that perhaps if he could have had his time over again he would have had no children, that he doubted if his sons would thank him, could they now speak, for the boon of life. What happened then to this miracle of living which so beset herself? Did neither Charles nor Bridget believe in it? Think it worth while? There was a little silence before she said: "Supposing you had fallen in love with Mr. Dereham? Would you still have refused him?"

"Yes, I think so, though it would have been more difficult and rather painful. But I hadn't fallen in love with him—I don't think I shall ever do that with anyone; I need, I fancy, rather to *grow* into love. I might have done that with Bob, but that I shall never know now. Anyway, we didn't talk very much about love—at least, not with a capital letter. He just asked me to marry him. We were perfectly frank with each other. I made my attitude quite clear and he made it equally so that he wanted the normal things of marriage. So that was that. We resumed our usual relationship—met occasionally

[205]

over business matters, lunched together once or twice and behaved like rational human beings. And I'm glad to say that he has now chosen a much more suitable wife elsewhere."

"Already?"

Bridget laughed at her mother's shocked countenance.

"As good as," she said. "You'd better hear about it, I think, but prepare for a surprise. I don't always, you know, go to the office on Saturdays and one such morning recently Bob rang me here about a matter of business which seemed to call for a little talking over, and as it was somewhat urgent I invited him to come along to tea here. We'd got fairly back to normal by this time, though I'd been avoiding him a little, I confess. He'd never been here before, and he met Gaby for the first time. The children were rather on tap, too, that afternoon, for Glen had taken Fenny out for a drive. And there you have it!"

"Have what?"

"The whole situation. You must please realise, darling, that Bob Dereham wasn't in love with me. We liked each other, we had a good deal in common and got on well together. The rest, I fancy, was just propinquity. Having reached the middle thirties without ever having fallen in love perhaps he thought the state mythical. However, there was Gaby with the children—the perfect domestic picture, and it was obvious to the meanest intelligence that he was quite bowled over."

"You mean he transferred his affections to Gaby?"

"I mean that he fell head over heels in love with her. At sight. And what is more, it would have happened even if I'd not been so appallingly frank and we'd become engaged. I'd never seen it happen before. Not there in front of my eyes. It really was an experience."

"And Gaby?"

"She was terribly embarrassed, poor darling. Still is. But she'd fallen for him, too, I could see—but much against her will, because of me. I had a lot of hard work to put in on her before I made her understand that I was out of it altogether and that Bob Dereham didn't mean a thing to me in that way. I think now that the next time he proposes to her she'll accept him. It's a very suitable match, don't you think? Gaby thirty-one to my twenty-five—and Bob thirty-four. And Gaby intelligent, booky—and wealthy. Not that Bob knew about the money. That worried him quite a lot at first."

"You leave me speechless!" said Pen, to whom, however, certain things which had puzzled her during her talk with Gaby now became very clear. She was torn between regret and concern over Bridget's attitude to marriage and pleasure that Gaby's life was going to follow the lines she had so long felt it should.

"Well, that's just as well," said Bridget, "as it's nearly one o'clock in the morning. Don't say anything to Gaby, please. Just watch the Engagement Column of *The Times*."

Pen rose, leaned over and kissed her daughter good-night, then, still silent, walked to the door. There, however, speech returned to her and she said, "I ought to tell you that Glen thinks this idea of yours is just a bee buzzing in your bonnet."

"You don't have to tell me—I've heard it dozens of times."

". . . and that some day you'll meet a man who'll sweep you off your feet."

Bridget smiled at her from her pillows.

"You never can tell," she said. "Good-night, darling. And don't stop awake thinking about me and my buzzing bee . . . I'm all right, I assure you."

But whatever her mother did, she herself stayed awake until the early hours of the morning, feeling that at twenty-five she had given up life or torn out its heart. But perhaps her tears were overdue and certainly they did not shake her resolution. If she wanted children all that much, she told herself, there were thousands of people who hadn't wanted theirs at all, and had thereby created for a harassed world a fine complex problem. I must take after Cousin Vicky, she thought. Or even Florence Nightingale, if I want to flatter myself. I dare say my strong urge to maternity would have ended by my being a shocking scourge to any family I might have had. Much better it should stretch beyond the boundaries of the merely personal.

Upon which consoling thought she fell asleep.

Chapter Four

IT WAS the first day of April, and a day so warm and sunny that the recent arctic days seemed to belong already to some other existence, when Doreen went to tea with Emmy Gaywood. It was some months since they had met, the severe winter having interfered with what had become a relationship of some intimacy. It was difficult to see what the bond was between them, unless it were dislike of "the family". Certainly Doreen found it of unending interest to listen to Emmy's version of ancient family history, not as Fryn would have done because she found everything concerning the family of the greatest interest, but because it amused her to hear talk so scandalous and malicious. It never occurred to her that Emmy, though entertaining and amusing, did not keep a strict regard for truth, and she would not have cared if it had. Nor did she know that truth told *with bad intent* (and wrong emphasis) *beats all the lies you can invent.*

Inevitably that sunny afternoon the conversation moved eventually to Danny, though Doreen had tried to keep it away from him. Now that Livvy was home, her father dead at last, Emmy supposed airily that Doreen would not see so much of him.

"I haven't seen him for weeks," Doreen told her, with well-simulated unconcern. "His mother's death has kept him at home, of course."

"Of course," Emmy agreed, not oblivious of the fact that Doreen made no comment upon Livvy's return. The death of her sister Cathy a month ago had taken Emmy, for the first time in years, to Bourne Manor, for Cathy had been the only member of the family with whom she was on any terms since her attitude to Audrey's escapade had alienated Cathy's daughter, Rose. She had sniffed at the air of Christian forbearance with which Rose had greeted her at her mother's funeral, but she had made no mistake. Rose and Larry's pleasant home in Chelsea was closed to her for ever. She regretted this but not her attitude to Audrey's romance. Audrey, of course, must be allowed her chance of happiness. People ought not to interfere. She had seen Livvy, too, and reported now to Doreen that she had seemed distinctly under the weather. Quite plain and "peaky-looking".

"Of all the odd marriages," she said, "that seems to me one of the oddest. Livvy's not at all the sort of woman you'd have expected Danny to want for keeps. She's smart, of course, and well turned out, even in these days, but she's so prim and starchy. She positively carries Boston about with her. But of course Danny always meant to marry money—and if he used to know how to make it he knew, even better, how to lose it. Livvy keeps a tight hand on hers—and of course she *runs* Bourne. Danny has simply no responsibilities at all. Well, that's one way of keeping a man, I suppose. All the same, I wonder she's cared to leave him so often and for so long. I suppose she's so sure of herself she just can't imagine him getting into mischief in her absence."

"Do you think he does?" asked Doreen, stubbing out her cigarette and keeping her eyes fixed upon the operation.

"How should *I* know?" said Emmy. "But I must say I can't help wondering why Danny took that furnished suite in that awful warren in town instead of staying at his Club."

Doreen said, carefully, "I think he found his Club a little stodgy. And Corridon House was comfortable and convenient."

"Oh, very convenient, I'm sure," said Emmy, with her tinkling unkind laugh.

"I mean," said Doreen, "he could take it for short periods, one week, or two or three. And everything was done for him and there was a good restaurant. He said he liked it because it was impersonal."

"Meaning, no questions asked. Yes, most convenient."

Doreen was a little puzzled. Was Emmy trying to discover if she had visited Danny at Corridon House—or did she know? That she and Danny met for lunch when he was in town had been known to her as long ago as the Greystones days, and she'd kept her word and told Danny to take her to the flat to tea afterwards.

"Did you ever lunch there with Danny?" Emmy asked suddenly.

"No—he always took me out. He knows a lot of lovely places. And he says the restaurant at Corridon House is always uncomfortably packed—and the tables too close together."

"So you never saw the place?"

"Oh, I used to call there for Danny sometimes when we were lunching together and he hadn't settled where we were going."

"But you never actually went up to his rooms? Not even for tea?"

"No," said Doreen, with firmness. It was a lie but she was used to telling lies by now and managed them well.

"Wise girl!" said Emmy. "You can't be too careful with Danny. I'm very fond of him, of course—he's such a relief from our stuffy

[209]

family. But all the same, he's a bad lad!" (Again the little tinkle of laughter.) "I wonder Dwight allows you to be friends with him."

"Oh, Dwight doesn't mind in the least. I mean, he'd rather I went out with a relative of his—even a distant one—than with someone he doesn't know at all. He used to be very jealous when I went to an occasional hospital dance in our early days."

Emmy laughed.

"People make the oddest marriages," she said. "You know, you ought to have married one of Danny's sort, and Dwight would have got on excellently with Livvy. Or with that girl of Lydia's— Fryn ; isn't that her silly name?"

"Oh, I don't know," said Doreen, though she looked a little startled. "Fryn's only eighteen and an awful kid for her age. And, if you ask me, Dwight didn't ought to have married anyone. He's not the marrying sort."

"He's rather a prig, of course. . . . How are the Spanish lessons getting on? Does the pupil progress?"

"I really don't know. I dare say."

"Why does Dwight want to be learning Spanish?" said Emmy. "It isn't as though he's a clerk."

"Oh, he seems to like learning languages. He takes after the rest of his family, I suppose. They all speak French as well as they do English."

"Oh, French, yes, that's a very different matter. My Uncle Ninian took his family to France when they were of school age, so that they all learned French easily enough. And, bi-lingual herself, Pen of course saw to it that her children are too. Then there's the French connection by her brother's marriage. David—the one who was killed in the first war. Gaby's father. But who would want to learn Spanish? You'd better look out, or you'll have Dwight falling in love with his young instructress."

"If he did," said Doreen, "it wouldn't make any difference. Dwight's not that sort."

"Well, queerer things have happened. What about Gaby sneaking Bridget's young man? I suppose you were at the wedding?"

"Yes," said Doreen, "but I didn't know he was ever Bridget's young man. He was a business acquaintance and her publisher, too."

"Well, she went around with him a good deal. I met them several times. And your charming mother-in-law went around with *her* publisher for years. Nothing in it, of course, but she married him two years after the death of his wife, all the same."

"I think you must be wrong about Bridget. She looked all right to me at the wedding. I mean, she didn't look as though she minded in the least."

Emmy smiled.

"I hear Gaby's buying the Richmond house from Pen, and that they intend when they come home to live there with Fenella and her family until they can get into Lydia's house. What's Bridget doing? She can't mean to go on living there."

"She's gone to Wyngates until she can find a flat in town."

"I suppose," said Emmy, "that Gaby's husband is really dead?"

"The War Office must have known when they sent her that letter."

"Presumed dead, yes. Ah, well, I dare say she got tired at last of slaving for Pen's brood. Worth taking a chance. Amusing, all the same, if he turns up," she added kindly.

Not being very interested in Gaby's wedding and not believing the story about her having stolen Bridget's young man, Doreen changed the conversation by asking after Audrey. Was the divorce going through?

"I've no idea. I've not seen her lately, and of course Rose and I are scarcely on speaking terms. Not my fault, I assure you. I was always very fond of Rose, for all she's such an addle-pate."

"Why aren't you on speaking terms?"

"I said 'scarcely', my child. Rose is always polite—she'd consider it un-Christian as well as the height of bad form to cut anyone. But she thinks I've encouraged the affair with Audrey and her major, which I certainly haven't. It didn't need encouraging, as far as Audrey was concerned—she takes after her Uncle Danny. (Audrey's *uncle*! How old that made him seem, thought Doreen.) Rose, of course, wants to impose *her* standards on everyone else, and she doesn't, I fear, move with the times, poor darling. She can't see that if Audrey and her major are in love they have a right to their happiness. She looked very miserable, I thought, at poor Cathy's funeral. And years older."

Doreen felt that at the funeral of her mother (of whom she was very fond) Rose had perhaps *felt* miserable, quite apart from her anxiety over Audrey, but this she did not say to Emmy. She said instead, "I'm sorry for Rose. She has always been very nice to me."

"She wouldn't be," said Emmy laughing, "if she knew you were meeting her brother in his wife's absence. Of course I haven't given you away."

"There hasn't been any secret about it," said Doreen. "If Dwight doesn't mind, why should Danny's sister?" But again she wondered how much Emmy knew (who seemed to know everything!). She had the sort of mind that ferreted things out—and prompted her to think the worst.

The "worst"?

Doreen pondered the word on her way home. She couldn't bring herself to apply it to her new exciting relationship with Danny, though she had never intended it to happen. Neither would it have done if she hadn't fallen in love with him. She had always thought the state "soppy" and had never expected to fall into it. But she had, and the rest had followed. She had been quite unable to put up any further resistance to his blandishments and attraction. She'd had no compunction about deceiving Dwight, since he so utterly neglected her as a wife, and in Danny's company always felt herself justified. That he was married did not worry her very much, either, for since Livvy was content to go away for months on end she found it hard to believe that she cared much about her husband. It must be his position, his title and Bourne that she cared for. Danny never discussed his wife with her, scarcely ever mentioned her, except to say she was away or coming home, but he had somehow managed to leave with her the impression that he, too, felt neglected and in need of consolation. Besides, he'd given her no peace—no peace at all. No woman, he said, had ever attracted him more than she did—or as much. Which was it?—she couldn't remember. When he made love to her she could think of nothing else. It left her helpless, and transported. Yet she thought, as she rode home on her bus, that, but for Danny's having taken the rooms in what Emmy called "that warren", she would still have been able to hold out against him.

Well, she hadn't, and she was glad of it, for during his stay in town during the arctic winter, she had been happy. Happy and satisfied, for Danny was not only a practised and skilful lover, he had used arguments which had fallen like good seed on fertile soil. One was only young once; and Danny, no longer in his first youth, had used the phrase, she knew, to persuade her that she was entitled to take what she wanted while hers endured. Everyone, he said, was entitled to Love. . . . But she had not expected to miss him quite so much, when his mother's death and Livvy's return had kept him down at Bourne. She had hoped, going this afternoon to see Emmy, to learn something of his movements, if there was any chance of his coming to town again. But she'd drawn a blank. She felt, however, that Danny would know how to find opportunities for their meeting again. Livvy hadn't always been in America when he came to town for short stays. It was nearly a month since his mother was buried. It seemed years. . . .

It was a mistake to fall in love. Heaven knew it wasn't what she had intended, but she'd known it was dangerous. She had never felt with Dwight as she did with Danny. It had been fun when she had first known Dwight, thrilling when he'd said he loved her and asked her to marry him. But she'd never loved or been in love with him, or with any other man. She hadn't disliked his love-making; she was normal, thank God. It was marriage she'd found irksome, until James had left them that money. Things had been pleasant enough then. She'd had a lovely house to live in and servants to run it for her, and the money to buy herself nice clothes—and the necessary coupons. It had all been very satisfactory until Dwight had gone all Puritanic because she didn't want any more children. . . . In a way, what had happened was his fault, though she hadn't thought of that side of it much, except as a justification for her falling in love elsewhere. . . . And scarcely at all since yielding to it. Everyone was entitled to Love. . . . She was made for love. The arguments were compelling, and she was an apt pupil. . . .

But now, as she rode home, she wondered how she was going to bear it if this was the end. Yet remembering her last afternoon with Danny she could not believe this possible. Emmy, she thought, had meant her to believe that Livvy's return would put paid to Danny's jaunts to town. All the same, she told herself again, though he had not been able to make month-long stays except in Livvy's absence, he had certainly come frequently to town. Emmy had probably only been "talking", trying to find out if there was "anything in it" and hoping to see her reaction. But I didn't give the show away, she thought, aware for the first time that if Emmy could be so mischievous and malicious in her talk about others, she was not above doing it about her if and where the opportunity occurred.

If you came to think of it, of no one they'd mentioned this afternoon had Emmy's comment not been full of hints. That Danny's marriage to Livvy was scarcely a success, that he was kept to her by reason of her money (which she herself would very much like to believe!); that Danny was a hardened philanderer; that Dwight liked Fryn too much, and that the Spanish lessons were only an excuse for further meetings; that Gaby had taken Bridget's young man (a plain statement this, not a hint); that her mother-in-law had been in love with Charles Anstruther all those years. . . .

No, this afternoon Emmy, though entertaining enough, had shown her claws. She had clearly wanted to know a good deal more about herself and Danny. All those questions about whether or not she'd visited him at Corridon House. . . . She was really quite a nasty old woman. She'd give her a miss for a bit. No sense in "starting" anything.

It was a week later as she came in from taking Barry to school, the telephone was ringing. She picked up the receiver to hear a familiar voice say softly, "Doreen? Know who it is? . . . Right first time. Well, when am I going to see you again?"

She said, "Do you want to?"

"You bet your life . . ."

"Where are you?"

"At the Corridon. I'm up for a week on business over probate of my mother's will. When can you lunch? To-day? To-morrow?"

"I don't know." Some instinct bade her not to jump at the invitation. "Won't you be very busy?"

"Not *too* busy. . . . To-day shall we say?"

"No. . . . I'll try to manage to-morrow. I'll ring you if I can't."

"Of course you can manage it. Meet me in the entrance hall at twelve o'clock. I'll book a table at your favourite restaurant. Don't be late. . . . Love me still?"

She did not reply to that. But a small secret smile came upon her face as she said good-bye and hung up.

On a hot evening toward the end of May Dwight travelled home in the packed Underground, oppressed, as ever, by the sight of humanity *en masse* and dispirited by a tiresome day at the office. Work there was slack and time hung heavily upon his hands, but recently he had enjoyed the designing of a small house a few miles out of London for a client who had obtained a licence to build. But now the hindrances seemed unending. He did not know, why these things should have depressed him so much to-day, since they were now the small coin of his days at the office, except perhaps that they seemed typical of the whole of his existence, at the office and at home. Everywhere frustration and a sense of life running to waste.

He wished it were his evening for his Spanish lesson. But that was two days ahead. Instead of Fryn, interested, serious and much bent on keeping him to the business in hand, he would spend the evening with Doreen, bored, dumb, and, the last few weeks, decidedly in the dumps. Nor would she understand that the hot journey fatigued him unutterably, for she seldom travelled on the Underground and did not loathe the hot weather, as he did. But Barry grew fractious in it and Doreen's handling of him did not improve his state or make for peace in the home. Indeed, nothing less like a home could he conceive of than the Battersea flat; the atmosphere of a home was quite beyond Doreen's powers to evoke. He wilted at the thought of the long years ahead of him with this lovely idle brainless creature, longed sometimes that she would grow as tired of him as he was of her; felt indeed that she already had, but that she stayed with him because he represented security and a refuge from the world in which she would be required to earn a living. And yet for some little while now he had had a feeling that there was someone else for Doreen in the offing; had even, to his disgust, played with the idea that she might leave him for another man. But the last few weeks something seemed to have gone wrong, if one might judge by her unusual snappiness and moods of silent gloom. Once she had asked him if he would divorce her if she were unfaithful to him. A hypothetical question he had called it, but now he wondered. He might, he'd said, if the other man could and would marry her—he could not envisage throwing even Doreen to the wolves. But now? . . . He abruptly snapped off his thoughts as he saw that he had reached his station, and rising pushed his way out of the crowded compartment.

In the street his mood was not improved by the size of the bus queue; but luck was with him. A taxi with its flag turned up came ambling along; he hailed it, got in, and with no further effort required of him and a refreshing current of air created by the two open windows, his spirits revived, so that on reaching the flat he greeted Doreen with an amiability of which he felt he would have been incapable a quarter of an hour ago.

And Doreen had a message for him which deepened his improved mood a hundred-fold. Lydia, it seemed, had phoned through to say that she had tried to telephone him at the office but found he had already left; whereupon she had got through to Doreen. Would she ask Dwight if he could manage to come along that evening for his Spanish lesson, instead of on the usual evening, as they were then dining with the Romaines. She had meant to suggest that he should go straight on from the office to Hereford Square and have a meal with them beforehand, but she realised that that would not now be possible. This, said Doreen to her husband, was a pity, for she had had no luck that morning with the shops and she was afraid there was only a very scrap meal. He would have had a better dinner at Lydia's.

There being only one comment upon this remark, and that not likely to please Doreen, Dwight said he had little appetite, and uncomplainingly ate the meagre rasher and fried tomatoes she set before him. Doreen was not in a talkative mood, and he thought she looked off colour, but as when he had recently remarked upon this unusual fact she had snapped his head off he was content now to register it without comment. Remembering Lydia's standing invitation to Doreen to go along to Hereford Square with Dwight whenever she felt inclined, he asked her now if she would like to accompany him, but she said that Lydia had asked her that and she had declined. She had rather a headache and thought she would go to bed early. And in any case she'd let Mrs. Mann go before Lydia had telephoned.

Dwight accepted this decision with a relief he was at small pains to dissemble.

His attention that evening wandered a little from lesson to teacher, and later he made her repeat some piece of explanation which he had perfectly grasped for the mere pleasure of emptying his mind of all thought but of her. It gave him a pleasure, sharp as a physical pain, just to look at her.

"Cousin Dwight," she remonstrated, "I don't believe you've taken in a word of that!"

He laughed.

"Oh, yes, I've quite grasped the point, thank you. . . . Why, I wonder, do you call me 'Cousin Dwight' when you are feeling particularly pedagogic?"

"I'm not feeling particularly pedagogic. I'm a very bad teacher. And you *are* my cousin, aren't you? To be exact, my first cousin once removed."

"Do we have to be as exact as all that? Besides, I prefer to think of myself as your second cousin."

"But you're not. Danny is your second cousin—the child of your mother's first cousin."

"How very depressing. Don't go on. I'd much rather think of Danny as no relation at all."

"How absurd you are! Do let us go back to the lesson. I think you ought to translate that passage again from the beginning."

"I will," he said, "if it will give you any pleasure," but as Fryn bent her head over the text-book, he murmured softly, "*And bright o'er Europe fell her golden hair.*"

Recognising the quotation, she said, "My hair's not golden and this isn't a globe of the world but a Spanish grammar. I don't think you're at all in the mood for a lesson this evening. You are really being very absurd. Perhaps we had better stop."

"Stop being absurd?"

"Can you? I meant stop the lesson."

"Why not? Our hour's nearly up. Let's talk."

"Oh, no. You must finish translating."

"Don't be so stern. We hardly ever have a chance to talk."

"What nonsense!—we talked for an hour before we began the lesson, and shall talk for at least another before you have to go."

"I meant, to each other."

The way they'd done, he meant, as he thought she knew, when he'd taken her home after her maths lessons at the flat. Did she know how he felt about her? He had no way of telling and could never persuade himself that she felt the same way about him. She liked him, yes; she liked his company, she liked to talk to him; but he did not believe she knew anything whatever about love. Which was just as well, since there was nothing to be done about the situation. He was married and she, twelve years younger than he was in actual years, was emotionally still a child. Also, she was his cousin, even though, as she so precisely put it, once removed. His Aunt Caro, in the dark backward and abysm of time that was pre-first war, had married her first cousin and Rose his Uncle Larry, whose degree of cousinship was precisely that between himself and Fryn, but it was no longer a habit smiled upon, either by society or family, so that even had he been free and Fryn as much in love with him as he now knew himself to be with her, any idea of their marriage would be distinctly unpopular. Certainly with Gilbert Hampton, whose views on the question were well known to him. But since it was out of the question, it wasn't marriage which was in Dwight's mind where Fryn was concerned. He wanted her presence and companionship and the very thought of the South Atlantic rolling between them made all his life look like a desert. Frustrated in his deepest emotions, he wanted the immense consolation of friendship with this child and did not stay to consider how precarious for her would have been a prolonged friendship with a married man. For he could not believe that he would ever leave Doreen. Not only because of Barry but because of herself. He should never have married her and the wrong he had done her by that act would hold him to her as long as she wished to stay with him. Some day she might leave him for another man, but failing that, so long as she could have her diversions, she would prefer life with him to life on her own. He was keenly aware that in imposing his version of married life upon her he was both cruel and unjust, the more so as he had made her believe he did it from an idealistic (and Puritanic?) motive, whereas he had long ago come to understand that but for his feeling for Fryn he would not have done it.

Physically faithful, he knew himself spiritually unfaithful. But there was nothing to do about it, no road back, as long as Fryn stayed. And gone? He did not explore that thought, for in an empty world what could anything matter?

He was a little stunned to realise how deeply this friendship with his young cousin had cut into his life, since they had begun to meet alone for her mathematical lessons. How sweet they had been, and innocent, continuing for him something which had begun for him that Sunday morning at Greystones a year ago, when she'd come with Meg and Bridget and they had all climbed Toys Hill, to sit down and talk and stare across the open Weald. Much as he was profiting from the Spanish lessons, he knew them for the excuse they were for getting her for yet another spell to himself. Not even the sense of guilt which oppressed him, rooted in his knowledge that they should never have been begun, could make him sorry he had suggested them. As he closed the Spanish grammar and gathered up his corrected papers, he stood looking down at her with a little smile. But for some reason Fryn flushed and looked away. Five minutes yet before their hour was finished, but she rose, not looking at him as she said, "Mother will tell me that I have given you very short measure."

"It wouldn't be true," said Dwight. "You give me, always, very full measure indeed."

She pushed her chair up neatly against the table and smiled at him, the flush gone from her face, leaving her very pale. Without replying to his remark she moved to the door and not waiting for him to open it for her, performed that office for herself and walked away.

Chapter Five

WHEN NEXT she heard Danny's voice on the telephone Doreen felt quite sick with relief.

"Doreen?" it said, in the soft tones she knew meant that he was speaking from his club. "I'm in town for a week. Can we lunch? When? To-morrow? Lovely. . . . Call for me at the Corridon, twelve o'clock. Don't be late."

It was nearly three months since Doreen had seen him and to the sense of emptiness that had dwelt with her for the first few days of that time had soon been added a frightening frantic anxiety which had now settled down to a desperate sickening certainty, for all she had avoided corroboration of her state. She didn't need to: she knew. Her misery, twofold at first—consternation at the position she found herself in and abject fear of the event that awaited her—was an engulfing sea in which, over and over again, she drowned. Only the little word "unless" had sustained what courage she had managed to dredge up from the depths of her despair during the last eight weeks. Unless—what? Sometimes it seemed only an empty meaningless word; sometimes, remembering Danny's protestations and remembering particularly that week when he came to town over his mother's will, she thought she had nothing, after all, to worry about, that perhaps this occurrence was less unfortunate, though no less terrifying, than at other times she believed it to be. It might be worth while going through with it if it meant release from her present existence, the entry into another that was shot through with all the barred colours of the rainbow. To-day, however, as she put down the telephone, the old delight at the mere prospect of seeing Danny again was crossed and recrossed by the knowledge that the familiar delights would not to-morrow belong to their hours together, but only the shock of the knowledge she was taking with her and must somehow find words to clothe. And words were not her strong suit.

She wondered how she would get through the lunch; what she could possibly find to talk about until the opportunity came to talk about the only thing that now occupied her thoughts. And suppose there was no opportunity? Suppose, as sometimes happened, their lunch together was just an interval between Danny's other engagements or his business appointments? Or suppose there was a film he wanted to see? . . . But that, at least, was unlikely, for it was so long since they had met that Danny would be sure to want to make love to her. Her common sense, which for so long had kept their association on a safe footing, told her (had told her for the past eight weeks!) that she had been a fool. Oh, if only she had not fallen in love! But she had, and so deeply that she had seemed to have no existence apart from Danny and his love-making. He was in love with her, too. How could she doubt it? He had used the phrase so often, delighting her heart, bewitching her senses, breaking down her last feeble resistances. But neither of them had ever directly referred to the fact that each was married. She, during her time with him, had clean forgotten it. Did he ever remember it? she wondered. Were the things at which Emmy had hinted really true?—that he had married Livvy for money and that it was money which sustained the marriage—so odd a one, Emmy had said. And though she blamed Dwight's neglect of her as a wife for what had happened, she knew that even if her life with him had been normal she would have betrayed him for Danny. That was the only clear piece of thinking of which she had perhaps ever been capable. For from the first she had acknowledged his fascination for her, known the friendship as "dangerous". In the end it was inevitable that he should sweep away all her caution, cut her adrift from her conviction that a girl was a fool to chance landing herself in a mess.

But she could not imagine how the "mess" had happened, for even her love for Danny had not altered her fear of child-bearing. It was love with which she had been concerned, the physical satisfactions to which, so Danny had so often contended, everyone was entitled. Love with a capital letter, which consumed the lovely creatures of her cinema world, which she knew she had never felt for any man until Danny had come into her life. Oh, God! she thought, why did this have to happen? Her fine world of romance seemed to be crashing about her; she prevented it only by remembering those hours of stolen delight, which she now opposed, as a bulwark, against her sudden sense of utter ruin and despair.

That evening, as she knew, Dwight was going to Hereford Square for a Spanish lesson, and she decided that she would go too, if Mrs. Mann was willing to come and sit in the flat, in case Barry should wake and find himself alone. Fighting her instinct to do no such thing but to betake herself to bed directly Dwight had left the house, she walked into the kitchen and asked her if she were free to come back that evening. She was, and almost at once Doreen regretted having asked her. But as the day wore on she thought that anything would be better than staying here alone with her thoughts and fears. Meg would probably be at home and at least she was good company, with her chatter of the gay times she had at the house of the Romaines, the plays and films she had been to see. Meg was human, not just brainy and booky, like her sister and so many of this family of her in-laws. And Lydia was kind and friendly, and even the young Jeremy, though he was not much given to talking. She thought him a solid sensible sort of boy, with none of Barry's nerves and tantrums, even if he did catch colds and every kind of minor ailment. These afflictions, Lydia said, he bore stoically, merely hoping that nobody would notice them. Yes, the Hampton family would take her mind off her own situation and she ceased to regret her hasty arrangement with Mrs. Mann.

She did not think, when she mentioned her decision to him, that Dwight greeted it with any marked enthusiasm; but enthusiasm was not a quality she any longer associated with anything he did or said. She knew that, quite apart from their relationship (which she thought, for all his good manners, he found as boring as she did), he was depressed by the state of his profession. There was nothing doing in his world, he said, and that he was gloomy about its future she had gathered from the conversations she'd listened to in his mother's house and at Lydia's. However, he said in his usual polite fashion that he was sure Lydia would be glad to see her if she felt like going, adding, "You seem a little under the weather lately—a change of scene may do you good." He helped her to wash up, then sat down with the evening paper until she was ready, which meant until Mrs. Mann put in an appearance. She was rather late, and the evening too hot for haste, so on the Embankment they picked up a taxi in which they sat in almost unbroken silence throughout the short journey.

Doreen's thoughts were troubled and elsewhere, and Dwight so looked forward to this fugitive hour each week in Fryn's company that, without knowing it, he a little resented his wife's occasional intrusions into the charmed circle at Hereford Square. If Fryn were for him the centre of it, it was also true that he found Lydia's house an attractive place, a genuine home, such as he had never known with Doreen. Somehow it seemed essentially right that this house where his mother's happy childhood and girlhood had been spent, and where he and his sisters had lived through so many happy days as young visitors, should now offer him the only domestic atmosphere in which he felt at peace and relaxed. And latterly there had been those honey-sweet hours with Fryn and a Spanish grammar. . . .

Thinking these thoughts he had almost forgotten Doreen's presence at his side until she said faintly, "How hot it is!"

He turned in surprise, for Doreen thrived on the heat, and saw that she was so pale her careful make-up stood out on her face like a clown's mask. He reached over and put the window on her side right down. "Stifling!" he said. "Aren't you feeling well? Would you prefer to go home? The taxi can drop me and take you straight back."

"No, I'm all right. It just came over me how hot it is in here."

"You look very pale. Are you sure you're all right?"

"Yes, quite," she said, a note of impatience in her voice. "Don't fuss."

Nevertheless, when they arrived at their destination she looked so limp, for all her natural colour had crept back beneath her make-up, that he asked her again if she wouldn't prefer to go back. But she shook her head and said that she had quite recovered, that it was only the heat, and that it would be cooler in the house. It was, but Lydia, greeting her, said, "Even you, my dear, seem to be feeling the heat this evening."

"Yes," said Dwight, "I thought in the taxi she was going to faint. I wanted her to go back in it."

"Oh no, she'll be better here than in the hot flat." (All flats were 'hot' to Lydia.) "We'll find you a cool drink. Go in and sit down. . . . Meg, get the ice, darling, and see where Fryn's got to."

Doreen, who now felt quite recovered, felt also quite terrified. Would Lydia guess? . . . make some revealing comment to Dwight? Oh, what a fool she had been to come! However, she went in and sat down in Lydia's pleasant drawing-room and finding herself alone quickly opened her hand-bag and taking out her looking-glass, examined her face with an anxious eye. She certainly looked rather "washed-up", though she was feeling almost normal again; and terror rose in her like a tide at the thought of what, either way, was in store for her. Remembering her hospital experience, she felt suddenly a little sick. She hastily put the glass away as the door opened and Lydia came hurrying in, followed by Meg. Casting a sharp glance at Doreen, she said, "Put up your feet. You'd better have a drink. Go and get the brandy, Meg."

"Oh no, please don't bother," Doreen protested, keeping her feet where they were. "I've quite recovered, and it's nice and cool in here." She wanted to say, "For God's sake, take no notice, leave me alone," and she quailed inwardly before Lydia's considering gaze. But she submitted to her attentions and heaved a little sigh of relief when she went away. And longed for the brandy, for though she had hated Lydia's obvious belief that she needed it as medicine she felt that it was the one thing which would pull her together mentally. Unusually abstemious for one of her generation, until she had met Danny, that gentleman had early taught her to realise how many inhibitions, how much misgiving and boredom, vanished beneath the magic spell of good drink.

The door opened again and Dwight came in with Fryn. They were looking at each other and laughing and the sense of their shared happiness struck her like a blow in the face. Though she had often told Dwight that he should have married someone like Fryn, she had never before seen them together in this fashion and the blow was repeated when Dwight turned his head and saw her and the laughter ran out of his face as if he had been transported on the instant to a world where such happiness had no place. How heartless he was!—not following her into the room but leaving her to the attentions of his relatives while he went off to look for Fryn! And she thought this for all her knowledge that to have been followed into the room and have had him, as well as Lydia, fussing over and commenting upon her state was the very last thing she had wanted. She had not seen this Dwight who laughed and talked in the open doorway with Fryn, for many years, only the polite young man who made no bones about the fact that she bored and no longer attracted him. Oh, what a mess everything was! She'd seen in that instant that Dwight was as much in love with Fryn as she with Danny. And Fryn? She didn't know—she knew nothing about Fryn. But this evening there was something different about her. She looked less like a schoolgirl, more grown-up. If she were in love with Dwight she'd probably have the same high-falutin' ideas about marriage and divorce as Dwight had. Or would she? And what about Danny? Nothing high-falutin' about his ideas. And Livvy's? She had no faintest notion, but some part of her mind had absorbed—only too willingly!— Emmy's story of Danny's having married her for her money. But now she wondered if that were true. Nothing was certain; she trod on sand. If Fryn was really in love with Dwight there might for him be a way out. But for her? That she wouldn't know until to-morrow, and that was miles and miles away, and this desert of an evening to be crossed first.

"How are you feeling, Doreen?" Fryn asked, hurrying forward, and now Doreen saw what was different about her. She had put up

[223]

her hair. And how well it suited her! Doreen had never seen her look more attractive.

"Quite all right now," she said, "thank you. It was just the heat."

"Yes, it's been terribly hot. It never seems to cool off with this Double Summer Time."

The door opened and Meg came in with the drinks, and the brandy for Doreen. As she handed it to her, she said, "What do you think of Fryn's hair-do?"

Doreen said that it suited her.

"You should see it when she drags it on top of her head."

Fryn laughed.

"It's much cooler that way," she said. "I suffer the discomfort of this only because of Meg's susceptibilities. She says that the other style makes me look like a charwoman."

"Mine has a marvellous perm," said Doreen.

"I meant one of Mr. Belcher's charwomen," said Meg, still busy at the tray. "But I expect they're all dead by now."

Not knowing who Mr. Belcher was, this did not clear up the point for Doreen, who thought how often this family talked of people she'd never heard of and who must, she'd once supposed, be friends, but who usually turned out, she'd discovered, to be some writer or artist. She had learnt on these occasions not to betray her ignorance.

Dwight said, "I rather liked the Belcher touch. It showed the nape of the neck, which in young girls is very attractive."

Meg laughed, turning round from the tray to look up at him.

"Cousin Dwight!—do you really look at the napes of girls' necks? You do surprise me!"

It surprised Doreen, at any rate, to hear him say it, but she felt that what he really did was to look at Fryn's and find *that* attractive.

Dwight's laughter answered Meg's. She looked across at him and said, "What do you want, Dwight? Sir Short Supply has temporarily vacated these premises. So we can offer you gin and vermouth, sherry or ale. Also soft drinks in variety. Oh—and gin and ginger-beer."

Dwight plumped for ale and as she poured it out for him she said, "Of course Fryn ought to have a perm. It would have to be a very expensive one, I'm afraid, to get large loose waves. She'd look awful with a corrugated head."

"I think," said Dwight, taking his drink, "that Fryn should be allowed to enjoy the one distinction left in the feminine world."

"Meaning an unpermed head? . . . Well, I fancy Fryn agrees

[224]

with you—at the moment, anyway. And, in a way, of course, it makes her sort of distinguished."

"Who—or what—is distinguished, if you please?" asked Lydia, coming in.

"The unpermed Fryn," said Meg.

"Poor Fryn! Why can't you leave her head alone? In any case, she's too young to think of a 'perm'."

"Nineteen in September," observed Fryn, taking her glass of orangeade.

"Don't remind me," said Lydia. "You'll all be grown up and flown before I can look round—even Jeremy, who, by the way, ought to be home by now. I hope he hasn't got drowned."

"Unlikely," said Meg. "He's an excellent swimmer. Odd, I always think, for someone as physically lethargic as Jeremy to be so energetic in the water!"

"I won't have the word 'lethargic' applied to my son, thank you, Meg," Lydia protested.

"I'll say 'lazy', if you like that any better, darling. What are you going to drink?"

"Orangeade, perhaps. . . . Feeling better, Doreen?"

"Quite normal, thank you," Doreen told her.

"That's good. I asked Bridget to look in this evening. Unfortunately, she has an engagement. We much appreciate having her so near."

"It was a pity," said Doreen, who felt she must say something to show how completely insignificant her indisposition had been, "she had to leave Richmond. She liked it there."

"Oh, but not to have done so would have created the illusion of a 'situation'," Meg said, "and Bridget would have hated that. I mean, living in the same house with the young man everyone expected her, and not Gaby, to marry."

"Very stupid, if anyone did," commented her mother. "And in any case, my child, that's one of the things which might have been better expressed. You've forgotten Glen and Fenny and the children. They feel rather badly, Fenny says, about not being able to give Gaby possession of her own house."

"I don't suppose they do, really," said Meg. "Though of course Fenny's just longing for us to go and give them possession here—especially as Glen has had to buy the house."

"It's lovely to think there won't be strangers living here," said Fryn, "after we've all gone."

"When do you go?" asked Doreen.

It was Lydia who answered.

"As soon as we can get berths after Gil comes home—which I hope will be early in September."

Doreen wanted to ask if Meg was going also: no one ever talked about Meg and her young man, these days. Perhaps she'd given him up . . . or he'd given her up. Or couldn't she make up her mind, or could nothing be done until Gilbert came and O.K'd the young man? . . .

The arrival of the son of the house interrupted this family talk. Not because Jeremy had much to say, even about his swimming. Had he had a good time? Yes, spiffing. Was he hungry? He was, rather. All he said off his own bat was, "Is this a hot-water night?" and being told it was, said they could have it all—he was very clean after his swim. He had then gone off to eat his supper.

"What about the lesson?" said Dwight, who had dropped out of the conversation since it had begun to concern itself with the general departure of the family.

"Are you sure it isn't too hot?"

"Not for me."

"Very well," said Fryn, and led the way out of the room.

As she smoothed out the Spanish grammar Dwight asked her if she had quite given up her idea of staying on and working at the Clinic with Vicky and Leah for a year.

With her eyes on the grammar, Fryn said casually, "Oh, I don't know . . . I haven't thought very seriously about it, and mother rather frowns upon it. She says father will think it's only a rather poor excuse for staying on here when they all go."

"And you no longer want to stay on?" he asked her.

"I think I ought, perhaps, to find a better reason," she said.

Did he imagine it, or was her manner to him a little changed now that she found herself alone with him? When he'd arrived, out there with the others, she had been her usual delightful self. And she spoke as though she had quite given up all desire to remain in England, throwing over her last excuse quite casually. Well, her father would never have agreed to it. He wouldn't want any reason for having to come back to England, whether it was to see a married daughter or a daughter engaged in "slumming". They all knew he had had enough of Europe to last him for the rest of his life. Gilbert's attitude he could understand, but not Fryn's. It changed her into a wavering uncertain person, which he was sure she wasn't really. What was it made her speak now as if she were quite anxious to be gone? His heart leapt a little painfully in his breast as he pondered this thought. But

[226]

there it was. She would go, and nothing could stop it. And if it had to be, then the sooner the better.

"What about the lesson?" he said.

It was a relief to find that Danny had arranged for lunch to be served in his rooms. A relief, but no surprise. It had happened before when they had not met for some time.

The flat was cool but noisy and Doreen walked to the window and stood looking down at the surging traffic, thinking of the last time she had come here . . . and of what had happened because of it. But miserable though she felt, she was not immune from the familiar compulsion of the gesture with which Danny took her by the elbow and pulled her round to him.

"Not a bit glad to see me, are you?"

"Yes, of course I am. It's been such ages."

"I'll say it has!"

She yielded herself to his embrace, to his kisses, with a consequent rising of her spirits. He hadn't changed: hadn't forgotten her. It was her, not Livvy he loved, though she'd kept him away from her all this time.

A few minutes later, mixing drinks at the little table in the corner, he said, "It must be over two months since we've seen each other."

"Ten weeks. Haven't you been in town at all that time?"

"Twice, as a matter of fact, with Livvy, my sweet. I hadn't the ghost of a chance of seeing you."

With Livvy, she knew, he stayed at the Mayfair. She said, "Does Livvy know about us—about our meetings, I mean?"

"She knows we sometimes have lunch together, of course. But Livvy isn't inquisitive, bless her!"

She said, stabbed by that note of affection in his voice, "Is she at Bourne?"

"Of course she's at Bourne, my sweet. It's where she likes to be. She adores it and has been away from it so much lately. Her passion for the place never ceases to amaze me . . . Try this."

She took the drink he offered her, surprised he should have said so much about Livvy when he need only have answered her question.

"Well, what have you been doing with yourself all this time?" he asked her, seating himself on the arm of her chair. She sipped her drink without replying, comforted a little by his presence, by the arm he slipped along her shoulders.

"Who's been taking you out?"

"No one. You know I don't go out with any man but you."

"Do I? But why shouldn't you? Or does Dwight object?"

"No, he wouldn't mind. But there isn't anyone, these days, except you that I've ever wanted to go out with."

"Flatterer! But don't tell me you've stayed quietly at home all this time, like a good little girl."

"I've been to Lydia's once or twice on the evenings when Dwight goes for his Spanish lesson."

"Can't think why he wants to learn Spanish, unless he means to build castles in Spain. . . . What other heady excitements have you been indulging in?"

"Only a week-end at Wyngates."

"My poor child!"

"Oh, I rather like going there—Mr. Anstruther's nice. He doesn't expect you to be something you aren't, or anyway doesn't let you see he wishes you were. The way Dwight's mother does, I mean."

"Pen's high-minded. Always was. And Dwight takes after her. She used to set me back quite a bit. She didn't—and doesn't—approve of me."

"Mr. Anstruther thinks a lot of her. Is it true he was always in love with her?—while his wife was alive, I mean?"

"I wouldn't know. Who says so?"

"Oh, I've heard it somewhere."

"Our dear Emmy, I expect. Have you seen her lately?"

"No. I did go to the flat quite a bit once. I used to find her amusing."

"And not now?"

"Not so much."

"She struck nearer home, did she?"

"I thought she was pumping me, rather, the last time I went."

"About—us? I hope you were discreet."

Discreet. Yes, she had certainly been that, she thought, but it did nothing for her now to hear Danny use the word. Discreet!—the word which described the knock at the door, announcing the arrival of lunch, now being wheeled in upon a trolley. The waiter quickly laid the small table in the window, was thanked and withdrew.

"Austerity, I fear," said Danny, "but as we haven't seen each other for so long I thought you'd like it this way. Right?"

"Yes," she said, realising afresh how she had hated the thought of lunch in public . . . how little she felt like eating any kind of lunch, austerity or otherwise.

Neither did she manage to make much impression to the contrary, so that Danny, so used to the young woman who appreciated her food, was moved to say, "What's happened to your appetite?" and to exhort her to drink up her wine. She did not much care for it, for to-day he had studied his own palate, not hers, and its dryness repelled her. Good food she understood and appreciated but nothing could conquer her liking for a wine that was sweet. However, she picked up her glass and sipped at the good Burgundy. Little as she liked it, she knew that its effect would be better than its taste, and for her the bottle was labelled not Volnay but Dutch Courage.

The meal came to an end at last; the debris wheeled out and black coffee brought in. Fortified, she made up her mind to speak, hunted vainly for words for a few seconds, then used the only ones that got the truth out bluntly.

"Danny, there's something I've got to tell you. . . . I'm going to have a baby."

He stared at her, then said, "Whose?"

She felt as if he had struck her across the face.

"Yours," she said.

"My dear child!—how can you be sure?"

"It can only be yours. . . . Dwight and I aren't married that way, any longer."

"Since when?"

"I don't remember exactly. A long while before you and I . . ."

"Good lord! What a thing to happen! What are we going to do about it?"

"Dwight would divorce me, I think . . . if you wanted to marry me."

"But I've a wife already."

"I thought that perhaps Livvy would divorce you."

"I wouldn't dream of asking her."

"But you've said so often that you love me. . . ."

"Of course I love you. You're adorable."

"But you were just having an affair?"

"Of course. So were you."

"At first. Then I fell in love with you. . . . I thought you had with me."

"Yes, so I did. But we were both married and I thought we both knew what we were about. It never occurred to me that you didn't know how to take care of yourself."

"I thought I did. . . . It was an accident. Please believe that."

"Of course I believe it. But that doesn't help us now."

"Oh why," she broke out, "didn't you leave me alone?"

"Because, my sweet, you so obviously didn't want to be left alone."

She made no rejoinder to that, unable to explain to herself, much less to put into words, that medley of emotions—physical attraction, longing, hunger, romantic yearning, and misgiving—that had gone to her loving. He would never understand that she wasn't the sort who had "affairs". Clearly, he had supposed she was. She had never before realised that.

He came over and sat again on the arm of her chair. Again she felt the comfort of his arm across her shoulders.

"My dear child!" he said. "Did I ever once lead you to suppose that our attraction for each other could ever conceivably break up my marriage—or yours?"

"No," she said. "I didn't want you to break your marriage . . . and mine was already broken. But I thought this might make a difference."

"No. Livvy's out of this. I suppose you've heard that I married her for her money and stick to her because of it?"

"I've heard it suggested."

"From our dear Emmy, I'm sure."

He waited for her to confirm this, but all she said was, "When you said you loved me I thought perhaps it was true."

"Did I say I loved you? Wasn't it 'in love', my dear? And so I am, but Livvy's the only woman I've ever loved."

She hadn't known there was any difference.

She said,"I don't understand that. If I'd loved Dwight I shouldn't have had anything to do with you."

"Weren't you ever in love with him?"

"No. I liked him, of course. But I liked the idea of being married and settled. And at first it was exciting. I didn't mind his loving me. . . . But I didn't want any children." She sighed and for a moment laid her head against his shoulder. "I was terrified. And I'm no good with children. Dwight despises me for that—and leaves me alone. He can't blame me for falling in love with you—or with anyone else."

"No. Serve him right. But you should have avoided complications. . . . What makes you think he'd divorce you?"

She was silent for a moment, then said, "I asked him once if he would, if I was unfaithful—and he said if the other man wanted to marry me."

"I heard a rumour about the gentleman being in love elsewhere."

"With Fryn? Yes, I think he is—but I don't know about her.

And in any case it makes no difference. You see, Dwight's like you about marriage. He thinks it's for keeps."

"But I don't—unless it's the right woman. I'm not as righteous as the high-minded Dwight."

She wondered where this conversation was taking her. Nowhere. Her situation was still unresolved.

"It's queer," said Danny, "to love a woman like Livvy and yet be unable to be faithful to her."

"Does she know?"

"I dare say she suspects sometimes. But she knows none of it matters. She doesn't let it worry her. . . . Look here, this is getting us no place. You know, of course, that you don't have to have this baby?"

She remembered that girl in the hospital, screaming her head off until they dosed her with morphia. She was devastated by the fact that Danny should know how to get rid of an inconvenient baby, that he should speak of it so calmly, and was painfully aware that she wasn't the first girl to whom he had given this piece of information. She said, "I'd be more afraid of that than of having the baby."

"You'd better think about it, my child. I'll do all I can to help you."

"No one can help me," she said. "I'll just have to go through with it."

"You mean you'll tell Dwight?"

"I must."

"But suppose he smells a rat?"

"I shan't bring you into it, whatever happens."

"You mean that?"

"Yes."

She could feel the relief that ran through him, as he said, "My word, you're a sport, my child!" Had she known it, he was so grateful for this assurance, for the way she was taking this unfortunate contretemps, which had put an end (he hoped but temporarily) to something he had much enjoyed, that he was fonder of her than ever before, and for once felt genuinely ashamed of himself. He'd never forgotten the unfortunate acquaintance of his who'd got himself in the same scrape and was forced into divorce and re-marriage. He'd been called in to see what he could do to prevent this disaster, and the young woman had sat tight, refusing all argument, saying over and over again, "He'll have to marry me—his wife'll have to divorce him. . . . No decent woman can want a man to stay with her against his will!" The grim humour of that scene had remained with him ever since.

"Well, don't tell him for a bit—think about the way out. I can give you the name of a good doctor—there'd be no risk at all. But I'm afraid it would mean going to Paris . . ."

Paris. How was she to get to Paris? What possible excuse could she find for such a trip? She could have laughed.

"I couldn't go to Paris. Isn't there a doctor in London?"

"None that I know of. Too risky, too. They order these things better on the Continent. Do go home and think of a plan. There wouldn't be any risk, I assure you."

She was stricken again by this revelation of illicit knowledge which bespoke experience, and somehow immeasurably cheapened her situation. She wasn't the first and she wouldn't be the last. Romance and love had tumbled together into the gutter, yet her love for him—the first she had felt for any man —was like a dagger in her heart.

"I don't want it to end like this, my sweet."

"It had to end some time."

Odd that she had never thought of that before. But she must have known it all the time.

"You make me feel an awful brute."

She stood before him, unable to speak, and he thought how lovely she was, even in her misery, and what pleasure she had given him. As a life-companion he could well imagine that she would be heavy-going; she was cut out for a mistress not for a wife. If only he could knock some sense into her over this contretemps, make her see that there must be ways of contriving this trip to Paris! But he didn't know what they were.

"Good-bye," she said, turning away from him, and picking up her gloves and handbag.

She stood quite still while he kissed her, then turned to the door. He opened it and followed her out to the lift-shaft. They stood in silence while the lift came up to them. She got in, the liftman pressed the requisite button. She looked up at him with a little forced smile upon her face as the lift began to move, and he raised his hand in a familiar gesture of farewell. She knew, in her heart, that she would never see him again.

Chapter Six

A FEW DAYS later, returning by way of the Park from a shopping expedition for her mother, Fryn saw Emmy Gaywood sitting beneath the trees near the Palace Gate. Before she could do anything to avoid a meeting Emmy had so obviously seen her that there was nothing to do but to walk across and speak to her.

"Well met!" said the old lady, her sharp green eyes belying the smile upon her badly-painted mouth, "I was just thinking of going in to tea. Do come and keep an old woman company. It's a very long time since I've seen you."

"Yes," said Fryn, who in fact had not seen Emmy more than three or four times since the encounter at Greystones, and had disliked each successive occasion, if possible, more than the other. Emmy, that figure in her mind of Romance and Rebellion, had been, upon acquaintance, a great disappointment. It was hard to believe that she had ever been anything but what she was now in her old age; a spiteful slightly ridiculous person, whose smoothest words had an edge and undercurrent to them; who seemed to take pleasure in other people's discomfiture and poked her finger into everyone's affairs.

"Well, come along, and let me hear all your news. I'm tired in all this heat, so let's see if we can get a taxi."

There was nothing Fryn wanted less than to have tea with Emmy Gaywood, unless it was having tea with her in the intimacy of her flat, in which so far she had managed not to set foot. But she was glad that an empty taxi came along as they left the Park, for she found it more than a little embarrassing to walk with Emmy in public, so youthful was her make-up, so very bright her hair. If only she would not decorate her face so much! It made her look ridiculous, whereas with her slim figure, the green eyes set beneath that remarkable brow, and her smart clothes, she could have looked quite distinguished.

"At the moment," said Emmy as they rode along, "I've actually got a maid. *Reason*ably capable, though in my youth she wouldn't have been considered so. What my mother would have thought of her I can't think—she was so lucky in her servants. But of course in those days we didn't hear all this silly talk of equality."

Arrived at the block of flats, Emmy paused in the hall to alter the "Out" against her name on the board to "In", then the lift whizzed them up to the fourth floor. ("So *much* nicer, being at the top!" said Emmy.) The door was opened by the new maid, who did not look as though she objected overwhelmingly to the fact that her mistress had brought a friend back to tea.

"Of course, you haven't seen the flat before, have you?" said Emmy. "This is my study." She indicated a room, of which the door stood open. "It's a very pleasant room, I think."

Casting a quick eye around, Fryn did not know that the room looked very much as it had looked that afternoon, nearly nine years ago, when Pen had confronted Emmy in it and had told her, with much truth and gratification, that she was a "silly vindictive old woman". The bookshelves lining the walls, the armchairs, the portable typewriter standing in its cover against the wall, the highly polished table at which, so Pen had thought, no serious writer could have writtten a word, the telephone, disguised as a mid-Victorian young lady, which stood upon it—all were the same. Even the hydrangeas in the false fireplace might have been the identical ones which had been the only things in the room that Pen had admired.

But on the blotting pad this afternoon lay a sheaf of written pages with a heavy weight upon them. Emmy, apparently, had begun writing again.

"I'm writing my memoirs," she said with a little smirk. "I find it a most amusing occupation."

"How very interesting!" said Fryn, thinking, Amusing. Yes, I'm sure she does. But perhaps here her unkindness would be tempered by her knowledge of the odd libel laws of England, about which she had once heard her great-grandfather talking to Pen.

"It's quite a relief to get back to the good old times," said Emmy, who had once so ardently thought them so bad. "Life has become so very dull, don't you think? I know people say we ought to find it an interesting time to live in, that we're living through a bloodless revolution; and so we may be. But it's made life very drab, with everyone so poor and shabby. Come along, tea is ready."

Abandoning the showing of the rest of the flat, she turned and led the way to the sitting-room, where tea was set on a small table near the window. Fryn noticed that the room was expensively and tastefully furnished and over the mantelshelf was a picture which was obviously of Emmy in her youth. Following her gaze, Emmy said, "That was done by an old friend of mine, Phoebe Lane." With whom you once lived . . . and with whom you quarrelled, went

[234]

Fryn's thoughts. She knew all about that episode—how Emmy had left home to live with Phoebe, who'd admired and adored her. Nobody knew what the quarrel was really about; but it had never been resolved. Emmy wasn't the sort who made up quarrels. She looked at the picture and remembered that her great-grandfather had said that Miss Lane was a better art critic than she was a painter. However, here she had made a colourful picture of a pretty, rather delicate-looking girl, which was a state Fryn did not associate with Emmy. No art critic, she was content to leave it at that. But she remembered hearing Cousin Andra once say that Miss Lane's sitters all appeared to have one foot in the grave—so odd. . . .

"Larry always said that portraits weren't Phoebe's métier," said Emmy. "He admired the illustrations she did for my war book very much."

Mistaken Shrine. Fryn had run the book to earth at last on her grandmother Bradfield's shelves, clamped between a *Life of Lenin* and a volume of Tchehov's *Short Stories*. But she found it as difficult to think of Emmy mixed up with all the blood and hazards of World War One as to think of her as the delicate, sensitive young lady of Miss Lane's painting. But noticing the past tense, which Emmy had used of the artist, she inquired if she were dead.

"Not as far as I know," Emmy assured her, and Fryn saw that she was only dead to *her*. The quarrel had somehow washed her not only out of Emmy's life but out of life altogether. She no longer existed, for Emmy. Grandfather Malling, she knew, had regretted the separation; he had thought Phoebe "good" for Emmy, and had maintained that everything she'd written since *Mistaken Shrine*—that was, after she had left Phoebe—was quite unremarkable. And there were those, like her grandmother, she had heard, who believed that Miss Lane had been responsible for more than the illustrations of the book, that at least she had wielded the blue pencil with discretion and excellent effect.

"Well, come along now, tell me your news," invited Emmy. However, it was Emmy herself who did most of the talking, asked all the questions and knew most of the answers. Had she been to see Gaby since her marriage? How did Bridget like living in town? Did Fryn think the young man had really jilted her for Gaby? Oh, yes, of course she knew that Bridget said she had refused him, but Bridget wasn't every young man's dream girl—too self-sufficient, detached. Was she making a lot of money over that children's book? Was she doing another? "And I suppose," she finished, "Miss L. P. Malling has turned out another masterpiece?"

[235]

"I believe she has nearly finished a book," said Fryn, answering the last question first, as was the only way with people who asked so many at once, and resenting the scornful note in her voice for author and work. "Gaby says it's quite the best thing she's done."

"Well, no doubt it will do well. *Such* an advantage to have married one's publisher! And quite in the best tradition. . . . Miss Braddon, you know, Isabella Beeton." Had she seen anything of Rose? Poor Rose, so *very* old-fashioned! making herself so miserable about Audrey, who seemed very happy, though it annoyed her considerably that the wife wouldn't divorce her husband and went on being friends with him.

Emmy laughed her little unkind laugh.

"Of course that pleases Rose very much, poor darling. All the same, she ought to leave Audrey to her own life. People interfere too much. When I was young I was interfered with all along the line. I had my life quite pushed out of shape by it. . . . Audrey has courage and I admire her for it. But it's easier now to be courageous in that way than when I was young."

"Oh, but you were quite a *serious* pioneer for freedom in your youth," said Fryn, who did not think much of Audrey's ideas of freedom. "I hope you will put all that in your book. About the mathematical tripos, I mean, and your not being able to take the Chartered Accountants exam."

"It's been done so often," said Emmy, with an air of boredom. "So many of the 'new' women of my generation have published their autobiographies. I shall skip most of that, and all my war service. It's all old stuff now and nobody cares to-day what you did in the First World War. Women, they say, are going to be a permanent part of the army. I'm much too old-fashioned, I'm afraid, to approve of that!"

(Fryn suddenly remembered another comment upon this innovation of women in the army, made by Emmy's sister, Andra Merrow, so much nicer an old lady, she thought. "I hear we've recruited—how many million women? Well, we shall have no excuse now if we lose the war.")

"By the way," said Emmy, "how are the Spanish lessons getting on?"

"Very well. Dwight's a very good pupil. He's naturally good at languages, of course."

"But why Spanish? . . . He'll never have any use for it, surely? Or does he intend to follow you all to South America?"

There was something in the way she uttered this last sentence,

[236]

with an almost imperceptible pause before the word "all", which struck Fryn as meaningful, but she said, "Well, even so, he wouldn't need to learn Spanish first. I think he just thought it was an opportunity put in his way and that he might as well take."

"Opportunity?" said Emmy vaguely.

"My being here, I mean—and our having got used to the role of pupil and teacher. We only had to reverse them, you see."

"Yes, of course. I quite see. *Most* convenient. What is all this I hear about your staying on for a year and working at that Clinic of Vicky Merrow's?"

(Did Emmy hear everything?)

"It's only an idea I had. Rather a silly one, perhaps. I don't suppose father will agree to it, anyway. He doesn't want to leave me behind."

"Parents are most interfering still, aren't they? If I were you— I mean if I really wanted to stay—I should stick to it."

"I don't think I want to do it quite enough to distress father," said Fryn. "Though I *should* like to have stayed in England a little longer."

After a pause Emmy seemed to decide to forsake her role of inciter to rebellion and said, "I suppose you see a good deal of Doreen, going to the flat in the role of teacher?"

"Oh, I don't often go to the flat. Dwight comes to us. And occasionally Doreen comes with him. She did yesterday. She wasn't very well—the heat, I think."

"But Doreen always seems to flourish on the heat. When the rest of us are expiring she usually looks as cool as an ice-cream."

"Yes, but in the eighties it becomes a little trying, even for those who like heat, perhaps."

"It's ages since Doreen has been near me. Do you know why? She used to come in quite a lot. But of course she's such a gadabout. Such a pity the Greystones venture came to an end so soon. Doreen was happy there. Of course she'd no idea of managing servants, but one didn't expect that. That woman Simmonds must have been a snag, anyhow—James spoiled her. He had left everything to her for years, but she knew better than to take with him the liberties she took with Doreen. But then, James, of course, like my mother, was quite a genius with servants. He knew how to get service and command respect."

"But those words are hardly any longer in the language," said Fryn, smiling.

"No, it's 'equality' to-day, of course, but so it was in James's last days. Yet he continued to get service and respect all the same.

But of course Mrs. Simmonds saw at once where she was with Doreen. Pretty enough, but hardly a lady."

"I don't think it was that," said Fryn, thinking that 'lady' was another almost obsolete word and that the label was pinned, anyway, on those whom it often didn't in the least describe. "It was the parties—the week-end company. She said she found them too much. She and Doreen got on very well, I believe, until the parties became such a regular week-end occurrence."

"Doreen must find it very dull at that flat, and I expect she doesn't care about having to pull her horns in, now that the Greystones income has gone. It must be very boring for them both. Such a silly marriage. Quite a misalliance."

"I'm so sorry," said Fryn suddenly, in what Meg called her 'interrupting' voice, "but I think I ought to 'phone mother—she expected me in to tea."

"You know where the telephone is," said Emmy, with the pained look of those interrupted just when they were getting well into their theme.

"Oh, poor you!" said Lydia's voice. "Couldn't you have got out of it?"

"I wasn't quick enough," said Fryn. Lydia laughed and said, "Well, escape as soon as you can. . . . Was the shopping successful?"

"Yes, I got all you wanted, I think," Fryn told her, thinking that if it had taken her as long as she'd expected, she'd probably have gone home by bus instead of walking through the Park, or have missed Emmy if she had. "Good-bye, darling," she said, and putting back the receiver, sat still at the desk for a moment, her eyes on the wad of manuscript beneath the paper weight. What, she wondered, would Emmy's autobiography be like? She seemed to be going to leave out all the really interesting things she had done. It would be an account, perhaps, of her late-Victorian upbringing, of her relations with her family—with Phoebe Lane. It wouldn't, she thought, be a very kind book. Emmy, so grandfather Malling used to say, had been quite a beauty in her youth. But beauty dwelt with kindness. An unpopular virtue, he used to say—having no place in this harsh century. Had Emmy ever been kind? She couldn't really believe that she had.

It was clear, Fryn thought, coming back into the sitting-room, that Emmy had not been diverted by her telephone manœuvre from the theme of Doreen and her marriage. As she poured fresh tea for Fryn and handed scones, she said, "Of course I feel very sorry for

Doreen. She's such a pretty creature it seems a thousand pities her marriage should have turned out so badly."

"Does Doreen say that it has?"

"Oh, no, not in so many words and she's very loyal to Dwight. She never criticises anyone but herself—says she's a misfit and that she's quite the wrong sort of wife for him. And of course she is, poor darling. She bores him very much—I could see that at Greystones and things, I gather, haven't improved since the move. I suppose that's why he doesn't mind her running around with her own friends. After all, a neglectful husband with a pretty wife must expect that."

From what roots, Fryn wondered, did Emmy's constant 'I gather' spring? Once it had doubtless been from Rose, the Family Chatterbox, giving away with her never unkind chatter situations which Emmy cherished and lovingly embellished. But Rose did not now see Emmy. Who then? Audrey? Meg said that Audrey was "sick" about not having got the divorce, and it wouldn't, she thought, have made her kinder to other people.

"But I don't think Dwight is at all neglectful," said Fryn. "I'm sure Doreen wouldn't say that he was."

"No? Well, of course you see a good deal more of the ménage than I do," said Emmy sweetly. "But after the intelligent women he's been brought up with, it must be very hard to live with such a brainless creature as Doreen. Uncharitable people, of course, might say he lets her run around with other men for his own purposes."

Fryn stared at her.

"I can't imagine what you mean," she said, with a little note of indignation in her voice she was powerless to prevent.

"Can't you?" Emmy's voice was edged with amusement. It was as if she'd said, "Oh yes, you can imagine it very well. Very well indeed." What she actually said was, "Doesn't it occur to you that it's very unwise to be a neglectful husband if your wife is as pretty as Doreen?—unless, of course, there's method in your madness."

Fryn continued to sit in silence, transfixed by the sheer malignancy of what this terrible old woman was saying.

"Besides," went on Emmy in that sweet reasonable voice which seemed to betoken concern and yet, Fryn knew, was doing nothing of the kind, "Doreen might get *involved* with another man. That would be a way out for Dwight, wouldn't it? He could then divorce her, of course . . ."

"Cousin Emmy, that's a most shocking thing to say. Nobody who knows Dwight could believe him capable of such a thing."

[239]

"Oh, ho!—Counsel for the Defence!" laughed Emmy.

"I'm sure you've no grounds for saying such things about Dwight."

"Well, perhaps I shouldn't say them to you."

"Why particularly not to me? They would be equally shocking said to others—more, because they mightn't know how very untrue they were."

"That's very disingenuous of you, Fryn."

"What do you mean by that?"

"Well—you can't really expect me to believe that you don't know that Dwight is in love with you?"

Fryn now felt a little sick. The hand holding the cup began to tremble so violently that as she returned it to its saucer, the hot liquid splashed on to her hand. The sharp physical pain for a moment counteracted her mental distress, and she was able to reply with a coldness that steadied her. Indignation was no good with this awful old woman. Coldness and contempt—two things she knew herself to be not very good at—were the weapons one needed here. She said:

"On the contrary, I can't imagine why you should believe anything so utterly ridiculous."

Emmy smiled sweetly.

"You are too modest, my dear. I know one person who wouldn't agree that it was ridiculous."

She wouldn't ask who: she wouldn't even try to guess. She could only refute this outrageous suggestion.

"But it isn't in the very least true. None of the things you've said is true. Dwight is my friend. He is also my cousin."

Emmy laughed, her green eyes fixed upon Fryn's cold shocked countenance.

"He is also unsatisfactorily married," she said. "In the circumstances, you must expect people to jump to conclusions."

"Circumstances? *What* circumstances, please?"

"Well, you're very close friends, aren't you? One way and another you contrive to see a good deal of each other. Then these lessons. The cramming over maths was understandable, but the Spanish lessons (to the uncharitable) look too much like an excuse on Dwight's part for seeing you—in favourable circumstances."

Fryn, though much shaken, managed to say calmly, "This is a theme I should prefer you to discuss with mother. Your point of view would surprise her considerably. I'm sure no one else shares it."

"Well, in Doreen's place, what would *you* think?"

Doreen. So it was Doreen she meant as the 'one person at least' who believed Dwight was in love with her. It was quite fantastic! She said, "I'm sure Doreen isn't so silly as to worry about anything so wildly absurd."

"I didn't say she was worrying about the situation," said Emmy with a little titter. "Quite the contrary, I should say. You see, I'm sure Doreen has some love-affair on of her own. So if Dwight is in love with you and you with him—well, there you are!"

"But the situation isn't at all like that, and I dare say you're as wrong about Doreen as about Dwight."

"And about you? Can you lay your hand on your heart and say you're not in the least in love with Dwight?"

"Of course I can. . . . I'm not in love with anyone. You have love on the brain."

She'd never thought of 'love' in Emmy's sense. She'd never even had the boy and girl love-affairs in which Meg had so early indulged. She didn't think of young men as sweethearts or possible husbands but only as acquaintances, and in Dwight's case, as a friend. Not only was he her cousin, but a person she very much liked, and who, she felt, liked her; with whom she shared enthusiasms and detestations, spoke the same language. Someone who was always interested and interesting, with whom she felt at ease. It was true that once or twice lately, and just for a moment, he had made her feel a little self-conscious—that evening when he had teased her and quoted Coventry Patmore instead of going on with the Spanish lesson, for example. But that was because she was always shy and embarrassed when someone paid her a compliment, even as glancing a one as Dwight's. But now Emmy's words, and the tone of her voice, the hard green gaze and her unkind laughter swept over their whole relationship like a blight, spoiling it for ever.

She reached blindly for handbag, gloves, and packages and got up. She had to get out of the room, away from that soft cruel voice edged with amusement; away from the hard raking eyes.

"Now, don't be a little goose, my child. I'm not suggesting you've encouraged Dwight in any way. I'm sure you've been *most* circumspect and a delightful companion for him. You're not to blame because it's made him neglectful of his wife."

"He's not neglectful. You know nothing about him. He considers Doreen in every way."

"Except, perhaps, the way that matters most—in a husband."

Fryn's blanched face flushed deeply. She knew what was meant but she couldn't believe she had really heard the fact put into words. Disgust and dismay rolled over her until she felt as if encased in ice, frozen to the floor. Then, as if a miracle had happened, she found herself outside the room, outside the flat, running down the stairs, as if the malignancy and cruelty that had been in that room had escaped and ran at her heels.

Outside she picked up a taxi which was setting a fare down and was driven through the blessedly normal London streets—home.

Walking into the sitting-room after going up to her room to see if she looked as mortified as she felt, she was greeted by a cheerful grin from Meg.

"Well, how was the Smiling Dragon?" she inquired.

"Most reptilian," said Fryn, and her mother, glancing up at her from her mending, saw upon her face that look of fatigue which came upon it far less from physical than mental distress. But this was not the moment to ask questions; nothing Fryn would hate more than to have to talk of something that had distressed her until she had wrestled with its worst effects upon herself. So she said, "You didn't walk home, did you, in this heat?"

"No, mother," she replied, but did not add that she had taken a taxi, since that would have surprised Meg to comment. For it was Meg who took taxis, Fryn went on Shanks's pony, to which, as Meg said, she was much addicted. Nobody, here in this room fronting the garden, would have heard the taxi, Fryn thought. She undid the small parcel of purchases she had made for her mother and passed them over to her.

"I hope they'll do," she said. "They were the nearest I could get. I'm afraid I had to give a coupon for the dusting gloves. I hope you'll think them worth it."

"Rather!" said Lydia, whose hands were her one vanity. Thin-skinned, they did not stand up well to domestic tasks and the long practice they had had since she came to England had not in the least broken them in.

"Thank you, my dear," she said, "putting the articles down upon the small table at her side. "Your grandmother's coming in this evening, so I must finish this mending. You know how she detests seeing piles of stockings and underwear about. But Jeremy will have no socks to wear to-morrow if I don't go on for a bit."

"Let me help," said Fryn, picking up a sock from the pile. "What time is she coming?"

"She said to supper, but that we weren't to wait."

"Grandmother never eats anything, anyway," said Meg. "No wonder she's so thin. And she talks what flesh she has off her bones."

But she doesn't talk Family, thought Fryn gratefully. Caro

[242]

Bradfield despised all such tittle-tattle. She'd probably forgotten there was such a person as Emmy Gaywood, for why should one remember it? Lydia thought, she'll talk about our policy in Palestine, in India and about the Conscription Act, all of which she disapproved of. Still outside all political parties, she disapproved of most things that were done by the Party in power and would have done so even if she had still belonged to it. Gilbert was probably right when he said she would be a very sharp thorn in the side of any party. At sixty-three she was a stormy petrel still: even more so. You never knew up what street she'd be hurrying or whether she was going or coming, he said, mixing his metaphors. How Ted Bradfield, that quiet steady Labour man, put up with her he didn't know, or what held them together. When Lydia said, "The same fundamental beliefs," he replied that he didn't see how that helped, since Caro would be certain to disagree with Ted's idea of how they should be implemented. Still, she was Lydia's mother and he bore with her good-humouredly, not unaware that she regarded him as a dyed-in-the-wool old Tory! Neatly darning the gaping heel of Jeremy's sock Lydia smiled at the memory of the measure of toleration these two people she loved granted each other.

As it happened, Caro did arrive in time for supper, but for once had little to say about the political scene except that we stayed in Palestine where we could do no good and were cordially detested by Jews and Arabs alike for trying, and were about to leave India (at least a hundred years too soon) where we could still have been useful. She dismissed the breakdown of the Anglo-Russian Conference with a despairing shrug. Clearly, for this evening at least, she had given the world up, and, as Lydia had done so long ago, they declined upon the personal, to her relief. And for once Caro was better informed upon family matters than her daughter. She'd had Rose to see her that afternoon; she'd come to tell her that Audrey's major had gone back to his wife.

"The fine high romance is over, it seems, and Rose regards it as a distinct answer to prayer. I'd qualify that a bit myself—and give some part at least of the credit to the persevering wife."

Fryn, who could find nothing to say in this uncomfortable matter, nevertheless remembered Emmy's assertion of an hour or so ago that Audrey was very happy. It gave her a sense, somehow, of relief to hear now that this opinion was ill-founded and confirmed her in her belief that everything she had said that afternoon of Dwight, Doreen and herself was fantastic and ridiculous.

"Well!" said Meg, "I'm bothered if I'd have had him back, if he were *my* husband. He deserves to have to live with Audrey for the rest of his life, if you ask me."

"Poor man!" commented Lydia. "What happens now to Audrey?"

Caro didn't know and clearly wasn't interested. Audrey, thank heaven, was not *her* daughter. Abruptly she switched attention to her grand-daughter. What was all this nonsense she'd been hearing about her and Redvers Green?

"It was just an idea I had—but I've quite changed my mind," said Fryn, not unaware of her mother's sharp glance at her.

"I'm glad to hear it," said her grandmother. "It's not your line of country at all—you're far too thin-skinned. You need to be tough for that kind of job."

"Would you call Leah 'tough'?"

"No, I wouldn't. But Leah has a vocation. You haven't. Or have you?"

"No, I don't think I have. But I wanted to stay in England and that seemed a useful way of doing it."

"And now you want to go back to South America?"

"Yes," said Fryn, and again felt her mother's considering gaze upon her.

"Very nice," said her grandmother. "And what about you, Meg?"

"Oh, I'm going home, too."

"To see if absence makes the heart grow fonder or if out of sight is out of mind?"

"Well, not exactly," said Meg. "But you're on the right track. I'm dying to see South America again. And, in any case, even if father consented, I don't want a hurry-flurry wedding and there wouldn't be time for any other sort before the rest of the family went off. You see, father's determined to get off at the latest by mid-September."

"You don't sound as if you're head over heels in love with your young man, I must say."

"I don't think I am. But I won't know until I get back home."

"And the young man? What's he got to say to all this?"

"Well, he's very reasonable about it. Now that he's got used to the idea. Fryn thinks I've treated him rather shabbily, don't you?"

"No," said her sister. "One would need to be *terribly* sure about getting married. . . . It would be awful to make a mistake."

"You have a pair of level-headed daughters, anyway, Lydia. I congratulate you. I get so sick of hearing all this modern stuff about Love with an enormous capital letter."

"Still," said Meg thoughtfully, "it would be very nice to feel that way—to be sort of rushed off your feet. But I don't seem to be made like that. I can't help feeling I'll see George better when I'm not seeing him at all, if you know what I mean. And of course I *may* find that I simply can't live without him. Though I don't think so. I mean, I may just find that life would be even nicer with him than without."

This clear exposition of her case Lydia found extremely comforting. She dismissed Meg from her thoughts, which reverted to Fryn, whose affirmation that she wanted to go back to South America had a little startled her, so assured was it, so much in contrast with her former statements which had shown so clearly how strongly she was drawn to this troubled land of her fathers. She felt sure that something had happened to have produced this *volte face*. This afternoon? If so, then Emmy almost certainly had something to do with it. It had not escaped her notice that Fryn had made a very poor supper.

However, whatever it was which had caused her to give up this latest excuse for staying on in England (and she could believe it nothing else, for indeed she was quite sure that Fryn had no vocation at all for the work Vicky and Leah were doing), it was a conclusion for which she was extremely grateful. It would have meant another unending argument with Gil. But now, when he came home in a few weeks' time they could all go comfortably off together, directly he got berths, and the sooner the better, she felt. For really it was time poor Glen was given possession of his house, and Gaby undivided possession of hers.

Fryn went to bed soon after her grandmother's departure. It was ten o'clock, but thanks to Mr. Willett, or, rather, to the Government's extension of his tiresome Summer Time idea, the sun was still high in the sky and the heat almost unabated. She decided to knock on Fryn's door and see if she was in the mood to tell her what the reptilian Emmy, the tiresome creature, had been saying to her. How unfortunate that Fryn should have run into her, and how still more unfortunate that she had not had the hardihood to excuse herself from the invitation to tea.

The voice in which Fryn bade her come in was reassuringly normal, and so was the sight of her sitting up in bed with a book. No one, she said, could go to sleep in this heat at half-past eight, even if the clocks did say half-past ten.

Lydia sat at the foot of the bed and agreed. To all but Jeremy Double Summer Time was a scourge. Besides, as Fryn said, there was no summer night sky. Only Jupiter.

"Did you find Emmy very trying this afternoon?" she asked. "She's quite the most deflating person I've ever met. One feels worn out for hours afterwards."

"She was—unspeakable," said Fryn. "However long I stay in England I'll never speak to her again."

This attitude was so unlike Fryn, whose interest in and curiosity about human beings of all kinds was so acute that she often let herself in for some very dull and boring hours (at least in her family's opinion), that Lydia said—carefully casual—"Care to tell me about it?"

She had always made it a rule not to force the confidences of her children and all her life had been rewarded by having her daughters, sooner or later, tip them neatly into her lap. Not Jeremy. He was another matter. She said, "Perhaps you'd rather wait a bit?"

"No, I think I'd like to get it off my mind."

Lydia still waited. She knew Fryn's way with confidences. She'd just screw up her courage and then out it would all come. So now.

"Emmy insisted upon talking about Dwight and Doreen. She said he was a neglectful husband—in what she called the way that matters most—and that he winks at her friendships with other men for his own purposes."

"I see. Did she say what they were?"

"So that he could divorce her because he's in love with me."

There was a slight pause before Lydia said, "Have you ever had cause to think so?" Though she knew the answer she could not but be relieved that it came so quickly.

"No. Of course we like each other, and we like the same things. But there's never been anything, not a single word. And Emmy has never seen us together, anyway, except that time at Greystones. Though she didn't actually say it, she inferred that Doreen shares her opinion."

"If so, Emmy probably put it into her head—and Doreen isn't as clever as Emmy. It would be quite easy to suggest a thing like that to her. But I must say I've never seen a sign of jealousy on Doreen's part toward you. Have you?"

"No, never. She doesn't like me much, but it isn't because of Dwight. She doesn't like any of us much, and I'm not at all the sort of person she'd like anyway. But according to Emmy, Doreen *isn't* jealous—because she's in love with someone else. So it suits her to believe that Dwight is in love with me and I with him."

Fryn in love with Dwight. No, that was certainly not true. Fryn was like the girl in Browning's poem—*it was not her time to love.*

[246]

She thought it wise, however, not to take up this point and asked instead why she had allowed such silly charges to upset her.

"Well, it's horrid to have such beastly things said about—about someone you like. And even about those you don't like very much. Besides, it's made me feel it's spoilt everything. I mean, I don't see how I can go on with the Spanish lessons after what Emmy suggested about them."

Lydia could guess what that was. She said, "But if you stop the lessons you are letting Emmy win a point. I should just ignore her innuendoes."

After a little silence, Fryn said, "Do you think Dwight and Doreen are really very unhappy?"

"They're not very suited, of course, and most of us could wish he had chosen a different sort of wife. But that's a common occurrence in families. Their public manners are very good. Whatever else she is or isn't, Doreen is an amiable creature. I sometimes think that should earn her more good marks than it does."

"I wish I knew why Emmy should have said all this. And why she should be so malicious and interfering."

"She's a soured old woman, my child, hugging a romance of her own which went wrong. It's an old story. It was old when I was born. It can't matter to anyone any more."

"She said people had interfered so much in her life it had been pushed out of shape."

"Well, even if that were true, which it isn't entirely, I think, it seems a poor reason for her interfering in other people's."

"You know, the odd thing was that she seemed to think she was doing us all a kindness. I mean Dwight and Doreen—and me. As if she were arranging or re-arranging our lives for us. And yet that wasn't it—quite. There seemed to be something behind it all—or someone, rather. What I think I mean is that she seemed to be trying to pay off an old score."

"With your Aunt Pen, doubtless. She knows her attitude to marriage and divorce, and though your aunt would have chosen a different sort of daughter-in-law it would make her unhappy if—if Dwight fell in love elsewhere."

"But why should she want to hurt Aunt Pen?"

"Oh, because as a mere schoolgirl she stumbled on the sequel to her precious romance, and later she thought it might comfort her to know about it. But it was the last thing Emmy wanted to know and she was convinced that your aunt had told her about it just to hurt her. She swore she would never forgive her—and she hasn't."

[247]

"I see," said Fryn, but she didn't look at all comforted, Lydia thought. Nor was she. For the first time in her life she had come face to face with sheer malice—revenge; and it revolted her. Her young face looked so pale and drawn that Lydia rose from the end of the bed and said they'd talked enough. Too much, for Emmy wasn't worth so much attention.

"You'd better try to go to sleep—put the book away for to-night. I'll turn out the light and draw back the curtains. There, that's better. It's a lovely night. Jupiter has the sky to himself."

"He has eleven moons with him," said Fryn, "but we can't see them. I think it's a pity." She didn't like this empty Double Summer Time sky. "He'll have a lot of other companions when we're all asleep."

Lydia imprinted a kiss on her young daughter's brow and laughed. But thinking that it was better she should have her mind on the night sky than on Emmy she went more happily away.

Left alone, Fryn twisted her head on her pillow and stared out at the bright planet which her grandfather had told her was the giant of the solar system. She remembered the phrase he had used of it— a handsome chap but inhospitable, for he was nearly five times farther away from the sun than was the earth, and terribly cold in consequence—always over a hundred degrees centigrade below freezing point. And moreover was enveloped in a heavy atmosphere known to consist mainly of marsh gas and ammonia. No argument about possible life on Jupiter, her grandfather had said, as there was about Mars. For who or what could live under such conditions?

An odd unexpected peace descended upon Fryn. Just to look at the sky made her feel that her grandfather was right when he said that we all behaved as though we still believed, like the old Greek astronomers, that the earth was the centre of the universe, instead of just an insignificant part of it, and that neither we nor our affairs were as important as we thought. To-morrow she would not believe this, but to-night it comforted her, for it washed out Emmy and her lies and left her free and unscathed.

Lydia, however, stayed awake long after Jupiter's companions had stolen into the sky. For though she had made light of Emmy's insinuations she was more than a little disturbed by them.

It had not escaped her attention that Dwight was fond of Fryn and happy in her company; but now she wondered if there was more in it than that, if Emmy, in her maliciousness, had stumbled on something she had missed. Was it so wild an improbability that

Dwight should have come to entertain warmer feelings for Fryn than those of a rather distant cousin? If one thought of his marriage, perhaps not. She wondered if she had started something by her suggestion of that mathematical coaching, for though it had pulled Fryn through her tiresome exam, it had led straight to those Spanish lessons. And it seemed to her now that Dwight might very well have had more in mind when he had suggested them than the mere learning of Spanish.

If so, what harm had been done? None, she felt, that was not remediable, in view of Fryn's own reactions to Emmy's insinuations and what she had said as to her own feeling for Dwight. She did not believe Fryn was in love with him; she was too little awakened, but for how long would this continue to be true if it was a fact that Dwight was even a little in love with her? The situation had undoubted elements of danger. Perhaps after all it would be wiser to discourage the continuance of the Spanish lessons, though after her advice to Fryn that to forgo them would be to give point to Emmy's statements it wasn't going to be easy. If Dwight were really being stupid over Fryn, he wouldn't willingly give up what remained of their time together, and even if he were not was unlikely to acquiesce in such a decision unless some very excellent reason could be put forward. Worst of all he might well embarrass Fryn to the point of candour, which might land them anywhere. For Fryn had nothing of Meg's faculty for looking at an awkward situation in which she might find herself as if it concerned someone else. She was too sensitive, too prone to be torn by her sympathies and affection.

The one thing upon which she could congratulate herself was Fryn's unexpected decision not to press for that year with Vicky and Leah; and it was none the less satisfactory because she felt that Emmy and her scandalous talk had moved her to it. If she went back on her decision, which she did not believe she would, then Gil must be primed—though his consent in any case was unlikely. But certainly Fryn must not stay behind. She must be removed from a situation which might result in heaven alone knew what complications and unpleasantness.

Having arrived at this point she remembered that hot evening a day or so ago when Doreen had come along with Dwight, and she had felt quite certain that she was going to have another child. She had not had three children for nothing, and was quite sure she was not mistaken. Well, could anything put a more effective brake upon a husband's wandering affections, supposing them to be wandering? Then why did she feel so uneasy? Surely not because of the wretched

Emmy's suggestion that Doreen was indulging in a love-affair? She didn't believe it. Doreen was stupid and a gadabout, but she knew, none better, upon which side marriage had buttered her bread. All the same, she wished she had not mentioned her belief about the baby to Pen when speaking to her yesterday evening on the telephone. Pen had been surprised but obviously delighted. But now she wished she had kept her opinion to herself, and felt that, in some odd fashion, she had precipitated something. But how stupid to allow herself to be alarmed in this fashion by the wretched Emmy's malicious gossip and suppositions! She gave herself a mental shake and taking some aspirin settled down to sleep.

In the morning she was cheered by the sight of an apparently normal Fryn to whom she said that perhaps, after all, it might be wiser to terminate the Spanish lessons. It might save her embarrassment. What did Fryn think?

Fryn raised no objection, and Lydia thought that over her pale face there stole an expression of relief. She said that Dwight had a very good grasp of the grammar, that his pronunciation was excellent, and that the rest would be easy for someone as good at languages as he was.

"Very well. I won't put him off for Friday, though you can find an excuse about the lesson if you prefer. But I'll have a word with him when he comes. I'll explain that we are going away a little earlier than we had expected, and that as they will themselves be still away when we return it will hardly be worth while to restart the lessons —especially as we are hoping to sail early in September."

"Are we going away earlier?" Fryn asked. "I didn't know we'd any plans."

"We have. I've just been on to that hotel in the New Forest which we all liked so much last year, and they can take us from next Wednesday. The New Forest and a little hotel like that aren't everyone's idea of a holiday, thank goodness."

It seemed to occur to her suddenly that she was saying too much and she stopped abruptly. Fryn had made no comment save to say "yes" and "no" at the appropriate places and to ask that one question. But her mother thought again that she was relieved. And naturally. This sort of thing made a young girl unbearably self-conscious.

Actually, Fryn was thinking, If father gets berths for early September, Dwight will still be away. . . . So after Friday she might not see him again. That fact sank into her mind like a stone into a pond, leaving a ripple of commotion behind it.

[250]

Chapter Seven

IT SEEMED to Doreen that she had sat in the flat for years, expecting to hear Danny's voice at the other end of the telephone, and knowing all the time that she never would; trying to find sufficient courage to write to his club, saying that she would be willing to go to Paris, but knowing that this, too, she would never do. Worst of all, trying to find the courage, and the words, in which to tell Dwight what he must soon know, in any case, and wishing that she were dead and only too miserably aware that she was alive. The idea of suicide came and went in her mind, like flashes of lightning, leaving everything much darker after they had gone. If one could just go to sleep and never wake up again! But sleeping drugs were not to be had without a doctor's prescription, and she could not face a doctor. And at the back of her mind all the time was the feeling that Lydia had guessed, and this added to her misery, for she might not hold her tongue. They'd all expected her to have another baby. If she'd had any sense, she thought, she could have fathered this baby on to Dwight long ago, when she'd first suspected her condition. There was one argument, she believed, which would have broken down his indifference and his neglect of her as a wife. But two things had prevented her, the fact that she was so deeply in love with Danny, and the fear that Emmy's talk of Dwight's being in love with Fryn was true, which would put him in the same case as she with Danny. But now it was too late. Everything was too late.

If only she knew what to do! If only she had the courage to take Danny's way out, the cleverness to find some plausible excuse for the trip to Paris. But she couldn't go on like this. There was this three weeks' holiday just ahead. Something had to be done or she would go mad.

On the afternoon of the last Friday in July, the heat of which seemed in some strange way to accentuate her general misery, Mrs. Mann had gone early, and unable to bear the empty flat any longer, she betook herself to the cinema, where she saw *Brief Encounter* which, however, did nothing to improve her state of mind, and only made her cry a little in the soft darkness before she hurried off to collect Barry from school. From now on until they went away in mid-August, she'd have him at home all the day. The thought depressed her unutterably.

But on the way to the school her mind filled up with the thought of Danny. That girl in the film had gone back to her husband . . . but then nothing whatever had happened between them. "A lot of fuss about nothing, if you ask me," the woman in front of her had said to her companion, who had laughed and agreed. But they knew nothing. Once you'd really been in love everything was different. She didn't see how she was to go on living knowing that everything between herself and Danny was at an end, that she would never see him again. Even in the family circle he would know how to avoid her, for he was not much given to family visits and was never invited to Dwight's section of it. He'd only to avoid Emmy's flat and to give up staying with Rose when he came to down, to be quite sure he would never encounter her. And if he wanted news of her, well, then he'd not give up these visits. She knew that he had urged her to get rid of this baby as much for his own sake as for hers, since then they could have gone on meeting. What had possessed her not to have taken the easy way out two months ago? She could have wept for her folly, and so little did she know about herself and her emotions that she was miles from understanding that part at least of her reason, for all her fear of childbirth, was that she wanted this child, as she had never wanted Dwight's, because she was so passionately in love with its father.

Barry, that hot afternoon, was in an unusually angelic mood, excited by having "broken up", and by the prospect which now danced before his eyes of the holiday by the sea, which he adored. He was very happy at school and already sufficiently disciplined by it to indulge less frequently in what Doreen called his tantrums. He was beginning to forget his beloved Serena and had ceased to ask for a sister of his own. Doreen took these improvements, as she thought of them, for granted, and never suspected that he had learnt to hide his inherent sensitiveness because she had laughed at it so often, and called him a baby. Dwight, on the contrary, Doreen knew, thought him a much-too-grown-up little boy, and held it to be a direct result of his unfortunate state of being an only child.

That evening, despite the overpowering heat and Double Summer Time, he went obediently to bed at six o'clock, for he did not mind going to bed so much when the friendly sun was in the sky and shining through his open window.

Dwight came in early, as he usually did on Fridays. He was fatigued by the heat and with little appetite for the casual meal

[252]

Doreen set in front of him. At eight o'clock, she knew, he was expected at Hereford Square for his Spanish lesson, and she guessed that the hot evening would induce him to take a taxi there, which was why he ate his unimaginative meal in so leisurely a fashion, and noticing how little she was eating, inquired if she was feeling the heat.

"It will be a good thing when we can get out of London in this temperature," he commented. "You look as if you needed a change."

While she was stacking the plates in the kitchen for Mrs. Mann's attention in the morning, he sat down with his *Times*. Before she had finished the telephone rang, and her heart jumped. But it could not possibly be Danny; he knew the safe hours of the day in which to ring her. When she went back to the sitting-room with the warmed-up coffee, Dwight was sitting hidden behind his paper, his long legs stretched out in front of him. But as she poured out the coffee he looked at her across the top of the printed sheet and said, "That was mother. She's asked us to go down for the week-end, and to leave Barry there until we go away. I refused because you seemed out of sorts. She laughed when I said I thought it was the heat."

Doreen's heart stood still; the coffee she was pouring into her own cup slopped over into the saucer, as she said, "Why?"

"She seems to think you're going to have a baby. I said it was the first I'd heard about it. I gather the idea came from Lydia."

So Lydia hadn't held her tongue. . . . She passed him his coffee, and as he took it, he said, "Well, are you?"

"Yes."

"May I inquire whose?"

"I can't tell you."

"You mean you won't?"

"Yes."

"Very well. What do you intend me to do about it?"

"I don't know."

"Then I'll tell you. I shall divorce you."

After a little pause, she said, "Once I asked you if you would divorce me—if I was unfaithful to you, and you said it would depend upon whether the other man would marry me."

"Well?"

"He can't—he's already married."

"Nevertheless I shall divorce you."

"So that you can marry Fryn?"

His eyes on the paper, he said casually, much too casually, "What has Fryn to do with it?"

"You're in love with her, aren't you?"

c.g.u.—9*   [253]

"Leave Fryn out of this. Your lover isn't asking for a divorce?"

"No—he thought we were just having an affair."

"And you weren't?"

"No, I was in love with him."

He believed that. He'd never thought her capable of the casual infidelity—she'd be too much afraid of results. Also, though she was empty-headed and a bore, she was not what men called a bitch. And that, he supposed, was why his purposeful neglect of her as a wife, so difficult at first, and now become a habit, had never struck him as dangerous. He even knew, in this moment, that he wouldn't have cared if his attitude had earlier driven her to illicit associations, since that would have given him the opportunity to get rid of her with an easy conscience. He thought this now without any sense of shame, seeing only the freedom ahead of him. Doreen was a bad house-keeper, an indifferent mother, as well as a faithless wife. Reasons enough, he thought, even if there hadn't been another. . . .

Yet, for all it had ceased to matter to him, she was still attractive, and not a stranger to physical passion, for all she would not willingly bear the fruit of it. Once she had given him more than his meed of physical satisfaction—most men would have found it enough in a wife who had borne him one child. Why didn't he? Other children he would have liked, but that wasn't the answer. He knew what the answer was, but he wouldn't think of it now.

"Why don't you say something?" she asked, sitting there stirring her coffee without the least idea she was doing it.

"There doesn't seem anything more to say."

"But you intend to divorce me?"

"Yes. You must get an affiliation order against this man."

"No," she said. "No. I can't have him brought into it. He's happily married—I don't want him to hate me. I've been a fool, that's all. Oh, Dwight, I know I've not been a very good wife to you; I know you're sick of me. But what am I going to do with a living to earn and a baby to keep?"

He saw the terror as well as the appeal in her eyes but he turned away from them.

"I will make you an allowance until you get on your feet again."

She knew then that there was no hope. He would neither forgive her nor allow her another chance. Their marriage was at an end. For a moment rage crossed her despair and a sense of just grievance, and she said, "But it was partly your fault. You left me alone. It's over a year since we were really married . . ."

"I wanted a wife, not a mistress."

"But you don't understand. . . . It wasn't as if I'd not given you a child."

"There was no reason why you shouldn't have others. You had a perfectly normal time with Barry. You just allowed yourself to be scared to death by something other women take in their stride."

"They've never been in a hospital, perhaps . . ."

He swept that aside, aware that he was being harsh and impercipient and not caring. So matter-of-fact, so unimaginative on every other side of life, why, here, should she be so neurotic and unbalanced? Without knowing it he had held that against her everlastingly. Had she been a sensitive highly-strung girl, he could have understood and forgiven it. He said, "Can you swear that if I had not neglected you, as you call it, you would not have taken this man as your lover?"

She couldn't. She'd thought so once and had dragged it in often enough as an excuse. But she knew it wasn't true. She said, "No. I did try. . . . But, you see, I loved him. I didn't intend this to happen. Neither of us wanted it. It was just an accident."

"You took good care there should be no accident with me. You're still in love with him, I suppose?"

She couldn't speak, but it wasn't necessary. He knew she was. "And you never were with me?" he said. "Why in heaven's name did you marry me?"

"You asked me so often. And I wanted to be married. I liked you very much."

"And you expect me to take you back knowing that you love another man?"

"No," she said. "I know you will be glad of the excuse to get rid of me. However much you deny it I know you are in love with Fryn."

"Leave her out of it. She's a child."

"She's eighteen—only a year younger than I was when you married me." The words poured suddenly out of her throat almost without volition. "If it wasn't for her you'd give me another chance. If it wasn't for her you'd not have neglected me the way you have—the business of children was only the way you justified it to yourself."

"It is not true."

"I think it is, even if you don't really know it. And how is it worse for you to live with me when you know I love someone else than for me to have lived with you knowing that it was Fryn you really wanted?"

He stared at her. He had never before heard her make so many remarks at once, nor heard from her a logical argument. Perhaps he had presented her with it. But all he said was, "Someone has been putting ideas into your head. And I can guess who."

Words deserted her again. She could never trust herself with words. She knew he would now unloose a torrent of them, which, as ever, she would find overwhelming. And he did. She sat silent beneath them, crushed but aware that he was being unjust. And Dwight was aware of it too, but that didn't stop him. His marriage was a mistake. And here was the chance to end it. He did not stay to consider that he had had of her all that he wanted, when he had wanted it, that she had never denied him and had been a generous lover. He did not even know that part of his fury against her was that she had been able to indulge her love, whereas he had had to clamp it down in his heart, afraid to declare it by as much as a glance, a word. . . .

She said at last, "There is Barry . . ."

"And how much have you cared for him?" he broke out. "You bore him unwillingly, you've washed and dressed and fed him—when you couldn't push the job on to someone else. You've never loved him. You don't like children. You've never even liked your own child. Or tried to understand him. You couldn't even save him from knowledge and sight of something no child should ever have known. You couldn't even see that your servants did what they were paid to do."

Mrs. Loder. Lody. . . . The name came creeping stealthily back into her mind, as if it knew how hard she had tried to forget she had ever heard it. He had never forgiven her that incident. He had been terribly unjust. She would not pursue it further or be dragged at the heels of an argument as old as the dreadful incident itself. She sat silent. There was no use in saying anything more. Whatever she said he would know how to discount it, to make it sound like nonsense. Then suddenly, as if the sight of him, sunk now in his chair, wearing a cold cruel expression she had never seen before upon his face, roused her to fury, she said, "They'll never let you have Fryn. In a few weeks' time they'll be going home. I hope you will suffer as much as I'm doing now."

"Shut up, damn you!" he burst out.

She rose and went out of the room.

He did not follow her. He sat there in his chair, unmoving, his thoughts playing not around Doreen and her lover and her predicament, but around Fryn whom he'd see in an hour's time. . . .

But he knew that what Doreen had said was true. Fryn was not for him. Oh God, how true it was!—Fryn was not for him. She was a child, utterly unawakened, to whom he would never dare utter a single word of his love. She would flee from him in horror. Even when he teased her too closely, she was embarrassed. He remembered that evening recently when she had walked out of the room, the sweet colour in her face . . . not looking at him, grown suddenly shy and self-conscious. Another year. Another year of companionship such as they'd known for the past two years, and which if it hadn't been all he wanted had been all he asked—just one more year and he could have brought her to love. But he wasn't to have it. Something had alarmed her, so that she had gone back on her last plan for getting permission to stay on a little longer in England. In a few weeks' time she would be gone. He'd not see her again for years. Perhaps never . . .

But he had known that day must come. What was it he'd hoped for before it arrived? That some day he would be free—free to pack up and follow her to South America? Had that been at the back of his mind when he had proposed the Spanish lessons? He could have done without them. He didn't know. Perhaps, unconsciously. What he had consciously known was that the lessons were the only way in which he could be sure of getting Fryn for those few odd hours entirely to himself. Emotionally asleep she might be, but he believed he could have awakened her if he had tried. But he hadn't. God! but he deserved a good mark for that!

Not until he had left the house—and without a word—did Doreen come back into the sitting-room. She had bathed her face and not troubled to put on any fresh make-up, so that she looked as pale as death, her eyes seemed to have sunk back into her head, as if she had been crying for hours. But she had not shed a single tear. She was miles from crying, frozen—possessed—by the demon of a corroding despair. She sat down in a chair by the window, listening to the sound of voices, of the lift everlastingly ascending and descending, to the summer scourge of a medley of loudspeakers. The heat was intense, the air still. The room pressed about her like a prison. She rose and walked to the window, to stand looking down into the well of the building. If only she had the courage, here was a way to put an end to it all—to get out, for ever. But she had no courage to face death; life was strong in her, and she turned suddenly from the window and sat down again, away from the window this time, in the chair in which Dwight had lounged and hated her. The whole evening stretched away interminably before her, like the long road that ran up Ide Hill which she had seen from her window every morning at Greystones and up which she had obstinately refused to walk. The world seemed empty, not even any longer full of the hopes and fears which had filled it for the last ten days. No use in sitting there. She might as well take some aspirin and go to bed. . . .

And then her eyes fell upon the copy of *The Times*, which Dwight had thrown down. She picked it up, and idly spread out its pages, but could, as usual, find nothing in it she wanted to read. But as she was about to throw it aside, her eye was caught by a familiar but unusual name, and she smoothed out the page, hunted down the paragraph again and read it.

On July 30th, at The Manor, Bourne, Dorsetshire, to Olivia, the wife of Sir Daniel Wingham, a daughter (Catherine Mary). Prematurely. American papers please copy.

Her heart stood still, but her mind raced backwards and forwards. With Danny to and from Boston, back to that first day of the spring when she'd had tea with Emmy and she had talked of her visit to Bourne for her sister's funeral a month earlier, and reported that Livvy had grown plainer and looked very "off-colour". So Danny must have known of this when first they'd become lovers. Why did that make her feel so cheap? When he had been urging her to get rid of his child and hers he had been looking forward to the birth of his and Olivia's. He'd wanted a daughter, she'd heard Rose say. . . . And but for what he'd called "an unfortunate contretemps", he'd have gone on with their relationship. Or wouldn't he? She didn't know. She had had predecessors, she knew. Why hadn't she thought that, like them, her little day would come to an end? Or had she? He had thought she knew they were only having an affair. Oh, if she only had have been! It was falling in love which had been so fatal!

Her misery poured over her like a flood-tide. She could not stand against it. She was washed by it clean out of the world, walled up in some well of darkness. Her mind ceased to function. She did not know how long she sat there, thinking of nothing, just letting the flood-tide of misery flow over and over her. But suddenly she sat erect, as if she saw a ghost, and stealthily into her stunned mind there stole for the second time that evening the name that for so many months Barry had kept alive for her. Lody. Mrs. Loder. . . . The curse of Greystones come home to roost, or whatever it was her mother-in-law had said about it. People said Lody had died very quickly, that she had managed things so well her neck was dislocated almost at once. Doreen shuddered. She sat there for a long time, feel-

[258]

ing very cold, as if it were mid-winter, and wondering if that piece of evidence were true.

Dwight listened to Lydia's little statement outwardly unmoved, accepting it with a few polite, conventional words. But the deep, agonised pulsing of his heart was suffocating, and though he heard himself uttering those entirely polite accepting words it was as if someone else spoke for him. He felt as if, in her kind, motherly and utterly reasonable voice, Lydia had snatched from him something of untold value.

His mind was very far removed from the Spanish lesson which followed upon this short and, to Dwight, appallingly painful interlude. For he could think of nothing save that this was the last time he would see Fryn alone. He had not been able to deny Lydia's contention that, according to Fryn, he did not any longer need a teacher but only to attend some good conversation classes. Yet this evening the play he was translating went haltingly, and it was clear that his mind was not on the business in hand. Fryn had sensed, when she had seen him upon his arrival, before her mother had said her say, that he was troubled about something, though it certainly had not appeared that her mother observed anything unusual. However, she corrected his mistakes, made no comment upon his unusual lack of idiomatic facility and wished the lesson was done. She had not expected their last lesson together to be like this, and she wished her mother had elected to say her little piece after, rather than before, it. For clearly, for some reason or other, Dwight had been in no state to be confronted with so summary and unexpected a decision.

It was he who closed the book, saying that he was feeling too stupid to go on, and apologising for wasting her time. Her concerned glance brushed his face as softly as might a moth's wing, and as briefly, and she inquired if anything was the matter.

"What should be the matter?" he asked.

"I don't know. I just thought when you came that you were worried about something. And then, mother's little chat. . . ."

The words came from her without volition, for if her mother's decision, so competently and reasonably voiced, about the lessons had anything to do with his mood, it was no part of the evening's work that he should be invited to put it into words. But all he said was, "I think that perhaps I'd better go."

"Oh, do stay for mother's coffee and sandwiches. Or she will be hurt and think she has offended you."

"How? By telling me so politely that she doesn't want me here like this—any more?"

Not quite quickly enough she said, "Oh, but she didn't mean it like that . . ."

"I know exactly what she meant. I don't blame her. In her place I dare say I should have done the same. . . . She suspects I'm in love with you, doesn't she?"

The colour ran up like a red flag into her face. But before she could think of anything to say, Dwight went on. "It's true, anyway. Surely you must have guessed it? Or has my conduct been so very exemplary?"

"Yes—yes it has. Of course it has. I knew you liked me. And I liked you. I thought that was all."

"But it isn't, Fryn. I'm so much in love with you that there's nothing I wouldn't do to keep you here in England."

"Oh, please, please don't go on. You see, I don't feel like that. . . I mean, I love you—I love you very much. But not in that way."

"Not yet. But if only we didn't have to be separated . . . if our friendship could just go on for another year, in its own way. . . ."

"Oh, do please stop. You've no right to say these things to me. I mean, you're not free to say them."

"And if I were? Would you listen to me then?"

"I . . . I don't know. How can I tell? Everything would be different, I suppose—I don't know."

"Listen, Fryn. I shall, soon, be free. . . . If you'd only make them let you stay on."

She looked at him with incomprehension clouding her eyes. What did he mean? That Doreen was leaving him? Then was everything that the wretched Emmy had said true after all? Her world, her happy little world, her tight safe sane little world began to reel about her. She felt a little sick.

"Fryn, darling. Listen. I'm divorcing Doreen."

"But—but mother says that she thinks Doreen is going to have another baby."

"She's dead right, but it isn't mine."

He saw the colour run out of her face so quickly that it a little scared him and he thought that this was no story for her ears. She had got up from her seat and stood there now staring at him, beyond speech of any kind. She wanted to run away out of the room, to save herself from hearing any more. But she was rooted to the spot and after a few seconds her mind cleared. She said, "You mean—you are giving Doreen her freedom so that she can marry the other man . . . in time. Before the baby is born, I mean."

"No, it isn't going to happen like that. The man is married."

"Then if you divorce her whatever will she do? Oh, Dwight, *why* must you divorce her?"

He said, "Why not? Most men would, in the circumstances."

"But not you."

"Oh, Fryn, don't you understand?"

The look on his face gave her the answer—Emmy's answer. He thought that if he divorced Doreen, now that he had good reason, that he, that she. . . . He saw that she understood and that she was inconceivably shocked.

"Fryn, Fryn darling, don't you love me at all?"

"No, never in that way, never. And not at all now, I think."

What a fool he had been to rush her like this! He had known she was not the sort to take such a situation with modern matter-of-factness. He had dished everything by his folly, and that moment of comprehension had converted him for her into a complete stranger, whom she did not even like. But he could not leave it there. As she rose from her seat he put a hand on her arm to detain her. She did not move, but she looked down at his hand on her bare arm and said, "Please take your hand away."

He obeyed, and watched her move to the door.

"Fryn, there's something I must say to you. Please come and sit down again and listen. I swear I won't touch you."

But she continued to stand at the door, her whole attitude refusing him. She did not want to hear what he had to say. Nothing he could ever say could cancel out what he had already said, what he had hoped, what he had meant to do—to try to do. All the shining fabric of their friendship and affection (in which Emmy's innuendoes had induced large cracks) had toppled to pieces at her feet. And there was nothing to do about it. Nothing could ever build it up again. She wished they had never met. She wished they had never been such friends. She wished, she wished. . . . Her thoughts went milling round and round, making her feel dizzy but not resolving themselves into anything that could be put into words. And she felt hollow inside, as if something had died in her.

His words reached her from a distance, across a whole continent of unhappiness. She wished she knew how to stop him, but she didn't. She stood there not looking at him, looking at the floor, wishing it would open and let her through.

". . . I've been a fool, Fryn—as big a fool as Doreen. Assuming too much, believing what I wanted to believe. For sheer arrogant stupidity there's not much to choose between us."

But she thought there was. He had neglected Doreen, and, as Emmy had hinted, for *her*. He had left her lonely and bored to find consolation elsewhere, whereas he was clever, with an interesting job and many interesting friends. Even if she had really been in love with him she could never have agreed that there was nothing to choose between his conduct and Doreen's.

His words poured over her. He was sorry to have hurt her, to have assumed too much. She must try to forget it all and remember only the happy hours they had spent together. . . . Oh, as though one remembered and forgot things at will! Why, even if she lived to be a very old woman she knew that all she would remember of this friendship was this last dreadful hour of it; and always she would wonder if what had happened to Doreen had happened because of her. And never never be sure. . . .

Unless—unless she went to see Doreen. . . . She would not mention what Dwight had told her about the love-affair and the baby. She need only speak for herself. . . . Whatever the result of such a meeting, it could not be as bad as this awful state of not knowing.

"Good-bye," she said to Dwight, looking not at him but at the door-knob which her hand encircled, as if she meant to flee if he made any move toward her. But he did not.

"Shan't I see you again?"

Not looking at him, she said, "I hope not."

"Do you hate me so much?"

"It's myself I hate, I think," she said, and turning the handle of the door, was gone.

Chapter Eight

AT ABOUT a quarter to eight that evening Charles Anstruther looked at his watch and decided to miss his train and go out to Battersea to see Doreen. He put it that way to himself because he had remembered that this was the evening of the week when Dwight went off to Hereford Square for his Spanish lesson, and also because it was Doreen he really wanted to see.

For he was uneasy about her—had been ever since Lydia had apprised Pen of her suspicions. And since he had telephoned Pen an hour ago to say that he had had a late appointment and would dine in town, he was aware that his uneasiness had deepened; for Pen had reported that she had just been speaking to Dwight on the telephone, mentioning Lydia's belief and inviting them all down to Wyngates for the week-end. But Dwight had said that Lydia's information, though interesting, was news to him, and had refused the week-end invitation. Pen, of course, having taken Lydia's guess as correct, had also taken it as evidence of a better feeling between the young people, and had clearly been puzzled and a little dashed by Dwight's ignorance of any such prospect, and by his brusque refusal of her invitation. Charles thought she would appreciate his going out to Battersea and having a look at things for himself. So he hailed a taxi and had himself driven to the flat, not remembering until almost there that there were occasions when Doreen accompanied Dwight to Lydia's. However, here he was and he must hope this was not one of them.

Taking himself up in the lift, he saw by the electric clock that it was close upon eight o'clock. If he was to catch the last train he would not be able to stop long, he reflected, as he let himself out of the lift, walked along to the door of number nine, and rang the bell. Nobody came. He rang again, thinking that he was unlucky, and Doreen after all had gone with Dwight. But in that case their woman should be in the flat, for he knew Barry was never left there alone.

He had just decided that his errand was in vain when the sound of something being awkwardly dragged along the floor of the hall caused him to ring once again. And this time Barry's eager little voice said, "I'm opening it—I can reach the handle now," and after a pause the door moved slightly inwards. Slipping in his hand and moving back the chair upon which the child had stood, Charles stepped inside.

"And what," he asked the small pyjama-clad figure, "are you doing out of bed at this hour, young man?"

"I woke up and it was so quiet I had to come to find mummy. I—I don't like it quiet, you know. She was doing something on the steps in the kitchen cupboard and told me to go back to bed. She gave me an orange and waited until I'd eaten it, then made me promise to go to sleep. And I did," he added virtuously.

"You seem to have wakened up again. Was it my ring?"

"No. It was a funny bang. Then it was all quiet again, and I didn't like it. So I got up but I couldn't find mummy. The cupboard door wouldn't open, either. I knocked and called and called, but there wasn't any answer. Then I was quite sure she'd gone out and I was beginning to be frightened when I heard your ring. Only of course I didn't know it was you. I thought it was mummy come back."

"Gone out without her key, eh? Well, now I'll let her in when she comes, but first I'll see you back into bed. Only this time you must stay there and go to sleep."

"All right. But I'm a bit frightened, I think. I don't like cupboards, you know, 'cos of Lody . . ."

"That was a very long time ago. We don't remember things like that. Now, come along. Remember you're on your honour to stay in bed this time and go to sleep. I'll come to see you soon."

"All right, but will you light my night-light in case it gets dark before you come? And could you stay with me for just five minutes?"

"Very well. Now into bed with you while I light your funny little candle. And it would be a good idea, wouldn't it, to have some hot milk? Would that help?"

"Oh, yes."

Charles went into the kitchen, took the milk from the refrigerator and put it on to heat. Then he tried the cupboard door. Locked right enough, and the key on the inside. . . . A penknife and a piece of wire should do the trick. But a sense of urgency assailed him. Barry, however, had first to be got to sleep. An aspirin dissolved in the milk might help. He went along to the bathroom, found the aspirin bottle and fumed at the time the tablet took to get properly dissolved. But at last it was done. He took the mixture along to Barry who, thank heaven, drank it without comment and obediently lay down on his pillows and shut his eyes. Charles hovered around for a few minutes, then saw that the boy was drowsy and stole away, leaving the door ajar.

[264]

He went quickly back to the kitchen and got to work on the lock with the penknife and a piece of bent wire which Doreen obviously kept for getting the tops off the milk bottles. His efforts with the key were soon rewarded, for he heard it fall out on the other side of the door, and through the aperture he saw that the light was on. The lock took a little longer, but that, too, yielded and, pushing open the door, he saw Doreen lying motionless upon the floor, an overturned pair of short steps near her feet. One horrified glance around told him what had happened, and worse, what she had meant to happen. He saw, as he stooped over her, that she was quite unconscious, and she had cut her head, for there was blood on the floor around it. Her face, guiltless of its usual make-up, was waxen; her hands ice-cold, and in the left one she clutched a piece of strap. Either this was a concussion from the shock of her fall, or a prolonged fainting-fit. Shut in here, with no air, for the cupboard (more accurately a box-room) had no window, anyone would have fainted, he thought, and without Doreen's terror of what she had intended to compass. Yet it must have seemed to her a place perfectly devised for her intention, for into the centre of the ceiling at intervals were driven large hooks, as if one were expected to be curing hams in Battersea. From one of these dangled the other part of the broken strap. It was clearly this faulty strap which had frustrated her intention (at least, of meeting death that way; he couldn't be sure that she hadn't encountered it in another). He felt her pulse, which was feeble, and then noticed a dark smudge on her throat, which before long would reveal itself as an evil-looking bruise. He must get help. She needed careful moving. He straightened up and after fetching an eiderdown from her bedroom and covering her up, went into the sitting-room and telephoned down to the hall porter, telling him that there had been an accident at No. 9 and he wanted a doctor at once. Would he please get on to someone in the neighbourhood and tell him the matter was urgent. "And then," he added, "perhaps you'd come up here and give me a hand."

On the floor of the store-room Doreen lay as he had left her, but for the moment his business was not with her, but with the tell-tale signs of her intention, which her own ineptitude or a fainting-fit, induced by fear and horror of what she was trying to do, had mercifully frustrated. He picked up the steps and stood upon them to unfasten the other part of the strap which had been left dangling, and then took a look round. Two of the walls were fitted with shelves and these were well-stocked with tins and cartons of all sorts and sizes. The top shelf, he realised, would be almost out of Doreen's reach on such a short pair of steps, even if she stood upon the top. Reaching up, he disarranged the things on it immediately in front of him, and taking down three of the largest tins disposed them carelessly about the floor, after which he replaced the steps as he had found them, and where doubtless they had fallen when she had kicked them away from her. Or had she turned faint before she had finished her grim preparations and fallen headlong, clutching the strap as she did so?

Looking round he was satisfied that the scene was now set for the story he was going to tell the hall porter and the doctor. It seemed to him a quite plausible reconstruction of a quite ordinary accident. There was nothing now, he thought, to suggest that the scene had actually been set for something far grimmer. Poor Doreen! Poor child! How desperate she must have been to have attempted so to find peace!

He felt very helpless when he looked at her. Supposing this was a concussion? What ought one to do for that? A memory of the day his elder boy, John, had fallen out of the apple tree came back to him. Ammonia to the nose, a hot-water bottle to the feet. Keep the patient warm. He put on the kettle, hunted for ammonia without success, and moved the cushions of the settee on to the sitting-room floor. There came then a discreet knock at the door, which he opened.

"Green, sir, the hall porter," said the young man who stood on the mat.

"Come in," said Charles, and having introduced himself led him to the spot where Doreen lay.

"Lord, sir, she does look bad. However did she come to do it?"

"It looks as if she was trying to get something down from the top shelf and over-balanced. Unfortunate that she was alone in the flat when it happened, save for my small grandson. Luckily he was awake and climbed on a chair and let me in."

"I saw the gentleman go out, sir—about seven-thirty it was. He nearly always goes out that time o' Fridays."

"Yes, I believe so," said Charles. "I think it would be best if we lifted Mrs. Lowe into the sitting-room. I've put the settee cushions on the floor so that she can lie flat, and some towels for her head. She's cut it rather badly, I'm afraid, and she won't thank us to-morrow for spoiling her cushions. If you'd just move the steps you will be able to take her feet."

"She's properly knocked herself out, sir," said Green.

[266]

"Yes," agreed Charles grimly.

She did not stir during their efforts, and as he covered her again with the eiderdown Charles looked down at her with an immense pity in his heart. There was so little he could do for her now save fill the hot-water bottle and hunt again for the elusive ammonia. Or smelling-salts, but the young women of to-day seemed not to use them.

He thanked Green and dismissed him, then went to deal with the hot-water bottle and gave up the hunt for ammonia or smelling-salts in despair. The bottle would be too hot for her stockingless feet, so he wrapped it in a towel, for even hot-water bottles these days must go jacketless, and took off her shoes—absurd high-heeled things that he would have guaranteed to throw anyone off a pair of rickety steps, and which anyone but Doreen would have removed, he thought, thinking also how pretty her feet were, with their pink polished nails and beautifully arched insteps. He put the bottle in position, drew down the eiderdown and thankfully rose from his knees and sat down in a near-by chair and waited for some change in her condition, hoping that she would open her eyes and recognise him, for that would make her feel better when she began to remember things. But she lay so still it seemed impossible to believe that she would ever open her eyes again in this world. . . .

What, he wondered, had made her try to kill herself?—and so horribly. (Shades of the wretched Mrs. Loder!) Fear of bearing this child? What then was fear? The alternative seemed so hideously out of proportion. A possible explanation slipped into his head, and if it did her a grave injustice, he would be grieved—even a week ago it was an idea he would not have entertained concerning her. He had not thought her light. . . . But it would explain Dwight's ignorance of her state when his mother had spoken to him on the telephone a few hours ago. And if it was so, what had Lydia and Pen between them let loose? Accusation and confession? A threat of divorce? But wouldn't that have been just what she wanted?—supposing that the other man wanted to marry her. If so, surely she would have told him the truth weeks ago, and of her own accord? Well, whatever had happened, and for whatever reason, it was clear that Dwight had marched off to console himself, it being a Friday, in the company of the young Fryn, not caring, perhaps not even aware, that he was leaving Doreen in the depths of misery and despair.

Fryn. She meant no harm, of course. She was a charming child, but she had made no more pretence about her liking for Dwight than he had about his for her. They were cousins, not very close,

[267]

certainly, and their friendship had been taken for granted. But Fryn was an innocent, knowing nothing of life and the traps it could lay for you, and she would not have realised the unwisdom of such a friendship with a young man reputed to be not too happily married and twelve years older than herself. But Lydia should have realised it. He wondered at her sanctioning these Spanish lessons, though she probably saw them as no more than a *quid pro quo* for Dwight's services over Fryn's uncertain maths. However, if Dwight had been fool enough to entertain any romantic ideas about Fryn he was doomed to a sharp awakening.

Nearly half-past eight. The doctor should be here at any moment. He went back for another glance at that horrible store cupboard. Yes, he seemed to have thought of everything. The scene was correctly set for the story he had told Green, that in more detail he would need, perhaps, to tell the doctor. But not to Dwight. That young man was going to get a shock. And shock, Charles thought, shutting the cupboard door, was exactly what he needed. On his way back to the sitting-room he looked in upon Barry and found him still fast asleep. By the grace of God, he thought, for a prowling Barry with his talk of locked cupboards would have made his carefully planned story look a little silly.

For a second or two he fancied as he stood looking down upon Doreen that her eyelids fluttered a little, that the dark lashes trembled upon her ashen face. He waited, hoping she would open her eyes and see him there and recognise him and be a little comforted. But she did not.

"Doreen!" he said softly.

Nothing.

"Doreen!" he said again, "it's Charles."

And then, as if his name called her back from the darkness, her eyes did slowly open and rest for a few seconds on his face before they closed again. Had she recognised him? He could not tell. Then he saw that her lips were moving. Her voice was faint and halting, but what it said was unmistakable.

"I'm . . . sorry . . . I . . . muffed . . . it."

"Don't say that, don't think it. You just fell off the steps and got a concussion. That is what everyone is going to believe."

There was no sign that his comforting words reached her along the dark road she travelled; nor could he persuade himself that the cold hand in his returned his gentle pressure.

The doctor, when he arrived, gave no trouble, accepting Charles's story of finding the patient unconscious on the floor in circumstances

[268]

which suggested an accident. All he said was, "A young woman in her condition had no right to be climbing about on steps and reaching up to shelves, anyway. I'm afraid she'll lose the baby. If you can help me get her to bed I'll have a look at her."

During the ensuing interval Charles went back into the sitting-room and smoked a much-needed cigarette. It seemed a very long time before the doctor came back.

"Her condition's pretty serious, I'm afraid," he said. "No, not the concussion—that might have been much worse. She's got her fine head of hair to thank for that. If it weren't for this pregnancy she would have been all right within a week. But she's had a bad shock, and I'm afraid a miscarriage is inevitable. If you can get hold of her husband, I think it would be as well. Meantime I'll send in a nurse and look in again a little later."

Luckily it was Jeremy who answered the telephone at Hereford Square, and he said, briefly, after his fashion, that Dwight had been gone about ten minutes, that Fryn had had a headache or something and had cut short the lesson. Good-bye—and he had hung up.

Pen, when he rang through to Wyngates to say he had been detained and would be staying in town over-night, was equally accommodating. "I shall be bringing Barry with me in the morning," he said, and this too she accepted. Not the least of Pen's qualities, he thought, as he replaced the receiver, was that she was not given to asking tiresome questions over the telephone.

It was after eleven when Dwight came in. His face was pale and drawn and he did not seem overwhelmingly pleased to see his step-father, who said, "You've been some time getting from Hereford Square. I rang through just before nine and was told by young Jeremy that you had already left."

"I went for a walk. I didn't know you were here. What was the hurry?"

"The doctor thought you should be here. Doreen has had an accident. I found her unconscious when I arrived. Fortunately Barry was awake and was able to let me in."

"An accident? What sort of an accident?"

"Get yourself a drink and I'll tell you."

"I don't want a drink, thanks."

"I should have one, all the same."

Dwight walked to the sideboard and poured himself out a whisky and soda. Standing there with the glass in his hand, he said, "Well? What's the mystery? What sort of an accident?"

"Officially," said Charles, "she fell from a pair of steps while trying to reach something on the top of the store-cupboard. But actually . . ."

As it had never occurred to Jeremy to mention that Charles had telephoned to speak to Dwight, nobody at Hereford Square knew that he was at the flat or suspected that anything was wrong there. Fryn, set on making her appointment with Doreen, fumed and fidgeted until Meg and her mother, rather later than usual, set out for their usual Saturday morning round of the shops. Then she hurried to the telephone, got through to the flat and was surprised to hear her Uncle Charles's voice.

"It's Fryn," she said. "I just wanted a word with Doreen."

There was a little pause before Charles said, "I'm afraid, my dear, that I have some very sad news for you. . . . Doreen died just half an hour ago."

"Oh, no! Oh, Uncle Charles! Why? I didn't know she was ill."

"She wasn't, but she had a bad accident in the flat yesterday—and she was going to have a baby, you know."

"What . . . what time?"

"In the early part of the evening. I found her unconscious when I arrived about eight. . . . Is your mother there?"

"No, she's at the shops, with Meg."

"Will you ask her to ring me directly she comes in?"

"Yes. Yes, of course," she stammered and put back the receiver without saying good-bye.

For a little while she sat there staring straight ahead of her, her thoughts heaping themselves around her like a wall, shutting her in with consternation and horrid conjecture. An accident, Charles had said. But what kind of accident did you have in your own home that could kill you? Charles had made it look as if but for the baby it mightn't have been fatal. An accident. Oh, what kind, what *kind*? Did he really mean that Doreen had tried to get rid of the baby?— girls who were going to have illegitimate babies often did, Meg had said. And if so, was it because Dwight had told her he would divorce her?—and because she had thought that Dwight and she, that she and Dwight. . . . Had it, perhaps, been *herself* Doreen had meant to kill? If she really believed what Emmy had hinted, and had thought it confirmed by seeing them together when she came to Hereford Square, mightn't she, perhaps? . . . Uncle Charles had sounded very upset, but as if he meant to keep whatever he knew to himself. . . . A sob rose in her throat as she thought suddenly that Doreen must have been lying there alone in the flat, unconscious, while

Dwight was saying all those awful things to her yesterday evening.
. . . It couldn't be true that she was dead; she was too young to die,
and too pretty! (Oh, I wish, she thought, that I had liked her better!)
But she *was* dead, and that made everything much worse. Much,
much worse, for now she would never be sure that her death, as
well as her unhappiness and the love-affair, had not, in some measure
at least, been her fault. Yet she had meant no harm; she hadn't
thought that Dwight felt about her in that way, except just once or
twice lately. . . . And she had done her best to discourage him.
She hadn't known how to handle him, what to say that should make
him understand. . . .

So now, she thought, despair wringing her young heart, however
long I live there will always be this awful thing that I shall never
know the truth about. That I shall never be able to bear to remember,
and never be able to forget. . . .

Hove—Farnham.
30th January, 1947—14th August, 1948.